A Hare's Foot

A Hare's Footprint

Celia Moore

Thank you for your support, love Celia Moore x

Other Books by Celia Moore
Fox Halt Farm and **Culmfield Cuckoo**

Copyright

Contact Celia

Website Celiascosmos.com
Facebook Celia Moore Books

Dedication

A *Hare's Footprint* is dedicated to Kate, my daughter and my dearest friend. I want to recognise Kate's endless encouragement and interest in my books and say thank you, darling.

There are so many other people I'd also like to thank and many of them are listed in my *Acknowledgements* but there are a few who are my cheerleaders and without their endless support, I might have given up - these people are my husband Paul, my friends Jen and Tracey, (who have both championed my stories from the start) Mum and Peter.

Thank you to everyone who's read Fox Halt Farm and Culmfield Cuckoo and afterwards, chatted to me about their experience, written reviews and/or told their friends about my books. Your feedback means the world to me.

A Hare's Footprint is the third and final novel in the Fox Halt Farm Trilogy and below is a quick recap of the story so far.

PLEASE NOTE: This catch up contains spoilers, so please skip it if you intend to read Fox Halt Farm and Culmfield Cuckoo.

The story since 1986

Eighteen-year-old Billy's summer job on an idyllic Greek island couldn't be further from her life on Fox Halt Farm, and soon the exotic Kostas sweeps her off her feet. Yet he discards her without a care, and Billy, devastated, throws herself over a cliff.

Richard is on the island, honeymooning with Janette, a woman he's been destined to marry for years. He runs his family's multi-national business in London. He should be on top of the world, yet underneath his dynamic exterior, he's weighed down with doubt. Richard saves Billy's life, but she is resentful, becoming introverted, secretive and distant from her family.

Daniella, Billy's mum, can't understand the appalling change in her daughter, and she contacts Richard to see if he can shed light on Billy's 'accident'. Richard and Daniella start a secret correspondence which continues for years, with Daniella eventually persuading Richard to employ Billy in his property company. Slowly, as they work together, Billy and Richard come to understand each other, and the death of Richard's mother is the catalyst of an affair between them, but Richard ends the affair, determined to save his marriage. Unbeknown to him, Billy is pregnant, and she turns to her childhood friend and neighbour Tom for help.

Billy suffers a devastating miscarriage and is told the resultant injuries from her cliff fall prevent her from having children. Again, Billy falls apart. Richard sends a work acquaintance of them both, Michael O'Rowde, to try to persuade Billy to seek help. Michael helps Billy recover, and in time, he persuades Billy to return to London to plan his celebrity style wedding to his fiancée, Jessie. Later, Billy lives and works with Jessie as they rebuild Jessie's childhood home, Culmfield.

Billy is happy at last, but then Michael presses her to work for him in London, helping him to review the future of his massive supermarket centred business.

Billy finds a new love, Ed, but this relationship ends when her dearest friend Saffi commits suicide, and Ed abandons Billy for a job opportunity in Dubai. Michael consoles Billy, and they start a long-term affair. Billy drops her best friend Jessie to continue her affair with Michael.

The foot and mouth crisis is the final straw for Billy's parents trying to hold on to Fox Halt Farm, and the farm is sold to Tom. The epidemic also cracks Tom's marriage to vet Martha, and they start to live separately. Martha and their children, William and Grace at Foxlands – Tom at Fox Halt Farm.

Richard and Janette realise they aren't making each other happy and divorce, and at the same time, Richard decides to sell his property business. Billy meets up with Ed again. The new relationship is platonic, but she hides it from Michael, and while Michael is at Culmfield at weekends, Billy returns to Hamsgate to be with her mum and to also help Tom.

Tom is killed in a farm accident, and then through the jealous actions of double-dealing Michael, Billy loses Ed too. Billy immediately ends the affair with Michael realising how he has manipulated her life.

Richard suspects that Michael killed Tom, and he shares his suspicions with Billy, and they confront Michael but unbelievably, instead of expressing remorse for Tom's death, Michael threatens to harm Billy's mother or Tom's children if they go to the police. A reluctant truce with Michael brings Richard and Billy together at last.

Billy buys back Fox Halt and starts to make it into a viable business, keeping the dairy herd and making artisan products from their own milk, selling it in their Community Farm Shop. After three years, Richard moves to live permanently in one of the holiday cottages at Fox Halt Farm, and asks Billy to marry him, but then Jessie and her daughter Mary, turn up uninvited at the farm. Jessie looks terrible, and Mary has a secret which she won't reveal – a secret that makes her unwilling to stay at Culmfield anymore. Against Richard's wishes, Billy offers sanctuary to Jessie and Mary, seeing it as a chance to rebuild her friendship with Jessie, putting her desperate desire to rekindle their friendship (and gain Jessie's forgiveness) over Richard, driving him away.

Michael is found dead, seemingly suicide, but evidence grows suggesting Billy murdered him. Richard, Jessie and Mary are all questioned. Richard takes over the reins of Michael's company while Jessie gets herself back on track. Jessie wants to sell O'Rowdes' but the sale stalls when the police discover anomalies in the company's accounts, leading to a fraud investigation. Billy realises it's Ed's sister who has sabotaged Michael's company as revenge for her brother's death, but she doesn't reveal this, and Sarah disappears without a trace.

Amir, Michael's chauffeur, murdered Michael because Michael was threatening to have him and his wife deported. Years before Michael raped Amir's wife, Nala – and Sharmarke, their son, is really Michael's. The police close in on Amir, but aided by Jessie (and a four-million-pound pay-out from a trust fund Michael set up for Sharmarke), he and his family leave Culmfield in the Rolls Royce that Amir killed Michael in. As they make their bid to escape, Billy accidently becomes embroiled. Amir kidnaps her, threatening to kill her if the police ever discover that he killed Michael.

Billy and Richard's relationship is challenged, but eventually, Richard realises Billy truly loves him, and they marry on Christmas Eve surrounded by friends and family. They are committed to rebuilding the farm and its various enterprises, and seven years later, Amir, Nala and Sharmarke are still nowhere to be found.

Prologue

17 June 2016

With eyes squeezed shut, I can still picture saliva bubbling from her mouth and a yellow discharge oozing from her nose. I throw my arms around her neck, pushing my fingers into her skin. 'I love you. Don't die,' I sob. 'No!'

A terrible crime has happened here - a crime I should have anticipated and prevented. The stench of death and guilt overrides my senses…

PART ONE

Chapter 1

DEVON – SIX MONTHS EARLIER— BILLY

Icy water soaks through my hair and into my cotton blouse, and a chill runs down my spine, making me shiver. It's clear from folded arms, pressed in tight to his hulking frame, that Troy Gloon won't be inviting me inside despite the sleet.

I shouldn't expect anything else – Troy has never had a good word to say about me since he opened his farm shop seventeen miles away from mine. He takes every opportunity to crow about how fabulous his business is compared to Fox Halt. Each chance he gets, he'll knock me, jealous my trade keeps growing while his stagnates.

My eyes scan his broad shoulders, almost the width of the doorway, and then they dart to his wrist – to a forked tongued snake tattooed around it. He places his hand on the door handle, clenching and unclenching his grip and glares.

'A clear-cut *no*, Mrs May,' he says, his voice a growl as he shifts his weight and then lumbers aside, letting a small white cat dash into the house. 'By six, tonight. Tell him – *no!*'

As two more cats skate past him, I consider stepping forward to see if he'll let me in too, but I don't, my feet are glued to the doormat, unnerved by his ultimatum.

'Okay.' I keep my voice level to hide the disdain I feel – I can't find anything nice to even think about this man. He curls his top lip, strides backwards and slams his front door in my face. Immediately, my body stiffens as I mull over his threat – if I accept the unexpected offer which I received an hour ago from one of Mum's friends, I'll regret it. Troy made it clear to me, he expected first dibs on all the factory equipment Andrew Arscott is selling – my mother's friend is retiring and closing down his local ice-cream making business. It seems Troy didn't expect him to give me the chance to buy all the machinery instead of him. He's livid.

At first, I turned down the kit because I'm so busy as it is, but Andrew offered me a few hours to think it through, his tone so encouraging that out of sheer politeness, I found myself saying I'd let him know later today.

How Troy knew that Andrew approached me about buying the gear, I don't know, but as I put the phone down on Andrew, my mobile buzzed again. This time it was Troy demanding that I come and see him. He refused to explain his problem or the urgency, but I could hear he was angry, so I decided to do what he wanted. I planned to let him rant for a while to find out if there was anything I'd done wrong, or if there was something I needed to worry about. I was trying to save more bad-mouthing of me – I've had enough of scathing comments already today – what the local paper published about me and my shop this morning was truly unbelievable.

As I take the first step towards my van, a filthy dirty and completely sodden hen nearly trips me up. She's clucking wildly, as though she's about to lay an egg. I gently pick her up and hold her firmly against me, one hand stroking her comb, trying to calm her. The hen quietens and blinks at me. Water drips off her beak. I can't see anywhere for her to hide from the sleet, still drenching and freezing us both. I turn back to the house. 'Here you are,' I whisper to her, 'this should be more comfortable for you.' Without a sound, I open the front door and release the grubby bird inside, smiling to myself.

'Right,' I say aloud to the rain. 'I'll think this through later, now though, I have to speak to Grace.'

* * *

I stop dead in the doorway of the farm office. 'What's that?' I ask, pointing at Grace's feet.

'Call yourself a farmer,' my assistant replies, her eyes fixed on a complicated graph on the screen in front of her. 'A golden retriever, perhaps?' Grace's voice is flat, not even sarcastic and unlike her usual bubbly self. It's the same tone she used this morning when I phoned her.

'It's a baby goat,' I say, answering my own question.

'Oh.' Grace continues to dash her fingers over her keyboard. To anyone else, she seems focused on her job, but I know better. She's been working for me for too many months, and I can discern when she's avoiding something. Grace doesn't want to return to the conversation we were having on the phone earlier. We were discussing buying a robotic and moveable milking machine that I plan to leave in the field, so our cows can be milked whenever they feel like it. However, the second-hand machine I'd like to buy is in Holland. Grace is my computer and engineering whizz, and I need her to check the robot over before I spend a lot of money purchasing it and then shipping it to the UK. She surprised me earlier because she point-blank refused to help me - totally out of character for her. Grace is like Tigger, up and ready in a flash, raring to go and always first to volunteer. Her negativity is baffling.

'I'm keeping an eye on her for your mum.' She glances at me, then her eyes flash back to her screen.

'Grace,' I say, feeling rattled.

She turns back, raising her thick black eyebrows in a vain attempt to look innocent. Grace isn't a talented actress, but she never stops trying. I've known her all nineteen years of her life - her dad Tom was my childhood friend, and Grace, her brother, and her mum are still my nearest neighbours.

The young woman takes after her dad, with his same olive skin and black hair. She's always been a tomboy, never a trace of makeup and as usual, her long hair is plaited in two simple braids secured with elastic bands. Even so, she's strikingly beautiful, normally with a grin that lights up her whole face.

'I won't take no for an answer,' I tell her, sweeping away a strand of my sodden hair from my eye.

She stares back at me, then leans down to stroke the goat. 'Your mum's called her Betsy - she always thinks of such great names. She said she's a Golden Guernsey, she is s— '

'Holland,' I say, not allowing her to distract me. 'Why won't you come?'

She raises a mug to her lips and slurps noisily. 'I explained on the phone. I'm busy.'

'But you're already scheduled to work for me. I need you there. It's crucial.'

Grace has her drink in front of her with her elbows resting on the desk. She shrugs.

'It's a Tuesday and Wednesday, so Freddy won't be here,' I say, knowing that if her boyfriend is away, she'll have nothing planned.

She pulls her mouth so far up in the corners that no-one could resist smiling back, but I try, shaking my head. The kid makes sucking noises and immediately Grace jumps up. 'Her bottle's in the kitchen,' she says. 'I'll be a moment or two. I have to warm it up.'

I block her exit, and she sits down again, looking up at me. 'I'll talk to the seller on the phone,' she offers. 'I'll tell you what you need to look out for. You can go on your own and watch the robot operating. See it for yourself, and I'll give you some checks to run on the software. You really *don't* need me there.' She frowns. 'What did Gloomy Pants want?'

Her nickname for Troy Gloon makes me realise how cold and wet I am, and I wipe my hand under my nose and around my chin. 'What do you think about us making ice-cream?' I ask, allowing her to sideline the milking machine problem for a moment. I value my assistant's opinion, she's not just energetic and enthusiastic, but Grace is clever too, Oxford University awaits her, but she's deferred her place to study maths and statistics until next year, to work for me instead.

She rolls her eyes, and I explain some more. 'Andrew Arscott rang me out of the blue this morning. He's retiring, shutting down the factory and he offered me all his ice-cream kit – every last screw and nozzle, for a price that seems too good to be true.'

'What's the Gloomy Gloon got to do with that?'

'He wants it, and insisted I had to turn Andrew down.'

'He's all mouth and no trousers, that man. Go for it.' Grace's normal zest and excitement has whipped up in an instance. 'You keep saying you want a new challenge but—' A cloud falls across her face, her vibrancy vanishing as fast as it bubbled up. 'But you're busy enough already? You never stop.'

I lean over Betsy, rubbing her between her ears. 'I think you ought to get her a bottle,' I say.

Grace doesn't move. 'And do you want to delve into a completely new business you know nothing about?'

'That's what's attracting me – I thrive on learning new stuff, and we'd have another product to sell.'

'Talk to Richard,' she says, now bouncing towards the kitchen. I press my close-clipped fingernails into my palm – Grace has hit a nerve. I don't want to discuss this with my husband, I'm sure his feelings will mirror hers, that I've enough to do already. I speak louder so she can hear me in the adjoining room. 'I told Andrew I'd give him an answer this evening.'

Heading into the kitchen area, I watch as she puts the milk in the microwave. 'He offered me first refusal; said he was sorry for me.'

Grace's eyebrows knit together. 'Sorry for you?' she asks, checking the temperature of the milk in the bottle.

'He saw that humiliating article this morning.'

She walks past me to kneel down next to the kid. I guess she wants to steer away from this subject too, in case I get upset again – the poor girl has already listened to a tirade from me right after I read the article.

I touch her shoulder. 'I need you in Holland. I'll add an extra day to the trip, so we can visit Amsterdam and do some tourist stuff.' I'm close to her desk now, and the pungent smell of her drink tickles my nose. *Ginger? When did Grace stop drinking coffee?* In this same moment, I spy a fluffy blue rabbit on the pile of computer magazines beside her keyboard. Cuddly bunnies are not Grace's thing – unidentifiable metal cogs, or a dog-eared manual on a new programming language, *yes* but definitely not furry toys. My eyes travel to her stomach, and the question is out before I've considered my words. 'Are you pregnant?' I ask.

Her pupils widen. 'You *can't* say anything to Richard. Promise me!'

I feel hot and cold at the same time. 'I can't keep this from him,' I say, my voice is unsteady.

* * *

Berkeley Square, London – Richard

I click away from a news update concerning severe flooding around Carlisle, trying to put the Rolls Royce I've spied in a wrecked building out of my mind. My computer defaults to my inbox. Straight away I see an email from Billy and my curiosity spikes. My wife rarely sends anything to my work address. The subject line reads, '*Can you believe this?*'

As I open the email, Arthur strolls towards his desk, an hour and fifty minutes late back from lunch – no apology or explanation. He glances at my screen for a second. 'Personal message,' he says, and then he smirks.

My jaw clenches. 'Funny,' I reply – Arthur is bright, sociable and easy to work with but every ten minutes his attention is diverted by something on his phone. It drives me to distraction, and I constantly nag him to save his private life until lunchtime or when he finishes work.

I've mentored this cocky young man for over a year, and mostly, he is a good student, but I am counting down the days until March, and his twenty-first birthday, when I will walk away from his family's company for good. Arthur has his late father Michael O'Rowde's ability to hear or see something once for it to fix permanently in his mind, but taking over a multinational business requires understanding and planning, not just a photographic memory.

'Have you completed those action points?' I ask.

'Done.' He sits back in his chair, hands behind his head and makes that silly smirk again.

'I suggest you start on them,' I say, standing up. I scoop up my laptop and a small plastic cow, which always sits on my desk – a token reminder of Billy and the farm. 'I will see you here at seven-thirty tomorrow morning.'

He has niggled me. Arthur should appreciate me more. I'm only here as a favour to his mother, my involvement starting as a commitment to help her out for a couple of weeks, then a few months but now it's been seven and a half years!

I work hard for this company, staying Monday to Friday in Richmond with Arthur, living in the O'Rowde family's luxurious London home. Okay, so the mansion-like house has every facility imaginable but it's not Fox Halt Farm, and I miss Billy desperately, only seeing her at weekends.

'Chuffing heck, I didn't mean to nark you off.' Arthur emphasises his posh public school accent, *narking* me off even more.

'Seven-thirty, and without a hangover,' I reiterate as I head for the door.

Arthur casts his eyes down to the floor and then looks up at me. He does seem sorry, but I am still annoyed, 'Think before you make stupid comments,' I say, and I consider ending this crazy arrangement right this minute – but I can't, I will not let Jessie down.

* * *

The taxi jolts, as the driver swerves to miss a cyclist who's ignored a red light. I hold my laptop tighter and start to read Billy's message which has a single attachment, an article about the Fox Halt Farm Shop from today's *Western Morning News*.

Billy was really excited about having a feature story in the Saturday supplement of our local paper and was let down terribly when it didn't appear this weekend. She phoned the journalist who'd interviewed her to ask why it hadn't been published, to be told there wasn't enough space after the editor had included many dramatic pictures of last week's floods. The article would come out this morning instead – and now that it has been printed, the story has been slashed from the expected double-page spread to just half a page.

There is a single photo of Billy outside the shop holding up one of the Fox Halt Christmas Hampers. She's hardly smiling, and the exterior of the shop looks drab. In 2008 when it was first built, the larch cladding was a radiant chestnut colour, but this picture makes its weathered silver hue look shabby. To be fair to the photographer, it had rained all morning, and Billy said the journalist took her snaps in a fleeting dry moment but still, I wonder why she didn't use one of the many indoor shots Billy said she took. The shop is brightly lit and decked out beautifully.

As I read beneath the headline, *'Why Buy Local?'* I see why the paper selected this particular image. None of Billy's passion comes across. Instead, it feels like she is demeaning supermarket shoppers. I didn't hear her being interviewed, but I'm sure she wouldn't have belittled anyone for not recognising the quality of the fresh produce she sells. She is quoted mentioning tough times and people watching their spending, especially at Christmas but there is no empathy. It gives the impression the shop is for moneyed people, educated enough to appreciate fewer food miles and premium products.

The dairy and also her cheese and yoghurt making businesses are mentioned briefly, but the journalist questions why Fox Halt products are limited. 'So, no toffee fudge ice-cream or clotted cream?' she asks. Billy explains both are available, but sourced from a dairy in Somerset. I turn the little plastic cow over in my hand, then I type, *I thought you knew Marian Helman. Why do you think she has been so caustic?*

Chapter 2

Fox Halt Farm – Billy

I long for Friday evenings and Richard coming home. I'm impatient for Crinkle's bark as she hears his car come down the lane – inaudible to me, but our border terrier always picks up on it. Her body stiffens, and her tail rises into a tight 'C', before she scratches at the door, dying to see him.

I'm excited to see Richard yet reticent too, wary of telling him about the ice-cream venture and anxious about how he'll react when Freddy and Grace say they're going to be parents.

Mum stands next to me in front of the Rayburn stove while I mash swede in an ancient saucepan. My mind wanders, thinking how we've always cooked like this together – the pans used by my family for decades. My attention runs on from the rhythmic clunking of the potato masher with its loose handle to the lop-eared animal nibbling the hem of Mum's apron. I don't think Betsy has left her side for days.

We have no experience of goats – cows or sheep would be our chosen specialised subject on *Mastermind,* but last Monday one of our customers told Mum about a kid whose mother had rejected it, cruelly butting it away. The man had tried to encourage the baby's mother to accept her, but in the end, he'd carried the four-hour-old kid to Fox Halt, knowing my mum is famous in Hamsgate, and (most of Devon probably!) for adopting stray or injured animals. The more hopeless the case, the more determined she will be to take care of it.

Mum bathed a couple of wounds on the baby's face, fed her, cuddled her and encouraged her to walk on wobbly legs, and Betsy has been indoors ever since. Mum's fashioned a nappy for the baby goat which, unexpectedly, Crinkle hasn't tried to rip off – instead, the dog keeps on licking Betsy's face as if she's her puppy needing reassurance.

'Saw Andrew Arscott in the shop, lunchtime.' Mum lifts her spoon to gauge the thickness of her white sauce.

'Right,' I say, scrubbing my hands through my hair in anticipation of the scolding I'm about to get. I may be nearly fifty, but Mum won't hold back, she'll be fuming that I didn't tell her about Andrew's offer. I sensed something was up as soon as I came into the kitchen this evening. My mother wasn't her normal self, not chatting about all the things she's done today, divulging all the trivial detail of Hamsgate news, or filling me in on the minutiae of our friends' and relations' lives that she loves to keep abreast of. I usually respond with a *yes* or *no*, not really listening, hoping my reaction is appropriate. However, this evening, Mum has been crashing the pots and pans and focused more on Betsy than me. I knew she'd say in the end what was upsetting her, but I was expecting it to be that, somehow, she'd discovered Freddy and Grace's news.

'He told me something interesting.' My mum stares at me, waiting for my confession.

'Oh,' I stall.

She frowns. 'Why didn't you tell me?'

'I want to talk everything through with Richard.'

'You haven't discussed it with him?' Mum breathes in slowly through her nose, her lips drawn in a tight line.

'I want to talk face to face,' I say, bashing the swede some more. Mum shoves her saucepan to the edge of the Rayburn then sits at the table and glares at me.

I stop and face her, waving the masher at her, bits of swede dropping to the floor, much to Crinkle's delight as she hoovers them up. 'Andrew rang me after he'd read that awful piece in the paper,' I say. 'He thought I might be interested in making ice-cream and I had to make a quick decision – it was cheap, he's virtually given it to me.'

'You've got time to make ice-cream?'

I nod.

'Have you thought this through?' she asks, getting back up to start on the gravy.

'I'll explain over dinner, Rich will be here in…' I check the cow-faced clock, 'fifteen minutes.'

There's an awkward silence between us until Freddy and Grace follow Richard into the kitchen. Crinkle and I tear towards Richard, both vying for his attention. I win, hugging my husband with Crinkle jumping up at our legs, desperate for him to give her a pat. I press my body into his, closing my eyes. I breathe in his familiar smell, and wish that I never have to let go. When I open my eyes, Mum is frowning at Grace. 'Where have you and Freddy been?' she asks in the same displeased tone she used to quiz me about Andrew.

'Are we late?' Grace winces, she'll hate upsetting Mum.

'Just expected you earlier than this,' Mum says, sounding disappointed now, rather than annoyed.

'We were at Foxlands, sorry,' Grace says as she heads across the kitchen to give Betsy a rub along her back.

'Is there something you want us to do, Mrs May?' Freddy asks.

'Daniella,' Mum snaps at him, reminding Freddy to use her first name for the thousandth time. She could tell Richard's son until she's blue in the face, and it wouldn't happen, Freddy's just uncomfortable with it. He tried calling her 'Gran' when Richard and I got married, but it only lasted until the end of our wedding day. They act like doting granny and grandson, him spoilt and her revered, but he likes using the familiar name he called her when he first met her.

'You're fine,' Mum says, her voice soft. 'Dinner's ready.' She smiles, but neither Freddy nor Grace look relaxed.

Richard kisses Mum on the cheek. 'I hope Billy did most of this. You ought to be putting your feet up, not cooking for us. It smells *so* good by the way.'

'Dad, have you seen the goat?' Freddy's eyes are fixed on Grace, who now has Crinkle and Betsy beside her, a hand under each of their chins. Both animals have their heads up, savouring her scratching them. Freddy moves to Grace's side and smooths Betsy's head. 'She's a cutie,' he says, and I'm not sure if he means Grace or the goat.

Richard steps towards the Rayburn, knowing Mum will hand him a warmed plate so he can start helping himself to the roast dinner. It's become a custom that he'll lead the way, dishing up his meal first from all the pans laid out on the top of the oven. It's what Mum insisted Dad did too.

As he sloshes gravy over mashed swede onto his plate, I wonder how to broach the subject of my impulsive purchase. I know he won't be happy that I didn't talk it through with him first, and I'm pretty sure he'll be dead set against me hazarding anything else when I'm already crazy busy. I just didn't want him to insist that I passed the opportunity over. I'd have felt I shouldn't go against his express wishes. Richard's been my rock while I've built up Fox Halt, and he's my husband. I would have reluctantly decided I shouldn't do it and I didn't have enough time to win him around. I'd have lost it all to Troy Gloon, and something inside me hates that idea.

I hope the prospect of him being a grandad again will distract him – perhaps he'll be more receptive to my new business plan. Richard pauses as he takes his full plate to the table. 'William and Mary not here?'

'Mary's at the cinema,' I say quickly, before Mum has a chance to reply. 'And you know William, he wouldn't be here without her.' I'm fibbing because I don't know where Mary is. She might be with Grace's older brother William, but nonetheless I know why they're missing this evening. I asked them not to come, reckoning it would be easier for Grace and Freddy to break their news if there was just five of us around the table. I asked Mary to stay away, telling her, I'd explain on Monday, and she happily agreed without a single question. '*No problemo,* Auntie,' she said.

The atmosphere remains stilted, and I'm questioning the wisdom of William's and Mary's absence. Mary would have made some intelligent observation, and we'd all be deep in a friendly discussion. Grace is usually animated, self-deprecating and full of stories. She'd generally keep the talk flowing, making us laugh too, but tonight isn't normal. Grace is quiet, glancing at Freddy every couple of seconds, clearly hoping he'll put down his knife and fork and tell his father about the baby.

'Rich,' I say at last, giving up on Freddy, ready to tell my husband about my recent purchase.

'Yes, Richard,' Grace says, performing her biggest smile at him. I guess she's panicking, imagining I'm about to tell Richard her and Freddy's news. She nudges her boyfriend hard in the ribs, and with this, Freddy pushes back his chair and stands up. 'We are going to have a baby, Dad,' he blurts out with everyone's eyes focused on him. I do my best to look shocked, opening my mouth a little, copying Richard's expression. I count a full five seconds of silence in my head, *one and, two…*

Richard licks his bottom lip and turns to Grace. He clears his throat and coughs. 'When?' he asks.

'May. Late May,' Grace says. Her eyes flicker.

'After my last exam,' Freddy adds, looking at Grace and touching her hand.

Mum leans so far forward, she's rocking on the front legs of her chair. She has a grin wider than the one Grace faked. 'Oh, wonderful,' she says, beaming at Freddy. 'So, you'll find a job around here when you finish university. You two are welcome to one of the holiday cottages if you'd like to live at Fox Halt. I'll babysit whenever you need...'

'Hold on, Daniella.' Richard places his hand on the back of Mum's chair, pushing the legs back down on the floor. His eyes are still on Grace. 'I take it this wasn't planned?'

'We're going to make it work,' Grace whispers. 'Freddy and I are pleased about it.'

'Less than twenty weeks.' I see Richard's muscles tighten in his forearms. 'You still have options,' he says.

My mouth goes dry. *Surely, he can't be suggesting an...* I can hardly think the word, let alone say it to myself. Something fires up in my stomach. *Never. No*! Grief for my lost child overwhelms me and my fear of what Richard might be suggesting stops everything in the room. I can feel sweat on my forehead, and when I realise Richard is speaking again, his words are hazy like I'm dreaming. 'You're only just nineteen, Grace. Freddy is twenty-three. A baby now will change everything for you both. What did Martha say? I take it your mother knows? Is that why you were at Foxlands earlier?' Richard hasn't looked at his son, still standing directly across the table from him.

'Mum thinks we'll be okay,' Grace says, her voice a little stronger than before.

Richard turns to me. I see so much uncertainty in his eyes. He keeps blinking. I bow my head, my breath catching in my throat.

'She couldn't stop hugging us,' Freddy tells his dad, and Grace laughs. 'That's after she nearly fell and had to grab hold of the table, her knees were wobbling so much.'

Richard doesn't smile back. 'And Freddy's mother?' he asks.

'We're driving up to Buckinghamshire tomorrow morning,' Grace says. 'We will tell Janette, then.' Freddy sits back down, but Richard still doesn't look at his son.

'Grace, you *are* so clever,' Richard says. 'You are going to Oriel College. That's one hell of an achievement. You have a brilliant future ahead of you. You must not throw it away.' At last, he glances at his son but then his eyes flash back to Grace. 'And you and Freddy should see the world before you think about having babies. You *cannot* have a child now, you are far too young.'

'I *have* travelled,' Freddy says. 'Dad, have you forgotten my two years before uni?' I can hear Freddy is struggling not to raise his voice. His hands shake. Grace reaches to touch Richard's arm. 'I'm happy about the baby,' she says. 'I decided to keep him and bring him up on my own even if Freddy wasn't sure. But he wants this too. Freddy's as excited as me.'

All I hear is *him,* and the word resonates through my body, thinking of the little boy I never had. *Him.* Their baby is a little boy. Freddy moves his hand, placing it gently on Grace's stomach, and then he stares at Richard until his dad looks back at him. 'When Grace found out she was pregnant,' Freddy tells his dad, 'she kept breaking down all the time. She was terrified. She kept on apologising to me, and I held her every moment I could, reassuring her everything would turn out okay. And we have talked about this – like we've never talked before. Grace and I love each other, and we both want *our* baby.'

'Don't feel pressured into this,' Richard says as if he hasn't heard Freddy. 'There is still time to reconsider. A child is forever. I'll say one last thing, Freddy.' Richard taps his fingers on the table, each tap reiterating how unhappy he is.

'What?' Freddy asks.

'Promise me you'll finish at Exeter.'

His son nods and smiles. 'I might even get a first.'

'Good.' Richard lifts his glass of wine, staring at Grace's pint of water. 'If you two are *both* sure, then congratulations are in order.' Mum and I quickly lift our glasses 'Congratulations,' Mum and I say together. 'Such wonderful news,' Mum adds.

Richard shakes his head at Mum.

'You know, Daniella, this isn't what is best for them.'

'Daniella and I are here if you need to talk,' I tell Grace.

'Or if you just want a hug,' Mum adds, holding out her arms to the young mother-to-be. Grace jumps up, slipping into her embrace. 'Thank you, Daniella,' she says, pressing her face against Mum's and kissing her on the cheek.

Richard is calmer than I expected. Freddy and Grace have been boyfriend and girlfriend since Grace was twelve years old, and I don't know how many times I've heard Richard caution them about the consequences of sleeping together. Freddy always shrugged off his father's embarrassing safe-sex speeches. I had expected the potential parents to be bombarded with, *'I warned you this might happen'* statements but no. No criticism at all about how careless they've been, but neither did I expect Richard to suggest Grace end the pregnancy, not when he knows how losing our child destroyed me. Not when he knows how much it still hurts, even after all this time.

Freddy pats Grace's belly. 'His name is Tom,' he says, looking at me, then at Mum and then at his dad. A tingle travels up my spine, and I watch Mum's eyes well up. 'Dear Tom,' she chokes her words out. 'After Grace's father, oh…' She lets out a long sigh. 'Your dad would be so proud, Grace.'

This isn't the right time to tell Richard my ice-cream plans, the baby is enough for him to take in. I'm off-balance, desperate for Grace to have her baby, hating seeing Richard so upset and I fear what will happen next.

Chapter 3

RICHARD

Monday morning and I'm punching out a text message to Janette. *'Can't sleep, 3am and not impressed. Need to be back at O'Rowdes' for eight!'* I press send and rub my eyes.

I was staring up at the bedroom ceiling until I saw Janette's text light up the room, and then I crept downstairs to the kitchen to reply to her, and to make myself a cup of tea. I spoke to my ex-wife briefly last night, saying how I'm constantly thinking about Freddy and Grace, and my worry for them – I can't be happy about the child. They are children themselves with no clue how a baby will mess up their lives. She warned me to tread carefully so I don't alienate them, but I want them to see what a massive decision this is, and how they are making the wrong choice.

Three more cups of tea and it's half-past five. As I close the lid of the Rayburn to toast a slice of bread, Billy appears in the doorway. Her hair is screwed into an untidy bun to keep it out of the way while she does the milking. Her blue overalls are spotless, but my nose detects the faint scent of cow muck when she kisses me, brushing my lips lightly with hers, 'Will you be okay?' she asks.

'I'm fine,' I say, retrieving my toast and watching her set the timer to microwave her porridge.

Billy sits down on the chair next to me. 'It's not your fault, Richard.' She has guessed what I'm thinking. 'You're a great dad,' she says.

I shake my head.

'Rich, stop beating yourself up.'

'I didn't spend enough time with him. I could have prevented this.'

She kisses my cheek as she reaches across me to pick up my cup. 'Want another one?' she asks.

I lift my cup so she can take the handle. 'I've been replaying the last few years through my mind,' I tell her. 'I regret how I have done so few father/son things with Freddy – how I used to let him spend hours at our neighbours in Buckinghamshire, and how, whenever we were in Devon, he always hung around with Grace. I should have tried harder. Been stricter with him, instilled more responsibility.' Tiredness makes me feel like crying again. Twice, Billy has found me sobbing. I haven't cried so much since Sharpie died. I went to bed on Friday night and held my wife so tightly that in the end, she asked me to ease my grip. I've hardly slept, and when I did manage to nod off, there was a split second as I awoke when I felt fine, but then I remembered the baby, and the black cloud of apprehension swamped me again.

Billy glances at my phone, the screen saying I have a new message from Janette, a single thumbs-up emoji. I pick up the phone and hold it out to her. She can read the conversation if she likes – there is nothing more in my messages with Janette than concern for Freddy and Grace. Yes, we are an affluent family, I have plenty of money, as does Janette, and there would be masses of support available for the new parents, but I'm still haunted by how Janette and I got it so wrong.

Billy doesn't take the phone. 'I knew Janette and I were too young to settle down,' I say, 'but still, I jumped in anyway, and then, we had the twins too soon. Janette and I had no-one to question if we were doing the right thing, my parents adored Janette, and all Sharpie wanted was grandchildren.' The microwave pings and Billy stands up to fetch her porridge. She runs a hand slowly over my shoulder.

'I appreciate how you have listened to me,' I say.

'I need to tell you something, Rich.' She smiles, but it doesn't reach her eyes.

'Now?' I feel frustrated, so exhausted that I wonder if I should be driving to London, but if I leave now the M5 shouldn't be stupidly busy. I don't want a drawn-out conversation with Billy about why I should change my mind about the child.

'I think you'll be cross with me,' she says.

'Oh?' I say, buttering my toast, no clue now where this might be going.

'Remember the article in the paper—'

'I thought we weren't mentioning it again?' I breathe in the comforting smell of the warm bread – always more promising than the eventual taste, even when I've smothered it with Daniella's homemade strawberry jam.

'Sometimes you need someone on the outside looking in to see things more clearly,' she says.

I frown at her. My brain is not up to philosophising. 'Can we talk about this on the phone, tonight?' I ask. She looks at me, saying nothing, and I can't read her face. Scarlet jam runs off my toast and slides across my plate, and I smile to myself, thinking how Daniella is always telling me strawberry jam won't set without adding extra pectin or some lemon juice, but she prefers leaving it runny. *Unadulterated Jam* she calls it.

'I've agreed to buy Andrew Arscott's ice-cream making equipment—' Billy's words rush out of her mouth. 'He's closing down his whole business. Says he's gotten too old. He virtually gave it away.'

'Damn!' I press my hand to my cheek.

'What?'

'I've bitten the side of my mouth.'

'You okay?'

'Fine,' I say, staring at her.

'You aren't fine, Richard,' she says, touching the hand I still have pushed into my face.

'Okay, I'm not. I'm pretty miffed that you have *not* discussed this with me. I think you would have guessed my reaction.' My voice is too loud, but I'm too tired to soften my response. 'You can't start a new business. You are nearly fifty – the shop is making money. The cheese side of things is doing well. You do *not* have time for anything else.'

'But—'

'No,' I say, holding up my hand. 'I finish at O'Rowdes' in three months. If Grace and Freddy don't see sense, then we are about to be grandparents. We plan to ease up a bit. I want to spend time with *you,* not have you running here, there and everywhere, trying to establish another business. You can't. You won't!'

'I won't?' Billy repeats and frowns as she tears at the elastic band holding her hair up, removing it and twisting it tightly around her fingers. 'You know what the farm means to me, and how much I want it to be a success?'

'So, you don't want to spend time with me?' I check. 'I'm telling you, Billy, I don't want you to do this. You are *not* starting a brand new venture. We should be looking forward to spending time together. At the moment, you have enough staff to cover you when you are away. We can get a motorhome. We'll go travelling.'

Billy shakes her head slowly. 'I don't want a motorhome.'

I stand up, and she immediately gets up too, throwing her chair back and facing me.

Silence. I imagine she doesn't know what to say next and I don't know either, but I won't back down. She turns and picks up the kettle. 'Tea?' she asks.

'I haven't got time,' I say through my teeth, slapping my fingers over my empty mug. Hating how this has flared up into a row when I'm about to leave for five days.

'Arthur will be okay if you're ten minutes late. He should be able to manage without his nursemaid by now.' I sense Billy is jibing at me, she never liked me agreeing to stay on at O'Rowdes'. She has never said anything negative about me helping Jessie, or argued against it as the time I've continued to run the business has gone on, but she has never said anything positive about it either.

'Ten minutes, that's all,' I say.

She makes two cups of tea; putting mine in front of me before quickly stepping away with hers, she uses her mug as a barrier, holding it up to her mouth, not drinking. 'We can have the ice-cream side of things up and running by June twenty-seventh, my birthday, that's exactly eight years since we opened the shop—' She pauses like she is waiting for me to confirm what a great idea this is but I say nothing. After a second or two, Billy continues, 'Freddy could manage the ice-cream business for us. Put his degree to good use. He'll be full of ideas - if anyone can sell ice-cream, Freddy can.'

I snatch up my unwanted drink and smack it down in the middle of the table, I glare at her. 'So, you were aware of the baby *before* you bought the stuff from Andrew?'

She flinches and I know I'm right.

'It's all second-hand, there's no new kit,' Billy says.

'Did you know about the pregnancy before Friday evening?' I feel the muscle above my eyebrow start to throb.

'Not when Andrew first approached me,' she says.

I take in a deep breath. 'You knew?' I ask again. 'And you didn't think to tell me?'

'Grace begged me to let Freddy tell you,' she says. 'What would you have done, if it were the other way around, Rich?' She puts her mug down next to mine. I wince, realising that this reversed situation would be impossible – Billy was unable to have children, and I shy away from continuing this argument, trying a new tack. 'I'm your husband. We tell each other everything, remember?' I tap the side of my head to emphasise my words.

'Freddy is *your* son. It was up to him to break the news to you, and I insisted they told you as soon as you got home.'

'So, your motive for this madcap scheme is it gives Freddy a job?' I check.

'There are a lot of good reasons.' Billy looks away, then back at me.

'Which are?' I snap.

'We are selling our excess milk, and it isn't making us a twentieth of what it would be worth as ice-cream.'

I try to estimate the different prices in my head, but my brain isn't functioning well enough to calculate anything. 'I would like to check that figure,' I say. 'Are you taking into account all the extra overheads? Go on, what other reasons?' I hold out my hands and gesture with upturned fingers, beckoning her to give me a list.

'I want a new challenge. Alright, Yes, I'm forty-seven, but I'm not ready to be written off. I love the farm, it's my life. I love learning new things, and it's another string to our bow, which has to be a good thing.'

'Would I ever see you, Billy? You work all the time as it is,' I say, picking up my car keys, trying to show her I don't want to discuss this anymore.

She carries on despite my keys now jangling in my hand, 'Mary can manage the cheese and yoghurt making. She could do it standing on her head. She'll look after the dairy, while I set up the ice-cream. It'll be fine.'

She's right. Mary could run the dairy, she's been involved with Fox Halt for ten years now, and she would be brilliant – reliable, astute and wholly dedicated to growing the business, but there's something Billy isn't taking into account, 'Mary has responsibilities at Culmfield,' I say.

Billy squares her shoulders 'Her heart's here, not at Culmfield. You know she'll jump at the opportunity.'

'I've got to go,' I say, and absentmindedly I swipe my cup to the middle of the table. Billy doesn't seem to react, her eyes set on mine. 'Where are your priorities?' I ask, 'Is the farm more important than us? I think you need to check all your costings carefully.'

Billy nods. 'Okay.'

'I can tell you, right now, I will *not* fund this scheme. Count me out.' I start moving to the door, and Billy reaches for my hand. 'I love you,' she says, kissing my cheek.

Instantly, my body relaxes a little. 'What will you do?' I ask, stepping away from her but she doesn't reply.

Chapter 4

Billy

Even with her wild red hair stuffed into a blue hair net and with her white coat and green wellies, Mary looks enchanting. For a second, her sparkle makes me feel old, but I shake the idea away. 'Why did you starve William and me on Friday?' she laughs, as she drops a floating thermometer into the pasteurised milk.

'I suspect you know why,' I reply.

Mary pushes her lips out and shakes her head.

'Haven't you seen William?' I ask.

'Spent the whole weekend with my darling brother.'

'Arthur?' I check, surprised, not because he's the only one of her three siblings who's left their family home, choosing to live and work in London, but because Mary has never given the impression she's close to him. She is a year older, and when I've spent time with them, Mary treats Arthur like an irritating younger brother, her fieriness and no-nonsense attitude oppressing his contrasting easy-going nature.

'He's been nagging me to go up to Richmond for ages. In fact, it was a laugh, he's got some cool friends.' Mary turns off the machine which is heating up the milk. 'What's William done?' she asks.

'Not William, his sister.'

She huffs like a disappointed child told a secret they already knew. Her reaction takes me back, to the time when Mary was a toddler, and I worked for her mother on the Culmfield Estate. I picture Mary in her favourite pale lemon dress with wide ruffles around its neck. I see her clearly, her chubby arms folded across her body and her nose wrinkled up.

'You knew about the baby?' I ask the nearly twenty-two-year-old version of the little girl in the yellow dress. Mary heads for the clipboards hanging on the wall opposite. She lifts one off its hook and records the details of the batch of cheese she's making. 'How did the expectant grandfather take the news?' she says, her eyes still on her notes.

'He feels guilty,' I say.

She scoffs. 'It's not *his* baby.'

'He's worried for Grace and Freddy. He says they're so young. Too young to be having a child when they have so many other opportunities, especially Grace's place at Oxford - he knows how hard she worked to get in.'

Mary stares at me. 'I still don't get it, why's Richard guilty?'

'He thinks he's been remote from Freddy at times, and he should have taught him to be more careful.'

She rolls her eyes. 'That's rubbish. Richard couldn't have done anything to stop them having sex.'

'When you have children, Mary, you'll be the same, feeling responsible for every little thing that happens in their lives. Judging yourself not to have been good enough. You'll gnaw over what you think you might have done differently that would have changed an outcome, or altered the way they behave.'

Her mouth opens as if she's about to reply, but then she shuts it again, and I guess she was about to say something that started with, '*How would you know…*' But like everyone who knows me well, like Richard did earlier, they steer away from subjects that could remind me of my miscarriage and my insides, too damaged to ever carry a child again.

I swallow hard, thinking how people don't need to *say* anything tactless to trigger these thoughts, such simple things set me off. Last week, William used a wrench to undo a nut in the dairy that neither Mary nor I could shift. As I watched William, my thoughts turned to how my son might have held the tool, imagining *his* eyes lighting up as he managed to loosen it for me. My heart jumps. *If only…*

It's been hard to listen to Richard and his views while hiding my own excitement of a new baby at Fox Halt. My eyes well up, and straight away Mary rifles in her pocket for a paper towel, 'Here, Auntie,' she says, handing it to me.

'They can't *not* have the baby, Mary. I couldn't bear it.'

'Grace and Freddy won't change their minds.' She flashes me a look of certainty making me feel a little better.

'Mary, after I've finished the deliveries can I talk to you about something else?'

'Give us a clue?'

'I need a sounding board. I want to tell you about my dreams for Fox Halt Ice-Cream.'

Mary whistles. 'Wowee!' she says.

'Yes, wow,' I agree.

* * *

A week until Christmas and it's been manically busy. Time's raced by, but still with everything going on, Mum found time to make me a fantastic new bobble hat and matching scarf from our sheep's wool which she spun earlier in the year. I adore the hat's bobble, and the pom-poms that she's sewn onto the ends of the scarf – their twisted strands are so soft to touch like silk.

I pull my hat further down over my ears and adjust my scarf to stop the cold creeping around my neck, and I drink in my surroundings –the morning sunshine glinting on the frost makes everything festive, the grass like tinsel.

Olive and Doris, two of my much-loved ewes, hurtle towards me, and they're soon nuzzling at the right-hand pocket of my coat where they know I'll have Rich Tea biscuits. This pair were orphan lambs, and we've had a special bond since I bottled fed them for the first weeks of their lives.

Richard leans on the gate. 'We are so lucky,' he says, his eyes fixed on the greedy Whiteface Dartmoors as they waddle back towards the rest of the flock, their long curly fleeces making them resemble Mum's knitted pom-poms.

'Beautiful,' I say.

He nods.

'Do you mind if we talk ice-cream?' I ask.

His gaze leaves the sheep and rises up towards the distant tors. He doesn't answer. I continue, regardless. 'The building will be the biggest outlay.'

'You need another building?' Richard straightens up, taking his elbows off the top rail of the gate.

'None of the existing ones are suitable. There needs to be plenty of space. It's got to be practical – good access, a prep room, packing area, storage for boxes, etcetera. I'll need a couple of large freezers too.'

'Right,' he says, his tone disinterested.

I keep my voice upbeat, 'I've given William the square footage I think I need. He said Sean and him could get it up in the second or third week of January. He's letting me have a proper estimate on Monday.'

Richard frowns. 'And planning?'

'That'll hold everything up.'

He kicks at the gatepost. 'I think you're being reckless.'

'I'll get Charlotte's friend to make the application once we are up and running.' I turn to go back to the house and start to walk away, hating his negativity.

Richard keeps up with me as we walk. 'Charlotte's friend?' he asks, shaking his head.

I feel more frustrated than ever; he must know who I mean. 'I can't remember her name at the moment,' I say, trying to conceal my irritation. 'The woman who sorted the dairy. She'll have no problems. Fox Halt is outside the National Park. I'll get her to apply retrospectively, and by then I'll have four or five staff working full time. The planners can't look unkindly on new local jobs in a rural community.'

He shakes his head again and makes a soft huff sound in his throat. 'I'd get permission first - it's a lot of money to pay out for a building you may have to take down.'

'I'll show you where I think it will go,' I say, looking into his eyes. I wish he'd smile and tell me that he loves my idea. He doesn't smile and I pick up speed a little, hoping my feet will warm up. 'Andrew Arscott said he'd help me install everything,' I say, slipping my gloved hand into his. 'By mid-April, we'll have it all set up, which gives us two months to tweak everything and then bam! We are off.'

'Billy.' Richard stands still, pulling me back.

I let go of his hand, 'What?'

'Stop saying *we*. I'm set against this,' he says. 'You're going about this all the wrong way. Forgetting the planning for a moment, where is the money coming from?'

'The bank.'

'Have you sorted a loan?'

I laugh.

'What's funny?' he asks.

'Not even I would go to Lisa Illston without costings and profit forecasts. She's no fool, but I'm confident she'll lend me the money.'

Richard shrugs and then he points to the cow shed. 'Will you be parking your ice-cream factory next to that?'

'I've found a better position.' I wait for him to ask where, but he starts to walk on again, taking long strides. I rush to match his pace. 'I've got a woman coming on Tuesday,' I say. 'She'll give me some more information before I finally decide.'

'A fortune-teller?' Richard jeers and I smile, unhappy with his sarcasm but at least we're talking about my plans.

'No,' I say, maintaining the grin on my face. 'She's a consultant from a company specialising in renewable energy. I want to put up a windmill, maybe two. The freezers will use a lot of electric.'

'Christ, Billy, I can hardly keep up with all this.'

'She'll also give me some information about heat recovery systems. She's been involved with a dairy in Cornwall who'll be carbon neutral in five years. That should help later, with the planning application.'

Richard stops again. 'You have one person on your side,' he says.

'Who?' I feel aggravated that he's thinking in terms of sides, me and ice-cream against him, but I stay calm, refusing to let him see that he's getting to me.

'Freddy,' he says, sounding annoyed.

'Oh.'

'Yes, he keeps calling himself the next *Mr Whippy*. I told him straight, it's never going to happen—' He watches my face.

I smile, refusing to react to his continued negativity. 'I'm glad, we went to check the sheep,' I say, relieved that his son is happy about my new venture, even if my husband isn't. 'There's nothing better than walking around the farm with you,' I tell him, reaching for his hand again.

He pulls me towards him and kisses me. 'Do you remember that first day you showed me around Fox Halt?'

'The day before Dad's sixtieth…' I pause, my body melting into his. 'Thirteen years ago…'

Richard releases me and stares into my eyes. 'It was longer than that.'

'It's thirteen years since Dad died.'

'Sorry, I thought you didn't remember.' He tries to catch hold of my hand again, but I stuff both in my pockets, hurt that he'd think I'd forget. 'I think of Dad so often,' I say, swallowing down the upset. 'Something will remind me, something he said or something he used to do. I'm sure he's looking over my shoulder all the time. He'd be so chuffed we're getting the farm sorted out.'

'He'd be proud of his daughter.' Richard smiles, his face lighting up. He checks his watch. 'We'd better get moving.'

'To see *the* site?' I ask, confused by his sudden keenness.

'No, we have to be in Ashburton by half past eleven, we have some motorhomes to look at.'

My heart sinks to my toes. I pull my scarf tighter around my neck. I'm not interested in a motorhome. *Does he know me at all?* 'Donna, no it was Dominique, Dominique Wade,' I say.

'Who?'

'That's the name of the planning consultant who worked on the dairy.'

Chapter 5

Billy

New Year's Eve and I'm standing in front of an open freezer overawed by its crammed contents.

I've come into the Culmfield kitchen to fetch more ice-cream supplies, and this freezer seems to contain every make, variety and flavour of ice-cream on the market. Jessie is suddenly next to me, pressing her face against mine. 'Lovely to have you here,' she says, squeezing my hand so tight it hurts.

'Are you okay?' I ask.

'Yes.'

I can feel moisture on my cheek. 'Really?'

She pulls away and half-smiles. 'I'm hiding,' she says.

'Sorry?'

'I can't do this—' Jessie releases her grip on my fingers. 'But I don't want to disappoint you.'

Since we met, over twenty years ago, Jessie and I have had highs and some horrible lows, but she's remained my closest friend. We share the same birthday - same day, same year, and for a long time, I lived here with her, both of us working together to get the 6,000-acre estate back on its feet. Jessie forgave the unforgivable when I had an affair with her late husband, but since Michael's death our shared secrets, shared hopes, and our shared devotion to Mary have glued us back together.

I shake my head. 'No way am I disappointed,' I say. 'You planned everything tonight and let me use your amazing home. You've invited everyone who's anyone around here. I'm so grateful to you.' Jessie has gone beyond anything I might have dreamt of, supporting my ice-cream venture - suggesting we held a grand New Year's Eve banquet in the Long Gallery at Culmfield Court with a fancy fish and chip supper, dancing and ice-cream. The invitations stipulated guests couldn't attend unless they were willing to consume tonnes of ice-cream – and give their honest opinion on every flavour and manufacturer.

When Jessie came up with the idea, I never imagined she was being serious. She is always so busy, and such an event seemed impossible to put together in the time frame. But she has done it, organising tonight's extravaganza all on her own.

I drop my gaze from her dark brown eyes and look down at my orange and yellow striped silk dress which Jessie spent hours in Exeter helping me choose, 'No-one will overlook you in that outfit, Billy,' she assured me. *Unless you are standing next to me,* I thought, taking in her sleek black hair, dimples, and slim frame. Her looks and her ballerina-like grace enthralled me from the moment we met.

'It's too bright?' I argued.

'It's a winter bash, and you'll be the sunshine. You look stunning. Buy it, please.' Jessie was determined.

I bring my eyes up from my dress to meet hers. 'What's wrong?' I ask. 'Everyone will be talking about tonight for ages. The place looks magnificent, the food was gorgeous and the Long Gallery is—' I pause, trying to think of the word to describe the atmosphere and revelry that I've just walked through to get to the kitchen. 'Buzzing,' I say at last – my is brain frazzled from the last-minute prep, event nerves and the glass of champagne Jessie insisted I had before the first of the party-goers arrived.

She blinks at me. 'Mary's still charming the pants off everyone in there. But I'm so sorry, Billy, I had to get out.'

Her frightened demeanour reminds me of another day. A day when she turned up with Mary at Fox Halt, her feistiness and seductive charm vanquished, and I realised how her husband had been controlling her for years, cleverly hiding the abuse. She was terrified – almost scared to death. But it was Michael who died, not his wife, and Jessie has returned to her daredevil diva self. This reticence, I haven't seen since Michael's death. 'Tell me what's upsetting you, and I'll sort it,' I close the door of the freezer, giving her my full attention.

Jessie smiles, an expression so genuine it makes me feel unexpectedly warm. 'It's the ice-cream,' she says.

I frown. 'Ice-cream, but that's the whole point of tonight?' I say, but now I reconsider what she's telling me. Jessie is a vegan, she would never eat ice-cream, and I was amazed she suggested tonight in the first place, promoting something she wouldn't eat. 'The ice-cream,' I repeat. 'This was *your* idea.'

'I wanted to help,' She brushes a finger across her cheek.

'But everyone stuffing themselves with dairy products was never going to sit well with you.' I wipe a tear from her other cheek and smile at her. I'm so glad that when Jessie decided to stop eating meat and dairy, we stayed friends - we talk about our views, but neither tries to change the other's mind. She comes and sees our animals, and she knows how hard we work looking after each one, and in turn, I respect her standpoint too, more so perhaps because she's seen the farm for herself.

'I feel a hypocrite, asking people if they want to try the Lush Liquorice or the Honest Honey, or whatever. I keep hoping they'll say no.'

'Don't worry,' I say. 'Just come outside for the fireworks, and see everyone off later.' I hug her. 'Thank you again for everything.'

'I'll skulk off upstairs then,' Jessie smiles and at the door she pauses. 'I did enjoy organising tonight,' she says. 'You must let me know if there's anything else I can do to help.'

* * *

Mary is shouting at the Lord Mayor of Exeter when I see her; the music is so loud and there is such a crush of people, it's the only way to communicate. 'Where's Mum?' she barks at me as I cross the crowded dance floor towards her, a tray of coconut ice-cream balanced in my hand. It's so hot that it's starting to melt.

'Making sure everything's okay with the fireworks,' I holler in her ear, wondering why I'm lying, maybe because I don't want to say anything negative about ice-cream. Richard still hasn't come round, even refusing to come tonight. *New Year's Eve and we are not together!*

Mary frowns.

'What's wrong?' I ask

'She's not letting them off, is she?'

I laugh, thinking how Mary's question is valid, I can see her mother relishing being involved with the explosives. A gentle tap on my shoulder breaks into my thoughts. I spin around to see William, 'Come on,' he says, holding out his hands to Mary and me. 'We'll miss the fireworks.'

I hesitate. 'Where's Jessie?' I ask.

William tugs my arm. 'Out there.'

Nearly two hundred people are gathered on the rear lawn, but the house's scale and its grounds mean there's plenty of space to view the spectacular display. Glittering red, orange and green sparkles reflect off the River Culm's black waters, two hundred yards away. I squeeze my eyes as the countdown to 2016 starts, loving the cool smoky air, so different from the sweaty atmosphere in the Long Gallery. With Mary and Jessie's hands in mine, I make a wish.

Chapter 6

RICHARD

On the driveway to Culmfield, a fallow deer darts in front of my car then leaps over the iron railings into the park. Billy is driving towards me, on her way home to Fox Halt Farm for the early morning milking while here I am arriving, to help clear up after the party. She doesn't slow her van as she waves to acknowledge me.

I wave back, wondering if, like me, she didn't sleep last night – even if she was in one of Jessie's *oh so* comfortable four-poster beds and no doubt, in the best guest room.

* * *

Sunshine streams through the mullioned windows of the Long Gallery creating white highlights in Arthur's blond hair. Jessie and I look up as he marches past us, heading for the grand piano sited at the far end of the room. Arthur holds his head high like a virtuoso about to open a concert at the Albert Hall. He is wearing jeans and an Aran sweater so he can't contrive a masterful flick of a tailcoat before he perches himself on the piano stool. Nonetheless, he sits in an unnaturally upright position while he waits for our full attention. He nods at us then stretches his fingers over the keys. The music brings the magnificent room to life.

His mother closes her eyes to listen to the opening bars, 'Beautiful,' Jessie whispers, before thumping a heavy marble bust of her grandfather which she was cleaning onto the windowsill beside her.

'I didn't know he could play,' I say.

'All the children can,' Jessie replies. 'We have a family saying that you can't have a Steinway and not play it. I play too, but Arthur is the most gifted of all of us. They say this piece is one of the ten hardest to master, and Arthur can make a pretty good job of all ten.' She picks the bust up again, having noticed she has missed a splodge of pistachio ice-cream under her ancestor's prominent nose.

'I never expected cleaning up to take so long,' I say, reaching up for a half-empty wine glass left abandoned on a bookshelf, between a large porcelain dog and a delicate-looking hourglass.

'Billy got off lightly.' Jessie smiles, 'heading off to milk the cows. Funnily enough, Mary had something vitally important to do this morning as well.'

I don't reply, turning to Arthur instead, 'You're full of surprises,' I say as I retrieve another glass, wincing as I pick it up, spying a water stain on the highly polished lid of the piano. 'Chopin?' I ask, pausing for a moment to appreciate the music.

Arthur raises an eyebrow, 'Étude - Opus Ten. Number Four,' he says.

Jessie comes to stand next to me. She touches Arthur's shoulder. 'This talented son of mine could do anything he wanted, Richard - I've absolutely no idea why he's chosen to run O'Rowdes'.'

Arthur ignores her comment, continuing to play, and Jessie resumes her mission to remove ice-cream and sticky fingermarks from all the works of art in the room.

I start to collect empty dessert bowls which are scattered on every horizontal surface. 'Do you remember the game, *hunt the thimble*?' I ask Jessie.

'Why?' she frowns.

'Because this feels like a grown-up version of it, I'm twice as tall and the thimbles are bigger.' I hold up a bowl. 'And the room is—' I cast my eyes around the magnificent room.

Jessie shrugs. 'Forty times larger?' she suggests.

'Something like that.' I smile, staring up at the spectacular ceiling, its white plaster moulded to illustrate scenes from the Old Testament. Jessie puts down her cloth and finds a new clean one. 'We raised nearly six thousand pounds last night,' she says.

'After costs you mean? Really?'

'I'm covering expenses,' she says, climbing up on a chair to polish a carved oak shield hung over one of the fireplaces.

I nod. 'That will make quite a difference to your charity.'

Jessie looks serious. 'It'll pay towards a safe place for a mum and her children, or a caseworker but not for long.' She looks down at the floor then back at me. '*WhatIf* has so much to fund. There are so many women and children needing help in Devon, last night's money won't go far at all.' Jessie's mouth turns up into a smile.' Do you know, Richard, I'm considering doing this again next year - without the ice-cream, of course.' She holds out an intricate silver bowl for me to take and grimaces. It's full to its filigree brim with vanilla milk. I shake my head. 'I think we can all do without that,' I say.

Jessie jumps down from the chair. 'Do you want to give me an update on your ice-cream war?' she asks.

I plonk my tray of glassware down onto a side table and sit down on a delicate-looking and gold-leaf covered chair, 'Billy is focused on the farm,' I say. 'She never stops to think about us.' I get up again, having spotted a glass hidden behind a cushion on another chair. I turn back to Jessie, glass in hand. 'She seems to have forgotten that I sold my business to be at the farm full time.'

'Well, that plan failed, didn't it?' she laughs.

My attention switches to Arthur, who has started to play a piece that is lifting the hairs on the back of my neck. The music, Ligeti's 'The Devil's Staircase', has quiet moments followed by colossal and vigorous parts. It's transporting me to the Paris Opera House. I can picture my old friend Saffi staring at me with his finger on his lips, telling me to be quiet so he can enjoy the music. The arrangement of notes is unforgettable, just like Saffi - I'll never forget him either, his vibrancy and his laughter. My thoughts run on to his terrible suicide, and then to Jessie's husband's similarly untimely death. I start to contemplate how different things might have been, if Michael hadn't died, leaving O'Rowdes' to Jessie - and if she hadn't asked me to help her with the business.

Jessie was desperate to obliterate all trace of her controlling dead husband, intent on selling the company, but the sale was delayed by a fraud investigation which grew in complexity and length as the level of the interference into the company's affairs and accounts was slowly and forensically uncovered. The woman, Sarah Lancaster, who'd messed up so much had worked cleverly and covered her tracks well and it took over two years to fully unravel - she still hasn't been found, obviously as good at hiding herself as she was at concealing false entries and deletions in Michael's seemingly meticulous files. Why she did it remains a mystery too, another person with a score to settle with Michael, no doubt.

Arthur had grown up expecting he would eventually, take over O'Rowdes', his siblings not caring about the company at all, and as the investigation dragged on, he became increasingly aggrieved about his mother's plans to offload what he considered to be *his* inheritance – Jessie eventually, agreed to keep the company for him. The upshot being me staying on as managing director while the teenager finished his GCSEs. After his exams, Arthur worked in the largest of O'Rowdes' Exeter supermarkets, undertaking a range of roles from night-shift shelf filler to checkout assistant, and both Jessie and I assumed he'd give up on his dream to run the company, allowing the sale to proceed, but instead, in the supermarket, he did every task assigned to him with gusto and pride, and everyone loved him – from the security guards to the store manager. He's continued to work hard, and now he is convinced he is ready to step into his late father's shoes.

Arthur has been with me in the head office for over a year, and on the sixteenth of March, I will leave him to it, to manage the company on his own. I wouldn't tell Arthur, but I'm certain he will be fine. He reminds me of his father. Determined, single-minded and clever – and like Michael, he is easy-going with people. He can make them do things they would rather not do, praising and cajoling them in equal measure. But Jessie, Billy and I all learnt to our cost that Michael was not all he seemed, and it makes me cautious of this particular son.

The atmosphere changes in a moment – the new music from Arthur's fingertips feels foreboding and mocking.

'—did it?' Jessie is staring at me, but I wasn't listening.

'Sorry?'

'The plan didn't work out, did it? To be with Billy at the farm. But I'm so grateful to you for everything you've done – I don't know how I'd have managed without you, Richard.'

I laugh. 'You'd have kicked everyone's backsides,' I say.

She shakes her head.

'Look at you, Jessie, setting up *WhatIf* and the tireless work you do for the charity.'

'Maybe now, but not when Michael died. I was a wreck back then.' She wipes her hands on the thighs of her scruffy jeans, and I think how Michael only ever let her dress in designer names. 'What's your version of the story?' she asks, and I guess she's back on the hot topic of ice-cream.

I fold my tall frame into one of the six faded Victorian fireside chairs lining the entrance to the gallery, and I immediately wonder how short people used to be back when they were made. I'm uncomfortable being so near the ground so I stand straight back up again.

Jessie laughs. 'Those chairs are just for show, they made them low to make the room look taller.'

'The song,' I say, grabbing the back of the chair I sat on.

'What song?' Jessie shakes her head, moving to stand behind the chair opposite me.

'Enjoy yourself. It's later than you think. You know it?' I ask.

She sings, swaying her body to the tune. *'Enjoy yourself, while you're still in the pink.'* I join in, swaying and holding my hands up – not noticing that Jessie has stopped. *'The years go by, as quickly as a wink, Enjoy yourself, Enjoy yourself, it's later than you think.'* I cough, feeling silly, and I see Arthur glaring at me. 'I want us to buy a motorhome,' I say to Jessie, turning my back on Arthur. 'We could explore the whole of Europe, drive to the Arctic Circle, park up overnight on the empty beaches of the Nordic fjords. We could see elephants in the wild, cuddle koalas. All kinds of things. We have both worked so hard for years, and fate has forced us to spend so much of our lives apart; a motorhome would be amazing.' I wait for her to say I'm right.

She smiles. 'Your wife thinks you're writing her off.'

'I'm not.'

'She thinks you're getting old before your time. Billy feels she has her life ahead of her, and you're expecting her to don a pair of moccasin slippers and sit with you watching daytime TV. She said you'll start talking about the pills you have to take for your high blood pressure, and whether or not you're constipated, or you'll be discussing how you've had a horrible allergic reaction to some medication or other, and you'll end up telling her in lurid detail all the nasty side effects, like unbelievably itchy balls.' Jessie laughs.

'She didn't say that?' I frown.

'Not exactly.'

'Billy wouldn't say *balls.*'

'She didn't. Testicles was the word she used. Inflamed and swollen testicles.'

Jessie moves to the front of her chair and sits down in it, looking up at me - she makes herself comfortable, as if she is about to tell me a long story. 'Billy has fought hard to save the cows and the farm,' she says. 'And she wants to keep doing it, making sure it remains secure.'

'But why?' I smack my hand on the chair creating a tiny cloud of dust. 'It's not like there's another generation of the May family to take it on. Billy saw how hard it was for her grandfather and her parents - and she's working twenty-four-seven. The farm leaves no time for us. I have enough money for a comfortable retirement. There is no need for the farm to be financially sound.'

'It's something inside her.' Jessie holds up her hands, 'It is engrained in Billy's psyche. She almost lost Fox Halt Farm once, and she's not going to allow it to happen again.'

Despite the low chair, I sit down in mine again and lean forward. 'How do I make her see sense?'

'Talk to her, see if there might be a compromise.'

'Hate compromises.'

'Why?' Jessie holds out her hands.

'No-one gets what they want.' I am up on my feet again and stretching up to reach the hourglass on the bookshelf behind me. I flip it over. 'Time is not sand in a jar. We can't turn our lives upside down and have this time all over again,' I say, watching the sand starting to fall. I hadn't noticed the music had stopped, but now Arthur comes back into the room and sits down at the piano once more and waits for our attention.

Chapter 7

Billy

Mid-January, and I am dying to get inside and thaw my toes out. The thick socks Mum knitted me for Christmas, and my woolly tights made little difference to how cold I was milking the cows this morning.

William follows me into the house, hanging his coat up while I kick off my wellies. I wonder what he's doing - coat removal suggests he's planning on being indoors for a little while. Now, I notice the rest of the four-man team who are erecting my new building, queueing on the front doorstep, obviously waiting for William and me to move forward, to make room for them in the small boot room. I frown. *This is odd.*

Normally at this time, I walk into the kitchen, and Mum would hand me a steaming mug of tea. A precursor to us having our breakfast together. But *this* morning, she has a drink ready for William too.

In seconds Sean, William's stepfather, and team member number three are in the kitchen with us. Sean introduced me to Number Three last week, but I don't remember his name, nor his connection to William or his stepdad. I was distracted, trying to solve a problem with some steel stanchions delivered in too shorter lengths. Mum smiles at them both. 'Jakub and Sean, sit down,' she says, her voice warm and welcoming.

Mum's apparently invited my workers indoors, and now I assume they'll be joining us for breakfast. My farm shop manager, Herbie, is the last to get his drink. He kisses Mum on the cheek. 'You're an angel,' he says, placing the steaming mug of tea on the table, so he can remove more layers of clothing.

Herbie lifts Betsy off the nearest armchair and starts to pile his discarded outerwear onto the seat. On the floor, the kid looks up at him with narrowed eyes. She bleats at him as if to say, *'Oi, this is my chair. Get off!'*

My manager smiles back at her, 'Goats should be outside,' he says, 'or slow-cooked for a good stew.' He laughs, ruffling the top of Betsy's head – Herbie's one of those people who seems to have a permanent grin on his face. He morphed from being one of the butchers in the farm shop to becoming the manager within eight weeks. Whenever I have a problem, he sorts it. He's one hundred per cent reliable, and he makes me laugh. I'm sure many of the shop's customers only go into the shop to see him and to have a chat. Despite being clean-shaven, tall and stick thin, he reminds me of Father Christmas because of the ever crinkled up sides of his eyes, wrinkled from smiling all the time.

Mum looks from Betsy to Herbie. 'Next Tuesday, I've got a little friend coming to live with her, very little, a pygmy goat called Bramble. Then, they'll *both* go out in the shed.' I know nothing about this either, but this time, I'm not surprised; Mum's always adopting waifs and strays.

Once he's unravelled his extra clothing, Herbie's half the volume, like a reel of cotton unwinding on a sewing machine. 'How's Jessie?' Mum asks – this is the first question she always fires at him. Herbie and Jessie have had an on/off relationship since they met, on the day Richard and I got married, their liaison made more volatile since Jessie gave up meat.

'Jessica? Fine, I think,' he replies. '*I think,*' is code for they've broken up – the pair make up and split up again every two or three months. They share the same sense of humour, and when they are together, they're always giggling like two love-struck teenagers besotted with one another, but other times they'll be aggravating the pants off each other with their polarised beliefs and opinions.

Mum serves the men their breakfasts first, in the same way her mother did – a hang back to the notion that husband and sons would need to be outside again as soon as they'd eaten. In one way, I'm secretly pleased my builders have their food before me, hoping they'll get back to work soon. Construction is a week behind already because the contractor who levelled the site kept delaying, saying the ground was too wet. 'Is it someone's birthday?' I ask Sean as Mum loads a third rasher of bacon onto his plate 'Is that why you are all in here?' I'm not happy about the invasion. I worried Mum will turn this into a daily ritual, she loves feeding people.

Sean shakes his head. 'Your ma said it was a right horrible morning and she said for us to come in.'

'It wouldn't be polite to turn down one of Daniella's famous breakfasts.' Herbie draws circles on his flat stomach with the palm of a hand, making me smile despite myself.

When Mum hands me a plate piled with bacon, eggs, mushroom and fried tomatoes, I realise I'm starving. 'Blue Monday,' she tells me.

'Blue what?' I ask, stabbing a mushroom and smearing it in egg yolk before stuffing it in my mouth.

'Today is supposed to be the most depressing day of the year. It's a combination of the weather, people's debt levels, the time passed since Christmas Day and the likelihood we've all given up on our New Year's resolutions – it makes everyone exceptionally low today.' Mum waves a hand around the table. 'I thought the boys needed a bit of a pick-me-up.' I shake my head – this is so typical of her, doing the utmost to brighten people's days.

Mary pushes open the kitchen door, coming in to fetch a drink for herself and Grace. In a moment, she'll be hunting out homemade biscuits or cake, or whatever Mum has stored away in various containers in the larder. My eyes dart from the new arrival to William who, as expected, hasn't muttered a word to anyone yet. I watch him sit up in his chair and grin at Mary. 'Morning,' he says, his eyes lighting up.

'Being spoilt, I see,' she replies, walking over to him and stealing the last remaining sausage from his plate. 'Thought you lot had wimped out for the day. I wouldn't have blamed you though, it's bleedin' frosty out there. Especially where you're working, that's like a real cold spot.'

The way William smirks at Mary reminds me of his late father, my best friend when I was growing up. For a fleeting moment Tom is at the table, not his son, and then I look away, a desperate sadness filling my stomach, and I wish his dad was still around. William snatches half the sausage back from Mary. 'But if you want to lend a hand for a while,' he tells her, 'we could do with someone to prise some of the timbers apart. The planks are glued together with ice.'

'The dairy is cold enough for me, thanks—' Mary laughs, 'but if you want a warm up later, pop over; I'm in there all day.' She winks at him, and I watch his cheeks redden.

At last, Jakub stands up. 'Better get on,' he says, taking a step towards the door. I smile at him, pleased one of my workers is keen to get back to the job. William and Sean follow his lead, thanking Mum as they leave.

The three have been gone five minutes before Herbie has wrapped himself back up in all his outdoor clothes. 'You can have your chair back,' he tells Betsy who immediately leaps up onto the seat, smacking her skull against Herbie's chin. 'Okay, Little Madam.' He rubs his face. 'I'll not dare take *your* seat again.' Herbie turns to me, 'I'm beginning to wish I hadn't taken two weeks off from the shop to help out with the building; I never expected it to be this cold.'

Mum responds quickly, 'There's a lasagne for one o'clock; make sure you're all back in again by then. That should warm you up.'

Herbie raises an eyebrow, 'With your legendry chips?'

Mum nods, and he gives her another peck on the cheek. 'You're the best,' he laughs.

As the door slams behind him, I shake my head at Mum. 'This has to be a one-off, just today. I can't have them stopping every three hours,' I tell her.

Mum shrugs. 'People like to know they are appreciated.'

I stop myself whining back at her that I value what William and co. are doing - and I'm paying them well. I keep my voice level. 'Blue Monday, that's it. Okay?'

* * *

I fling a carton of cardboard wrappers for Mary to catch and restack in the dairy, and I think how lucky I am to have her working for me. She's the closest I'll ever have to a daughter.

'What's so funny?' I ask when her smile has lasted three more pitches of the lightweight boxes.

'It's just something William said.'

'Have you ever thought about being kinder to him?'

She laughs.

'Mary, you are mean to that boy.'

'I'm not. I'm his best friend. Who else does he talk to?' She's right; there doesn't seem to be anyone else he's close to. William is always quiet unless Mary is around, and then it's like she's pushed an *on* button. He'll take his earplugs out and have a proper conversation. I shake my head at her. 'You know how he feels about you, and you tease him mercilessly, it's not fair.'

Mary catches another box, but this time, she shoots it back at me. 'What else can I do, Auntie?'

'Tell him you'll never have feelings for him.'

'And break his fragile heart?'

'Don't you have any feelings for him?' I ask, throwing the box back to her and watching as she adds it to her stack.

'Like a brother, a fab, bestest, older brother.' She breathes in slowly and stares at me. 'I still love Sharmarke. So many years, Auntie, and still my half-brother haunts my dreams. You said time would make it better. Well, it sure hasn't.'

'But have you never wondered if you might be happy with William?'

Mary sticks her hands on her hips. 'No.'

I let go of my box and copy her stance, feeling like Wonder Woman with hands on hips, legs slightly apart, facing her. 'William is good-looking,' I say, 'he's thoughtful, intelligent and hardworking, and he'd always love you faithfully. Surely, he's a better prospect than never loving anyone, ever again?'

'I love you,' she says, shaping her two index fingers and her thumbs into a heart shape and holding them up to me. I copy the heart back to her. 'What about the Dale sisters?' I ask, lifting my now empty pallet and leaning it against the wall.

'Cara and Lorna?' Mary frowns hard at me.

'You must have noticed how they hang around him. Won't you be upset if William ends up with one of them?'

She screws her nose up like a rabbit, showing her perfect teeth. 'That ain't goin' to happen,' she says.

Chapter 8

Billy

Valentine's Day, and Mum knows what Richard is up to because I heard them whispering at the bottom of the stairs last night. I'm not one for surprises. I hate people wasting their money on something I don't like and having to pretend I'm delighted. There'll be a horrible sarcastic pixie inside my brain, saying, *'Honestly, you really think that's my taste?'* or *'this stinks worse than cow pee,'* or wickedest of all, *'is this all I'm worth?'*

After the time, when Richard gave me a Christmas card which read, *'Christmas is a time for exchanging presents'* and him adding in red capital letters, *'I WONDER WHICH ONE OF MY GIFTS YOU'LL EXCHANGE THIS YEAR?'* we made a pact. I buy my presents and give them to him to wrap for the designated day. It's safe, and I'm always genuinely thrilled.

I love the orange tulips and sentimental card which were magically lying on my bedside table when I awoke this morning. And, as I've already told Richard, waking up with him pressed into my back with his arm over me is all I want. Whatever it is that Richard has dreamt up for the rest of the day, I'm pretty certain I'll loathe it. He went outside ten minutes ago, saying he'd be back in five with my *special* present.

Now I see him, and I'm living my worst nightmare. I can see the grin on his face from the kitchen window, across the yard and right through the massive windscreen of the biggest motorhome I've ever seen. My heart sinks. This only confirms how little Richard understands me. The more he tries to sell the idea of *'Driving our Dream,'* the more stubborn I become about my ice-cream aspirations.

As I walk closer to *'the van'* - which is how I keep referring to the motorhomes he keeps showing me in his caravanning magazines, my stomach feels like it's filled up with cement. I want to cry. I'm not sure if Richard doesn't understand how much I don't want a motorhome, or worse, he knows but he doesn't care what I want. He's driving over my ambition, steamrollering over it.

Richard signals for me to get in the passenger side. 'Before you yell at me,' he says, 'I haven't bought it.'

I feel my heart lift a tiny bit, grateful that this might not be a permanent fixture in our lives. 'Why's it here?'

'Why do you think?' He's so excited.

I try not to show my disappointment or resentment. 'So I can have a test drive?' I ask.

'Nope.' Richard's eyes sparkle.

'No?'

'I'm driving.'

'You're driving?'

'Yes.' He grins, like a child opening the Christmas present he's been begging his parents for.

I shake my head. 'I'm not being funny, but this thing is enormous, and you're not confident manoeuvring a tractor in a field. You are really proposing to drive it?' I scratch at the palm of my hand, imagining what the shiny vehicle will look like after Richard has bashed it.

'It'll be fine, I promise.'

My heart drops to the back of my heels, searching for somewhere deeper to sink.

'It's hired,' he says in a tone intended to reassure me. 'But it's the same model as the one I want us to buy.'

'Did the rental company record the condition of every panel before you drove it away?'

'I expect so.'

I frown. 'You don't know?'

'Jessie collected it for me,' he laughs. 'She's driven it over, and Mary followed her in her car. They are driving back to Culmfield now.'

'You let Jessie loose in this?' I say, waving my hand wildly around the white leather interior. 'Are you mad?' I swore I'd never be driven by Jessie again after the first time I was in her car, she drives like a Formula One racer, and Richard knows that. Jessie is the last person - after Richard - whom I'd permit to drive this monstrosity.

'Jessie drives the *WhatIf* minibuses all the time,' Richard says. 'And she was keen to see it. She was really impressed and

Mary thought it was great too.' My fists clench into tight balls, thinking how Jessie and Mary have been in on this 'surprise'. They both know how much I hate the idea of travelling around the world … *and the traitors have told him they like the darn thing!*

'How long before you are ready to leave?' Richard sits back in his seat.

'For lunch?' I check. 'You said we'd have lunch somewhere nice.'

'Lunch, dinner and breakfast, that is your Valentine's surprise. William has agreed to milk tomorrow morning, and Mary is in the shop. The dairy is sorted too – Gloria and June know exactly what they need to do.'

'And you've taken tomorrow off?' I ask, taking in all the co-conspirators he's recruited against me.

He nods.

'Oh,' I say, feeling cornered with no way out of this; every argument I put up he'll knock down.

'We don't need to be back until tomorrow evening. Daniella has packed up some provisions for us, and she's sorted out bedding, towels, and some other items she thought we might need – she's putting everything on the kitchen table as we speak, we will just need to scoop it all up to take it with us. You and I will be walking Piggy on Kennack Sands later. I've reserved a table at Polpeor Café for lunch.'

Mum too, I think. 'Her name is Crinkle,' I say, niggled by his persistence with the unkind nickname. In truth, other than him driving, what he's planned sounds idyllic, but it's not what I want to do. 'Give me half an hour, and we can go,' I say, turning away from him to climb out of the motorhome, 'but I'm driving, that's final.'

'I am driving,' he says, his words slow and deliberate. I take in a deep breath as I stare out the passenger window, counting slowly, *one and… two and...* On *five,* I turn to face him. 'You know you can't drive this, and I'm not sitting next to you for three hours scared to death you're going to hit something.'

Richard takes the keys out of the ignition and stuffs them in his pocket. 'I've had lessons.' He grins.

I laugh. 'You haven't.'

'In Richmond, in the afternoon and evenings. I have a certificate if you would like to see it.' He leans towards the glove box in front of me to fish it out. I touch his arm. 'I believe you,'

I say. Frustration seeps through me, realising how committed Richard is to his retirement plan. 'Listen, Rich.' I force a smile. 'I'll try and enjoy this weekend, you've obviously made lots of effort, but a motorhome is *not* part of my long-term plan.' I'm not quite able to meet his eyes, not wanting to see the hurt I'll be causing. I continue, 'But I'm driving the first two miles to the main road, the lanes to the A30 are so narrow, and the granite walls will win if you hit them. *And* I'll drive the last two miles on the way home too. Okay?'

'Agreed.' He holds up three fingers with his thumb pressed over his pinky finger like a scout salute, 'I promise, Caravan Club Honour,' he says.

* * *

When I woke up, I never imagined I'd be savouring a pasty on the Lizard Peninsula while a seal hangs out in the emerald green water below me. Crinkle is laid out at our feet, soaking up the winter sunshine, and I am warm enough to ignore the salty breeze cooling my cheek and nose - the only bits of my body exposed to the elements.

'I love it here,' I tell Richard. I mean it too - on the rare occasions we make a trip to Cornwall, we always head for the Lizard, it was where my parents spent their honeymoon and where I came with Mum after Dad died. The unspoilt landscape set against the dramatic sea is stunning. 'Thank you,' I say, and something lurches in my stomach as he smiles and leans in to kiss me. So soft and so sensual. I run my fingers around his neck, pressing my lips hard onto his. As I move closer, pasty crumbs spill to the floor in front of Crinkle's nose. She's upright in a split second, searching out the tiny morsels in the grass, then burrows her nose between us, making loud snuffling noises.

'We could do this for weeks at a time,' Richard says. 'Get this one a passport.' He strokes Crinkle's head and talks to her. 'You can have scraps from our plates from all over the world,' he says. 'Your own blog too where you can list your favourite global culinary delights.' Crinkle tilts her head, listening intently to everything he says. When Richard takes his hand away, a little whine, sounding like she's deflating, slips out of her mouth. He turns to me. 'Ice-cream?' he asks.

* * *

As the first spoonful dissolves in my mouth, I delight in its cool silky deliciousness, and my thoughts drift…

Richard touches my hand. 'Did you hear what I said?'

'No, sorry.' I shake my head.

'It doesn't matter,' he says as he ladles up his own chocolate fudge dessert. He looks disappointed, making me wish I'd been listening – with the two of us alone together, I should be paying him more attention. 'What were you thinking about?' he asks.

'The cows.'

Richard puts his head in his hands. 'Can you *not* let go, even for a day?'

I extend my answer, 'The ice-cream *and* the cows,' I say, hoping he'll ask me to tell him more. I'm finding making and implementing my plans so hard without his support. Up until my ice-cream proposal, Richard's always been ready to give advice or just sit and listen to ideas. Jessie, Mary, and Mum are all taking careful notice of everything I'm doing, but speaking to them feels like I'm being unfaithful to my husband. I should be sharing with him. He's silent, his face still covered by his hands. I give up. 'You said something before, but I wasn't listening. What was it?'

He sits up and stares at me. 'It's something Mary said to me earlier, how you were so happy Grace is keeping the baby.'

'Yes,' I murmur, a lump rising in my throat.

'Sorry, darling,' he says.

I nod this time, grateful that after months of listening to his fears about Grace and Freddy messing up their lives, he's realised that I've never agreed with him. I listened in silence, unable to confront him with my own terror that he might pressure them into something we'd all regret.

'It doesn't matter,' I say, and I stroke my wrist, not looking at him. It *does* matter, but I don't know how to tell him that I wish he'd accept they want to continue with the pregnancy. I want him to know how miscarrying our baby twenty-four years ago and being unable to have another child still hurts, pain and regret weighing in every part of me.

'You mean the world to me, Billy,' he says, as he reaches forward to rest his hand on mine.

I bite down my sad thoughts. 'Let's get down to Kennack Sands,' I say. 'Get settled in. We can play ball with Crinkle on the beach and enjoy the sunset with glasses of wine in our hands—' A thought hits me. 'Can we park there overnight?'

'Not officially, the carpark is closed until Easter, but your mum knew someone who is the friend of the man who runs the café next door. Daniella explained who they were, but I don't remember exactly - anyway, she has asked them to hide a barrier key for us to use.'

* * *

The tangerine sun dips below the horizon as water laps against our feet, and we kiss. Crinkle drops her ball between us and whines. How fortunate we are that Mum knows everything and everyone. She's allowed us to have this beautiful isolated beach to ourselves. *Thank you, Mum.*

* * *

RICHARD

As the sky darkens and the sunshine we enjoyed for the last two days vanishes, my phone buzzes on the dashboard. Billy checks the caller ID. 'It's Arthur,' she says.

I squeeze the steering wheel. 'I said not to ring me.'

'It might be urgent.' Billy moves to lift the phone.

'Leave it, please.'

Her eyes stay set on my mobile. 'You're still the managing director. He may need an okay on something,' she says. 'Why isn't it transferring to answerphone?'

'I turned it off.'

'Really?' She glances at me.

I nod, wishing I had turned the phone off too. To be fair, until now, no-one has contacted either of us. It has been heaven - focusing on each other without a single work distraction.

A text pings in and Billy looks at me. 'Can I read it?'

'Okay.'

Billy pulls her glasses out of her pocket and starts to read the message. '*CB unhappy YOU were not in the meeting today. Need to talk. Must get back to her pronto.*'

There is a double roundabout in front of me, and I'm working out the best position in the road. 'Text him back, will you? Say I'll be back with him this evening and we will discuss it over a pizza then.' There is a motorbike intent on overtaking. The rider's unpredictability makes negotiating the tricky junction scary. 'Organ donor,' I say under my breath to the leather-clad biker as he roars by.

I notice Billy's body stiffen. 'Arthur's sent a thumbs-up emoji,' she says. Her body stiffens.

'Are you okay?' I touch her arm.

'Yes.' She turns to me but she doesn't look okay.

'What is it?' I ask.

'I was hoping you'd stay tonight.'

I wanted to be at the farm too but whenever I leave, it hurts. This feels like ripping off a plaster and getting the pain over and done with. I consider asking Billy to text Arthur back and say I'll ring him when we get to Fox Halt, or I could put him on speakerphone now, but I dismiss the idea, I don't want to deal with work right now. I shake my head. 'I'll go tonight.'

'How many days left?' Billy asks. I can hear her disappointment.

'Twenty-seven.' I lift my hand off the wheel and punch the air. 'And then, *whoop, whoop,* freedom!'

* * *

On the kitchen table, an A4 sheet of paper covers up three unopened envelopes. I read aloud the short message scribbled on it in Daniella's shaky writing. *'Look in I C F, you're in for a bit of a surprise!'* The Ice-Cream Factory has stuck as a nickname for the new building - ICF for short.

I hand the message to Billy, my attention switching to an ancient Cadbury Roses tin positioned next to the mail. As I lift the lid of the container, the honeyed smell of marzipan and apricot jam from Daniella's homemade Battenberg cake fills my nostrils. I move to fetch two plates, but notice Billy is by the door staring at me. 'Aren't you coming?' she asks, her hand wavering on the door handle, waiting for me.

'I want a piece of cake and a cup of tea,' I reply. 'That was a long drive, and I need to leave again in fifty minutes -Jessie and Mary will be here at six to take the motorhome back to Ashburton. I hoped we would empty it before they arrive.'

Billy looks at the floor and then back up at me. 'I'll empty the van on my own when you're gone,' she says. 'Just a quick look? Let's see what it is.' She watches as I pour hot water onto a tea bag, and then, while I fetch the milk, I hear the front door click behind her.

'Me and you for cake then,' I say to Crinkle, even though the little dog can't have it because the marzipan would make her sick. She wags her tails as I head to the larder to find the biscuits Billy keeps for the sheep. I hand her a whole one. 'It's no wonder you love me so much,' I say to her curled-up tail, but she is too busy crunching to hear.

As I check to see if any of the post is for me, I spy a bright orange '*Signed For*' sticker on one of the envelopes addressed to Billy. Picking this letter up, I think I know what is inside, guessing that when she opens it, she will have a problem on her hands, and maybe a serious one. I stuff the last delicious morsel of cake into my mouth, sliding the ominous envelope under the other two. I will leave before Billy finds it. 'Arthur, thank you for the excuse,' I say aloud as I head upstairs to pack my bag to leave.

Chapter 9

Billy

I try the number again only to hear the same three short pips and then silence. Stowing my phone in my jeans' pocket, I gaze at three piles of stainless steel in all shapes and sizes that have been dumped on pallets in the corners of my new building. I tremble, wishing I'd pulled a coat on before I left the house. The newly poured concrete floor is still drying and the moisture rising up from it renders the already cool air wet and colder still. The snow-white walls make it feel like I'm in the world's largest fridge.

Crinkle is suddenly at my feet, and I can hear footsteps outside. My eyes follow Crinkle's trail of dirty paw prints back to the entrance door. 'Oh,' I say, my smile falls away. 'I was expecting Richard.'

'Where is he?' Mum walks towards me, her hands deep in her mucky Barbour jacket.

'Demolishing your cake.' I frown.

She smiles. 'You had a good time?'

'It was lovely, having him all to myself for two whole days. We laughed so much.'

'But?' Mum says, not looking at me as she raises Crinkle up into her arms.

'He's leaving tonight. I thought he'd stay.'

Mum stares at me with a look that signals she knows I'm not telling her the *whole* truth.

'He's not interested in this.' I wave my hand around the room, and I feel a sudden compulsion to spin like a child. Round and around, I stretch out my arms as I whirl in circles, relishing the space inside the building that only exists because I have a dream. I stop and push my arms back down. 'He hates it,' I say, the walls spinning in my eyes.

Mum won't take sides. 'Good job you like puzzles.' She nods towards one of the heaps of metal.

I shake my head. 'I rang Andrew, but his phone seems to be dead.'

'He's gone.'

'Gone?'

Mum turns on her heels with Crinkle still in her arms. 'This rascal's heavy,' she says. 'Let's get back indoors. We can talk inside in the warm.'

'Give her to me,' I say, happy to carry the dog to avoid more mucky footprints on my clean floor.

'I'm fine.' Mum takes a step towards the exit.

'Let me.' I reach for Crinkle, but my hands are immediately wet. 'Where's she been? She reeks!' I wince at the acrid smell emanating from the animal now in my arms.

Mum smiles. 'I fetched her out of Betsy's and Bramble's pen. I caught all three of them playing in the water trough. They've made it so filthy, I'll have to fence off a new area tomorrow.' She rolls her eyes. 'I can't believe how much mischief two kids can get up to, *and* I'll make sure this one stays away from them too in future.' Mum pats Crinkle's head.

I hold out my palm to show Mum a lump of goat poo that's stuck to my hand. 'Bath for this little monkey,' I say.

* * *

Richard is loading the dishwasher as we walk in. 'Oh my!' He straightens up, staring at Crinkle.

I squeeze the dog into my chest to stop her from squirming free to greet him. 'She's been in with the goats – she's having a bath,' I say and Crinkle flattens her ears. She looks at me, mouth open, showing the whites of her eyes.

'Billy, I need to go.' Richard makes a stride across the flagstone floor towards me but then stops. I was expecting him to wrap his arms around me or, at least pat Crinkle, reassuring her that a bath wouldn't be so bad. But he'd get pretty mucky if he came closer to either of us. I make my best attempt at puppy dog eyes, hoping to melt his heart, hoping he'll change his mind and stay, but Richard leans over Crinkle, his hands shielding his clothes, and he kisses me gently on the lips, 'Thank you for Cornwall.' His eyes linger on mine, and I know he's waiting for me to say thank you too.

'Yes,' I whisper. The word sticks in my throat, and in seconds he's gone.

* * *

I plonk Crinkle into the bath, taking my upset out on her. I stroke her head as I turn on the tap, 'Sorry,' I say, and she lifts her paw onto my hand like she's trying to say, *'It's okay.'*

When I finish, I'm as wet as the dog and the whole of the white-tiled room is spattered in brown stains. 'Why's all Andrew's stuff here?' I ask Mum as I lift Crinkle out of the bath.

'A lorry turned up this morning, with it all,' she says, starting to dry Crinkle off – to the terrier, this is a game, and she keeps biting the towel. 'The driver said the new owners of Andrew's farm paid him to load everything and deliver it here.'

'He's sold up completely?'

'Sounds like it. Can you get another towel? Billy, this one's soaked.'

I head to the airing cupboard, shouting back at Mum, 'What do you mean, sounds like it?'

'Liz Cole says he's in Ibiza,' she calls out.

I throw the fresh towel over Crinkle and gather her up in it, taking over the drying. I decide not to ask who Liz is because if I'd been listening to Mum properly all these years, I'd know everyone in Hamsgate and the surrounding villages.

'He's gone to live with his niece over there,' Mum continues, 'she runs some sort of retreat. Apparently, the niece has been on at him to go over there for ages – mightn't've meant for good, though – but Andrew took it as a permanent offer, sold up lock, stock and barrel. He flew out ten days ago.'

'Do I know Liz?' I ask, drawing in a deep breath, hoping this isn't going to be a long-winded explanation with the woman's complete life history.

'Andrew's neighbour,' Mum replies, and I feel relief at the simple connection. 'Liz cleaned his house for years. She said you went to school with her son, Nathan? I told her I didn't think so, but she sounded sure.'

I shake my head. 'I don't remember any Nathans,' I say, thinking how Liz must be a saint. I've been in Andrew's house once with Mum, and two things come straight to mind – a parrot in a cage in his kitchen which had flung seed, feathers and bird mess onto every surface, and high stacks of old faded newspapers piled up against the walls. I wouldn't want to clean for him for a day, let alone years. 'I can't understand why he didn't say he was leaving,' I say, 'I wanted to see how everything was laid out. He said he'd help me plan where the different elements should go.' My voice is high, and I must sound like a spoilt child. Crinkle squeaks. 'Sorry, sweetie,' I say to the towel, loosening my grip and accidentally letting the dog escape. Crinkle rubs her head along the bath mat, drying her cheeks off on the rough pile before charging off to find her favourite chair.

'When he got here, the lorry driver wouldn't unload your stuff - he said he hadn't been paid to do it,' Mum says after we've chased Crinkle along the hall and into the kitchen.

'So, you gave him some extra cash?' I check, now trying to get a dry towel under the wet dog.

'Mary and William sorted it for you. They unloaded it all. Did you know they went on a date on Saturday?'

I frown, wondering how many more surprises this evening will bring. 'A date? No. They're just friends.'

'Mary said they tried out the new Chinese in Exeter, the same one Grace and Freddy went to when it first opened. The Golden something.' She frowns trying to remember the name.

'Did it go alright?' I ask, still unconvinced.

'Mary said it was *sick* - she had to explain that means good.' She laughs. 'Have you heard that before?'

I stop listening because I've just picked up an envelope from the table. I wave it at Mum. 'Did you sign for this?'

'Shouldn't I have?' She stares at me as I rip open the letter. I feel sweat on my top lip. I cannot believe what I read.

'What is it?' she asks. I can hear she's still worried about signing for its delivery.

'An enforcement notice, saying I can't have the ICF. I should've got planning,' I say. 'But I thought it would be fine, especially once it was up and employing people. I didn't want to be tied up in bureaucracy for months—' I look at Mum. 'The building is hidden away, I didn't think anyone would know it was there. This could ruin everything.'

Mum presses her fingers over her mouth. 'You can't demolish it?' she says. 'Not after all the money you've spent.'

'I'm calling Richard,' I say, tossing the notice onto the table. 'I hope he'll help.'

Chapter 10

Billy

As she walks into the kitchen, Mary's eyes fix on the cake tin. 'Did you have a great time?' she asks me.

'It was…' I pause then whisper so Jessie can't hear – her mother followed Mary into the house but Jessie has walked over to Mum to kiss her on the cheek and say hello. *'Sick,'* I say quietly to Mary. I slip my phone in my pocket, giving up on Richard answering – I've tried to get through to him for twenty minutes without success.

'So, Nan-Dan snitched,' she whispers back, not looking at me as she cuts herself a piece of the Battenberg cake. 'Do you want some?' Her knife is poised, ready to cut another hefty portion.

I shake my head. 'Why didn't *you* tell me?'

Mary lifts her shoulders in a shrug and then Jessie speaks to me. 'Did you have a great time?' she asks, her focus more on the cake than me. 'Gosh, there are times when I seriously consider my life choices,' she says, lifting the cake tin to her nose, delighting in the smell of the marzipan.

Mary is about to stuff in her second enormous mouthful, but she stops. 'I'm sure that Nan-Dan would make you a vegan one—' She laughs, 'I'm pretty sure too – it will be delicious.' Mary licks her lips.

'Who brought you up, Mary?' Jessie tries to look stern as her daughter finishes the slice of cake in a second mouthful.

Mary holds out her hands, raises her eyebrows, shakes her head and shrugs again.

Jessie grins at her before turning back to me. 'How was it?' she asks again.

'Like our honeymoon all over again.' I smile, and I wonder if she knows how I'm really feeling. Jessie is like Mum, she can see through me – *it was like our honeymoon, that's true,*

Richard and I were so connected and happy, our minds centred on each other, *but* I'd have rather stayed here with us working together on something – him sharing my enthusiasm for Fox Halt and appreciating how wonderful it is, him keen to secure its future too.

'You should encourage him to buy a motorhome then, and you could go off in it all the time,' Jessie says.

'Are you being serious?' I frown at her. 'I'm not interested in retiring or even slowing down for that matter.' I wave the enforcement notice at her. 'But it might happen yet,' I say, handing the letter to her.

She doesn't look at it. 'So what's your plan?' she asks.

I smack the paper she's holding with the back of my hand. 'You know what this is?' I frown.

'Something to do with planning?' Jessie says, her eyes still on me. 'What will you do?'

'Phone Rich. Get his advice. I was trying to get him when you arrived.' I retrieve my phone and hold it out to her.

Jessie looks at me in the same way Mum does when I'm going out for the evening and she disapproves of my outfit. It won't be that it's too revealing, more likely, the opposite – her expression and scan from head to toe will wordlessly say, *'Can't you make more effort than that?'* Often, I'll just turn around, head back to my bedroom and find something other than jeans to wear, apply a bit of makeup and tidy my hair, hoping she won't look so disdainful when I see her downstairs. 'What?' I ask Jessie, recognising the same look of condemnation.

'You *can't* call him.'

'Why not?'

She takes my mobile and places it on the dresser. 'He has been on the phone to me all the way here. He's upset.'

'*He*'s upset?' I emphasise *he* – it's me who's upset, I should have been ringing Jessie, not him, she is *my* best friend, not his. Her voice is calm. 'He told me about the planning.'

My mind spins. *How did Rich know? Did he tip off the local authority?* I grab the notice and wave it at her. 'Is Richard behind this? You can't see my new building unless you're poking around the yard. And if someone did see it, they'd never know it wasn't another agricultural building – that would be permitted development, I wouldn't need consent.'

Jessie glares at me, and I guess she's shocked that I could suspect Richard. Her words are slow and precise. 'He saw the envelope and guessed what it was. That's why he left as soon as you came back from the ice-cream factory. He knew you'd expect him to help.'

'Isn't that what a partner is supposed to do?'

Jessie takes in a slow breath. 'Not when they don't want their partner charging down the wrong path. He felt if he advised you, it would give the wrong message. I'd like to knock your heads together, at least lock you both in a room until you sort this out, but I'm hoping for now, you'll accept one piece of advice.'

'What?'

'Do *not* ask Richard about it, and when he rings you later, thank him for organising such a lovely surprise.'

I raise my eyebrows, trying to think who else I can turn to about the notice.

'I'm serious, you can't keep ignoring Richard's feelings, and he has to stop burying his head too. Now, where are the keys to the motorhome? I've got to get it back in an hour.' She holds out her hand.

'You can't get to Ashburton in an hour,' I say, checking the clock, but I rethink. The way Jessie drives, she can. 'I haven't even unloaded it yet. With everything that's happened since we got home, I completely forgot.'

Mum is on her feet. 'Mary and I'll do it,' she says.

'No, Daniella. Billy and Mary can unload it.' Jessie reaches for Mum's hand. 'I'd like you to take me to meet this famous Betsy of yours. Mary's told me about her. I love goats.'

Mum beams. 'Come on,' she says and as they bound out the door together, Mum has her arm linked into Jessie's, and she's explaining about Bramble too.

Richard's name flashes on my phone, and my heart jolts, wondering, if he's right about the ice-cream. *Should I give it up? No, I won't!*

* * *

'Thank you,' I say, '-a wonderful and thoughtful surprise.

* * *

From across the car park, I see Troy Gloon has dark circles under his eyes – I guess he's had a heavy night, or perhaps he hasn't slept, and for a tiny fraction of a moment, I feel sympathy towards him. I didn't sleep either, working out my plan for today. He doesn't see me as he lifts his massive legs off the seemingly fragile road bike. He pushes the skeletal machine towards me, the cleats in the soles of his shoes tipping him backwards slightly, making him walk on his heels. He focuses on the buttons of a small computer fixed to his handlebars, clicking them in quick succession, and I guess he's checking his time for the eleven-mile ride from his home to his work place. As I watch him, my blood boils.

I step forward, my back to the rear entrance of his shop. 'Morning,' I say, my voice light and excited like I'm from the National Lottery and about to announce he's won the jackpot. He doesn't look at me, stabs a key into the lock of his back door, twists it and yanks the door open. I summon every ounce of courage, determined not to cry like I often do when things aren't fair. 'Stop,' I tell him, my voice fierce.

He snaps his head around to glance at me like a cow annoyed by a fly. 'What are you doing here?' He scowls.

'You know why.' I feel calmer now - while I waited for him to arrive, my chest thumped at the thought of confronting him, still worried about the notice.

'To say I can have all Andrew's kit, after all?' His flippant response makes me angry. 'That's why you told the council what I was doing; you thought a poxy notice would make me roll over and give up?' My tone is thick with disgust for his underhand trick. 'I'm here to tell you it won't work.'

He stares me straight in the face, 'Ha!' he says, his eyes open wide and his eyebrows raised.

'I will get consent.' I ball my hands into fists. 'It may take a bit longer, but you informing on me was a waste of time.'

'No idea what you are talking about.' He steps into his shop, making me see red, and my hand flies out to catch the hem of his cycling jacket, but I grab at air. He's about to shut his door in my face, however this time my reaction is quicker, and I jam my foot in the gap. He forces the door against my trainer, making it feel like the small bones in my foot are being crushed together. 'No!' I yell.

Troy releases my foot. 'It weren't me. Wish I had, though,' he spits. 'Whoever told the planners, good on them.'

He puts his thumbs up, smiles and walks inside, leaving me questioning who else it might have been.

* * *

Dominque Wade's secretary tells me that her boss will arrive at precisely ten o'clock. She says, 'Dominque won't second guess circumstances and will not advise over the phone.' The secretary has the same lovely lilt as Sean, but she doesn't sound like someone to disagree with. I'm not going to argue. In fact, I respect the consultant's professional approach, even though I crave her reassurance that everything will be fine. I haven't slept, my mind whirring over and over how I'm going to fix this. I take off my glasses, rub my eyes and then put the small writing pad I had ready to make notes on, away in my overalls. I try to decide what to do until ten.

The three heaps that William and Mary stacked up in the ICF take up about an eighth of the floor area, and I've spent an hour assessing what's here. The first pile is made up of tanks of different sizes and some large, scary-looking machinery. The second pile is a jumble of pipes, connectors, fixings, electrical boxes, cables and switches, but it's the third pile that's the most intimidating because I'm unsure what most of it is. I recognise fans and gas bottles fitted with various pressure gauges and a stack of mats, but there are also six black rubble sacks stuffed full, which I haven't dared open yet.

Start with Heap 1, I tell myself, pushing down the handle of the pallet truck I've borrowed from the dairy. I need to separate everything out, placing each individual element onto more pallets to see them better.

* * *

Dominique opens her file and looks up at me. 'I think you'll be okay,' she says, and I feel I've grown taller with relief. I've shown the consultant everything around the farm, explaining how I've got this far. I've talked through all my plans and projected figures and I stressed how the ICF is hidden amongst the other farm buildings – how it can't be seen from the nearby tors, or any part of the National Park. I also told her about the renewable energy infrastructure I want to use, but all the time, up until now, her only reaction was a nod.

It was satisfying having someone listen because this is what I've missed from Richard. I don't necessarily want his approval, but a spark of interest would be great. I want him to realise how passionately I feel about my new scheme, and have him try to understand. But then, I suppose, he knows me too well – the last thing he wants to do is to encourage me with something he's set against.

'It'll be okay?' I check, staring into Dominique's eyes, trying to reassure myself that I heard correctly.

'It would've been better if you'd gone through the proper channels, but yes, I think we can get this through retrospectively.' I watch as she writes something on one of the copy plans that I've given her. 'Everything depends on the nature of your development and how the building or business will affect your neighbours.' She lifts her eyes and frowns. 'To be honest, I don't see why you were issued with a notice.'

'What do you mean?' I collapse down on a stack of pallets and look up at her.

She smiles. 'In normal circumstances, I would have expected the council to have sent a planning officer around to have a look and talk to you like I have. I know they're short-staffed, but issuing control notifications only creates more work for them in the long run. I suppose we can be grateful it's not a dreaded 'Stop' notice. That would have forced you to completely cease what you're doing straight away. They've given you time to comply and remedy the breach, so that's in your favour.'

'I won't have to take it down?'

'Unlikely,' she says.

'And I can carry on with my plans for producing ice-cream? Can I put up the windmills too?' I probably sound like a child whose been told they can try every piece of confectionary in the sweetshop.

'Again, most likely. Send me copies of the information you've shown me this morning, and include a summary of all the points you made so eloquently to me today. Once I have that, I'll talk to the Inspectorate and sort the planning. I think an appeal, and the costs and disruption that would lead to, has to be the last resort. There is something, though.' Dominique perches on the pallet next to me.

I twist my body towards her. 'Have I forgotten something?' I ask, holding out my hands, palms up as if to say that's it, I have nothing left in my arsenal.

'Is there a neighbour or a disgruntled customer who might have put the authorities onto you? It would be best to think of ways to get them on board before I do anything else.'

'There's no-one. I've racked my brains. My mother has too, and she knows all the gossip around here. We can't think who it might have been.' My thoughts after dismissing Richard turned to Troy, but this morning's encounter makes me feel certain it wasn't him.

'Someone must have, Billy. If you suddenly realise who, then let me know right away, and we'll discuss how we might smooth things out with them.'

I nod, my mind turning to my bruised foot. Dominique stands up, holding out her hand for me to shake, 'Let me know when I can buy your ice-cream,' she says.

'Twenty-fifth July,' I reply, not hesitating as we both walk towards her car. My launch day has changed to the Saturday before my birthday because I now have something in mind which will work best on a weekend. 'I'll deliver a whole carton to you as soon as it comes off the production line. What's your favourite flavour?'

'Rum and raisin,' she says.

As her beaten up Land Rover pulls away, I write *Dominique – Rum and raisin* in my notebook, pausing before I close it. *Was it Richard who stirred up the planners?*

Chapter 11

Billy

I've just finished in the farm shop. I don't normally work Saturdays, but two of the girls wanted the day off for a friend's wedding, so Mary and I stepped in – and it's been fun working with her all day, unpressured with time to talk to customers.

'Tea?' Richard asks, placing the kettle on the Rayburn to boil. I scan the table where he was sitting as I came in, immediately spying a brochure laid open on a double-page spread headed, *'Worldwide Safari,'* its pages held down carefully with a cow and bull salt and pepper set. I cringe, imagining the conversation he wants to have about this possible trip.

'I only came back for this.' I wave a bit of paper with Liz Cole's address on it. 'I've got to be there in eight minutes. Do you want to come?'

He huffs, and I try not to glare at him, frustrated by his averseness to anything to do with my ice-cream plans – I feel like running outside, charging to the middle of Home Field and screaming so loud they'll hear me in Okehampton!

'I'll be an hour,' I say, smiling sweetly, 'back in plenty of time to go to the pub.' All I want to talk about is the ice-cream factory, and that's the one thing he refuses to chat about. He wants me to be excited about the motorhome he's ordered, and he's desperate to discuss all the places we'd visit, but that's the last thing I want to do.

* * *

Liz opens her front door to let me in. 'You remember Nathan?' she asks, waving a hand towards the young man standing next to her. I notice the top joints of her fingers are bent at forty-five degrees, and think how painful they look. Before I have a chance to answer, she turns back inside, expecting Nathan and me to follow. I don't remember him. What's more, he must be around

Mary's age. So, we couldn't have been at primary school at the same time. Nathan turns towards me, his eyes still on Liz as she continues down the hall. He touches my arm. 'I'm Oscar,' he whispers, now holding out his hand.

I shake it. 'Oscar?' I frown.

'My dad's Nathan, but it upsets Nan if I correct her.'

'I'll call you Nathan, then?' I smile, hoping to reassure him. I'm happy with our collusion - remembering how my grandad used to confuse me with his wife, Annie, my grandmother.

'Thank you, Mrs May,' he says, 'She's already flustered having someone different here today. I like to keep a routine if I can, it's simpler for her.' He nods his head, indicating he'd like me to go ahead of him.

'Call me, Billy. You live with your nan?' I ask as I squeeze past.

His response is so quiet, I can hardly hear him. 'Since I left university. I work from home and Nan is great. She has good days - when she's the wonderful lady I grew up with, she'll remember almost everything. She has a wicked sense of humour. Really wicked—' He pauses as we reach the sitting room. 'I'll make drinks,' he says loudly.

'Coffee or tea?' Liz looks around at me; her neck is stiff, preventing her from turning her head fully. Her piercing blue eyes fire into me. She fluffs up a cushion on her threadbare settee and points for me to sit down.

'Tea, please,' I say.

She presses on the arms of her chair as she sits down opposite me. 'You want to talk about Andrew?' she says. 'Such a lovely man.'

'Yes,' I reply, thinking how she appears lucid. 'Andrew sold me all his ice-cream-making machinery, and I thought you might know someone who used to help him make the ice-cream.' I speak slowly. 'I'm hoping they might give me some advice about putting all his equipment back together.'

'He's a farmer.' She creases her thick untidy eyebrows into a frown. 'Andrew wouldn't be making ice-cream. He sells all his milk to them Milk Marketing Board people.' She calls into the kitchen. 'Nathan, tell her, the maid's got it wrong.'

Oscar's head appears in the doorway. 'I'm not sure,' he says then disappears again.

He returns carrying a tray which he puts down next to his nan. There are three mismatched bone china cups, a teapot swamped in a patchwork tea cosy in the shape of a hen, and a tea strainer. The milk jug has a little lace net over it, the net weighted with buttons around the edge to hold it in place over the rim of the jug. I haven't seen one of these covers in years. I want to comment but decide I shouldn't. Oscar passes me my drink, dropping a slip of paper on my lap and I see there's something written on it.

I slip my glasses on and read, trying not to draw attention to what I'm doing. I don't want Liz to realise I'm not listening as she tells me every last detail of Andrew's house. *'I don't think Nan will be able to help. Please don't pressure her.'* I sit back in my chair and sip the hot tea. 'Does Andrew have any cats?' I ask.

* * *

Oscar walks me to my car. 'There are odd days when she'll be fine,' he says, 'but mostly, Nan lives in the past.'

'I remember those special moments with my grandfather too,' I say, recalling the wonderful man who lived with our family until he died when I was in my twenties. The moments I treasured back then, minutes when Grandad was his old self. These are memories I cling on to, and the ones as a child when he spoilt me rotten, his storytelling and our little secrets. How he'd wink and say, *'we don't need to tell your mum.'*

'Did your dad go to Hamsgate school?' I scratch my fingers into my scalp, hoping I have time to wash my hair before Richard and I go out.

'No, Nan and Grandad came to Hamsgate in 1984. My father was too old then to go to the village school, but he went to Okehampton College. You might have known him there.'

I press the button on my key fob to open my van, 'I don't recall him,' I say, shaking my head

Oscar takes in a deep breath. 'My father left my mum. He ran off to Spain with Andrew's niece. My nan hasn't spoken to him in years.' His words quicken. 'Lately, Nan keeps thinking I'm him, and it's made more difficult because she doesn't remember Mum or that they had me.'

'My grandfather used to mistake me for my gran sometimes,' I say. 'That was weird too, but I was lucky in a way, because it reinforced to me how much he loved her. My grandmother died before I was born. His confusion was like pulling back a curtain on the past; I could peep through and imagine what she was like. It must be hard for you, Oscar – your father abandoning you and your mum.'

We stand in silence by my car. After two uneasy minutes, I have to say something before I move to leave. 'I hope our paths cross again, and good luck with your nan,' I say. 'Seriously, if you need a bit of help or want someone to talk to, then ring me.' I hold out my business card. 'Anytime,' I say.

He grips the thin card between his thumb and forefinger, but doesn't take it. 'Thanks…' He pauses, and I think he wants to say something else, but seconds go by and he doesn't.

'You've got my number,' I say, letting go of the card. 'Please ring me if you want.'

As I drive away, my thoughts return to the ice-cream factory, and the prospect that I'll have to unjumble everything myself. When I get back, I'll start to trawl through *YouTube* videos. *Surely, there'll be something useful on an online forum somewhere?*

* * *

Herbie looks over my shoulder, folds his arms against his white coat and laughs at me. 'Bills, you've slogged for hours on that blimmin' computer. In two days, have you managed to find anything useful?'

'Bits and pieces,' I say, stretching my neck out, wondering if I like him calling me *Bills*. That's what Tom used to call me, and I feel a jolt in my stomach every time Herbie does it – especially as he often uses the same inflection. Tom was always joking with me too. I refocus my eyes, away from my computer screen, scanning the small office which is tacked onto the back of the farm shop, taking in the hygiene certificates lined up evenly across one wall and then the red and blue rosettes pinned above them that we've won, mainly for our Foxy Lady Cheese.

'Where will you start?' He smacks a folder down on the desk next to me.

'With the milk tank. It's exactly the same as the holding tank in the dairy. The trouble is I can't install it until I've worked out the whole layout,' I explain.

He nods. 'I want your opinion on something.' Herbie

beckons me to follow him into the shop. He points to an eye-catching display he's made of pickles and preserves, 'That's better, isn't it?'

'Looks great.' I struggle to sound interested when my mind is still stuck on a diagram I was figuring out before he wandered into the office.

'You should've asked me to help you.'

I'm sure he knows I'm not concentrating on his new arrangement so I swap around the front jars of three types of local honey. 'I prefer that,' I say, standing back to check.

'I could have helped,' he says, his head on one side staring at the jars I've switched around.

'You'd have helped me search the internet?' I laugh, knowing all too well Herbie's disinterest in anything digital and his distrust of technology.

'Not that.' He puts the jars back to their original positions. 'The different coloured labels stand out more like this,' he says. Herbie's right, but I don't want to talk about his display. 'What then?' I ask. 'Do you have a hidden talent for installing muddled up machinery?' My hands are on my hips.

'Come on,' he says before turning to Mum, who's helping behind the counter this morning. 'Danielle.' He waits for her to look up. 'We're popping out for a mo - back in twenty mins, is that okay?' Mum nods as she slips a sausage roll into a paper bag for her customer.

Herbie opens the front door of the shop. 'It's a five-minute walk,' he says.

He marches me along the main road before turning into a short driveway marked with four wooden signs on a tall post. The notices sit one above the other. I read them aloud.

'RIVENDELL,'

'Beware of Fairies and Unicorns,'

'WELCOME to the FUN HOUSE,'

'A Magic Boo & Tiny, a VERY BIG Dragon live here.'

'What's a *magic boo?'* I ask Herbie.

He shrugs. 'There's your solution,' he says, now pointing at a thatched cottage at the end of the drive, its front lawn adorned with foot-high, red, white, and green windmills, all whirring violently in the breeze. Dotted amongst the toy windmills are at least fifty smiley-faced gnomes. Fairy lights are strewn in ribbons over the cottage's arched doorway, and I watch them flash white, then green, then red. 'Gino Bianchi,' he says his eyes following my gaze.

'Gino?' I frown. 'Is he Italian, perhaps?'

'What makes you think that?' Herbie looks at me from under his glasses, like a professor considering a pupil's remark.

'Don't know, really,' I say, smiling at him and thinking this seems like a total waste of time. I'm wondering how I've never noticed this place before, I must have driven past the driveway a thousand times, probably more.

'If he can help you, he will,' Herbie says. 'Gino worked with Andrew Arscott from the start, and I'm pretty sure Andrew would never have gotten his ice-cream business off the ground without him. Be warned though, the man's got fourteen nephews and nieces. Nothing, but nothing comes before them.'

I scoff. 'He can't have that many.'

'He has. I assure you, Billy – and don't let him start talking about them because you won't get anything else done.'

I look at my watch, then back at Herbie. 'I haven't got enough time to knock on his door right now. Do you have his number? I'll ring later when I've finished the deliveries.'

'Back in the office, I do. Don't call him this afternoon though. Try tomorrow, at eleven, that should be okay.'

* * *

While Herbie searches for the telephone number, I move the honey again. I'm certain my manager will notice soon enough, but it will make him smile. I smile too – at last, there's a glimmer of fairy light hope that I might have found someone to help me.

* * *

My phone call to Gino destroys my expectations. I'd assumed he'd have an Italian accent or at least a hint of one, but his voice is Devonian, as strong as my mother's West Country burr. He's to the point. 'I don't drive,' he says, 'If you pick me up right now, I'll come over and tell you how it all works.'

I'm at the fairy-tale house again, and as he opens his door, I see Gino doesn't look like how I'd envisaged either. I'd conjured up a sort of modern-day Gandalf – a wizard with straggly white hair and a long beard, wearing stout leather boots. His narrow eyes strike me first, black-brown like Jessie's with large black pupils, which focus on me for seemingly a whole minute. I stare back at him, and neither of us speak. I can't decide if his lower eyelids are outlined in makeup or if it's his long dark lashes that give an illusion that he's wearing eyeliner. He's dressed immaculately with a suede waistcoat, and spotted tie.

We don't say anything until we pull up in the farmyard. 'Where are you planning on making the ice-cream?' he asks, giving me the distinct impression he's got something else he wants to do.

'There,' I say. I point to my new building.

He opens the van door and turns to me as his feet touch the ground. 'I'd like an A4 pad of paper, and then I can make you two or three sketches to show how it should be set up.'

'Two secs,' I say. 'I'll need to fetch the paper, then I'll show you where everything's been dumped.' I find myself running towards the dairy to find what he needs.

'I'll wait here,' he calls to my back.

When I return, Gino is gone, and I find him inside the ICF standing next to what I guess is the pasteurising tank. 'Here you are.' I pass him the pad.

'Where did you think the freezers might go?' he asks, folding up the front page of the pad.

'I have an idea based on some layouts I've found online. I've roughed out a proposed floor plan. Would you like to see it?' I ask.

'Nope.' He begins pacing out the length of the building.

'It's forty-five feet by thirty if that helps,' I say, and I watch as he stands still, writing the dimensions down in neat block letters.

'I'll show you what's best,' he tells me, not looking up as he draws out his plan.

'Alright,' I say. I have a sudden fear he's about to take over. I don't want to be side-lined, this is my project, and I need some good advice, that's all. I watch his pencil darting over the paper, his frowning concentration and his tongue just visible between his set lips. *How will I keep control of this?* I ask myself.

Chapter 12

Billy

Gino waves a hand at the first pile of equipment. 'I'll run through what you've got here,' he says. He pulls two sets of red post-it notes from his pocket. 'You'll need these.' He holds them out to me on the flat of his hand like you would a sugar-lump to a pony. 'I tell you what's what. Write it on a sticky note and slap it on whatever I'm pointing to, okay?'

After an hour my head throbs, taking in everything he's said whilst writing labels as fast as I can, trying not to waste his valuable time. As I scrawl a name on the last of the notes, Gino turns to leave. 'Can you take me home now, please?' he says, looking at the exit to the ICF.

* * *

My passenger has his hand on the door, about to dive out of the van and head into his cottage. 'If you need clarification on something, then you can ring me,' he says, 'but as you know, I'm very busy, so I'd prefer it if you didn't.'

I nod, immediately disappointed and overawed by the enormity of what I now need to do on my own.

'Listen.' Gino slams his hand on the dashboard, making me jump. 'If you speak to them, you might get the people who bought Andrew's place to sell you the freezer units too, if the freezers are still there? I've heard the new owners plan to demolish both buildings where we used to make the ice-cream, making way for an Olympic-sized pool.' He stares at me and smiles for the first time since I picked him up this morning. A smile that is full of warmth that lights up his dark brown eyes. 'Could be worth a call,' he says.

* * *

Back in the ICF, I'm armed with sellotape, using it to firmly secure all the post-it notes, terrified that I'll come in here tomorrow morning to a sea of red on the floor, where all my makeshift labels have peeled off.

That done, I lay everything out around the building in a close approximation to where Gino drew it on his plans.

'That looks incredible,' I say aloud to myself, feeling chuffed but checking my watch. I see it is half-past ten, I've missed lunch and tea, so engrossed in what I was doing. Mum brought me drinks every hour or so, and each time I told her I'd be in a minute. I yawn, suddenly exhausted by all the physical and mental strain of the day. The thought of getting up at six tomorrow to do the milking is not helping, but now I grin. *It's worth it.*

* * *

I've got the song 'You Spin Me Right Round' stuck in my head. It was the first thing I heard playing on Radio Devon when I turned the radio on in the parlour, and the poor cows have had to listen to me singing the chorus over and over no matter what was being played later. I'm still singing to the cows as I let them into the field. Mum taps me on the shoulder. 'I came to see if you're alright. You were shattered last night.' She leans her arms on the gate next to me.

'I'd never have got myself into this if I'd realised how hard it was going to be,' I say.

Mum turns to me, her eyebrows raised. 'Maybe that's just as well. There's been many things I wouldn't have started if I'd known how many obstacles there'd be. We always get there in the end, though, don't we?'

I touch her hand, 'Love you,' I say. 'You're an inspiration, and look, you're still working.' I nod towards the bucket of eggs she's carrying. She'll be cleaning them all in a minute, stacking them in boxes for me to take to the farm shop.

* * *

'*Big Bertha*.' I read the note stuck on the holding tank and smile, thinking how I like the nicknames Gino gave various parts of the equipment. They make the task of fitting everything back together seem less scary. I've manoeuvred this massive tank which will store the milk from the parlour, to the furthest corner of the building, to the spot nearest to where we milk the cows. I've set *Bertha* next to *Pasty Pat*, the tank where the milk will be pasteurised. I'm now working on connecting these two parts up, determined to stop at four o'clock so I'm in the house by the time Richard gets home.

* * *

I'm sitting at the kitchen table, having just watched Richard drive out the yard to head back to London, and I feel almost a sense of relief that the weekend is over. Things aren't getting easier between us, despite me doing nothing on the ICF since Friday, and despite me not mentioning ice-cream once. Every time we started a conversation, it died with a lack of enthusiasm from either of us.

Mary tramps into the kitchen, stopping and staring at me. 'Auntie…' She shifts her light frame from one white trainer to the other.

'What is it?' I ask.

'Do you have time to discuss something?'

'Later,' I say, my mind still on Richard. I run through in my mind everything I have to do today. 'Three o'clock? Shall I come and find you in the dairy?'

* * *

In the office, I find Mary kneeling on a swivel chair, staring over Grace's shoulder at her computer. Grace flicks her screen from a page of trendy looking prams to the accounts' database.

'I'm so happy, you're letting us pay for a new pram,' I tell her, trying to ease any guilt she might have about being caught not working – she has no need to feel embarrassed. I've never seen anyone rattle through tasks like Grace does, and I've not discovered a single mistake in all the months she's worked for me. Mary turns her chair towards me by twisting her waist, and she smiles. 'I hope your ice-cream business does well.' She laughs. 'It better make a small fortune if it is going to fund all the baby stuff you keep offering to buy.'

'That's unfair,' I say. 'Grace has found nearly everything second hand, and besides, it'll be nice for her and Freddy to have a brand-new pram.' I'm longing for the baby to arrive, probably as excited as his prospective parents. I'm so pleased Grace and Freddy are moving into one of the holiday cottages before the baby is born. They'll be living across the yard from our house, and I'll get to see the little one all the time. I clap my hands, forcing my mind away from daydreaming about the baby. 'What do you want to talk about?' I ask Mary.

She scrambles to her feet and holds her hands out to me. 'Another long-term customer cancelled their order this morning. They said they'd be buying their cheese and yoghurts elsewhere in future. That's the third who's stopped buying from us in a fortnight.'

I feel cold; it's a long time since any of the local businesses stopped buying from us. Most are steadily increasing their orders, not cancelling them - my thoughts of babies vanish. 'Which customers?' I ask.

'Evans Café in Okehampton, today. Last week, it was the coffee shop in Hatherleigh, and before that, the butchers in North Tawton—' Mary sounds like she is on the verge of tears. 'I told them there wasn't anything to beat us, and asked if we needed to change anything so they'd stay - but all three have been adamant. I can't understand what's happening, can you?'

Our sales always fall off in the New Year while customers make recompense for Christmas indulgences, but the cafés and butchers normally keep a trickle of orders coming in. 'Would you like me to speak to them?' I offer. 'See if I can find out anything. I can ask if you've offended them?' I smile.

'No, Auntie.' Mary frowns. 'You know I wouldn't upset *any* of our customers. I always go the extra mile. They love me.' She's right. Mary's been involved with the farm and the dairy since she was thirteen. All our customers immediately adored the red-haired teenager who earnestly talked about our products, often having them in fits of laughter because she was so passionate about the farm. Customers asked where she was when she wasn't around.

Grace folds her arms tightly across her ever-increasing chest. She looks at Mary, then at me. 'I offered to spy on them and find out what they are replacing our products with, but Mary refused to let me do it.'

'But, Mary,' I say, 'I think that might be a good idea. Grace could sneak a photo of their menus or their counters, and then you'd soon be able to spot what's changed. You don't think it's Troy Gloon, do you?' Mary and Grace shrug their shoulders at the same time.

'And what should we do about the show?' Grace asks, and I notice how Mary glares at her. Grace's reaction is to turn back to her screen.

'Show?' I look from one to the other.

Grace spins back to face me. 'Devon County Show. I rang the secretary yesterday to see if we could set up our stand a bit earlier this year, but she was surprised to hear from me. She said she hadn't received our booking, and has given our usual spot to someone else.'

'Who?' I check.

'She said she couldn't tell me.' Mary sits down heavily, forcing her chair to run across the concrete floor towards Grace. 'I don't know how it happened, Auntie,' Mary says. 'I posted everything before Christmas. I've been trying to get another spot, but I've failed.'

I won't be angry; I can see Mary is upset. 'It doesn't matter,' I tell her. I turn to Grace. 'It's a bit slack. Why don't you pop into Okehampton and do some sleuthing?'

She jumps up, grinning. 'Being paid to eat Evan's homemade doughnuts – ask me to do that whenever you like.' As Grace pulls her coat on, I touch Mary's arm. 'Don't worry about the show,' I say. 'It's one of those things. I'm sure we'll find out soon enough why these customers have found a new supplier. I'm so proud of you for stepping up, and so, *so* grateful for the way you put your heart into the dairy.'

Mary blinks several times before she speaks. 'I'm grateful to you too, Auntie.'

'For what?'

'Making me be nice to William.' She smiles.

'You enjoyed the Chinese?'

'We laughed and laughed. He's good company. I've only ever talked to him about work before. We went for a ride together yesterday afternoon too. 'And,' she pauses, her face reddening. 'He kissed me…' she says.

I wait, feeling a *but* coming.

'It didn't seem right,' she says, at last. 'I pulled away from him, and I left.'

'Did you explain how you felt?'

'I tried to, but I'm sure I've hurt him. He said it was fine when I texted him last night. He told me he was happy just spending time together.'

'Well, today is the ideal time to put that right.' I grin at her. 'It's February twenty-ninth today. You can make him a leap year proposal.'

'Marry William!?' she almost shouts.

'Why not?' My voice is calm.

'Because I don't want to and if I ever I do find someone I want to spend the rest of my life with - which I won't, I'll be doing the asking, anyway, leap day or not. I'll plough up Gully Field with forty-foot-high letters saying, *'Marry Me'* so whoever the lucky chap is, he'll see my proposal from Nan-Dan's bedroom window.'

I laugh. 'Why from Mum's bedroom?'

'Duh— because it's got the best view of the field.'

'Shame you can't plough,' I laugh, glad she looks more cheerful now.

'I can, actually. I ploughed two fields for William last September. I helped him out when he was inundated with apples to press.'

I nod at her, my eyes widening. 'Ooh,' I say. 'A lady of many talents.'

She smiles. 'And they'll have to signal '*yes*' in semaphore from the top of Primrose Mound.' Her smile disappears. 'But it's never going to happen. I'll *never* stop loving Sharmarke, and I can *never* marry him,' she says, leaning over Grace's computer to shut it down.

'I'm sure William's happy taking it slow,' I say, not wanting to dwell on Sharmarke. 'Be honest with him, and William will be honest with you.' I feel a hypocrite. *When did I stop telling Richard everything? ...when did I last think about how lucky I am to have him?*

Chapter 13

BILLY

I can't believe how the year is rushing by. We are three days into March. Daffodils seem to adorn every hedgerow and I love the bright yellow flowers – they make me feel cheerful just looking at them.

The new owner of Andrew's farm insisted I take everything I needed, saying he wanted the place cleared out as quickly as possible, and what's more, he'd only accept a truckle of Foxy Lady in payment!

I'm driving William's largest tractor away from Andrew's former home with the trailer behind me, loaded so high it is probably over its legal weight limit. *It's not far back to Fox Halt and the route is fairly flat,* I tell myself, fingers crossed and hoping my precious cargo will round each bend. I wish I'd been less rash, divided the load and made two trips. This journey seems endless.

My sense of relief on reaching the farm disappears as my thoughts turn to where I'm going to stack my haul – I'll have to clear some of the factory floor to make room until I'm ready to rebuild it. That could be weeks because I keep obsessing every last detail, focusing on one thing at a time, refusing to move on until each element is oiled, cleaned and polished.

As I finish unloading, I think how there's still so much to do. For example, I have to source and buy all the raw materials for the ice-cream, sort packaging and make a marketing campaign. I crush the keys to the ICF in my hand, squeezing so tightly it hurts. I'll make a project plan with a timeline to get a proper idea about what I need to do and by when. I need something down on paper to reassure me that I can really do this.

* * *

'What's so interesting?' Richard asks with no hello and no kiss, and I guess it's because I typed the last word of my sentence before I closed my laptop, looking up at him just one nano-second too late.

'Hello, darling.' I get up and wrap my arms around him, kissing him. My words are like honey, but my insides are vinegar, hurt by his lack of greeting– *Heck! We haven't seen each other for five days.* 'Traffic bad?' I ask, keeping my voice upbeat.

'No.' He taps the top of my computer.

'You're a bit late,' I say, burying my hurt and now feeling bad that I didn't run into the yard as his car pulled up, hating the way that this weekend has already started.

'Sorry.' He sits down at the table, and I wait for him to explain why he is an hour later than normal, but instead, he starts to tear the cellophane off a magazine that arrived for him this morning. He obviously doesn't want to explain.

'I've cooked your favourite dinner. It's ready.' Again, I try to sound excited he's here.

'Thanks,' he says with no enthusiasm, hardly seeming to listen as he flicks the pages of the magazine he's opened.

I nod towards the Rayburn. 'I've put your wine over there to warm up a little. Do you want a glass?'

He shakes his head. 'What were you doing when I came in?' He lifts up the lid of my laptop.

'Nothing much,' I say, avoiding telling him because I don't want another argument. I'm tired. I push the lid back down, almost catching his fingers. 'Are you hungry?'

'Actually, do you mind if I have a shower before dinner - it's been such a busy day. I'm whacked.' He gets up before I reply and heads upstairs.

I have no inclination to do anything now, not chase after him or shout that I've had a hard week too – I moved everything on my own today from Andrew's old farm. It was a slog, and I'm so tired that concentrating on my project plan was pretty impossible. My brain is frazzled, and my energy sapped. Nor do I tell him how I rushed my plan to finish it before he arrived. I sit down where he just sat, putting my head in my hands, and wait for him to come back downstairs.

Richard places a hand flat on my back between my shoulder blades. 'What were you working on when I came in?' He kisses the back of my neck. I shiver. He smells delicious, the same aftershave I noticed the first day I met him. It's his smell; it always makes me feel safe. The tone of his question is softer, but I'm not sure he really cares what I was doing – it was just that it was taking priority over him.

'Something for the ice-cream factory,' I say, not wanting to be specific –if I told him that it was my schedule for the next three and a half months, he wouldn't want to look at it anyway. 'Dinner?' I ask, getting up. It's just Richard and me tonight; everyone else is at Martha and Sean's for their fifth wedding anniversary and a special family dinner. Mum invited herself along, thinking it might be nice for Richard and me to spend an evening alone together.

He steps back. 'Is it chicken and broccoli lasagne?'

'Yes,' I say, and he smiles, his face lighting up, and my heart jumps – there is nothing in the world that matches the way my body reacts when Richard looks at me like this.

He puts the first forkful in his mouth and pulls a face to show how much he's relishing it. 'You know, darling?' he says.

'What?' I smile, hoping he is about to say I've made nearly as good a lasagne as Mum does.

'The only thing that would beat this is sitting with you, having this same dinner parked up at the edge of a Norwegian Fjord, watching the sunset on the water.' Suddenly, I don't want to be here. I push my seat back to stand up. Every chance he gets, he brings up the motorhome. Richard claps his hand on mine. 'Where are you going?'

As I get up, I don't have an answer, his hand still trapping mine – I don't know where I intend to go. I want to be away from this intimate situation. It feels contrived, and I'm uncomfortable. I don't want to discuss our retirement options or plans to travel the world. Tears well in my eyes. I'm tired, and fed up with his lack of support for what I'm trying to do.

'Sit down, Billy.' He's angry. I was expecting sympathy. He can see I'm upset. I sit back down, but I can't look at him.

'We need to sort this; we are going in two different directions, and I'm questioning how you feel about me. Do you love me?'

'Yes,' I say, but my voice is sputtery.

He jerks my hand. 'Are you sure?'

'You are my world, Rich,' I say.

'It doesn't feel like it. All you seem interested in is the farm and that damn ICF. When did we last talk? *Really* talk?'

I'm lost for words. All I can think of is how I wish it wasn't the *damn* ice-cream factory, that he'd be proud of me having a dream and pursuing it.

'Are you not going to talk?'

I frown at him, staring into his eyes, knowing if I tell him how I feel, it'll upset him more. I don't want to lie. I stand up. 'I'm not hungry. I'm going to bed. Today's been tough.'

'Go on then, but running away won't solve anything.'

I'm halfway up the stairs before I stop, realising he's not following me. Richard is letting me go. I turn around and head back down, and he's eating his lasagne. I march across the kitchen and sit directly opposite him. 'Cards on the table time,' I say. 'You listen to me, and I'll listen to you, and there has to be some middle ground. We're not leaving this table until we agree on something.'

'Okay.' He puts his knife and fork down and pushes his plate away.

Chapter 14

RICHARD

Women! Sometimes, I wonder if my life would be easier without them. Daniella and Mary have been trying to find ways to bridge the rift between Billy and me, supporting and defending each of us in turn, but nothing seems to help.

Our new motorhome arrived yesterday, coinciding with my last day at O'Rowdes' and my official retirement, so I'm ready to - *actually, I am unsure what I'm ready to do. I feel lost.* Billy works every spare moment installing the kit from Andrew Arscott, but I've avoided the ICF, determined not to show one iota of interest. Despite appearances, I do care, and I want Billy to succeed. But at the same time, I'd like us to spend some proper time together, undistracted by the cows, milk vending machines, the farm shop or cheese and yoghurt.

We managed to agree something - that we'll go away for ten days in October and have a whole month off in January, but the horrendous battle to get Billy to concede to this has spoilt all the fun of planning where we will go. There is no real buy-in from her, no exclamations about where she has always wanted to see, and no delight at the thought of us exploring new places together.

Jessie is adding to my woes today - although her intention is to do the opposite, wanting to ensure my first day of freedom isn't a big let-down, but her plan is not making me feel better. I have a brand-new football in my hand, and I keep banging the sides of it, enjoying the noise and the vibration through my fingers. It's like a giant stress ball, relieving some of the tension I'm feeling. I am contemplating keeping it and not handing it over to Betsy and Bramble.

As a *WhatIf* minibus pulls up into the farmyard. I feel crabby - grumpy that Jessie is expecting me to meet all its passengers. She has designated me as her positive *male* role-model for the day, providing me with two pages of instructions about what I need to do – her directions mainly focusing on how not to be intimidating to vulnerable women and the children. *WhatIf* is the charity that Jessie set up after her husband died. It helps victims of abuse, and Jessie has told me in general terms about the history of some of the families coming to Fox Halt today. She even had Billy and me acting out some non-threatening scenarios last weekend to reassure herself, as well as me, that everything would be fine.

The purpose of the *WhatIf* visit is for the children to see the animals. Jessie has organised the three hours with precision - the children will feed the lambs, and the ducks and hens, they'll be able to collect eggs and maybe try to milk a cow. There is time to spend with Crinkle, William's two sheepdogs and our cats —and a carefully supervised visit with Banjo and Soup, our two ancient Dartmoor cross Shetland ponies, with Billy making sure no-one has their fingers nibbled, toes squashed or hair munched.

The pièce de résistance will be Betsy and Bramble's antics with the football. Nothing is to be rushed or pushed, but Jessie asked us to stick to her timetable as best we can.

* * *

I help a toddler feed a lamb with a bottle of warm milk, and while I'm watching her, I find myself tuning into her mother's conversation with another of the mums. '…it was all my fault. I shouldn't have wound him up. He was lovely in public, I thought no-one would believe me, but Jess understood.'

The four-day-old lamb stops wagging its tail and nudges the bottle so hard the child lets go. 'Look,' I say, 'he's drunk the whole lot.'

'Feed that one.' The girl points towards another lamb, and her mother turns to me, 'Can she?'

'Of course,' I say.

The woman blinks at me, a rapid-fire of fluttery lids. 'I've not heard my Elsie ask to do something before,' she says, smiling at me then jolting her eyes away to watch her daughter run towards the new lamb. *Why hasn't she asked for things before?* I wonder.

'I'll need to hold that lamb. Maybe your mum can help you with the bottle,' I say, darting to catch the animal before it knocks Elsie over. 'This lamb is five days older and much stronger than the one you fed just now.' I look at Elsie's mother 'I don't want your daughter to be frightened. Do you think we should feed a smaller lamb instead and leave this one to be fed by one of the older children?'

Elsie stops and stares at me. 'Not fright'ed,' she says.

'I can see you aren't scared,' I reply, 'but wait a moment for your mum and me to help you.'

* * *

Jessie slams the side door of the minibus shut, and then she holds out her hand to me, 'I don't think today could have gone better,' she says. 'You are both animal tamer and child tamer.'

'I had a great time,' I tell her. 'It's made me appreciate the farm again.' I open the driver's door for her to get in.

She leaps up onto the seat. 'Good,' she says.

Crinkle is by my feet, looking up with wide eyes, waiting to be picked up. As I scoop her into my arms, Jessie winds down her window. 'I expect you'll be getting some pretty heart-breaking thank-you letters next week,' she says, leaning out of the window so she can kiss me on the cheek.

'I'll reply to them all,' I say. I step back so she can drive away. I hold Crinkle's paw and move it as if the dog is waving, keeping her foot moving until the bus, and the children, who are all waving back, disappear out of sight.

I twitch my nostrils, suddenly aware of a horrible smell, and I realise that my hands and chest are soaking wet. I shake my head. 'I don't need to ask where you've been, Piggy,' I say, and as I walk towards the house to take Crinkle for a bath, I nearly trip over a football, punctured and plastered in muck.

* * *

Billy

I place the primroses by the granite, reading the last line of the inscription aloud. *'A kind and gentle farmer.'* I kneel quietly beside the grave for ten minutes before I trace my fingers along the indents of my father's name. 'Can I sell them, Dad?' I whisper, tears sliding down my cheeks. This feels wrong, wicked even.

The horrific idea germinated from a tiny seed in the first week of January, and it's taken root and grown away inside my mind. It's so massive now that I can't ignore it anymore. I think

I have to sell half of my cows. The seed was planted the day after Jessie's New Year party, when I analysed the results of the ice-cream sampling. At first, the outcome made me smile because two cheaper supermarket brands had out-scored Fortnum & Mason, and Harrods, but after that, I scrutinised what made some ice-creams taste better, determining it came down to one thing, the butterfat in the milk.

My hypothesis was confirmed on Valentine's Day, when Richard bought me ice-cream in the café on the Lizard. As soon as I tasted it, I realised it had the flavour and texture I wanted to replicate, and that particular ice-cream was made using milk from Jersey cows, not the black and white Friesians I have at Fox Halt whose milk is not so creamy. I could carry on regardless, using our own milk and buying in some Jersey milk and cream from the Somerset dairy who already supply the farm shop—but I want my ice-cream to be 'grown' here. *How can I call it Fox Halt Ice-Cream unless it truly is?* Anyone can say something is packaged or bottled in a certain place, but it would mislead our customers into believing it's wholly produced on the farm.

That's why I feel I need to replace half our herd with Jerseys —but how can I even consider this option? Generations of Mays have kept Friesians at Fox Halt, and the herd has been painstakingly bred. I know each cow individually and all their quirky ways —observing them closely for signs of illness or upset, noticing the smell of their breath, a limp, or how they might have withdrawn from the herd, or if they are lying down too often - or hardly at all. I track how much they are eating, checking the amount of milk they're producing. I notice if they are being bullied, the lustre of their coats, any bruises or abrasions - all sorts of little signs from a slightly lopsided posture to a watery eye. I know and love them all; I don't just care for them.

How could I ever decide which to keep and which to sell? And I know a big fat zero about Jersey cattle. If I bring in new stock, I'll need to start again, discovering all their personalities and foibles. It will be hard work settling them into their new surroundings. I don't even know if I would have to keep the different breeds in separate fields.

Mum loves all our cows too, and like me, she knows each one - but it's Dad I feel more guilty about: In 2001, the foot and mouth crisis led to Fox Halt being sold to William's dad. Our cows survived the disease, but Mum and Dad didn't come out well. The farm was virtually bankrupt despite me pumping money into it for years from my well-paid city job. Mum was seventy-four, and Dad was seventy and I had a life away from the farm. Tom, William's dad, agreed to keep our herd intact, planning that Dad would still help with the cows after the sale. But my dad had a massive stroke, dying on the day they were due to move. I'm sure it was too hard for him to leave Fox Halt and the animals.

Later, I bought back the farm and made it viable at last, I can't betray my father and sell the cows, *can I?*

My father loved Fox Halt, and I often think if I'd not gone away to university to study for a new career away from farming— if I'd decided to take on the farm when I left school, things might have turned out differently - my wonderful dad might still be here. Buying the farm back and fighting for its survival is my way of making it up to him, and if Mary or Freddy make a go of the place after I'm gone then that would be amazing. I sit back on my heels, still staring at Dad's name, 'So, what do you think?' I ask him.

Chapter 15

Billy

I rarely visit the small cemetery beside Hamsgate church because to me, it's not where Dad is. He's everywhere on Fox Halt – always behind me, watching over my shoulder. I sense his presence so often. But today, I wanted to talk to him face to face, and I thought this was a solution. But he's not granite and black etched words; he is soft and warm, he's a smile where I can see all his teeth. 'I miss you so much,' I say.

'You okay, Auntie?' Mary calls to me as she battles her way up the steep bank to reach me. I don't reply because she can see my face is wet, and I'm sniffing. 'Saw your car and wondered what you were up to. Is it your dad's birthday?' She checks the dates cut into the headstone and realises it's not. 'You never come here. What's wrong?' Mary drops down on her knees next to me and places a hand on my shoulder.

'I needed an answer to a question,' I say, turning to her and wiping my cheek with the back of my hand.

'Sounds major?'

'It is.' I sniff.

'Has your dad given you an answer?' Mary squeezes my shoulder, and her sympathetic gesture makes me want to cry even more. I take a deep breath. 'You turned up, so no, not yet.'

'What's the question?'

Her face is so earnest. I try to smile, trying to make things seem less bleak. My voice is a whisper. 'I need to sell half the cows.'

'Gripes? That *is* major,' Mary says. 'Why?'

'For the ice-cream to be good,' I say, swiping away another tear. 'We need Jersey milk mixed in with the Friesians.'

'You *cannot* sell Petunia 717!' She pushes her shoulders down hard. 'I adore that cow.'

'I won't,' I reassure her. 'She's not only your favourite, you know, we all love her. She saved my life once, or at least stopped me getting seriously hurt— I was driving a calf back to his mum after he'd squeezed through a hole in the hedge, but the mother came for me, thinking I was threatening her baby. Petunia saw what was happening, and she charged at the other cow, giving me time to escape.'

'Aah what a darling, I didn't know that, Auntie - I adore her even more now. Why don't you get extra cows for the ice-cream and keep all the Friesians?'

'Our acreage won't support more cows; besides, I don't need more milk, I need a different kind.'

'Creamier?'

I nod. 'Yes.'

'What about less drastic action, like swapping a quarter of them instead? After all, we still need milk for our cheeses and the yoghurt. We can't change our existing recipes, our customers would go bonkers.' She knots her hands together. 'What's Nan-Dan going to say?'

I shake my head, leaning forward and removing a dead flower I've noticed amongst the bunch I laid on the grave. I roll its delicate stem between my index finger and thumb.

Mary makes a low whistle. 'She can't stop you, Auntie; it's you running the farm now.'

'It's her farm too. Mum loves those cows as much as you and I do.'

'Ask her, Auntie. See what she says.' Mary stands up, trailing a hand across my back. 'I'm sorry, I've got to go,' she says. 'We've got skittles tonight, and I've been late for the last three matches. William's threatening to drop me from the team if I'm late again. I've to get back to Culmfield first; the new tenants in the Dower House keep belly-aching about the track. I have to see if it's really as bad as they are making out.' She turns, then runs down the steep bank. I drop the single dead primrose and pick up the jam jar of flowers instead. 'Was that your answer, Dad?' I ask, my words now directed to the single patch of blue in the sky. 'The same one you used to give me as a child, *ask your mother?'* I wait for a signal of confirmation, but the patch of blue fills in with cloud and I think Dad has gone. He's headed back to the farm.

* * *

'Those are lovely,' Mum says, watching me position the jar of primroses in the centre of the kitchen table. 'I was just thinking about your dad – he loved primroses. I heard the door handle, and I stood there, waiting for him to stroll in. All these years, and I still expect him to come through the door, kiss me and ask what's for dinner.' She sits down at the table and looks at me. 'What's wrong?' she asks, immediately getting up again.

I walk up to her and put my arms around her waist. I press my lips together before I whisper into her neck. 'How would you feel if you looked over at High Meadow tomorrow morning and forty-eight of the cows weren't black and white?'

'You mean Jersey coloured instead?' she asks, pulling away from me.

I'm shocked by her quick understanding.

'Gino Bianchi told me when he came over to help you sort the machinery. I met him in the yard – you'd left him by your van while you went to fetch something. He took one look at the cows in the field, and the first thing he said to me was, 'Friesians? You need higher butterfat than that.' In fact, that was all he said before he walked off towards the ICF.'

I stand there, in the middle of the kitchen, staring at her, feeling hopeless.

'Never!' Mum shouts at me, 'How could you think I'd ever agree to that?' In the next second, she has marched outside, leaving the door wide open.

* * *

Jessie roars her Ferrari through the gates of the Woodleigh Café carpark, pulling up hard in the space next to my van. Before I have even grabbed my rucksack from the passenger seat, she's standing by my driver's door. 'Morning, lovely,' she says with a big grin spreading across her face.

'You're cheery,' I reply, feeling jaded in comparison – I tossed and turned all night, thinking about Mum's refusal to talk about the cows.

'Been here before?' she asks, waving vaguely towards the café.

'No.' I stare up at the imposing former coach house. I imagine that it's an annexe for an impressive stately home, but the mature trees behind it hide any other buildings that might be nearby.

'It's got good reviews,' Jessie says, holding open the door of the café, letting me go ahead of her to get to the counter. Jessie knows I'm paying – I only rang her an hour ago to ask to meet up, so I owe her big time for changing her day around to see me. She said this place was about halfway between Fox Halt and Culmfield, and she'd like to see what it was like.

The man behind the counter is looking out the window at Jessie's car. 'Bit posh for round here, ain't it?' He is speaking to the glass, but his comment is obviously meant for us. He turns his head and makes a sad clown face at Jessie.

Jessie smiles at him, 'Would you like us to go?'

'If you don't mind.' He grins. 'Might raise our customers' expectations, seeing that in our carpark.'

'Don't worry, Billy's shitty van next to it lowers the tone right back down,' she says.

'I'll have you know I washed it yesterday,' I snap back at her. 'It's all this rain, it gets filthy in the lanes.'

The man ignores our bickering. 'Ladies, what can I get you?' he asks, opening his hands, holding his palms up.

'A latte and a black decaf coffee, not too strong,' I say, without checking with Jessie; she always has a black decaffeinated coffee. 'And a piece of that too, please.' I point at a mouth-watering carrot cake.

'This is vegan?' Jessie asks, tapping her finger lightly on the glass dome covering a fruit and nut flapjack.

'Yep. My daughter made it this morning,' the man tells her, pushing his shoulders back, obviously proud of his daughter.

'Two pieces, please,' she says.

'Two?' I check.

'I need the calories.' Jessie looks serious, 'I have a feeling this will be painful – I guess you want to discuss Daniella and her not agreeing with your plans for the herd. I'll have to listen to you complaining for the next half an hour, I expect.'

'That's what friends do, Jessie; they listen.'

The man waves the large knife he's about to use on the carrot cake at me, then at Jessie. 'Are you two always like this?' he asks.

'Yes.' Jessie laughs.

'But we love each other, really,' I say, putting my arm around my friend's shoulder and pulling her towards me.

* * *

'My earliest memories are of cows,' I tell Jessie as I slide two chairs across the wooden floor so we can sit down at the only empty table. 'I do understand Mum's loyalty to them.' I feel lucky to have Jessie's focus on my troubles as I continue. 'I remember when I was a toddler, I must have been about two years old, Mum tripped over me in the kitchen and she poured a large mixing bowl full of still-warm milk over my head. I close my eyes, and I can still feel it running through my hair and down my nose. Our milk was put in churns back then to be taken away but we always kept back two bowls each morning for ourselves. Mum's accident created such a mess and Dad wasn't pleased he had to ration his milk on his cornflakes and drink less tea.

'I also remember when I was small, back when our electric came from coal power stations, and the government was in dispute with the miners. Of course, I was unaware of the politics, but I can still see Dad storming out of the shippen in a terrible rage because the power had gone off again. His milking machines were electric, and he still had cows to milk. The parlour had a back-up generator, but it was worn out and difficult to keep running. My father was easy-going and gentle, so him swearing about the power cuts and shouting whether Ted Heath or someone in his 'ruddy' cabinet would like to come and help him milk his cows with no 'bleddy' electric is something that'll always stay with me.'

Jessie picks up her first flapjack, so I keep talking. 'And Mum's childhood was the same as mine, all about the animals – her parents working sun up to sun down with the cows. Relishing the miracle of calves being born, looking after them throughout their lives. She'll talk for hours about her father milking his cows by hand and the small herd he had. The bull they borrowed from their neighbour who broke every gate on the farm – I do see why she's set on keeping our pedigree herd together. I want that too; just have less of them. And like our family has always tried to do, I want to make a living from the farm as well.'

Jessie closes her eyes as she savours her flapjack.

'Another drink?' I ask, pointing at her empty cup.

She nods. 'Please.' Before I can get up, a young waitress is asking what we'd both like. I notice her Yorkshire accent is the same as the man who served us before, and I wonder if she might be his daughter and whether a family run this friendly place.

As the young woman walks away, Jessie tilts her head, which I assume means I can keep talking, and she's ready to listen. I don't need encouraging. 'Grandad grew up with cart-horses,' I say. 'They pulled wagons, and he used them for ploughing, and one of my most treasured photos is of him with his shires, Blossom and Pleasant. I think I've shown it to you.'

Jessie nods, wiping golden crumbs from her lips, and I stop, waiting for her to say something, but she waves her hand at me as a signal to go on.

'My grandad slowly replaced his horsepower with tractors,' I tell her. 'And he bought in other machines too to help make the work easier, and that's what I'm doing, taking Fox Halt into the future. Grandad kept ponies and horses on the farm, and like him, I still want the Friesians, but unlike my grandfather whose ponies became pure indulgences, I want my treasured animals to make money too.'

'That was exceptional,' Jessie says as she finishes her second flapjack. She leans back on her chair. 'I remember you telling me how your grandfather delivered milk with a pony and cart when he was a boy.'

'I showed you a photo of that too with the churns in the cart and Grandad's youngest brother next to him, holding up the measure they used to dip out the milk for their customers. Grandad told me some great tales about the things that happened on that round and the characters they saw each day.'

Jessie touches my hand. 'I do understand all the history of the cows,' she says. 'But what's your plan now?'

I shrug. 'I still want the Jerseys. I just need to make Mum see why.' Jessie looks at her watch, 'You need to go,' I say.

Jessie puts her empty plate and cup back on the tray. 'Do you have a strategy that might get Daniella to listen?'

'I haven't got a clue how to do it—' I pause, and smile at her, 'but it's nice to be able to talk to someone.' I stand up, expecting her to push her chair back and get up, but she doesn't move. 'Billy, sit down, please; you haven't finished your cake.'

I wonder if there's something about Mary she wants to discuss. After all, I see her daughter more than she does these days. 'What's wrong?' I ask.

'We're here for a reason,' she says. 'At this café.'

I raise one eyebrow, 'What do you mean?'

'Because of Richard.'

A familiar heaviness settles inside my stomach at the mention of my husband's name, waiting for another lecture from Jessie about how we need to sort ourselves out. 'What's this place got to do with him?' I shake my head.

'Because every Friday night, since you told him about the ice-cream - right up until last week, he stopped here on his way back to Fox Halt.'

'But this place is fifteen miles - and *only* twenty minutes away from the farm, why would he break his journey back from London here?'

'To delay getting home, preparing to face you and the way you are hell-bent on your own selfish project which you know he's set against.'

I look down at my unfinished cake, unable to take this information in and unsure how to respond. Jessie doesn't say anything either, she just stares at me. At last, she speaks. 'Richard's got no excuse to come here now, not since he finished at O'Rowdes'. No excuse to have a light-hearted conversation with Josh, the chap who joked about my car or Olivia, one of Josh's daughters. '

'You know their names?'

She nods.

'You said you'd not been here before.'

'I haven't, but Richard talks to me. He's described this place and the family who own it. This café became important to him. A haven, I suppose.' Jessie reaches over for my hand but I move it away, angry that Richard has confided in her. I feel tears of self-pity threatening. She keeps talking, her voice gentle but firm like I'm her child, and she needs to tell me off; she doesn't want to, but she has to. 'He has no escape now, no excuse to have some friendly banter or time out – you mustn't ride roughshod over him. Richard's hurting: you have to see that.'

I bow my head.

'You need to talk to him and your mother. Speak to them both, reconsider your priorities, and see how you are upsetting them. Don't lose what you have while striving for something more – be careful, Billy.'

Chapter 16

Billy

I open the door of my van, and right away, Richard is beside me. 'Why are you so late back?' he asks, a deep frown across his forehead. 'The deliveries don't usually take this long.'

'I—' He doesn't let me finish.

'The vet has been. I wish you'd been here.'

'Is everything okay, a calving?' I check, dread rushing up inside me - I'd heard a text land on my phone when I was in the café, but I hadn't looked at it, and afterwards, I forgot about it, my mind full up with what I should do about Mum and him.

'It is, *now*. They're fine,' he snorts. This doesn't feel like a good time to say where I've been. Also, I don't trust myself. I feel snarky about how he's always turning to Jessie when he's got problems. *Maybe he should have rung her and asked for her help?* 'Come on, show me,' I say, trying to sound in this moment and not in the world where questions about our future stomp all over my brain.

'It's twins,' he says, turning to me as I struggle to match his strides towards the barn.

'Gosh, I thought it was Winnie, she's due to calf today. The twins aren't due for five or six days.'

'I know. I checked the app.' He glares at me, wielding his mobile in my face. We have an amazing program on our phones that tracks our cows' histories, holding data we previously stuffed in drawers and cupboards in the kitchen dresser. Now tonnes of information about each animal is available with a swipe of a finger across a screen. He holds the phone lower for me to see, showing me the calving wheel - each segment of the pie chart relates to a cow, colour coded to say if she's pregnant, or due to be put in calf, or has calved.

'There.' Richard points at the screen. 'Three-Four-Two not due until Thursday.' All our cows have names, but numbers are easier to enter into the app, and since each cow has two ear tags marked with their unique number and their hindquarters are freeze marked with the same number, it's easier sometimes to refer to the cows by their number.

As we stare over the gate at the two perfect black and white heifer calves, I touch Richard's hand. 'I met Jessie, that's why I'm late back.'

'You bumped into her on your round?' He frowns. 'That's odd, she's not often near here. She had a new case?'

'I was her case this morning.'

'What do you mean?'

'You know how good she's at listening to people's problems?' I say, intending a double meaning, hinting at the fact that she and Richard speak to each other on the phone all the time. Their conversations used to be about O'Rowdes', but it seems to have become about anything at all that might be troubling either of them. 'We met at Woodleigh Coach House.'

'Woodleigh?' His face reddens.

'It was Jessie's suggestion. She told me how you used to stop there to delay coming home.' He rubs the back of his neck, staring at me.

'Look, Rich, we need to talk, properly this time. Somewhere away from Fox Halt. We could have lunch?'

* * *

Richard and I are in another café, part of a local National Trust run foundry with a working waterwheel. The tearoom is in the shape of a decagon – each of the windows has a different view onto the waterwheel, its race or the well-kept gardens.

'This place, for example.' Richard looks around the room. 'I've been searching for somewhere to volunteer, and here, they rely on people who've retired, giving up their time for free. I need something else besides helping out at Fox Halt.'

I feel hurt that the farm is not enough for him, but I don't say so; instead, I nod and scoop up another spoonful of my spicy tomato soup.

'I like being around people with interests outside the farm,' he says. 'And with you so busy, I want to find something else for a day or two a week, somewhere close to Hamsgate.'

'You need an escape from your selfish wife?' I say, wondering what else he hasn't told me.

Richard laughs, but not the laugh where the skin around his eyes wrinkles up. It's half-hearted, and I think I'm near the mark, my obsession with the farm is driving us apart.

As I finish my soup, I remember another time when I nearly drove Richard away, when I chose rebuilding my friendship with Jessie over him. Now, I'm putting the farm first. I know it's hopeless, trying to *tell* him how much I love him, I need to *show* him. 'I'll get someone full time to do the milking,' I say, thinking quickly. 'Then we could do more things together. There wouldn't be such a massive commitment to be at Fox Halt then, especially the late afternoon milking, which makes doing anything else so tricky, always having to get back to the farm for the cows.'

I can't read his expression, but then he says, 'If you do get someone, they'll probably have to live in. Could they have a holiday cottage?'

I keep the idea running, hoping he sees I'm keen to find something that might make things better between us. 'The cost of accommodation would come out of their wages, but it'll fall short of what we're getting on the holiday lets,' I say. 'We might get some tax relief though; I'd have to check.'

'I'll do that,' Richard smiles at me, and I'm shocked. I've forgotten what it feels like to have him offer to help.

Two new people bustle through the doors, throwing down giant rucksacks and taking their coats off in such a noisy way that I wonder if they know that there are other people here who were enjoying the tranquillity of the place. I turn back to Richard, trying to ignore one of the newcomers who's reading out the menu to his companion - shouting each word as if she can't see the list in tall capital letters on the blackboard right in front of her. 'Actually, I'd prefer to find someone local,' I say. 'I can put an advert up in Mole Avon, and if they lived close by, they wouldn't need accommodation.'

'Daniella is bound to know someone.' Richard laughs, and I see the creases I love so much; he's really laughing. 'If anyone can locate someone nearby, looking for a job, she will.'

'True.' I laugh too, feeling happier, thinking we might be smoothing things over a little.

Richard looks stern now. 'Could you trust someone else with the cows?' His eyes gaze into mine.

The man yells across the room as he gives their order to

the lady behind the counter. 'Jacket potato with the cheese first, or the beans in first?' I bet she'd like to pour hot beans over his head - he is annoying. Everyone is upset, exchanging furtive glances and raising eyebrows from one table to the next - but in true British style, no-one complains.

'I need *you*,' I tell Richard, my voice barely a whisper against the noise Baked-Bean Man makes as he clomps back to his friend. 'I love you so much - *much* more than the cows. Besides, I could milk once a week, just to keep an eye on them. The other thing to consider is the robotic milk—'

Richard cuts in, 'The one sat in the field doing nothing?'

'At the moment,' I agree. 'But I'll get the young cows accustomed to it, and when they are used to it, then slowly but surely, all the cows can be milked like that.' I pause, waiting for him to look at me again, 'If I do this, would you still want to volunteer somewhere?'

'Yes.' My heart sinks. *Will we ever sort this out?*

* * *

The app on our phones is brilliant but we still have to keep paper records relating to all our animals and these are 'filed' in the dilapidated pine dresser in the kitchen. The Victorian piece of furniture is stuffed to bursting, so when I'm doing farm admin, I sit next to it, working at the kitchen table. Mum always did this before I took it on, and it just feels right to be sitting here with a mug of tea and with Crinkle balanced on my knees. It is hard to move my mouse with her head resting on my arm, but I haven't the heart to move her.

I've posted a job advert on Facebook, and I'm making a list of all the things our new herdsperson needs to know. *'741 always wants to come in first with 153, but make sure you only let 153 in first (on her own) or she'll kick everything in sight. 788 MUST be milked by hand, NO CHOICE, do it, or YOU and all the machinery will be broken. 567 has five teats close together – the robot can't cope, so put the clusters on by hand…'* My list runs into a second page, saying which cows prefer the left-hand side of the parlour and which the right, who to leave until last, and how 099 coughs from when her udder is wiped until she has the last clean off with antiseptic— *'don't worry, she always does this.'*

I try to recall every little quirk, and I plan to write this out again in numeric order for William and Mary to check because they milk the cows too, and might think of something I've missed. Richard is sitting next to me, making another list, a note of places who might want volunteer help. 'Have you said about Joy's ear?' Richard asks, leaning across me to read my screen. Crinkle starts to lick his wrist, then she gets up from my lap and steps onto his. It feels like a proper family moment, all of us so close together, and I'm caught up in the cosiness. 'Rich, how do you think I can get Mum to talk about the possibility of getting some Jers—'

He plonks Crinkle back on my lap and gets up. 'I don't know how you can even think of upsetting her. The Fox Halt Herd is her history. Keeping the bloodlines going was your father's obsession. Give it up, Billy, I beg you.'

'But—'

'No buts - just give it up.' He strokes Crinkle's head. 'I'll see you later. I'm meeting someone at Lydford Gorge. They need someone in their ranger team.' He snatches his car keys from the top shelf of the dresser. 'Think about this from other people's points of view for once.'

As his car starts up in the yard, I throw my body back into my chair and sigh - I don't want to allow a stranger to take charge of the cows, I don't want to hurt Mum either, but this the way forward for the farm, I am convinced I'm right.

Chapter 17

Billy

Two weeks later, and I'm standing in a paddock in Laugharne in south-east Wales. Richard refused point-blank to come so I'm here with Jessie.

There is an icy breeze which cuts right through you, but the sun glints off the galvanised roofs in the farmyard, and with the stone walls around me blocking the wind a slight warmth percolates through my fleece-lined coat.

As I watch, Jessie scratches the neck of one of the Jersey cows we've come to see. The heifer swings her head around, blinking, as if to say, *'That's nice, don't stop.'*

'Mulberry,' I tell Jessie who frowns, not understanding. 'You said her fur was red. It's called mulberry. Jerseys are either fawn or mulberry coloured.'

'Ooh, don't you know a lot?' Jessie laughs, running a hand softly down the cow's neck.

'I've a lot more to learn.' I press my hand to my forehead. 'But I have a new motto—' I tell her, *'Less cow to feed, more cow to milk.'*

'You made that up?'

'No,' I say, glancing around at the beautiful young cows around us. 'It was something I read in the *Farmers' Weekly* last night. Thanks.'

'What for?' Jessie frowns.

'Coming with me today, I know it must have been difficult for you, but I *sooo* appreciate it.'

Jessie shakes her head. 'It wasn't too hard; I'd already scheduled a day off. I thought you were about to thank me for driving us here.'

'Thank you for that too,' I say, trying to forget how scared I've been for most of the two hundred and seven miles to get here. Jessie drives too fast, even in a cattle lorry, but it would have been a slog driving both ways on my own, so I am grateful and it's been nice to have Jessie all to myself - I'll be taking it a lot slower on the way back. I just wish Richard was here; this could be a pivotal moment for Fox Halt Farm.

'You must have this one. I love her already, she's so placid and—' Jessie pauses, looking over her new friend, over her back, along her body and down her legs. 'She's got the best feet. They're really—' she hesitates again, 'black.'

'Definitely,' I agree, patting her cow. I look down at its cloven hooves. 'Mmm, very black.'

Jessie nods slowly, pushing her chin out like she knows everything there is to know about livestock. All she really knows is they have two eyes, a tail and four legs, one in each corner. 'And those three as well,' I say, pointing at a small group standing close together, all watching us with wide, inquisitive eyes. 'The one on the right looks the best here. They're obviously friends though, so if I choose one, I'll have to take the trio.'

'Buttercup and Daisy Mae too.' Jessie points at two more cows, eyeing us from the furthest corner of the small field.

'Buttercup and Daisy?' I say, 'Is that the best you can come up with?'

'Daisy Mae,' she corrects me, 'They're great names.' Jessie laughs. 'See the way they stare at us, and then how they touch noses. They remind me of school girls whispering about a boy they like.'

'I can only take five,' I tell her.

'Do you have a Buttercup or Daisy Mae at Fox Halt already?' she asks, ignoring my comment.

'Not the point. Mum won't like them, she always chooses unusual names.' My voice falters as I mention Mum.

'Billy,' Jessie is nearly shouting. 'You haven't told Daniella about us coming here?' She stares at me, her eyes wide in disbelief.

'I *wanted* to tell her but I was too scared. I don't need to lose any of the existing herd this way. These cows will be extra, and I can gradually add to their numbers over the next few years, instead of selling any of the Friesians.'

'So, why didn't you discuss it with her?'

'Because I know she'll still hate th—' The owner of the

cows grunts at me. 'Which ones?' I think he says, but his accent is strong.

'All eight,' I reply to whatever he said, suddenly deciding I want them all. I wrap my fingers around the wad of notes in my pocket. 'I can pay for five in cash, and I'll make up the rest with a transfer into your account right away.'

* * *

The cows load easily, and in half an hour we're driving away. 'Look at that, isn't it beautiful,' I say, pointing to a rhododendron smothered in lilac blooms. 'Stunning, isn't it?'

Jessie grins as she sees the bush. 'I understand, *now*.' She shakes her head. 'Why it had to be today.'

I smile too. 'Yes, to coincide with Mum's Women's Institute visit to Lanhydrock to see the azaleas and the rhodos. There's a dinner afterwards in The Hamsgate. She'll be late home.'

'You're putting off the inevitable, you know?' Jessie says, looking at her phone to finish the text she was typing.

'Yes, but Mum's always happy in the mornings, and when she sees Buttercup's beautiful face, her heart will melt and we all know she's unable to turn any animal away. It'll be fine, I know it will.'

Jessie holds up crossed fingers. 'I hope you're right,' she says. 'I take it that's part of the reason Richard wouldn't come with you today?'

'He told me straight. He said I mustn't, *but* he's against everything I'm doing so—' I hunch my shoulders and sigh, 'I did it anyway.'

Chapter 18

Billy

I feel Mum's presence, and when I lift my head from my pillow, I wish instead of looking up to check, I'd snuggled into Richard and pulled the duvet over our heads. She's standing in our bedroom doorway with her arms folded. I look at the clock. 'It's five AM, Mum,' I whisper. For a whole minute, she glares at me until I break the silence again. 'You've seen them?'

Mum steps back, disappears, and then I hear her bedroom door close. I try not to wake Richard as I get up to follow Mum into her room. I clamber onto her bed on Dad's side and prop myself up on one of her pristine white pillows. 'Mum.' I touch her back and realise she's fully dressed.

'I heard them,' she mumbles into her pillow. She raises her head slightly, but she doesn't turn to look at me. 'I couldn't understand why the cows were so close to the house.'

'You went outside to investigate?'

She sits up, but her eyes are fixed straight ahead on a painting of the hotel on the Lizard where she and Dad spent their honeymoon. They met the artist on the cliff and insisted on buying it there and then before it was even finished.

'The old stables seemed like the best place to keep them,' I say, 'They'll be in there for the next month while they're in quarantine. Two or three in each stable. They're big stables, and they're small cows.' I'm rambling now, not really thinking what I'm saying. I can't bear how mad she is.

'Where are the rest going?' she asks, still focused on the picture.

'That's it, eight.'

'Just eight?

'Yes.'

At last, she turns and locks her eyes on mine. 'Billy, why don't you talk to me?' Mum's voice is more disappointed than angry. 'It's always secrets with you.'

'I knew you'd find out, but I thought this was the best way to get them here.'

She shakes her head.

'I truly believe the Jerseys will be good for the future of Fox Halt, and I'm not going to sell any of our herd.'

'Five generations, your great-great-great-grandpar—'

'Yes, I know,' I cut in. 'I know how much the bloodlines, the history and the quality of our herd means to you. It means the same to me too. I've been racking my brains for weeks, trying to think how we can swap half of the herd to Jerseys, and this was the only solution I could bear. We'll gradually build up the Jerseys as the Friesians go, and we won't keep any of the Friesian calves for the next couple of years.'

Mum moves to the door, leaving me sitting on the bed. I can see she's about to cry. I chase her along the landing and down the stairs. 'Mum, wait.'

'No.' She dives into the downstairs bathroom, and I hear the lock being rammed across. I stand outside in the hall, debating with myself, wondering if I should shout my arguments through the door or wait and explain everything quietly when she comes out again.

Eventually, I decide to sit at the kitchen table, where I can hear the bathroom door open; my body grows colder because I daren't move to fetch my dressing gown and slippers in case I miss Mum's reappearance.

'What's up?' Richard asks as he walks into the kitchen.

'I'm waiting for Mum.' I pick up the kettle and wave it at him. 'Tea?'

He nods. 'She's in the dairy.'

'No, she's in the bathroom hiding from me.'

'I assure you she's not. I saw her go in five minutes ago from our bedroom window.' He frowns. 'I take it she's *not* happy.' He takes a deep breath in, as if he's about to launch into an 'I told you this would happen' speech, but I cut in, 'She hasn't given me a chance to explain.'

'Don't worry about the tea. In fact, I'm surprised you can be even bothered to make me one.' He takes his cup from my hand and thumps it back down on the shelf.

'What?' I shake my head, my mouth open.

'Because I'm surprised you are willing to do anything for anyone else - all you ever think about is yourself, Billy, it's always you, you, *you*. Do I want to spend the rest of my life with someone who doesn't consider my wants, my advice, my happiness?'

'This is for the farm. It's for all of us - we have to diversify, keep up with markets - Fox Halt has to keep moving forward. Maybe you should leave. Do you ever think about what I'm striving for and what makes me happy?'

Richard is halfway back up the stairs. 'You had better get dressed and talk to her. Maybe Daniella will forgive you, but I won't. You've gone too far this time.

* * *

Mum turns a screw that presses a cheese mould, squeezing out the liquid inside. She is forcing it down too fast, which could affect the eventual appearance of the truckle. 'Didn't see you leave the house,' I say to her, trying to forget Richard's stinging words and regretting the way I bit back.

Mum shrugs at me. 'I climbed out of the window.'

'You're too old for that,' I laugh, hoping to lighten the mood.

'And too old to know what's happening in my own home too.'

'Mum, listen.' I catch hold her of her hand. 'Hear me out.'

She sits down on a stool next to the cheese presses and stares at me.

'The Friesians *are* special,' I say. 'I know that - just like you, I've grown up with them, doing little chores as a toddler which has grown into hours of commitment today and every day - day in and day out. The cows have shaped how we have turned out - and up until the foot and mouth outbreak, it was the only life you'd ever known. I saw the sacrifices you and Dad made, never complaining, making sure all our animals were cared for and well-fed. I know how important the farm was to Dad, and I'm sure he'd be delighted we are making Fox Halt Farm thrive. I just want to keep it a success - for Dad, as much as anything else.' My eyes start to well up.

Mum doesn't say anything, rubbing the back of her neck, her face like she's got something sour in her mouth.

'I want a strong future for Fox Halt,' I tell her. 'I hope Freddy and Grace's children might take it on, – or Mary and maybe her future family,' I say. 'I want *our* Friesians at Fox Halt forever; with the same bloodlines we can trace back through generations. That's what I truly want, the same as you.' I feel like I did when I was a small child – Mum staring so hard at me, it's like she can see through my skull. I'm four years old, trying to justify why I cut the mane off my most precious toy – a wooden horse Grandad spent hours whittling for me. I had no reasonable explanation for what I did. I'd simply found a pair of scissors and wanted to try them out. I reckoned like human hair and animal fur, the horse's mane would grow back.

'And those animals in the stables?' she says at last. 'How do they fit in with your grand plan?'

'Once the confinement period is over, I'll keep them in separate fields away from the Friesians. Also, they are the ideal age for me to get them used to being milked by the mobile robotic milker, which I'll leave in the field with them. We'll sell most of our Friesian calves in the next few years, keeping the Jerseys' offspring instead. As some of the Friesians come to the end of their working lives, the Jerseys can take their place until we have a fifty-fifty split.'

Mum's face is stony. I continue. 'We'll ease the Jerseys in. We can find out about the breed to see what works with them. The Friesians are high maintenance, but Jerseys have a reputation for being tough and sturdy, so they'll be less work.'

'So, you're planning on buying in extra milk with the higher butterfat for now,' she says.

'But my aim is to use just our own milk in the long term.'

'Don't ever go behind my back like this again.' Mum gets to her feet. 'I can't trust my own daughter. How do you think that makes me feel?'

* * *

RICHARD

I glance up from my phone as Billy walks in. 'Forgotten something?' I ask. I've hardly seen her the last four days. Every spare minute she has, she is working on the ICF. I am sure she is avoiding me, so I don't have a chance to complain about the new cows, the ice-cream, or the fact that I never see her because she is always working. This seems to be the new way it is between us. No longer arguing, just side-stepping each other. She smiles at me, a half-smile and then she starts to rummage through the dresser. 'What are you looking for?' I ask.

'A piece of paper with a model number on it.' She fans a wad of A4 receipts, and I nod at her before turning my attention back to an article which a former colleague has emailed me.

'What are your plans today?' Billy asks. Her hand is on the door, ready to rush back to the ICF.

I look at my phone and scan my list. 'Repairing the hayrack and then, Daniella asked if I'd help with a bit of a spring clean in here.' I wave my hand around the room, feeling deflated. I can't imagine the Fox Halt kitchen ever being tidy.

'You okay?' Billy takes a step towards me.

I frown at her. 'Yes.'

'You're not,' she says, coming another step closer.

'Okay, I'm not – I'm having a bit of an identity crisis.'

Billy smiles. 'I thought that yesterday when you didn't tell Tania you'd finished at O'Rowdes'.'

I feel better already. It's nice to have her attention for once. Billy stares at me. 'So why didn't you tell Tania?'

'Because I no longer have a title, I suppose,' I shrug as I place my phone down carefully on the table, 'I've lost my badge of honour, I've nothing to indicate how hard I work, or how successful I am. I've been avoiding telling anyone I've retired, imagining they will think I am lazy or worse, so comfortably off that I don't need to work, and that I'm rubbing my fortunate situation in their faces. I would hate them to believe that.'

'Rich, you've worked so hard for years and look at all the time you've worked for O'Rowdes', living away from the farm—' She pauses, 'And when you were with Janette, you worked all the time then too, missing the twins and Freddy growing up, especially the girls, you hardly saw them.'

'I know it is silly,' I say. 'I have really looked forward to retiring, but I miss the camaraderie too, my old work acquaintances, and I miss people requiring my opinion. I miss making decisions.'

'Do you want a coffee?' Billy says, now next to the Rayburn and holding up my mug, and there is something in her tone which makes me feel she is in no hurry to leave.

'Please,' I say, 'but I'll make it, you sit down.' My chair

scrapes on the flagstones as I get up, and Crinkle opens one eye to check what's happening - closing it again when she decides it's nothing interesting. 'I am happy, Billy.' I spoon coffee into mugs. 'It's adjusting, that's all it is, but—' I pause, placing the drinks down on the table. I look into her eyes, 'But there is one thing that keeps nagging me - it's impossible to make more time, and seconds and hours are slipping away. Time is precious; we need to be making the most of it.'

She looks back at me on her way to the larder to find the biscuits. 'Everyone finds change hard, we all do but it will be fine. In a month, you'll be wondering how you ever had time to work.'

'Do you think so?' I am unconvinced and certain she hasn't grasped what I was trying to explain.

'Yes of course you will. Wait and see,' she says.

Chapter 19

Billy

Suddenly, it's the first Sunday in April, and the rain we've had for the last nine days has turned to snow. Soft flakes land on my eyelashes, and I'm happy, watching it swirl in the air. It's only forecast for this morning, and the ground's too sodden for it to settle. I stand still for a moment, enjoying it, breathing in slowly, noticing the tingle inside my nostrils from the cold.

The headmistress of Hamsgate Primary school lent me chairs and tables for today, even helping me stack them on my trailer to transport them to the farm. Now, as I step into the ICF's packing area, I see a ramshackle classroom with twelve children of varying ages sitting around the tables in groups of four. They sit up straight and fold their arms when they spot me, shushing each other to be quiet.

I walk past them to the whiteboard I've fixed to the wall, and I grin at Gino, who is standing across the room from me. He's brought his whole family together to help me today, and they are all here, despite the weather; all his nephews and nieces, his brothers and sister and their partners. Two of his nephews are older, I guess sixteen and seventeen, and Gino even persuaded them to come.

'What flavours of ice-cream can you think of?' I ask, and all the children wave their hands at me, keen to answer. I notice they are all sporting colourful badges with *'Chief Ice-cream Taster'* written in small letters under their names. 'Okay, Jack, you set us off, name a flavour, just one, please,' I say.

I start to write *'mint-choc-chip'* on the whiteboard with Gino now next to me. 'Have you got another pen?' he asks. 'I'll help, and that way, we can get to try the ice-cream more quickly.' A cheer from all the children suddenly rings out inside the echoey building. The noise is deafening, but then Gino holds a hand up, and the children quieten in a heartbeat.

The Bianchis try as many flavours as their stomachs will hold and there is a vote at the end for their favourites. It's the messiest and noisiest tea party I could imagine, but as I wave goodbye to my tasters, I've decided which will be the first ten flavours of Fox Halt Ice-Cream.

* * *

I find Richard helping Mary in the parlour. 'Well, that has to be the most fun customer survey ever.' I laugh. He nods and then turns back to the buckets he was washing. I feel like grabbing one and pulling it over his head. I cannot believe he isn't happy for me.

* * *

We milk the cows with a relaxed air, knowing the job will take two hours, and there's no point trying to rush, talking to each animal as we work. 'See you again later,' I tell Fizz. I rub the top of her tail before letting her out into the yard. As the morning sunshine hits her coat, she turns her head and pokes her tongue out at me.

'That's what she thinks of you,' Richard says, striding into the parlour to fetch some of the milk that I can't put in the bulk tank. Some cows have recently calved, and the colostrum and bacteria levels in their milk is too high for human consumption, so this spare milk Richard will feed to the calves.

'You're a bit early,' I reply, letting in a new cow. 'I'll have some for you in five minutes.' Richard has started feeding the calves when I'm milking, and it's about the only time at the moment when we feel like a team. Looking after the calves is one of my favourite jobs. Richard loves it too, never moaning about the stupid hour we get up, never complaining about interrupting his afternoon activities to feed them again. The youngest animals need extra feeds during the day, but Mary and sometimes Mum, do these. We all have a soft spot for the babies – the fresh straw and their milky diet makes them smell nice, and they're always happy to see us. We keep them in twos or threes, so they have company of the same age and size, but they still rush up to the front of their pens as we walk in, nuzzling our coats and breathing a warm hello.

I'm standing behind one of my gentlest cows, Bliss, and I'm taken by surprise when she suddenly fires dung down the front of my overalls. 'Nice,' Rich says. 'Seems like no-one is keen on you.' I smile back at him as muck drips from my chest to my toes, determined not to cry. He's hit a nerve. *No-one,* he means Fizz and Bliss, *and him too.* I hate the animosity between us, even here, where I think we work well together. He feels he's got to have a dig at me. 'Just bad timing,' I tell him, wiping some splashes of muck from my chin with a paper towel.

Crinkle starts barking. She always lies on the rubber mat outside the tank room until I finish milking. It's rare to hear her make a sound. 'Something's wrong,' I tell Richard. 'Can you take a look, please?'

Richard throws down his empty bucket, and in half a minute, he's back. 'It's *your* brown cows. They're in the yard, taking it in turns to munch your mum's rose bushes,' he says.

'No! Could you shut the gate onto the lane and I'm sorry, but I need you to get them back in their field. I can't leave these ladies at the moment.' I wave at the cows being milked.

'Okay.'

'Dammit,' I say. 'I couldn't have turned the electric fencer back on when I gave them extra grazing last night.'

Richard is about to leave, but then he stops and looks at me, 'It is obvious, Billy, you are doing too much. You can't concentrate on anything properly. I am not surprised you forgot.'

'Please go and shut the gate,' I say. 'Then get them back in the field – rattle a bucket of food and they'll follow you.'

* * *

The next day, Crinkle barks again. This time, I'm in the ICF, removing a rusty pipe fitting, focusing more on how stupid I was to allow the Jerseys to escape than on the screw I'm undoing. I drop my screwdriver and dash outside.

Eight cows lift their heads at once. They know they shouldn't be here, blinking at me before they turn back the way they've come. 'Need a hand?' Mary calls from the dairy steps.

'Please,' I say.

She ambles towards me. 'Nan-Dan said these monkeys were out yesterday too.'

'Yes,' I say, noticing Mary's eyes are starry as though she's been crying, or hasn't slept.

Mary smiles. 'All morning, Nan-Dan has kept on about her roses being ruined, until in the end, I offered to buy her new ones.'

'She's pretty mad about it,' I agree, blocking Buttercup's

bid to investigate the garden of one of the holiday cottages, waving my arms up and down in front of her like I'm trying to fly. Buttercup blows heavily through her nostrils at me, changes her mind and heads towards the field again.

'If it makes you feel any better, Auntie, when I made the offer, Nan-Dan soon 'fessed up that they might flower even better in June with a harsh pruning now.'

'She didn't tell me that, 'I laugh as we follow the last cow into the field. Buttercup and Daisy Mae are now in the lead, strolling along like they're in a beauty pageant, heads high, blinking their eyelashes on every step.

There's a clicking noise when we reach the electric wire that I set up to stop the Jerseys eating all the fresh pasture at once. The wire is on the ground, and each time the current shorts on the wet grass there's a loud click. 'Look,' I say to Mary, 'I thought yesterday the cows had tripped over the wire, pulling it onto the ground, but the same three posts are knocked down again. It's weird that the electric is on, and they still got out.'

Once we have the fence back up, I study the single strand of wire that has kept our Friesians on the right side of the fence for years. Buttercup saunters up towards me, and then right before our eyes, she demonstrates how she and her friends escaped, nudging the top of one of the posts with her nose, pushing it until it starts to lean, and now Daisy Mae starts doing the same thing to an adjoining post.

Mary and I watch spellbound as the clever pair work together, collapsing the fence in ten seconds– the plastic hook on the very top of each post has insulated them from shock. 'I can't believe this,' Mary says, placing both her hands on top of her head. 'They're cool, aren't they?'

I sigh. 'A tad too cool. I need another strand of wire to feed through the top clips on each post. That should stop them doing this. I'll get some more wire from Mole Avon, this afternoon,' I say.

'Better padlock the field gate until then.' Mary pulls the wire and the posts towards the hedge out of the way. We can't leave everything like it is in case the cows get caught up.

'Two padlocks, perhaps.' I laugh.

'Can I come?' Mary asks, continuing to roll up the wire.

'To Mole Avon?' I check. Her tired eyes worry me. 'Afterwards, shall we take Crinkle for a short walk?' I suggest.

Walk is our secret code word that we've used for years meaning, we need to talk. Walking making it easier to air thoughts – moving and not directly facing each other.

Mary looks at me and smiles. 'Yes, a walk – we should reward Crinkle for her excellent guard dog duties. You never know, thanks to her we may have got the cows back before Nan-Dan saw them?'

I shake my head. 'She always knows,' I say. 'Mum misses nothing. I'll come and get you when I'm about to leave.'

I watch Mary as she heads back into the dairy, seeing her heels press on each concrete step. She normally jumps them, missing the first two. *What's wrong?* I wonder.

Chapter 20

Billy

It's not until I'm back in the van, having been into Mole Avon and bought everything I need to stop the Jerseys breaking out again, that Mary says anything, 'How about Okehampton Castle?' she asks as I turn the ignition.

'The castle?' I frown.

'To take Crinkle for a walk. It reopened this weekend after the winter break. Have you been there?' Mary holds on to Crinkle. The word 'walk' was the dog's cue to leap from the passenger footwell onto Mary's lap, and now Crinkle is whining with her nose pressed against the passenger window. Mary tries to quieten her, rubbing her neck. 'Ssshhh, girlie, in a minute, not yet, sorry.'

'I haven't been there,' I say. 'I have to admit, though, every time I drive past, I think how odd it is that it was built in a valley. Surely, castles should be on hills?'

'There's a woodland walk along the Okement.' Mary has unwittingly used the *w* word again, and Crinkle pricks up her ears, eyeing Mary then me, waiting for me to turn off the engine so we can go.

* * *

The sign in the carpark boasts that the ruin is the remains of Devon's largest castle begun soon after the Norman Conquest. I don't get a chance to read more because Crinkle strains on her harness, desperate to say hello to a woman with two pugs. I clench her lead tightly, waiting for the lady to pass the entrance kiosk so she's out of sight.

Mary reads another information board as I pay the entrance fee. She tells me, 'The castle was last owned by the Earl of Devon until he fell out with Henry VIII. Afterwards, it sank into disrepair. There's supposed to be ghosts,' she says.

'Do you want an ice-cream?' I ask her. 'It's a nice day.'

Mary makes a tiny smile. 'You want to try it, don't you?'

'It's the same brand Grace said they have in Evans' now. Same supplier as their new cheese too. I don't understand, it doesn't look very special, does it?' I whisper.

'I'm buying them.' Mary holds up her bank card.

* * *

The castle ruins are an archetypal tumbledown fortress, and the setting evokes the Knights of the Round Table. I imagine Stephen Spielberg going doolally over its potential as a film set, admiring its twisted walls and the haunted shape of the keep, high up on a grassy hill. We walk for forty minutes in the woods, throwing sticks for Crinkle and chatting about Grace, the goats and Mum. 'Could we sit over there?' Mary asks when we reach an empty picnic site.

'I'm imagining Arthur riding across there,' I say as we sit at the nearest table. I point to the wide river below us.

'My brother? No.' Mary shakes her head.

'I meant the pulling-a-sword-out-of-stone Arthur, Excalibur. I can picture Lancelot and Maleagant jousting down there.'

Normally Mary would laugh, but she doesn't. I want to ask what's wrong - query if more customers have cancelled orders or if there's another problem with the dairy, but I feel I have to wait for her to tell me. She picks up Crinkle, holding her high in her arms, shielding her face. 'William and — ' she pauses, putting the dog on the seat next to her, then she stares at me. 'We slept together.'

I'm unsure what to say as she starts to bite her thumbnail. I shrug then raise my eyebrows, but this doesn't prompt anything further from her so, eventually, I ask, 'And?'

'I didn't intend it to happen, you said to be honest, so I told him about Sharmarke.'

I frown. 'After you said to William you'll never love him, you had sex with him anyway?' I can't believe how she is treating the kind and thoughtful young man from next door.

'No, Auntie. I told William *everything!*'

'Everything?' I check, my hair standing up on the back of my neck. There are seven of us who know *everything*, and there's a tacit understanding between us; that's how it will stay. Buried - forgotten and safe. Bile rises up my throat, and I close my mouth, trying to hold nausea at bay. I'm sweating.

'I had to; it wasn't fair keeping the truth from him.'

I press my fingers onto my forehead. I can't look at her.

Crinkle senses something is wrong and pushes her nose into my thigh. As I stroke her, I know I'm about to be sick. I wrench my legs through the gap between the bench and the table and run towards the river. The ice-cream comes up easily, but I don't feel the normal relief from being sick. My legs give way, and I collapse on the grassy river bank.

'He won't tell anyone else.' Mary has run after me.

'How could you ask him to keep it from his mum and Grace? He'll have to tell them too,' I say.

'He promised he wouldn't.' There are tears in her eyes. 'He loves me, and I know he won't. He agreed they need to keep believing his dad's death was an accident.'

'It would have been kinder to let William carry on thinking that as well,' I say.

'He needed to know the truth.' Mary is resolute.

I shake my head. 'You're wrong.'

'You weren't there—' She pauses. 'And you said be honest with him, didn't you?' Mary is almost shouting as she kneels beside me. Crinkle, still tied to the picnic bench, is desperate to get to us and she's dragging the table towards us. Mary runs to her and then kneels back down next to me. 'It was good to tell him,' she says, scratching Crinkle's ear. 'I've felt guilty for years knowing it *wasn't* an accident.'

'Why didn't you just say you'd found out Sharmarke was your stepbrother? That explains why your feelings are so mixed up.'

'But it wasn't like that.' She is going to cry, and I hate it.

'Sorry, darling, I shouldn't be angry with you,' I say.

'Like I said, Auntie, you weren't there. Last night in the pub, William was so quiet. He's not normally like that with me, and he kept on ordering tequila shots, one after the other. I nagged him to tell me what was wrong, and eventually, he said it was his dad's birthday.' I nod. The date never loses its significance for me either. Tom's death is always harder on his birthday. 'He told me something I didn't know before.' Mary shuts her eyes, pressing her hands together before she speaks again. 'He believed he caused his dad's death. He told me his father was rushing because of him, and that was why the accident happened.'

I stare at Mary, not believing what I'm hearing, not wanting to believe it. She continues. 'William was angry because his dad had said he wouldn't make it to see William in a Young Farmers play that night. There were two punctures in the tyres of a trailer which his father needed to use the next morning, and his dad said by the time he'd fixed them and checked everything else over, he'd be too late for the performance. William stormed off, mad at his father for putting work before him, but he said by the time he got home to Foxlands, his temper had cooled, and he felt guilty, realising his dad always tried to be involved with everything Grace and he did. Straight away, he went back to apologise but at Fox Halt, he found his father wrapped up in the tractor's prop shaft. There was nothing William could do; his dad was already dead.'

'No,' I say, feeling sick again, mortified that our secret had been destroying William, suddenly understanding why he's so withdrawn and how deeply his dad's death has affected him. He was thirteen. He's spent ten years blaming himself. 'What have we done?' I say, crossing my arms across my chest and folding forward, a deep ache in the pit of my stomach.

'Been judge and jury.' Mary shakes her head. 'We let his family believe it was an accident, thinking it would be easier that way. It seemed the best thing to do. Yes, we were virtually certain his dad was murdered by *my* father, but remember how frightened you were.'

I stand up slowly to head back to the picnic table. I hold my head in my hands as I sit down on the bench again. Mary is beside me. 'Look, you were too scared to tell the police, terrified my father would take revenge on more innocent people. He threatened to hurt Nan-Dan, Grace or William if you revealed the truth.'

I lift my head to look at her. 'But now, your father's dead too, we could have told William a long time ago.'

'That's wrong. It was three years later that my father died, William and his family were getting their lives back together. We did what we thought was right—not stirring everything up again. Making allegations about my father seemed pointless. He was dead, and it would have kicked up a right hornets' nest. An inquest would have literally dug up the past. Exhuming his dad's body and trawling over everything again. Think of the press intrusion and the media storm it would have generated. And it would have been horrific for Sharmarke and his family too.'

'So why did you tell William?' I ask. 'Why last night?'

'Because he started crying his heart out in the pub. He was drunk, and everyone was staring at him. I started crying too, and that's when I made him leave with me. We walked out, pretty much holding each other up, not talking anymore, neither knowing what to say. William, with his guilt about his dad dying because of his selfishness, and me with my own guilt about not telling my best friend what really happened.'

'And you ended up in bed together?' I ask.

'Listen.' She sounds impatient. 'William didn't want his mum or Grace to see him upset and drunk, so I drove him back to Culmfield. We went straight up to my bedroom because I thought he needed to sleep off the alcohol, but he wouldn't stop sobbing. I wondered if he hadn't cried before, and this was years of regret pouring out of him. I couldn't bear how miserable he was. He said over and over how his dad would never see his grandchildren, how he'd never hold baby Tom. It broke my heart, Auntie. I lay on the bed next to him and stroked his hair, trying to reassure him it wasn't his fault. But then he suddenly sat up and yelled at me, 'Stop saying it wasn't my fault!' William has never shouted at me before. Never.' She shakes her head and stares into my eyes. 'That's why I told him everything.' Mary gets up and stands next to me, waiting for me to say something, but I don't know what to say, and we stay there - me hunched over, her looking down at me.

Mary breaks the silence. 'William stared at the floor for ages. He held my hand so tightly, taking it all in and then he looked at me and suddenly his mouth was on mine. We just kept kissing. He made me forget and made me feel like it didn't matter who my father was or what he'd done. We made love, and it felt good, like we were making up for all the loss and pain - and then we woke up together.'

'Are you alright?' I get up and touch her hand.

She links her little finger into mine. 'One minute, I want to see him to make sure he knows how much I care about him and the next, I'm afraid he thinks everything has changed between us, but I still love Sharmarke, and I always will - and now, William has to keep a terrible secret from his family. I feel like running away, but that won't solve anything, will it?'

Chapter 21

RICHARD

Crinkle makes a low growl as she lies sphinx-like facing the door; her ears are pricked, and her tail is straight out behind her. 'What's up, Piggy?' I ask, abandoning an email I was reading on my phone and walking towards her. She is up in a split second and starts scratching at the door, desperate to get outside.

As I open the door, I see a smart new Range Rover parked next to Billy's van. I recognise it straight away. It's the one Arthur bought himself for his birthday - another of his preoccupations when he was supposed to be working, choosing all the extras he had to have.

Crinkle bolts off, heading for the ICF, barking like mad, then snarling at the closed door. When I follow her I hear raised voices inside. Before I go in, I grab Crinkle's collar to take her back to the house, quickly shutting her in the kitchen - she is not allowed in the new building, and Billy's been mad at me before for letting her in there.

* * *

'You should be at Culmfield.' Arthur is angry. 'Stop wasting your time here.'

Mary stares back at him, shaking her head slowly.

'Look,' he shouts. 'If I hadn't been in the estate office, then God knows what the tenants would continue to get away with. When did you last review any of the rents, Mary?'

'How dare you go through my office?' Mary spits back, 'How dare you come here and tell me what I can and can't do.' Her eyes are bloodshot like she's been crying, and their redness against her loose red hair would make me hold my hands up and surrender, but Arthur doesn't back down, and I grab his arm as I think he is about to strike his sister. He spins round to face me. 'Oh, so you are around,' he jeers. 'I thought you just spent your time these days lazing around with your feet up.'

I ignore his snub. 'You need to be keeping your own house in order before you throw stones at Mary,' I say.

He yanks his arm from my grip and rubs his wrist. 'What's that supposed to mean?'

'I've just received a long email from Christianson, begging me to come back, he says, you are just—' I pause, looking up at the ceiling, trying to recall the exact words. 'He said, you are so busy posturing, you are achieving nothing.'

I don't know how long the brother and sister have been rowing, but Arthur is as volatile as Mary, and my challenge to his ego ignites a volcano inside him. He seems to grow two inches taller and wider, and he's already taller and broader than me. He lifts his shoulders back, breathes in and then launches himself at me, two hands at my neck, pushing me back against something sharp, I hear my shirt tear, and then the force of me hitting it knocks the machine he's pushed me against onto the floor. I fall next to it with Arthur on top of me, his grip on my throat getting tighter.

I hear Billy and Mary yelling at him to stop, and the hollow thuds of Billy pounding her fists into his back. I shut my eyes against the agony of my throat being wrung. *I can't breathe!*

Suddenly Arthur lets go, jumping to his feet in one easy spring. His words are slow. 'You are not worth it,' he says as I sit up, holding my neck as I splutter.

Billy is by my side, her arms wrapped around me. Tears run down her face. 'Go, Arthur.' Her voice is ferocious, even more severe than Mary's. 'Get out, now!'

Arthur strides away, his nose in the air while Mary rages how much she hates him. She follows him, saying she's going to check he actually gets in his car and drives away, swearing twice. Like Billy, she never swears. I think if she had a gun in her hand, she would shoot her eldest brother dead.

Billy stares at her palm. 'You're bleeding,' she says.

I nod toward the machine on the floor next to me. 'I caught my back on that,' I say, 'It's smooth though, I can't see anything sharp. It felt like a nail.'

'That's the front. I was working on the back this morning. There was an old screw I was trying to get out when the cows escaped again; it was probably that.' She examines my back. 'It's stopped bleeding, but you'll have a bruise,' she says. 'How's your throat? It's really red. Is it sore?'

'Not too bad.' I cough as I stand up. 'I'll be fine, let's go in. I expect Crinkle is going barmy – she is the reason I came over. She knew something was wrong.'

Billy opens her mouth as if to say something, then closes it and shakes her head.

'What?'

'I discovered something dreadful earlier,' she says. 'That's why Mary was in here, we were talking about William.'

'There's nothing terrible about that young man.' I laugh. Billy doesn't smile as she stares at me. I wait, but she says nothing more. 'Go on,' I say, sitting back down on the floor, suddenly feeling like I might faint. Shock must be kicking in. *Hell, he was strangling me!*

'I don't know where to start,' Billy says.

'At the beginning.' I swallow, aware of how tender my throat is. I feel sweaty all over.

'William,' she says, but stops again.

'William what?'

'Two things.' She stares at the machine on the floor lying next to me.

'Which are?' I prompt, in the softest tone I can muster, concerned Billy's finding whatever it is so hard to tell me but frustrated too, that she doesn't just come out with it. I want to get back into the house; it's freezing in here, especially sitting on a cold concrete floor. 'Come on, Billy.'

'Alright.' Billy bites her bottom lip then her words rush out. 'William has been blaming himself for his dad's death. He thought it was his fault.'

'Why would it be his fault?' I frown at her. This makes no sense.

'Tom and William had an argument just before, and William thought his dad was careless with the prop shaft because he was distracted and trying to rush. All these years, he's been guilt-ridden. Mary told him last night that it wasn't an accident and how it was Michael who'd killed his father.'

'She told him Michael killed Tom?' I rub my neck.

'Yes.'

I wipe perspiration from my forehead.

'Are you okay?' Billy touches my shoulder.

'No!' I push her hand away. 'We all agreed. We said we'd never say anything – it was best that way.'

'But William's been blaming himself, if you had known that, you'd have never kept it from him, would you?'

'No.'

'No?' she checks.

'No—' I say again, 'I'd never have let him suffer like that. I would never wish that on anyone, let alone a thirteen-year-old. Poor William.'

'We have to tell Martha.'

'Because?' I place my hands onto the floor to push myself back up.

'We've done enough damage already - William can't be expected to keep this from his mum. We must tell her the truth, and I think we should go over there right now, the sooner the better - not Grace though.'

'Why not Grace?' I frown.

'Distressed expectant mums can miscarry.'

I close my eyes, feeling crass, remembering how Billy lost our baby the day after her beloved Grandad died. I touch her arm to convey that I am sorry for not thinking how Grace would be distraught, finding out that her father was murdered. I want to say so much more to Billy, comfort her about Ross, the name she gave the baby she miscarried, and tell her how I know it still affects her, but I don't know how to. After all these years, neither of us seem able to even start that conversation. It's painful for me too, but how I wish losing our child wasn't still so raw for her.

Billy puts her hand on mine and smiles. 'It never goes away, does it, Rich? I think of him, so often.'

I'm unsure if she's talking about Tom or Ross. I nod slowly, staring into her eyes, trying to read what she means.

Billy answers my unspoken question. 'I see William, and I see his dad. They're so alike, physically, I mean.'

I nod again, thinking how we never talk about Tom either - not about how she misses the friend she grew up with, or how their close friendship was almost certainly the reason Michael killed him; whether it was unintentionally, in an argument, or on purpose, it doesn't matter, her friend is still dead. With all this loss buried deep inside my wife, perhaps it's no wonder she obsesses about the farm. We should talk. 'Let's go indoors,' I say. 'I think I need a hot shower, I am cold and starting to ache all over.' I laugh. 'I'm too old for rugby tackles like that.'

'We ought to tell Martha *and* Sean,' Billy replies. 'She'll need Sean's support.'

'Billy, I want to go in.'

'We ought to go over and see Martha now. We shouldn't leave it. We've done enough damage already. We can't let William suffer any more than he already has; he can't be expected to keep the truth from his mum.'

'You want to go now?' I ask.

She sighs like she is tired of me not listening to her when it is her not listening to me. 'Yes,' she says, 'Grace is working 'til five. We can tell Martha before she gets back to Foxlands.'

I shake my head. 'I don't think we should.'

'What?'

'We shouldn't tell Martha. You said William's promised Mary he won't say anything. It was just him who's been affected. Martha's not blaming herself. Grace isn't either. Let sleeping dogs lie, Billy. Let's not make this any worse than it is already.'

'Is your tetanus jab up to date?' Billy asks, examining the spots of dried blood on her hands.

'You're always checking that. Yes, it is.' I start to walk to the door. 'Are you coming in?'

Billy shakes her head. 'You have a long hot shower. I still have a cheese delivery for Mark Davies-Smart – with all the drama this afternoon, it's still sat in the dairy ready to go.'

Chapter 22

Billy

Martha and Sean are dismantling lambing pens when I arrive. 'William's bottling cider, we haven't seen him today,' Martha says, assuming I'm at Foxlands in search of her son. 'He's in the Cider Barn.'

'I'm not here to see him,' I say, wishing I was and I wasn't about to tell my neighbour I've been effectively lying to her for years, keeping a shocking secret about her husband's death. Sean looks up as he unties a hurdle and calls out to me. 'Sorry, we haven't put the guttering on your building yet.'

'Don't worry.' I smile at him. 'I know you'll do it when you can. I need to talk to you both about something else. Could we sit down?' I wave a hand towards some straw bales pushed up against one of the hurdles.

'Is Grace okay?' Martha's suntanned face is suddenly grey.

'She's fine,' I reassure her. 'It's about Tom.'

* * *

The lambing shed has a small kitchen, and Sean has fetched a mug of tea for Martha. She hasn't moved or said anything since I explained about Tom's death. Her eyes are fixed on a muddy stain on the wall. Sean sits down, wrapping an arm around his wife. He turns to me. 'We'll tell Grace after the babe's born.' His voice is soothing. 'You go, Billy, before the lass gets home. I'll be looking after this one.' He kisses Martha's cheek, and my heart breaks for her.

* * *

I suck in the cool morning air, concentrating on this new day and a new beginning. Holly Needham, my new herdsperson, stomps towards me. She looks bright and cheery. Fired up, ready to start her first day with the cows. 'Bang on time,' I call to Hols, grinning, trying to hide my exhaustion. It wasn't Mum who found Hols, as she likes to be called. It was me with a chance phone call to Bicton College.

'My parents are always up early, so it wasn't hard. I'm a morning person anyway. My alarm is always set for five, whether I'm milking or not,' she says.

I like her positive attitude and the long explanation. This was the trait that persuaded me to employ her - she answered all my questions in full, providing more information than I needed or expected. Hols described in detail how her apprenticeship placement had ceased when the farm she was working on was sold and how, although she's only seventeen, her parents are dairy farmers, so she has lots of experience.

Her skinny legs, clad in tight jeans, disappear into Wellingtons that swamp her. I guess she's borrowed the boots from someone two or three shoe sizes bigger than her. I shake my head, and she smiles at me. 'Dad's,' she says, pointing at her feet. 'He made me wear them - said I'd give the wrong impression turning up in trainers. Do you mind?' she asks.

'No,' I say and her face drops. I realise she's misconstrued what I meant, 'Trainers are fine, but your feet will get wet.'

'Sometimes, but it doesn't bother me. I warn you though, my trainers do stink, but Mum goes bananas if I put them in the washing machine. I can only throw them in there when she's out.'

'Pop them on, and we'll get the cows in,' I say.

She opens her car boot and sits down on the edge to change. The trainers are grey-brown and reek like rotten eggs.

'I'm planning on you doing nothing this morning,' I say. 'If you can watch me and ask questions, that'll be great.'

She pushes her shoes on with the laces still tied. 'Not help at all?' Her brow furrows as she looks up at me.

'No, but this afternoon it will be the other way around. You'll do everything, and I'll watch. You can ask me questions, but you'll need to tell me what you think the answer is before I reply, and I'll only step in if something you do is dangerous.'

'Okie dokie.' She's on her feet. 'Let's go.'

'It will be hard,' I say, as she opens the gate to Home Field, 'I have to let you make mistakes, but I don't think you'll learn otherwise - and I won't feel confident leaving everything to you if I don't give you a chance to prove yourself.'

In the parlour, I hand Hols my checklist, a pen and a large notebook. She frowns as she takes them from me. 'I've just given you a list of *all* the things you need to learn about our cows,' I explain. 'But I'd like you to make your own notes too. They'll mean more if you've written them yourself.' I watch as she opens the book. 'One last thing,' I say. 'A long time ago, when I first started work, someone said to me, *you will make mistakes. If you don't, then you're not doing anything.'*

I smile, thinking back to that first day working for Richard, and him telling me it was alright to make mistakes. Back to a time when I misunderstood him, and disliked him intently. 'We all make mistakes, Hols,' I say, 'but I beg you, don't cover them up. Tell me, and I'll support you. We'll sort them out and find a way to stop them from happening again.'

'Okie dokie.' She nods, and I hope she's not too young to understand what I'm trying to say.

* * *

Hols pushes her seatbelt closed, ready to leave, but then she reaches across her car to pick up the boots from the passenger footwell. She waves them at me. 'I'm glad I can say goodbye to these,' she laughs.

Chapter 23

Billy

I stare at my project plan spread out on the top of *Pasty Pat,* pressing my finger on the fifth of April, today's date. *You're behind,* I tell myself, shaking my head and sighing.

All the shelving should be up, *and* everything I need stacked on it, but that feels way off. I need to service the mixer today. It's not picking up everything from the bottom. It only requires an adjustment, not the whole thing taken apart again. I have to keep myself from nit-picking and try to let things go if they're working sufficiently well, continually telling myself, *eighty per cent is probably good enough.* If I work to perfection, there's no way I'll open on time. I run my finger down to the twenty-fifth of July, breathing in deeply, thinking, *one step at a time,* 'You will get there,' I say aloud, drumming the palms of my hand on the tank.

I'm delighted with what I've achieved so far - I've worked along the production line, servicing each element, ensuring it runs smoothly before moving on to the next. I didn't need specialised skills, only determination to find things out and apply the information I discovered, ticking off each item on my list within the timetable. Well, not the actual allocated time slot because I'm four days behind, and I have no leeway. I have to catch up. I need to focus on just the things I need to do, not do any more than what's essential - there's no time to add little extras that I feel would be nice.

My thoughts turn to Gino, and the day he helped me start this. I remember standing outside his whacky home and the four signs on the post - *What's a Magic Boo?* I wonder. The ping from a text breaks my musing. It's a message from Mary. '*Walk?*' is all it says.

'Are you in the dairy?' I type back, but she doesn't reply.

* * *

'Is Mary in there?' I ask Grace, nodding at the closed door to the production area.

'Said she'd back by twelve.' Grace looks at her watch. 'Oh, it's half past already.' She raises an eyebrow. 'She's not normally late.'

'Grrrrr, tenants.' Mary charges into the office. 'Arthur!' she huffs, flinging her handbag onto the desk next to Grace.

'What's happened?' I ask.

'I need a cup of tea first,' she says, turning to head back out again to fetch a drink from the farmhouse – there's a kettle in the kitchen area adjacent to the office, but she and Grace prefer using the kitchen in the farmhouse, probably because it's cosy in there. Mum is often indoors too, ready for a quick hello, and there's always homemade cookies or cakes to pilfer. 'What would you like?' Mary checks, looking at me then Grace

Grace is on her feet. 'I'll get them.' She's waddled out through the door before Mary, and I reply. She knows we'll be happy with whatever she brings back.

'It's the Dower House lot again,' Mary says, watching through the window as Grace crosses the yard. She turns to me. 'I met them this morning to approve the place where they want to site one of those stupidly expensive aluminium-framed greenhouses.' She sits down heavily in the chair next to mine. 'They were late. They didn't apologise for keeping me waiting for forty minutes, and then they insisted I look at a damp patch in their kitchen. They want me to organise and pay for the re-rendering of the whole darn house. I told them straight, I'd get a builder to check it out, but then they started demanding a rent reduction until it's fixed.'

'What's Arthur got to do with it?' I frown.

'He keeps going on and on about how I should instruct a property agent and let them manage all the tenants – but they won't, will they? I don't know how much my friend Mollie spends on her lettings bloke, but I do know he takes a woolly mammoth sized commission, *and* he still rings her every five minutes to get the okay on everything he does. It'd be a complete waste of dosh.'

'Richard would recommend someone.'

'Actually, a reliable agent isn't the problem, Auntie. In truth, it's Arthur himself. He's still tormenting me about working here and neglecting Culmfield – he won't shut up.'

'Oh,' I say, letting her get it all off her chest. Arthur's not my favourite person either. I can't believe he attacked Richard.

'He keeps on insisting that I concentrate on running Culmfield, and it's wearing me down a bit. He knows how much I love it at Fox Halt, and he knows I feel no real tie to the estate. Sometimes I think if he cares so much about it, he should inherit the house, not me. Max and Mikey see it as a ridiculous amount of work for a home that constantly needs oodles of money spent on it, but Arthur adores the place.'

* * *

Grace hands a mug of tea to Mary. 'Got biscuits too,' she says, holding out one of Mum's cookies to Mary. Grace looks at me. 'This is the last one, sorry. I wolfed the rest. I'm so hungry all the time at the moment, and biscuits—'

'You have it, Grace.' Mary waves the cookie away wafting its rich cocoa aroma towards me; it must be still warm.

'Is that what you wanted to talk about?' I ask Mary, 'How you can keep on top of all your estate work and still work here—' I pause, distracted for a second as Grace scoffs down the last biscuit. 'Am I expecting too much, asking you to manage the dairy?' My fingers are crossed behind my back. I hope not.

'That was about Jim Reeves.' She laughs.

'Is he a new customer?' I ask.

'Hardly, he's been dead since 1964.' Mary looks at Grace and touches her keyboard, 'Will you call up, 'Welcome to my World' on iTunes?' she asks and in seconds, the song plays through Grace's computer. 'Listen to the lyrics,' Mary says, pulling at her earlobe.

'…Welcome to my world
Built with you in mind.
Knock, and the door will open.
Seek, and you will find.
Ask, and you'll be given
The key to this world of mine…'

Mary smiles. 'How could I resist that?'

'Aha.' Grace grins back at her. 'So, it's my darling brother you want to chat to Billy about?'

'Yes, William and his damn *country and western* music.' Mary frowns. 'He played that song to me last night while I helped label his cider bottles. If he keeps on like that, I'll fall in love with him.'

'I don't mind,' Grace says, muting the music. 'If you ask me, you two are meant to be together. My darling bruv's been in love with you forever and you'll be the best sister-in-law in the whole world.' Grace's eyes are wide as she turns to me. 'You agree, Billy, don't you?'

When I don't answer Grace continues, 'They're really good together – like, a real lovely couple. William even had a conversation with me about something other than farming last night. Everyone sees how much happier he is lately.'

'I've got to go,' I say, not wanting to pressure Mary about her feelings for William in front of Grace. 'I have to start putting the shelves together in the ICF.' I pull a tattered bit of paper out of my jeans pocket, and show it to Grace. 'Would you sort this for me?' I ask her.

Grace takes the paper, unfolds it carefully then flattens it out. 'No worries,' she says as she scans the note.

'I know it's not dairy work,' I say, 'but can you order all that for me? I've listed the suppliers with the best deals. I can't see me finding time to contact them for a few days, and I need it all pretty much right away.'

Grace clicks her keypad, and her screen comes back to life. 'Right away,' she repeats.

As I walk towards the ice-cream factory, I text Mary, *'I'm in the ICF until 3.45. Come and chat some more, if you want xx.'* I slip my phone in my pocket but then I pull it out again, and I send Mary another text, *'Knock, and the door will open!'* I imagine her smile when she reads it.

* * *

Richard

As always, Billy is up moments before the five-thirty alarm.

'Shall I press snooze?' she asks as the buzzing starts.

'Please,' I say, rolling over.

It's nearly eight before I wake up again. I feel awful, not because I overslept, but because I'm groggy and achy. I force myself to get out of bed and into my work clothes, determined to find Billy to apologise for not feeding the calves. I know she'll have done them by now. Mondays are Hols' day each week, the day when she is in college, so while Billy milked this morning, I was supposed to be looking after the calves.

Billy has finished both the cows and the calves when I find her and she is now pressure washing the parlour walls. I walk towards her, but with her back to me and the water blasting, she doesn't hear me. I tap her on the shoulder, and she spins around, deluging me in water. She directs the nozzle away quickly, but too late, I'm soaked. 'Sorry,' she says, throwing the gun to the floor as if it's suddenly red hot.

I laugh. 'My fault, creeping up like that - anyway, it's me who needs to apologise to *you*.'

'Why?' She shrugs.

'The calves, I'm sorry, I overslept.'

'It doesn't matter, I enjoyed doing them, and you'd earned a lie in - you've fed them every morning this week.'

'I enjoy it too,' I say, looking down at my sodden jeans. 'I've learnt all their little habits, and it's a great way to start the day.' I sniff and shiver, both at once.

'Are you okay?'

I sniff again. 'I think I'm coming down with a cold.'

'Well, you can have another lie in tomorrow Hols is in charge of the calves from then.'

I frown. 'She's managing them *and* doing the milking?'

'Bedding them up, everything. What's the point in her being here otherwise?' Billy picks up the washer again and holds it up to me. 'Really sorry I got you wet. You'd better go and change.' She turns to start cleaning again. Her news about Holly and the calves stings. I've grown attached to them. They are all little characters, and it's great watching them grow. I love listening to them guzzling their milk - it's calming too, making it feel like nothing else matters. I feel a sudden empathy for Billy, allowing someone else to take over the cows. She's known the whole herd since they were born.

Billy doesn't restart the washer. She must sense me staring at her back because she turns around, reading my disappointment. 'You can always help her,' she says.

'I will go and change,' I slide my hands over my freezing cold thighs. 'I will get breakfast started; give Daniella the morning off.'

Billy doesn't look impressed; she knows what I will serve up won't be a patch on her mum's. 'I'm not being funny, Rich,' she says. 'You don't look so good. Leave breakfast, have a bath maybe, warm up. Perhaps go back to bed for a while?'

'Okay,' I say, already wondering if my weary body is up to cooking. My legs ache and my head pounds.

* * *

I make Daniella a cup of tea. 'Sit,' I tell her, pointing to the chair next to Crinkle's; there are two cats already stretched flat out on this seat, but I know she will place them both on her lap.

'But—'

'No buts, I'm making breakfast, that's final,' I tell her.

Daniella concedes, scooping up our three-legged ginger tom called Sainsbury because he was rescued after being discovered caught up in a bag for life - the vet couldn't save his leg because the plastic handle had been wrapped tightly round his paw and gangrene had set in. He adores his rescuer, and reaches up to Daniella's neck, kneading his claws into her shoulders hugging her.

'Nice to do this for *you* for once.' I scan the inside of the fridge. 'Eggs?' I ask her, aware Daniella is watching my every move as Violin, the second cat, copies Sainsbury, jealous that he might be getting more attention than her.

'They are in the larder.' She smirks because I ought to know she doesn't refrigerate eggs. 'The Jerseys have left my roses alone for four whole days,' she says, emphasising the number *four*.

'Yes,' I say, concentrating on placing the frying pan on the Rayburn; my hands are shaking.

'Funny—' Daniella stops, noticing my trembling. 'Are you still cold, Richard?'

'I am. I've changed out of my jeans, and I'm here stood next to the cooker, but I am still frozen. What's funny?' I ask.

'How they broke through the original fence, Billy assured me they'd be less work than the Friesians. I'll *never* accept them being here, you know that?'

I nod, not feeling up to a discussion, and I start rubbing my arms, trying to get my circulation going.

'Richard, leave it.' Daniella is on her feet, heading towards me. 'You go and have a long hot shower; you were silly getting those logs in for me. You should have had one right away - like I told you to. I'll make breakfast.' She grabs the packet of sausages I'm holding. Too cold and tired to disagree, I nod at her once more.

* * *

After my shower, I don an extra jumper, but I'm still cold when I go downstairs again.

'So, Mum did breakfast, after all?' Billy grins at me as she comes into the kitchen – no doubt assuming I didn't put up a fight when Daniella insisted she'd cook. I'm sitting next to the Rayburn in Crinkle's chair with her balanced on my knees. I'm coated in dog hair, but it's the warmest place to be. I can't sum up the energy to explain.

Billy creases her eyebrows into a frown. 'You alright?'

'I can't get warm,' I say. 'I'll have some breakfast, that should help, and then I'll go back to bed. Actually,' I say, suddenly feeling a bit nauseous, 'I think I'll go up now.'

'What about your breakfast?' Billy checks.

'I am not hungry. I would rather go and lie down.' I look at Daniella. 'Sorry, you've cooked, and I am not going to eat it.'

Daniella smiles. 'Don't worry, Richard. Would you like a couple of hot water bottles? I'll bring them up in a moment.' She is already taking them off their hook inside the larder.

'Please,' I say, pushing Crinkle onto the floor and getting to my feet. I feel like I'm ninety as I shuffle my first step to the door still aching from head to toe.

'I'll bring these up to you,' Billy says, taking the bottles from her mother. 'And I'll get you an extra duvet too, from one of the spare rooms. You'll be fine once you've got yourself warm again, won't you?'

Chapter 24

BILLY

Despite the cold, Jakub turns up wearing a tee shirt and shorts. 'Sorry I'm a couple of minutes late,' I tell him. 'Richard isn't feeling too good. He's gone back to bed. I was taking him up some hot water bottles.' I slam the front door shut behind me, expecting Jakub to step back, ready to follow me to the ICF, but he hasn't moved. He is simply staring at me. I stare back until I feel I have to fill the silence between us. 'I didn't think I could put up the shelves on my own,' I say.

'We go then,' he replies.

I now understand why my helper is clothed for a summer's day. It's because he works at breakneck speed, fetching the next piece we need, putting it in place so I can hold it and then screwing it up in seconds. He's lightning fast.

An hour rushes past, an hour since I left Richard in bed, and I feel I need to check on him, but it feels wrong to leave Jakub alone, continuing to work without me. 'Do you mind waiting ten minutes in the kitchen while I check on Rich?' I ask as we complete the first section of racking.

'I carry on,' Jakub says, shaking his head, 'I'll do some bits that will make it quicker when you get back.'

'Are you sure?'

He waves a hand, gesturing me away and picks up another bracing strut.

* * *

Richard is asleep under two duvets and sweating. I peel away the top quilt and touch his brow; he feels damp and cold, and his skin looks translucent grey. 'Can you get up, Rich? I want to take you to the doctor.' I whisper, kissing his forehead.

He opens one eye. 'Let me sleep for a bit.' He closes his eye again.

'Rich, I think you need to see the doctor. I'm calling the surgery. I'm sure they'll send someone out to see you.'

'I'm not that bad.'

'I think you are. I want to get you checked out.'

He turns over and mumbles. 'Give me fifteen minutes, and I'll get up. You can drive me to the surgery then.'

* * *

Jakub shakes his head at me. 'Too much,' he says, taking just two of the twenty-pound notes from my hand.

'But you expected five hours work,' I say. 'You could have done another job today – you've lost out because of me.'

'I don't work each other Monday because I take my son to school after he spend weekend with me. This is a favour for Mrs May. Sean said she need help. I thought he mean your mother.' I wince at his loyalty to my mum, not me, and I remember his odd behaviour when I met him this morning – he thought he'd be working for Mum.

'Will you come and help me next Monday?' I ask. 'If we start at eight, we'd have all the shelves finished by five.'

He shrugs. 'Maybe.'

I push the rest of the money at him, 'Take it please,' I say. 'And maybe, you'll work for me again next week?'

'Breakfast and lunch from Mrs May, your mother?'

'Okay,' I say. 'You come at eight, and there'll be breakfast at ten.

'And lunch?'

I nod, pushing three more twenty-pound notes into his hand. 'Take this too, please.'

* * *

As I walk into the bedroom, Richard is still lying in bed. He holds out a hand to me. 'Billy, help me, can you? I don't seem to have the strength to even sit up on my own.'

'I'll phone Dr Pines,' I say.

'No, help me, and I'll go to the surgery. It's not an emergency. It's probably just flu.'

By the time I have him dressed and to my van, I wish I'd asked Jakub to stay and help. Richard is so much taller than me and supporting him down the stairs when I was terrified he might fall was awful. He rests on my arm, taking a breather, and then I virtually lift him into my van. Mum is beside us, desperate to help me, but I won't let her.

'I can't believe you are like this now when you were walking around the yard this morning,' she says.

'Should I take you to the hospital, instead?' I ask Richard as I do up his seatbelt.

'The surgery is just fine.'

* * *

Dr Pines is on the phone in seconds. He looks at me, still holding the phone to his ear. 'They can get an ambulance here, in twenty minutes, or you can take Richard into the EMU now. They'll see him straight away.'

'Billy will take me,' Richard says, trying to stand up, and I grab his arm to steady him.

'I'll take him,' I agree. 'Exeter, Wonford, that's where I'm going? Will there be signs for the EMU?'

'Yes.' The doctor sounds keen for us to go.

Richard and I are at the door, about to leave the consulting room when I turn back to Dr Pines. 'Do you know what's wrong?' I ask, realising in all the haste we hadn't checked. 'They'll do tests,' he says.

* * *

Richard has a side room to himself because he's been sick and has diarrhoea, so although the doctors think it's pneumonia, he's being isolated in case it's the Norovirus.

The ward staff let me stay all night in the chair beside his bed wearing a plastic apron to cover my clothes and disposable plastic gloves, but now I need to go home to fetch pyjamas, slippers and a wash kit for Richard. I need a shower too, and I need to change into some clean clothes - I'm still in the ones I was working in. The shelves were plastered in dust, so every bit of me feels disgustingly dirty. Mum is desperate to see Richard, so I'll bring her back with me later. Jessie said she can drop her home whenever she likes.

Freddy wanted to visit too but because of the possibility of the virus he's going to stay away, in case Grace then the baby are infected in turn.

I'm about to head off when Dr Ryani, the lovely doctor we saw earlier this morning, comes into the room. He sits on Richard's bed, asking his patient to listen. Richard makes a small nod, his eyes half-open. 'I have some good news and some bad news—' he says and then he taps the front of the thin file he's holding. 'And then another bit of good news.' The doctor smiles at me.

I sit up in my chair. 'Do you know what's wrong?' I ask.

'Yes, we do Mrs –' He checks his notes.

'Billy,' I say. 'Please, call me Billy.' I rest my hand on Richard's shoulder.

Dr Ryani starts to speak again, this time directing his words to me. 'The good news is we know what's making your husband so ill.' He turns to Richard. 'I'm sorry, but the bad news is that you have contracted sepsis, maybe from the wound on your back, but it may be from an entirely different source. We will probably never know where the infection originally came from.'

I press my fingers hard into Richard's shoulder, feeling guilty. I haven't looked at his back since I checked it had stopped bleeding. He hasn't mentioned it again, and I'd forgotten about it, my focus on the bruising around his neck after Arthur nearly throttled him. 'What's the other bit of *good* news?' I swallow.

The doctor looks from me to Richard and then back to me again. 'The good news is we've pinpointed the exact strain of sepsis, so we'll start administering the appropriate antibiotic in just ten minutes or so.'

'That *is* good, isn't it?' I hesitate, recalling a man I saw on TV a few weeks ago, who'd lost both his feet, part of his nose and a part of his cheek because it took so long to determine which particular form of sepsis he had. His doctors couldn't treat him without knowing the correct antibiotic to fight it.

'Yes, it is, but there's something you must understand –' Dr Ryani looks me straight in the eyes.

I breathe in hard. 'What?'

'Over the coming days, the antibiotics will likely cause Richard to feel worse than he does now. This is common and to be expected. He *will* get better over the next few weeks, *but* you need to be ready for your husband to look and feel much sicker than he does now.'

I almost shout as his words sink in 'Weeks?'

'Three or four.' The doctor steps back. 'Sepsis is serious. We'll keep monitoring whether the drugs are working.'

I nod, not wanting to voice my next question, too scared to hear the answer. *What if they don't?*

Chapter 25

RICHARD

Billy seems to be here every time I open my eyes. Daniella and Jessie visited me, but my brain is foggy, I can't say when they were here. I'm sweating. Too cold. Trembling, struggling to breathe - the oxygen mask makes it impossible to get comfortable.

Again and again, someone checks my temperature and blood pressure. Beeping machines, doctors, nurses, and specialists, all in confusingly coloured tunics– *too many names!*

Day or night, I don't know.

Pain in my chest. Aching everywhere…The sepsis is winning - destroying me. *Can I just sleep? Please?*

* * *

BILLY

Richard's been in hospital for three days, and I've come home to have a shower and to pick up Mum so she can see him later. Mary walks into the kitchen, and I imagine she's come to get drinks and some of the cookies that I smelt before I even entered the house. Mum blocks her path. 'Carry Crinkle down to see Betsy and Bramble, will you?' This sounds like an order rather than a request.

'Carry?' Mary frowns. 'What's wrong with her legs?'

Mum points at Crinkle. 'Haven't you noticed?'

'What, Nan-Dan?'

'That poor dog hasn't sat in her chair since Richard left.' Mum jabs a finger at Crinkle, sitting by the door. Crinkle must reckon she's in trouble because she ducks her head and looks away. 'You've been on that mat twenty-four-seven,' Mum says to her. 'Not touched your food either. I even cooked you Special Chicken this morning, and you just sniffed it.'

Mum looks back at Mary. 'The goats may cheer her up. She won't come voluntarily though, you'll have to carry her.'

Mary touches my elbow. 'Will you be here when I get back?' She looks as tired as I feel, and I immediately wonder what's happening in her world. I've been so focused on Richard, I haven't given anyone or anything else a thought.

I smile. 'I'm here until two,' I say as she lifts Crinkle up.

'No need to mope,' she tells the dog, 'He'll be back soon.'

I open the door to let her and Crinkle outside then sit at the table, expecting Mum to put a cup of tea in front of me like she normally does when I come in for breakfast. She's already lifted the kettle off the Rayburn. 'How is he?' she asks.

'He hardly slept last night. He thinks he's going to die. He keeps saying he is too weak to fight. Caroline, the nurse, you—'

Mum cuts in. 'The one moving into a new flat today?'

'I don't know, sorry. She was there yesterday. She had the tattoo on her wrist, and you asked her where she had it done? You are *not really* considering getting one, are you?'

'Not sure - maybe a black and white cow, here?' She stresses the colours *black and white* as she touches her ankle.

'You're joking?'

Mum shrugs. 'She's moving into a flat in Alphington, and she explained exactly where it was, so I posted her a *Happiness in your New Home* card when I got back from the hospital yesterday - I put yours and Richard's names in it too.'

'Mum,' I say, standing up and hugging her. 'You are so caring - I wish I was half the person you are.'

She holds me for a minute, not saying anything until I let go and sit back down. 'I remember what it was like—' She stops, like she's remembering something.

'What was like?' I prompt.

'When I moved into the cottage by the shop, all that upheaval. The cards meant such a lot.'

I remember too. How anxious I'd been when Mum left Fox Halt to move into a small terraced cottage in the centre of Hamsgate. How I worried was about her saying goodbye to her childhood home after seventy years of living there, leaving all her family's history behind. If Dad hadn't died, they would have moved together, and it might have been easier for her, but she didn't complain, saying how cosy the cottage felt and how lovely it was to have caring neighbours just footsteps away.

'So, Caroline,' Mum says, shaking my focus away from that awful time when I lost my wonderful dad, selling Fox Halt, and Mum being forced to abandon all her animals. 'What about her?'

'She was great,' I say. 'She helped me try to get Richard to realise it's the antibiotics *not* the sepsis that are making him feel so bad. In the end, we decided I should come home for a couple of hours, and then Rich might see I'm confident to leave him. That I'm sure he'll still be alive when I get back. He'll stop imagining I'm sat there waiting for him to die.'

'Are *you* alright?' Mum asks.

I look into her eyes, the exact same greeny-blue colour as mine. 'I cried all the way home - it is so hard being strong for him when I feel my world's falling apart.'

'He *will* get better, Billy. You must believe the doctors.'

'But he might give up. That's what I'm so petrified of,' I say, clasping the handle of the large mug of tea she's just placed in front of me.

'Freddy and Grace are going in at one o'clock, now that there's no virus to worry about - those two are bound to cheer him up.' Mum smiles. 'I told Grace to take the afternoon off. I hope that was alright?'

'She can take as much time off as she needs. The dairy admin isn't important. I just hope they can lift his spirits.'

'Grace will have him grinning from ear to ear as soon as she walks through the door. The things that girl comes out with - often, she'll have me laughing so much, my jaw hurts.'

'I hope so,' I say. '-But I think it will take more than Grace to make him feel positive. He is really, *really* low.'

Mum picks up her mug. 'Would you mind doing a bit of ironing for me after you've drunk your tea?' She nods at a wash basket overflowing with sheets, pillowcases and towels.

I frown. 'That's the linen we use for guests,' I say. 'Have you got friends coming to stay? Did you tell me, sorry?'

'No—' She stops then changes her answer. 'Yes, friends.'

'Don't you want to put them off? With Richard so ill. You'll want to spend time with him, not look after them.'

'I only invited them yesterday.'

'Why?'

It's Franklin, Sid and—' She pauses.

I close my eyes because with a nasty premonition about who the next guest is.

I say the name slowly, 'Janette, you've invited *her* to stay here?' I stare at Mum in disbelief.

Mum doesn't respond, allowing me to absorb the news that Richard's ex-wife will be standing in this kitchen and sleeping upstairs – in sheets I've ironed! And Martin?' I cough the name of Janette's new husband, 'Am I sleeping on the couch?' Janette and Richard have remained friends. They do, after all, have three children in common – who they both adore. I asked Mum to tell Janette, his dad and his daughters how ill Richard is. 'But Janette and Martin could stay in an Exeter hotel near the hospital. Fox Halt is thirty miles away.'

Mum's tone is uncompromising. 'I invited Martin but he's on a lecture tour in the US for six weeks. Janette and Sid will share a room, so you won't need to give up your bed. They're all so worried, and it was the least I could do.'

'And Harry, is she on her way too?' Harry is Sid's twin sister, they're really Ariadne and Cressida, but Richard's mum gave them nicknames which stuck. Harry lives in New Zealand with her Kiwi husband. She has a family, but I imagine she'd soon hop on a plane to see her dad.

'No, but I promised to tell her if Richard gets worse.'

I nod. 'That's why you sent Mary away, so you could tell me about Janette?'

'I admit I did consider not telling you, Billy, and you finding them here tomorrow morning. At least, there's only three of them, and they'll be leaving after a day or so – unlike the eight Jerseys I discovered you'd moved in permanently without a single word to me.' She's up on her feet now, opening the cupboard where she keeps the ironing board.

'I might have crawled out of the bathroom window too if I'd found Janette in her nightie on the landing,' I laugh, 'Leave it, Mum, I'll do it,' I say as she reaches for the iron.

'I'm still not happy about the Jerseys,' Mum says, not smiling, not even the slightest rise in her voice, which might have lightened how miserable she knows I am feeling.

'You don't expect to discuss the cows now?' I snap.

Outside Mary shouts to be let in, and when I open the door to her I see she's more plastered in mud than Crinkle. 'I couldn't catch her,' she says. 'Those rascal goats kept shielding her from me, like they wanted her to stay and play.' Crinkle smiles, her tongue hanging out as she pants.

'Have you got anything else to put on?' I ask Mary, wondering if I should hose them both off before I let them in.

'Nooo.' She sounds sarcastic. *Why would she have spare clothes?* 'Will you lend me something?' she asks, wiping a splash of mud from her chin.

I nod. 'Of course,' I say. 'Take her through to the bathroom, will you?' I open all the doors as wide as they will go so neither she nor the dog has a chance of smearing mud onto them. 'I'll find you something to wear, and fetch some towels.'

'What's that?' Mum frowns at me.

'A carrier bag for Mary's wet clothes, so she can take them home,' I tell her.

'No.' My mother shakes her head. 'I'll stick them in the machine for her. They'll be rank by the time she gets around to washing them, wet and filthy and sat in plastic.'

'Okay,' I say, wishing I'd thought to offer to wash them for Mary. 'When are *they* arriving? Have you told them visiting times?' I ask Mum as I head down the hall to help Mary.

'Later this afternoon, but I suggested they left visiting until tomorrow. It would be too much for Richard after Grace and Freddy have been in. Grace is bound to wear him out.'

I don't know what to say now, wondering if I'm selfish, still not wanting them here when I know seeing his dad and his daughter will be such a tonic for Richard?

Mum calls into the bathroom, 'Franklin's taking us all out for dinner at The Hamsgate. I've booked a table for seven.'

'Seven?' I check, unsure if she meant seven o'clock or seven people – if she meant the people that would be the three of them plus Grace and Freddy, Mum *and me?* 'I hope they don't expect me to go. I'll be at the hospital,' I say, thinking how there's no way on earth I'll spend an evening with Janette.

'Seven for seven. He wanted Grace, Freddy, William and Mary to go too.'

'That's eight, or aren't you invited?' I say quickly, opening the door so I can hear her properly.

'Mary can't go. Something's happening at Culmfield.'

'So, what time exactly will they be here?' I ask.

'I'm not sure.' Mum's tone indicates I'm asking an irrelevant question, but it *is* relevant. I want to make sure I've left for the hospital before they arrive at the farm.

'And are you still coming back with me?' I ask, feeling done in. I'm tired from spending three nights in a chair and exhausted with worry about Richard. Tiptoeing around Janette is the last thing I need.

'Yes, Freddy's picking me up from the hospital after his seminar. He's coming back here anyway, for the meal.'

Everything is planned, so I'm going to have to put up with it. *I can easily avoid the woman for a couple of days, can't I?*

'Will you help me make up the beds after you've done the ironing?' Mum asks, and I now realise she is carrying a bucket full of all the things she needs to clean the bathrooms.

'No,' I say firmly. 'I'll make them up on my own. It's too much for you. We agreed you're not to do them anymore. I'll clean the en-suite and the downstairs bathroom too, please just leave it, Mum. Let me sort it all.'

'I'll help you, Auntie.' Mary stands in the hallway in my overlarge clothes with Crinkle wrapped in a fluffy pink towel which I meant for her to use on herself. It'll be demoted to a *dog towel* now. I can see Crinkle has been tearing at it, like she always does when we dry her off - her revenge for making her have a bath. 'I've only got two small deliveries to make, I have time,' she says, smoothing Crinkle's damp ears.

'Please explain to our customers why you're dressed like that,' I say. 'I don't want them to think you've had some sort of breakdown - you always look so immaculate normally.'

Mary laughs. 'Auntie, I'll give you a hand later. You won't have even finished the ironing by the time I get back.'

'Don't worry, sweetie. I can do everything,' I tell her, not knowing how long it'll take or if I've even got the energy for it. All I want to do is get back to the hospital and hold Richard's hand. Mary pouts, and immediately I realise she wants to help. I guess because she wants to talk. Mum stood by the bathroom doorway while we dealt with Crinkle, so if there is something private she wants to tell me, she couldn't have said it then.

'Oh, if you *do* have time?' I backtrack. 'It'll be quicker with two of us. I'll come and find you once I've ironed this lot.' I point at the overflowing basket.

* * *

The sweet fresh meadow smell of fabric being steamed provokes happy memories of growing up. Carrying me back forty years, me settled in a chair next to my mum while she ironed – a precious hour when she was still.

While Mum ironed the family's and the bed and breakfast guests' linen, she wouldn't be charging around doing all her usual daily chores, and it became a special time when we'd talk. It was always one-sided, me telling Mum my hopes, dreams and fears. I had no secrets back then. Unlike now, when I hold back from her because it often feels simpler that way.

I storm through the pile of ironing, thinking how I'd never could have predicted I'd be flattening out a sheet for my husband's ex-wife, so she'd have smooth, fresh cotton against her skin – *naked skin – yuck!*

* * *

As I walk across the yard to fetch Mary, a rattling noise grabs my attention, and when I turn towards the strange noise, I see a man climbing out of the goat pen; he waves a grubby paper cup at me. 'Hello, Billy,' he calls out, and now I recognise who it is. It's Arthur. 'I came to see Mary, but the dairy is locked,' he tells me.

'The office is closed,' I say, feeling anger instantly boil up inside me. 'What are you doing?'

'I want to see Richard, but I hate hospitals, so I'm here to persuade my sister to come with me.'

'I meant, why were you in with those two?' I point at Betsy and Bramble.

'I couldn't resist saying hello,' he says. 'Mary has told me all about the goats, but I had my coffee in my hand and that one—' He waves at Bramble. 'Grabbed it in his mouth.'

'You were rescuing your cup?' I check.

Arthur waves the Costa Coffee cup like a victory flag. 'I didn't think it would be good if he ate it,' he says, 'So, yes. Voilà!' He holds the cup above his head and grins.

I look from the thick-set, bearded man to the tiny Bramble, thinking, *you are at least three times taller than her. It shouldn't have been difficult.* I bite my tongue. 'You want to see Richard? Really, after the other day?'

'I want to say sorry. I was a dick. Sis got me fired up, and then when Richard told me what Erik Christianson had said, I lost it. I owe him a massive apology – without him, O'Rowdes' would've been in the shit, and Erik was right; I was posturing. I want to assure Richard that I'm knuckling down now.'

Richard wouldn't be in hospital if Arthur hadn't pushed him, but he's admitted he was wrong. He's young, and we all make mistakes. 'Let's find your sister,' I say fed up with how today keeps getting worse. I could have done with Mary's help, and I feel prickly towards Arthur. He nearly strangled Richard. He should never have lost control like he did.

'Yes,' he says, throwing the filthy cup on the roof of his pristine Range Rover, then following me to the dairy.

I press in the door code and Arthurs stares at me. 'She's locked in?' he says. 'Is that how you keep her here?'

I'm not sure if he's joking. 'Grace isn't here to meet visitors. She's seeing Richard, so the office is locked, and this is the access to the production area.' I could explain there's no lock on the inside. Mary can let herself out anytime, but I don't.

'Thought sis and I could go in a minute. You'll let her off early, won't you?' he asks as I open the door.

'No,' I say, remembering Mary telling me how he's trying to persuade her to give up working here and annoyed he assumes she can drop everything to suit him.

'A bit early then? I'll wait in here.' He moves to step over the threshold, his hand about to push the inner office door.

'Arthur, don't come any further, please. Wait on the step. You've probably got goat shit on your shoes; I don't want you trailing it in here. I'll get Mary to come out to see you.'

He stops. 'You're always so damn cranky. Richard must have been happy to spend five days a week away when he was working at O'Rowdes'. He must be pleased he's got sepsis, and in hospital. Glad to get away from you for a while longer.'

My grumpiness must seem uncalled for, but he's annoyed me. 'I'll be two minutes,' I say in a more conciliatory tone, trying to sound welcoming. I resist the urge to slam the door in his face, leaving it wide open as I disappear inside.

Mary picks up two trays of yoghurt and a box of cheese, balancing them in her arms. 'I haven't done the deliveries yet,' she says, as I walk into the dairy, 'But if you open the doors, I'll stick these in the van now. I can go straight off, once we've finished indoors.'

'Your brother's here. He wants to speak to you,' I tell her.

'How dare he show up here again.'

'He says he's sorry,' I say, taking the yoghurts.

* * *

'You don't want to go with Arthur?' I check, feeling like an umpire between the siblings. Mary looks at me. 'Not today. Not after Grace and Freddy. Richard will be whacked. Arthur and me visiting as well is too much.'

'But I want to see him.' Arthur is petulant, like the child I remember when his older sister was unfair to him.

Mary regresses too. 'No, Arthur, Richard is too poorly. We'll go another day when the antibiotics have kicked in, and he's feeling better. In a day or two, maybe.' She steps around him, clicking her van open before she slides the box of cheese into the back, turning the refrigeration on.

Arthur takes the yoghurts from me then follows her, saying, 'We'll go in for just ten minutes.' He passes Mary the trays. 'Richard's done so much for me. Hell, I need to apologise. I've driven all the way from London to see the poor fellow.'

'No. You should have checked with me first,' Mary tells him, turning to me. 'Shall we get started on the paperwork? You need to get back to the hospital.'

Arthur huffs. 'Right then, I'll go on my own.'

As he climbs into his car, he lowers his electric window. 'Ten minutes won't do any harm.'

Mary turns her back on him, grabs my arm and pulls me towards the house. 'I need to talk to you. It's about William—' she says and within a couple of minutes, Arthur's car screeches out of the yard, the coffee cup tumbling off its roof and bouncing along the ground.

PART TWO

Chapter 26

Billy

My heart jumps, seeing Richard sitting in a chair. This is the first time I've seen him out of bed since he was admitted. 'Missed you,' he says, smiling his best smile - one that reaches his eyes and scrunches up the sides into three deep wrinkles. He's lost weight, you can see it in his face. *He was thin enough before,* I think, but I console myself with how much better he looks; his skin isn't glowing, but it's lost its grey pallor.

I sit on his bed. 'Didn't Grace and Freddy keep you entertained?' I try not to stare at the clear plastic tube running from somewhere behind his left ear and into his left nostril. 'That looks uncomfortable,' I say when Richard notices where I'm looking.

He shakes his head. 'It's better than not having it at all. It's so frightening when I'm gasping for breath. You look exhausted, darling.'

'Did Grace and Freddy stay long?' I ask, steering away from how I feel.

'Until two nice porters collected me for an MRI scan. It was good to see them.' He smiles again. 'I'm glad you're back.'

'Did Arthur come in?' I ask.

'Arthur O'Rowde?' Richard frowns, reaching forward to put his hand on mine. It's a slow movement, taking all his strength and concentration.

'Yes, Arthur O'Rowde, he wanted to say he was sorry.'

He shrugs. 'Maybe he came while I was being scanned.'

I keep my voice level, as I don't want to upset him, admitting how I felt like garrotting Arthur when I first saw him, so angry about him hurting Richard. 'He drove down especially from London,' I say.

'Oh.' Richard raises an eyebrow.

I run the back of the hand he isn't holding, down his cheek, away from the oxygen tube. 'I'm sure Arthur is sorry,' I say. 'He must feel bad, knowing he probably caused you to be in here. He wanted Mary to come in with him, so he drove to the farm to fetch her.' Richard's eyes close, but I go on, not wanting to sit here in silence. 'Mary refused to go with him, and we told him it would be too much for you after seeing Freddy and Grace this afternoon. She suggested postponing it for another time, but he said he'd stay just ten minutes. Maybe he listened, and he'll come in another time—'

'I am pretty tired, actually.' Richard's voice is raspy, and he blinks at me several times. I hate having nothing to rest my back on, so I gently lift his hand off mine so I can fetch one of the plastic chairs designated for visitors from the corridor.

As I place my new chair in front of his, Richard looks at me for a split second before shutting his eyes again. I want to hold him, but I don't know where he might be hurting, and I'm frightened of disturbing any of the equipment surrounding him - instead, I touch his knee. 'I love you,' I whisper. 'I love you.' I yearn for his arms around me. *Get better soon, please...*

* * *

The hospital allows two visitors at a time, so as Franklin and Janette appear in the doorway of Richard's room, I start to gather up my things, ready to make a quick exit, but now I overhear Janette talking to Franklin about how long Richard is likely to be kept in hospital. 'Six weeks,' I repeat, not believing what she just said.

'That's what the nurse told me.' Janette turns to her ex-father-in-law. 'Didn't he?'

Franklin puffs out his chest. 'That's indeed what the good man conveyed. The fellow said, it could be even longer.'

Sid and I were about to get a coffee in the hospital cafeteria - I like Richard's quirky daughter, and I haven't seen her in ages, so I jumped at her suggestion to go to the café, but now I don't want to go.

I watch Richard's closed eyes, wondering if he's heard he'll be stuck in here for longer than we both anticipated. He doesn't move a muscle, so I assume he's asleep, not resting his eyes like he often claims when his eyelids grow heavy.

Janette places her chair as close to Richard as she can, like she's staking a claim on him - *Richard and Janette are friends,*

I tell myself, *because of the children – they have nothing else in common anymore,* but I'm jealous. She touches Richard's hand, and I stare, transfixed.

'Billy, you look worse than Dad.' Sid breaks into my thoughts. 'Sepsis isn't contagious, is it?' She looks concerned.

'No,' I reassure her. 'It's hard to sleep in here, that's all, there's always light and noise, or the night staff moving around doing their obs or dealing with warning bleepers.'

Sid loops her arm through mine, 'Let's get you some coffee then, and maybe some breakfast,' she says, using her heavier frame to wrench me away from Richard, her grandfather and her mum.

* * *

In the hospital restaurant, my phone vibrates in my pocket, and I pull it out to check who's calling. 'It's Mary,' I tell Sid. 'She wouldn't ring unless something's wrong.'

I answer the call in the area where phones aren't prohibited and then head back to Sid, who's still sitting at our table, guarding our cooked breakfasts. It looked so good before, and I was ravenous, but now I don't think I can eat a morsel. I sit back down and push my plate away.

'What's wrong?' Sid asks.

I move to pick up my teacup and accidentally skid my phone across the table towards her. 'A Hygiene Emergency Prohibition Order,' I say, my voice breaking up.

'An order?' Sid frowns, pushing her lips downwards and outwards like a bull dog.

I nod. 'An Environmental Health Officer was in the yard when Grace arrived this morning – he closed the dairy down.'

Sid fires questions at me, allowing no time to answer. 'And he served a notice on Grace? Mary is the manager, isn't she? And the notice is for poor hygiene?' She picks up my phone and hands it to me. 'That's terrible. What will you do?'

I sit back in my chair, feeling defeated, struggling to process the phone conversation I've just had. 'Mary wasn't there,' I say. 'She had a flat tyre this morning and was late. The officer said a member of our staff hand-delivered a letter to their office, which included incriminating photos of the dairy. They said they had serious concerns about the dairy's cleanliness and hygiene.'

Sid frowns. 'But Daniella gave us a tour; it is spotless.'

'This morning it wasn't.' I shake my head. 'Mary's just given me a graphic description. Someone's made it look like Betsy and Bramble spent the night in there. The officer walked in, took one look and shut us down straight away.'

'Jeepers, Billy, for how long?'

I put my head in my hands. 'Two weeks minimum.'

'What can I do?' Sid asks, touching my arm.

'Nothing, darling, but I do need to get back to Fox Halt to support Mary - and I need to help her sort this out. She's pretty shaken up. She's in charge, and stupidly she is beating herself up about this happening. She kept on apologising.'

Sid is on her feet. 'Don't worry, Mum, Grandie and I can stay with Dad for a few hours, until you get back.'

'I can't leave him,' I say, trying not to cry.

'Dad'll be fine,' she says, 'You go.'

I look up at her. 'I don't want your mum being with him,' I blurt out, and now I've said it, I carry on. 'I'm your dad's wife now. I want to be there holding his hand. He's putting on a brave face, but he's terrified underneath. I wasn't going to say anything because I knew it would upset you, but he was choosing hymns for his funeral last night.'

Sid's eyes widen as she sits back down. 'Dad's not dying, is he? Should I tell Harry to get on a plane right aw—'

'No, sweetheart,' I cut in. 'He's *not* going to die.' I catch her hand, squeezing her fingers. 'He's strong; he'll beat this.'

'Are you certain, Billy?' Sid asks, sitting back down.

'He loves you all too much to give up. It's the drugs making him feel sick - so ill that he believes the sepsis is going to kill him. The antibiotics are pretty potent, causing him to feel really depressed.'

'Is depression a known side effect then?' Sid picks up her phone as if she's about to Google the answer.

'It seems so, and that's why we must keep reassuring him. Having you and your grandad here means the world to your father.'

'I'll cheer him up.' Sid smiles. 'I always do - I'll tell Dad about a crazy mess I got into last week when someone expected me to be a chap. Sometimes I wish I had a sensible name, but I'm not a Cressida, am I?' She's up in a flash. 'Cressida MarcFenn, pleasure to meet you,' she says in a pretend Cockney accent.

'You're undeniably Sid,' I laugh.

She smiles. 'Go and see Mary,' she says. 'Stay for three or four hours if you need to. We'll hold the fort here. I'll text you a picture of Dad in a mo, with a big fat grin on his face.'

* * *

Mary lays out ten A4 sheets of paper along the edge of the kitchen table. 'These are copies of the pictures the Environmental Health guy brought with him. They're the ones their office received. Look,' she says, leaning forward to touch the first one and staring at it. 'Please don't tell me not to be concerned. You haven't seen these and you haven't been in the dairy yet!'

I pick up the last photo, unable to grasp what I'm looking at. The picture is like the others, a close-up image, and this one shows the corner of the packing counter smeared with muck and golden hairs. I take up a second picture and stare at that again. Bramble's white hair is caught up in one of the muslins we use to line the cheese moulds. It's disgusting.

Mary holds out a crumpled sheet of paper – it looks like she has screwed the letter up and smoothed it back out again for me to see. 'Lies,' she says, smacking the page. 'They say we allow Betsy and Bramble free range from the house to the kitchen and into the dairy. That the animals can roam through all the food processing and storage areas.'

I grab the note and read it slowly– the letter is signed, *Fox Halt Farm Dairy Employee* with our address in brackets underneath. I have tears in my eyes, and I sniff at the moisture building up in my nose – an all-too-familiar reaction when something happens that makes me furious. 'This says they complained to the manager three times about the hygiene, and they've been threatened with losing their job.' I stare at Mary, thinking how awful this must make her feel. 'I don't recognise the writing, do you?' I ask.

Mary shakes her head. 'You'd better see it for real.'

* * *

Before we enter the dairy, we don our normal protective gear. I feel sick with apprehension, which turns to anger as we step into the preparation area – the bath, where the milk is processed into curds and whey, is smeared with dung with goat hairs stuck all around the rim.

I check out the rest of the room and the packing areas in silence, ready to scream and unsure what I can say to Mary that might make her feel better. There is hair and droppings on every tank, on counters, on our packaging, the fridge and door handles. It's wicked that someone's done this on purpose. I can't understand who would be so callous. I employ Mary and Grace full time, but there are two ladies in the village who work part-time here too. This is not just my livelihood, it's theirs too. I try to keep my voice even. 'Call the police?' I say.

I pick up the order sheet to see which customers we will be letting down, trying to think what to tell them.

'I've called them,' Mary says. 'They'll send someone as soon as they can. They said not to touch anything.'

I jam the order sheet back on its hook, and another terrible thought crashes into my head. 'Have you been in the cold store?'

I watch in despair as Mary casts her eyes to the floor. *Oh no!*

* * *

My breath catches in my throat as I cast my eyes along the shelves, seeing goat hair dusted everywhere. 'I thought two weeks to clear this mess up,' I say. 'But they'll deem everything contaminated, won't they?' I shake my head at Mary, taking in the neatly laid out truckles of cheese, turned every day and cared for meticulously.

'All gotta go.' Mary scratches her head through her hair net. 'We're going to lose six months' stock.' Half a year is the minimum time we cure our Foxy Lady Cheese, but some of our extra mature cheeses are more than two years old. It breaks me, thinking how all this cheese will have to be chucked away. I move to swipe my arm along a shelf to bring everything crashing to the floor, but I stop, remembering the police. They'll want to check for fingerprints and take more photographs. 'Has Mum seen this?' I ask, suddenly imagining her horror too. She's helped me right from the start getting the dairy running, thrilled to bits with every prize we've won.

'She's helping Grace ring customers,' Mary says. 'They are asking them to take all our products off their shelves and telling that that there won't be anything coming from Fox Halt for the next three weeks.'

'Is she okay?'

Mary wrings her hands together. 'I don't think I've ever seen Nan-Dan so mad. If she finds out who did this, they're done for—' She pauses. 'She'll get Betsy and Bramble to trample them to death.'

'I'll go and see her,' I say.

'No.' Mary brings her hand across my body to stop me moving. 'Leave her, she's happy talking to our customers, they're as shocked as she is, and they're giving her tonnes of sympathy.'

'Are Grace and Mum offering them compensation?'

'Yep.'

I massage my temples, trying to feel more in control. 'What are they saying happened?' I ask.

'Sabotage, that's the truth, isn't it?'

I don't answer, racking my tired brain. *Who'd do this*? I remember the enforcement notice. It's got to be the same person, trying to hurt me again. *What could they do next? How far will they go?*

'It's so unfair,' Mary says. 'The onus is on us to prove that it's a deliberate targeted attack and that the so-called whistle-blower doesn't exist. We have to get our staff to corroborate that the goats have never been near this place.'

I think about Troy Gloon, wondering if he is behind this; he said I'd regret taking Andrew's stuff, but when I confronted him last time, I felt sure he knew nothing about the enforcement notice. I picture his red eyes and his snarling mouth and hear him mocking me, '*It weren't* me.'

Mary is telling me something else, and I tune in again to listen, '... everyone we supply has to display notices warning customers not to consume any Fox Halt products they've already bought. We—' she shouts the word *we* at me, '*We* have to pay for embarrassing and discrediting notices in local papers telling the world the dairy has been closed due to hygiene concerns. Who did this, Auntie? This could ruin Fox Halt.'

'Why did they do it?' I say, shaking my head.

Chapter 27

Billy

I've been back with Richard for twenty minutes and my phone bleeps. I panic, thinking Mary has another problem, and then I freak out some more when I see it's a text from Grace. I scan the message quickly. *'Meet up in five- for five? – in Katrina's Coffee Bar in the maternity wing. Need to ask you something?'*

I want to ask if there's a problem with the baby, but I can't do that by text. My heart races, fearing something bad is happening – maybe today and all the break-in stress was too much for her. I kept out of the office, letting Mum and Grace deal with customers, while I helped Mary with a list of all the things she needed to sort for the next day or so. My mind charges on. My mouth is dry, and I lick my lips, telling myself to calm down, *breathe, count to ten,* then I text back a thumbs-up emoji.

I kiss Richard gently on his mouth. His eyes are closed, and he doesn't react. 'I need to meet Grace for fifteen minutes I'll be back straight afterwards,' I whisper, watching his eyelids for a flicker of recognition but again there's none. I scribble a note and leave it on his over-bed table, held down by a glass of apple juice he hasn't touched. I walk out of the room, then practically run through the hospital corridors to get to Grace.

Relief washes over me as I see her, and she's smiling. She's not upset. *Thank you, God, she's okay – the baby's okay.*

'Six weeks!' Grace shouts, and everyone stares at us. She instantly slams a hand over her mouth, shocked at how loud her words came out. 'Oh, fiddles, poor man,' she's whispering now. 'And poor you, Billy, in here every day. I've been coming into hospital once a week for the last six, for antenatal classes, and that's just two hours at a time – that's enough.'

I smile. 'Maybe it won't be that long,' I say, still unable to believe it myself. 'How's Freddy?' I ask.

'Takes everything as it comes. He's been visiting his dad a lot, but he's studying hard too, and as you know, he's like really, really excited about the baby.'

'Doesn't he come to the classes with you?'

'Not today.' She smooths a hand over her huge bump.

I feel uneasy again. 'Why did you want to see me?'

Grace opens up a sheet of folded A4 paper lying on the table in front of her and reads the title on the page, *'Feelings and Relationships in Pregnancy and Beyond.'* She looks up. 'This was today's class. It was only for the mums-to-be so we could discuss any concerns without feeling like we couldn't say humbug things about the daddies.' Grace starts reading again. *'Pregnancy brings about big changes to your life, especially if this is your first baby. Some people cope with these changes easily, while others find it harder.'* She looks up as if she's waiting for me to say something.

'Was it useful?' I'm perplexed about where this is going. She said five minutes, and I want to get back to Richard to encourage him to eat something. He's lost his sense of taste and isn't bothered with food but I brought in a pasty Mum made, which he usually loves, and one of the nurses said she'd heat it up for him. Grace rocks backwards and forwards in her chair. 'So far, the classes have been good but today's was not so useful.' I've lost track of our conversation. I focus on her face, trying not to think about Richard.

'You know me.' She smiles. 'My attitude is that stressed is, in fact, desserts spelt backwards - if I'm tense, I turn to cake. I get on with things.' Grace pushes out her cheeks. 'Chocolate is my friend.' She isn't fat, except for her gigantic baby bump, and despite her love of sweet things, Grace is normally stick thin. Bounding around like Zebedee from *The Magic Roundabout* probably burns off all the calories she consumes.

'I thought perhaps your class today triggered something you were concerned about, and that's why you texted me?' I say, pressing my fingers to my mouth and, noticing how sore my bottom lip is where I was unconsciously biting it as Mary and I went through her list of most important things to do. It feels surreal, the dairy being shut and us drawing up a contingency plan.

'That's right,' Grace says. She points to the room she's been in for her class. 'I got all fired up in there,' she says. 'That's why I messaged you – I was supposed to be doing a role play. I got the right evil eye from the woman running the class, I tell you. Made me feel like I was back at school. Here's, the bit,' she says, reading aloud again, '*Pregnancy is a special time for you and your partner, and there may be lots of other people who are interested in your baby, such as your parents, sisters, brothers and friends.* It just made me think of you, Billy, and how wonderful you've been to us, and how excited you are about Tom. I wanted to tell you how much Freddy and I really appreciate it, even if Richard is still down on us all the time.'

For the first time, Grace looks sad, and I wish Richard would be pleased for them. I lean over and touch her belly, like she's let me do a hundred times. 'He'll come round, Grace,' I say, staring into her eyes, trying to look confident, even though I'm not. It's too late for an abortion, but last week I saw my husband give Freddy a pamphlet he'd ordered. '*How to have my baby adopted.*' He didn't even try to hide what he was doing from me. I start to count, trying to put it out of my mind... *one and, two and...*

'There is something we want to ask,' Grace says. 'I left the class early so I could talk to you.' She places her hand on mine.

'Ask,' I say.

She waves her hand in front of her face, 'Sorry, I might cry, but I've been rehearsing it since I decided I had to ask you – so I may be able to hold myself together.' She pauses, looks away and then back at me. 'But I might not. I might cry.'

'Say it.' I'm agitated.

'You might cry too – but I really want to ask you. Please don't be angry with me if I upset you. But I do want to ask...'

I dive into my rucksack and find the envelope containing the hygiene notice and I pass it to Grace, its contents still in it. 'Do you have a pen?' I ask her.

She holds up a biro.

'Write on that.' I point at the envelope still in her hand.

Grace frowns, and I smile back. 'Write your question down, and if I can't answer, I'll screw that stupid document *and* the envelope up. If I'm angry with you, I'll tear them both to shreds, but if I'm crying too much but want to reply, then I'll write my answer under your question. How does that sound?'

I read over her shoulder as she writes. '*Freddy and I want to give Tom a special middle name. We want to call him Tom Ross MarcFenn. Can we?*' As I read Ross, my heart stops. The name I wanted to call my baby, the baby I miscarried: mine and Richard's lost child. Grace passes me the pen, and I'm not crying – yet. I'm happy, but I don't think I can make words come out of my mouth, '*YES,*' I write, in letters so big they reach from the top to the bottom of the envelope. 'Thank you.' I hug her. 'Thank you, thank you…' I can't stop saying it.

'…something else.' Grace is talking into my neck. I can't hear her properly, so I let go, sitting back in my chair. 'Sorry?'

'Last night, William and Lorna Dale came back late from tilling one of our fields. I overheard her ask William about a Range Rover she'd spied parked up inside the gateway at the top of your lane. They were both driving tractors, so Lorna could see over the hedge. She said she thought it was odd, and she didn't recognise the car – but William laughed it off saying it was probably a couple of young farmers seeking a bit of privacy, but now I'm wondering. *Could it have something to do with the dairy being trashed*?

'What colour was the car?' I ask.

She shakes her head 'You'll have to ask Lorna.'

'I will,' I tell her, thinking about Arthur's Range Rover, then dismissing the idea, as there's no reason for him to attack my business. Yes, he doesn't like Mary working at Fox Halt, but he wouldn't go that far. 'Tom Ross MarcFenn,' I say the baby's name slowly to Grace, loving that something wonderful is happening when everything else is falling apart. 'I think your dad would have liked that too.'

Grace's eyes fill up. 'I wish Dad was here,' she says. 'He'd have been the bestest grampy ever.'

'Yes, the *bestest*,' I say, a lump building in my throat.

Grace stares out the window. 'How many tickles does it take to make an octopus laugh?' she asks. She is still looking out when she delivers the punchline. 'Tentickles.' She glances at me. 'I'd better go. Freddy will be waiting.'

I stand up. 'Thank you again. It means such a lot,' I say.

She nods, and I can see how tricky she is finding it to smile, all her rushing around and her zany act, so opposite to William's quietness – but like her brother, she is masking her deep feelings about losing her dad.

A tear runs down my cheek as I watch her and Freddy hold each other tightly, as tightly as her belly allows.

* * *

Richard is no better and no worse – still so weak he can't walk to the bathroom, so it's bedpans and bed baths. He's sitting in the chair beside his bed, as he has for the last three days, making a distinction between day and night in the windowless side room – spending his days in the chair and night time in bed. He wants to get into bed now, and doesn't complain as he struggles to lift himself onto the bed. I tell him Grace's joke as I put the covers over him, hiding how my heart hurts seeing him like this. He smiles. 'I don't mind if you go home. Go and get a good night's rest in our bed,' he says. 'You're exhausted.'

'I wouldn't sleep,' I tell him, pulling the blanket and sheet up so his shoulders are covered. 'Not without you. I'd worry what's happening here.' I'm relieved that the staff turn a blind eye to me sleeping in the chair next to Richard. I'm frightened it's not really allowed so I haven't offered to leave when the official visiting time ends, and so far, no-one's commented about me staying.

Just after six o'clock, Caroline, the nurse Mum sent the moving in card to, strides into the room. 'Morning,' she says brightly. Richard is still asleep, so she walks straight to me, leaning over to whisper, 'They intend moving him to a ward later today.' Ever since a virus was ruled out, I've been expecting Richard to be moved to a ward, but each day he's stayed put. 'Oh, great.' I smile. 'It'll be nice for Richard to have some company.'

Caroline grins, waving a hand around the small room. 'And have some windows to the outside world too.'

Suddenly, I'm anxious. It's been nice having our own private space, I think, more relaxing for Richard, he can be restless without feeling guilty about disturbing neighbouring patients. Also, no irritating ward companions are snoring their heads off all night. Richard opens his eyes, focuses briefly on me and then spews vomit down my arm; he gasps to breathe.

Chapter 28

Billy

In the Intensive Care waiting room, Janette ends her phone call. 'Harry better make it in time,' she warns me, hatred in her eyes. She's convinced that Richard's rapid deterioration must have started last night, and I should have recognised the signs. If I hadn't been so neglectful, Harry would be nearly here now. She avoids looking at me again, staring out the window that looks out onto a tarmacked ancillary area with four skips and a line of wooden sheds. 'Do you have any idea what it's like?' she asks, her eyes now on something I can't see from where I am sitting.

We've been getting up and down every couple of minutes, dancing around each other desperate to hear how Richard is, both banished to the waiting room while the doctors treat him.

'What it's like?' I repeat, keeping my voice level, trying to ease the tension that's been building since they rushed Richard, lying on a trolley, into the emergency department. He was struggling to breathe and the fear in his eyes ripped me apart as I ran next to the porters, trying to reassure him.

Just after this happened, Janette and Sid arrived at his normal ward to find an empty bed - and by the time they walked into this waiting room, Janette was frantic. Last night, we arranged that Janette and Sid would come in to see Richard at eleven, and then I'd head back to Fox Halt - later on, Mum and Franklin would be here, allowing me to be at the farm for a while, knowing Richard wouldn't be alone, but all that changed in a heartbeat when the doctors decided to whisk Richard into Intensive Care.

Sid's putting more parking time on their car. She's phoning Mum and Freddy too, leaving her mum and me alone together for the first time ever. If this was going to happen - I would never have chosen this moment.

We are like two caged animals stalking one another. 'What's what like?' I ask Janette again, not caring but trying to be civil. My mind is full of Richard being sick and unable to breathe at the same time. I think of his terrified eyes.

'Having a daughter and three grandchildren so far away?' Janette clears her throat before she continues, still glaring at me. 'Seeing them just twice a year and missing so much as they grow up.'

My insides cramp. *I can't know what it's like BECAUSE UNLIKE YOU, I COULD NEVER HAVE CHILDREN.* I want to shout, but I say nothing, casting my eyes down to the stained carpet. I squeeze the pressure point on my right hand between my index finger and my thumb – this was something Grandad showed me when I had a tummy ache as a child. It never fails, but I think it's because I always picture his smile and soothing reassurance; 'You'll be right as rain in a mo, maid.'

'...miles away.' Janette is still talking to me.

'Move to New Zealand then,' I say, trying not to snap, still pressing my hand and telling myself to breathe. 'Or come down here to live so you can be near Freddy and Grace. What's stopping you? Exeter University has a great reputation. Martin could get a job there easily.'

'Martin works for the National Film and Television School. There's nothing like that here.' She moves elegantly across the room on her impossibly high heels to sit on the chair next to me, and like a jack-in-the-box, I spring to the window. I'm now transfixed by her small hands and how smooth they are compared to mine, calloused from working with the cows, made larger too by constant manual work. I can't pull my gaze away from her manicured fingernails and the red polish. I'm the polar opposite of this petite and beautiful woman.

The ward sister swings open the door to our room. 'One visitor at a time.' She looks from me to Janette and then back to me. 'Sorry, that's the rule.'

* * *

At first, I don't see Richard. My attention is caught up in the scene laid out before me. It's as if I'm on a Hollywood set for a spaceship – where the passengers and crew are in life-suspending capsules. Richard lies on the futuristic styled bed surrounded by a sea of monitors all constantly beeping and lit up with graphs or numbers. He gazes at his feet which are sticking out from under the bedcover.

'I can't remember,' Richard says to me, pulling his oxygen mask away from his face so I can hear what he's trying to say. 'Billy, I can't keep track.'

'It's alright,' I tell him, stroking his face with the back of my hand, relishing the touch of my skin against his. 'The drugs are making you a bit woozy, that's all.'

'I know it's Friday because it's written up there.' He glances at a whiteboard at the entrance to the room.

'Sweetheart, it's Saturday. Someone's forgotten to change it.' His face feels cold. I straighten the crisp cotton sheet and blanket, so his feet are covered up properly. 'Do you want an extra blanket?' I ask, but there's no response; he's asleep.

As I sit down next to him, a woman walks in. She doesn't even glance at Richard, holding her hand out to me. 'I'm Dr Saluke. I'm the heart specialist looking after your husband,' she says, scraping the plastic chair she has in her other hand along the floor then banging the chair down in front of me.

'Heart?' I say, frowning at her as she sits down heavily, her knees brushing mine.

'Yes, heart.' She is abrupt, as if this is a stupid question.

'My husband has sepsis,' I say, my hands hugging the back of my head. It feels like it might explode, and I'm holding my skull together.

'Which is seated on his heart valves. They are being eaten away, and at a later stage, we'll have to perform an operation to repair the dama—' She stops, and my eyes dart to Richard, who's suddenly restless. A bleeper fires off, and in less than a second, a nurse and the doctor are trying to calm him as he flails his hands around his face, knocking the oxygen mask. He's wheezing like he did this morning.

'Pain!' Richard cries out. 'Too much.' He starts to cough.

'It's okay.' I stroke his wrist, which I have caught in both my hands. 'They'll find you something to stop it.'

His eyes are wide as the nurse encourages him to breathe slowly and deeply. He swipes the mask away with his other hand and sputters something at me, which I can just make out. 'I want to die, Billy, sorry…love —'

The doctor lifts the mask back into the correct position, talking to him softly. 'Some people feel like they want to keep fighting, and others just want to be comfortable and let things happen as they may. You don't have to keep fighting,' she says.

Her words cut into my skin like a dagger, taking me a second to realise I've been stabbed. 'You can't say that!' I shriek. 'You're his doctor; you ALWAYS have to help your patients. Never—' I breathe in hard, trying to resist the temptation to shove her out the room. 'You can NEVER do anything that can't help - you telling Richard he can give up if he wants to is *not* helping him. He needs to stay positive. He can't give up!'

Dr Saluke shrugs at me. 'I'll sort out some more morphine that will *help* with the pain.' She emphasises the word help. 'Your husband is very ill, and I promise I'll do everything possible to make him better, but he needs to want to fight this himself too.'

I stand up, and this time it's me invading her personal space. My face is far too close to hers, but I need her to listen. I stare into her dark brown eyes, not blinking. 'Tell Richard he can get through this, tell him that the antibiotics are working and loads of people have damaged heart valves repaired. Hope, Dr Saluke, give him hope.'

Chapter 29

Billy

In front of the hospital's main reception desk, Harry and Sid hug each other, oblivious to me and everyone else. The pair are identical twins, not completely alike because Sid is heavier than Harry, and where Sid's blonde wavy hair reaches to the middle of her back, Harry's is cut into a precise bob which has been neatly feathered, giving an air of sophistication.

'I'll take you up.' Sid grabs her sister's hand, which Harry extends to her in the same split second. I walk away to head back to Fox Halt, deciding I'll say hello to Harry later.

* * *

Mum stands by my van as I get out. 'I've made you some breakfast,' she says, waving to the open door of the farmhouse.

'That's kind,' I say, 'but, sorry, I haven't got time.'

'He won't be here until mid-day, you've got twenty minutes, and Mary has it all sorted. You *do* have time, and you need something proper to eat.'

Mum is not going to take *no* for an answer, so I gather up my things and follow her to the house. She talks all the way to the front door. 'Did the specialist really tell Richard he didn't have to fight on?' Mum frowns. 'She can't have said that.'

'That's exactly what she said. It's so PC, isn't it? And so negative. Richard hooked up to all those amazing machines with his own dedicated nurse and everyone else doing all they can to keep him alive, and she says he can die if he wants to.'

'Terrible.' She stops, her eyes on mine, waiting for me to say something else, but I'm quiet, craving a little peace just for a moment. Mum visited Richard yesterday, seeing for herself what it's like for him now. He has his own space again but not a peaceful side-ward, the new Intensive Care room is full of machines, screens and beeping, *always beeping*… Every second, another beep confirming he's still breathing.

Mum continues to wait for me to say something.

'Terrible,' I repeat, hoping my tone conveys that I don't want to discuss this. My eyes well up, remembering the woman's shocking words and my terror that Richard would give up, tired of the pain and the battle to breathe – both his body and his mind sapped of any will to go on.

'He's fighting,' Mum says, picking up on my worry. 'He won't let the sepsis beat him. You have to believe that.'

I sit down at the kitchen table but everything around me feels blurry and unreal. 'I believe the extra oxygen is forcing fluid away from his lungs,' I tell Mum. 'And it helps to prevent the fear when he's struggling to breathe. I know he's *not* being, or even feeling sick anymore – but I'm *not* sure how much more he can take. This is wiping him out.' I pick up a slice of toast which Mum has buttered and coated with my favourite honey, but as I bite into it, I'm unaware of any taste. My brain is on repeat, going over and over the doctor's words about Richard's right to choose to die.

Last night Dr Saluke was cruel again, insisting I had to go home to sleep in my own bed. 'We truly believe he'll make the night,' she said. 'There's nothing you can do here. Get some rest, and we'll ring you if your husband's status changes at all.' She made it crystal clear I couldn't stay.

I was desperate to get back this morning, but visitors aren't permitted in the Intensive Care unit until after eleven when the doctors have finished their rounds. I was allowed to ring for an update before then, but that was all. It feels like my world has stopped.

'What about the pains in his stomach?' Mum asks.

'Better,' I say. 'I wish I could stay overnight…' My voice trails off as I spy a smart Range Rover arriving in the yard, and I continue to watch from the kitchen window as Arthur steps out of it.

'He's here,' I tell Mum, but she's disappeared. I feel my chest tighten, knowing I'm going to have to face him. I spoke to Lorna about the car she'd seen, and it did sound like Arthur's. After that, Mary and I pieced together a scenario where Arthur might have been the felon who attacked the dairy. I said how Arthur could have managed to let himself into the dairy by noting the door code when he stood behind me, waiting to be let in to see his sister. Later, Mary checked with her local garage who told her that her flat tyre had been let down. It wasn't punctured, and she said her brother had an opportunity to let the air out while her car was parked at Culmfield that night. He'd come back late to the house, saying he needed Jessie's signature on a document for the morning. Apologising profusely that he'd been so disorganised, not realising she had to sign it too.

Mary decided Arthur flattened her tyre so she'd be late for work in the morning, giving her no time to clean up before the authorities arrived to investigate the alleged filth. We may have put two and two together to make five, but it feels plausible, and Arthur's already made it clear he's set against Mary being at Fox Halt. Although, I can't believe he'd go to such extremes.

Mum's already convinced he's to blame – she found places all over poor Betsy and Bramble where someone yanked at their fur, and it took four of us, Mum, Mary, Grace and me, forty minutes and probably forty treats and forty cuddles, to coax the goats into letting us take some decent photos of their bald spots for the police. 'If I get hold of him,' Mum said.' I'll wrench out his beard one hair at a time, then his eyebrows – and after that, the hairs in his nostrils.' Every time she sees the goats, she spends half an hour smoothing their coats and telling them new tortures she has planned for Arthur.

Mary is sure too and she has forced her brother to come here today, threatening that if he didn't apologise to me, she'd have him arrested. She warned him she has plenty of evidence, and there will be a minimum of six months in prison for the criminal damage he'd caused or even longer when the court considered the massive financial loss and his cruelty to animals – it might be ten years.

I imagine that this wasn't a calm exchange between brother and sister. I've seen Mary's temper before. I suspect there was much gnashing of her perfect white teeth when she insisted he had to say sorry *and* come up with a plan to physically put things right. He has to show me that he truly regrets being so stupid and reckless or we will discuss our suspicions with the police.

I step outside, still doubting Arthur is the real culprit. I've a niggling suspicion about Troy Gloon – he's gaining business now the dairy is shut down, our reputation in tatters, and he did threaten me, saying I would regret buying Andrew's kit.

As I approach the dairy, my face heats up with embarrassment. It might be anger, though, because if it was Arthur then I'm about to speak to the person who has closed us down in such a humiliating and horrible way.

I catch up with Mary at the entrance to the processing area. She's insisting that Arthur puts on a white coat before he enters the processing area. 'That won't fit me, I'm too big,' he protests, pushing it away.

Mary thrusts the coat back at him, swiping him across the face with a sleeve. 'We keep extra-large ones for visitors who need them. Take off your suit jacket – then it'll definitely fit. Don't worry about the wellies.'

I frown, wondering why she's already made him put on a hairnet, beard net and gloves when nothing has been cleaned up yet. The police have completed all their forensic work so there's no need to worry about spoiling any evidence. As they move on, I slip on a coat too, only because I'm glad of a delay.

In the area where we make the cheese, I see three of the office chairs set up in a triangle pattern. Arthur and Mary have already sat down, and Arthur has his back to me. As Mary sees me, she stands up. 'I've forgotten something. I'll be back in a moment,' she says.

Arthur doesn't swivel around to face me, even though he must know I'm here. His belligerence proves to me we've made a mistake – he's angry about being forced here when he's done nothing wrong. But now I reconsider. *Is he feeling so guilty, he's unable to face me?*

I grab the back of one of the empty chairs to steady myself, and I stare at the back of Arthur's head. At that moment, I decide to work on the basis of *guilty until proven innocent*. 'Do you have any idea what you've done?' I ask, stepping around him to sit down.

He pulls up one side of his mouth, seeming to sneer.

'Do you?' I ask again, happy with my ambiguous opening gambit.

'I hope so,' he replies, folding his arms and moving so that he's more upright in his chair.

'You hope so?' I repeat, frowning hard, flummoxed by his stance and his confidence.

'Yes,' he says. I stare at him. Arthur doesn't say anything

else, and it feels like neither of us wants to make the next move.

This seems to be a game I've started without knowing the rules, not even checking out my opponent first, and we're still silent when Mary returns. I look around the room then back at Arthur. 'Are you planning to help clear this mess up? Are you sorry?' I glare at him, but he doesn't even blink.

Mary scowls at Arthur too. 'You told me you were sorry. You said this was a moment of madness, and you didn't consider the consequences. Apologise to Auntie and explain how you intend to help us get over this.' Mary's voice grows louder and more menacing with each word. 'Or I'll give your infantile name to the police,' she warns.

Arthur doesn't reply. His face is expressionless so Mary goes on, talking through gritted teeth. 'If the police work out it was you, but Auntie Billy believes you are sorry, she'll ask them not to prosecute you – *but* you must convince her that you truly regret being so stupid.' I watch open-mouthed as Arthur shakes his head and grins at his sister.

I stay quiet, allowing him ample opportunity to say he's sorry for what he has done. I think now he *is* guilty, but part of me still isn't sure – his attitude is so odd. If he did sabotage the dairy, I wonder if he couldn't have appreciated the scale of the damage he'd cause, destroying the business for months. I'm too tired to think of a candid remark to help initiate an apology, so we all now sit staring at each other. Nobody is speaking.

At last, Arthur looks directly at me. 'You don't get it, do you?' He unfolds his arms and starts to click his thumbnails together. He turns away to focus on the floor. The rhythmic clicking of his thumbnails is hardly audible at first, but as it continues, still without eye contact, I feel myself getting hotter. I wipe the sweat on the palm of my hands onto my jeans. Mary shakes her head. She must be as confused by his behaviour as I am. *Click… click… click…*

The aggravating noise suddenly stops, and Arthur lifts his head. He stares at me again. 'Why buy local?' he hisses, leaning towards me, so far forward it feels intimidating. 'Rather a poor appraisal of your precious little shop, wasn't it? That was just the beginning, you know?'

'What do you mean?' I lean back to get away from him.

'The damning article in the local rag, I arranged that.'

I jump up so fast that my chair is forced backwards, crashing to the floor. 'You got Marian to put that spin on it?'

'Not your *local* ice-cream, only high-end customers, the crap photo?' His smile suddenly reaches his eyes. I can't reconcile the man in front of me with the child I spent hours with when he was small - the boy who liked to cook and play with the ponies. I changed his nappies, held him when he was scared, and I read his favourite *Thomas the Tank Engine* book to him night after night until he fell asleep. I want to check Mary's reaction to this confession, but I can't tear my eyes away from his snarling lips as he continues. 'Amazing what changes can be made when O'Rowdes' want a whole page advert every week for a couple of months.'

'Our customers finding new suppliers, are you behind that too?' Mary's on her feet, hurdling my fallen chair to stand next to me. It's like she's caught fire.

'One of O'Rowdes' local subsidia—' He doesn't finish because Mary throws an elbow across his face, catching him hard on the nose. 'You jerk, how dare you?' she growls.

He wipes his fingers under his nostrils and inspects them to see if there is any blood. I see Mary's disappointment when there isn't any. As she makes to slap him hard on the cheek, Arthur seizes her arm.

'Let go!' She pulls hard against him.

'Calm down, Mary. This isn't about you,' he tells her.

'Wha—'

Arthur doesn't let Mary finish, nor does he release her arm, which she frantically tries to free. 'I'll let you go,' he says, 'but only if you promise not to clout me again.'

'I'll cuff your eyes out - what you've done turns my frickin' stomach.' Mary moves her head until her nose almost touches his. 'You are *not* my brother, not anymore!'

Arthur looks at me. 'I contacted the planners too. I *will* finish you and this place for good. Watch your back, Billy May.'

I turn away, reaching for the fire extinguisher hung on the wall. I rip it down, my hand on the lever to fire it. 'Let her go.' I aim the nozzle at his neck. Suddenly, he loosens his hold on his sister and stands up. He's a foot taller than Mary and me, and he's out of the door before either of us can think to stop him. I shout after him. 'Stop!'

Chapter 30

Billy

When Arthur slams the outside door, Mary turns to me. 'Give me your phone.' She sounds so certain, I quickly dig my mobile out of my pocket. 'Here,' I say, passing it to her.

Outside, Arthur throws his suit jacket into his car before he jumps in too. Mary is in front of me, striding purposefully, but she isn't rushing. His driver's door makes a solid closing sound, and we both see Arthur fiddling with his key fob and his frustration when his car doesn't fire up.

With Arthur not getting away, Mary and I reach the car, and I watch as Mary opens the back door. 'Get in the front, Auntie. He's going nowhere.'

Blindly, I do as she commands.

'Your car won't start?' Mary asks Arthur, her tone innocent like she hasn't seen him smacking his fists on the steering wheel. I look round at her as she does up her seat belt in an easy everyday movement as if she expects her brother to chauffeur us somewhere. 'Annoying, isn't it?' she says to him, 'Pretty annoying for me too, discovering I had a flat tyre at six o'clock in the morning, and it was bloody peeing down.'

I copy Mary, pulling my seat belt across me too, no rationality in my action, too livid to think for myself. I speak to Arthur's cheek as he tries again to start the car. 'Why did—'

Mary interrupts. 'I want to get this right, Arthur,' she says. 'You deliberately smeared shit and hair over the dairy.'

Arthur ignores her. Mary leans forward, 'You weren't mad at me for managing the dairy. You planned to ruin Fox Halt Farm?'

'What have you done, Mary? Why won't my car start?' He looks daggers at her reflection in the rear-view mirror.

'I fished your car keys out of your jacket when you started talking to Auntie. I disconnected a cable in the ECU, not that you'll know what that is or how to connect it up again.'

'Why would you do that?' he asks.

'Why would you want to destroy the farm? The ECU was because I thought you might possibly want to get away before we'd finished talking to you – actually, it does feel good giving you a taste of your own medicine.'

'Get out.' Arthur undoes my belt. 'Both of you.'

'Tell me why, Arthur?' I say, pushing all my weight into the white leather seat in case he tries shoving me out.

'To ruin *you,* not the farm. You will pay for what you did. You wrecked my life.'

'My affair with your dad, is that what this is about?'

'Murdering him, that's what. You killed Dad, even if the police haven't got enough evidence to prove it, I know it was *you.*' Saliva shoots out of his mouth as he says *you.*

'It wasn't Auntie,' Mary says, lifting her phone as if she's about to text someone.

'You covered my dairy in filth to revenge your father's death? You believe I killed him?' I say, feeling hollow; everything Arthur's done is because of a misunderstanding from a boy who lost his dad. His loss and rage growing day on day, his rage focused on me.

'I want Dad here, not you,' Arthur shouts into my face.

'Your father was evil,' I tell him, turning my body to face him with my back pressed against the door. I keep my voice as calm as I can. 'Surely you remember how he controlled your mum. It was your father who wrecked lives, not me. Believe me, you are far better off without him.'

'So, you admit it, you kill—'

'I did *not* kill your father. I'm glad he's gone though.'

'Mary, get this car started. I need to go.' Arthur leans over his seat, reaching into the back, grabbing his sister by her shoulder and shaking her. Mary's coat's too big for her skinny frame, so he's only gripping the material, but it must hurt.

'I will,' she replies, her eyes filled with loathing, 'but only because I don't want you here for another nanosecond. Arthur, you're wrong, so darn wrong. It's not true. It wasn't Auntie.' Mary unbuttons her coat and wriggles out of his clutches. 'As soon as you're gone, I'm phoning the police.'

He pushes her back against the seat. 'Go ahead – you haven't got a scrap of proof, just like her when she killed Dad.'

He nods his head towards me. 'I've been *very* careful.'

'Release the bonnet,' Mary yells at him. 'If you even know how to.' Mary kicks her door open. 'Auntie, come on.'

I hesitate, unsure of what to do. I wonder if I should tell him who really killed his father.

'Auntie.' Mary is determined there is nothing more to say. She wants me out of the car.

I decide telling him how his dad died will only cause more grief, and his memory of his father will be completely destroyed, discovering how his father raped Nala. I climb out of the car, pausing to look at Mary, who's fiddling low down in the Range Rover's engine. She looks up. 'Call the police?' she says, digging in her pocket to give me back my phone. 'Okay,' I say as I walk back to the dairy. In the office, I put my head in my hands, listening as the Range Rover revs up, pressing my fingers into my hair until I hear Arthur drive away.

* * *

Mary massages my shoulders. 'That's nice,' I say, appreciating the tension in my neck being squeezed away.

She stops rubbing. 'He knows my feelings towards Fox Halt. I love this place,' Mary says, sitting down on the desk beside me. I even discussed with him what I should do to stop more customers cancelling their orders.' She pauses. 'Oh shit!' She slaps her hand on the edge of the desk.

I jump. 'What?'

'I gave him the letter to Devon County Show. It was in my car when I got to Richmond, I'd forgotten to post it, so I asked him to do it for me. He said he'd sent it. He's lied about that too.' Mary smacks the desk again, this time with her hands in fists. 'What did the police say, Auntie?'

'I haven't rung them,' I say.

'You haven't?' She frowns.

I shake my head. 'I was getting my thoughts together. What will your mum say if I get Arthur arrested?'

'You haven't got a choice. He'll keep persecuting you.'

'What about telling him it was Amir who killed your dad, that Sharmarke is his stepbrother, about the rape and the threats your dad made to stop the truth coming out?'

'No.' She gets out her phone, enters her key code and holds it out to me. 'Call them.'

'Mary, this is a big deal, consider your mum. How will she feel about her eldest son in court? Her child in jail?'

'What about Fox Halt Farm, you, me? Think about what he'll do next if you don't,' she says.

'This will affect O'Rowdes' too. If I make the call, the press will be onto it right away – the bigshot supermarket boss at war with a lowly farm shop owner, what a David and Goliath story that is going to be, they'll have a field day.'

'Mum doesn't care about O'Rowdes'. She's only hung on to it for Arthur. He's brought this on himself.'

'I *will* call them, but I have to speak to Jessie first,' I say, resting her mobile on the palm of my hand for her to take back.

She ignores it. 'When will you speak to her?' she asks.

I balance my phone next to hers. 'Right after you've checked these to see if we have a decent recording of what he said in the car.'

She scoops the phones up and smiles. 'Between these two, there has to be something the Crown Prosecution Service can use. My brother is heading for prison, there is absolutely no doubt about it.'

Chapter 31

Billy

In the kitchen, Mum looks up as I tell Mary. 'In one respect, he's done us a favour.'

'It went alright, then?' Mum interrupts.

'What do you mean?' I frown at her.

'Arthur is going to help to put everything right. You were discussing favours?' Mum picks up a cooking timer and sets it for the pie she's just slid in the oven.

I look at Mary then back at Mum. 'The only favour he did us was losing Devon County Show. It was down to him we haven't got our stand next month, but since we won't have anything to sell, it won't matter, will it?'

'Arthur affected your booking, how?' She frowns.

'Can I explain later, Mum?' I say, reaching for the kettle, 'I want a cup of tea.'

Mum steps out of my way and nods at me. 'I rang the ICU,' she says, and suddenly, the frantic ticking from the timer matches my racing heart.

'Is Richard okay?'

'Yes. Polly said he's having a CT scan tomorrow.'

'What for?' I try to picture a nurse called Polly. *Maybe she's one of the doctors?* Mum probably knows all their names, shift patterns and most likely, their life histories too.

'I didn't ask,' Mum says. 'Don't you know?'

'No,' I snap, immediately feeling guilty for being short with her. 'Sorry, I don't know,' I say more softly, 'But I think I should get back there as soon as I've drunk my tea.'

'Can I come too?' she asks. 'I want to take Richard in some Battenberg cake. Janette said he's no appetite. It might tempt him.' Instantly, I'm annoyed that Janette is discussing

Richard's lack of interest in food with my mother.

I inhale deeply, telling myself to let it go. It doesn't matter, Janette is only trying to help. 'You can come, but I'm paying for a taxi to get you home again later,' I say. 'Do you mind a taxi, Mum?' I ask – Jessie's been in so many times, often going miles out of her way to take Mum home. I don't feel I can ask her to help again.

'Taxi's fine.' Mum wraps her arm around my shoulder, and I press my face into her neck. Her familiar smell and the gentle rise and fall of her chest, making me feel safe.

'I'm heading outside again,' Mary says. 'I need to start clearing up. Sid's going to help me later, which is good.'

I step away from Mum. 'I expect she'll rope Harry in too,' I say.

'Auntie, what about the case?' Mary is frowning at me.

'Case?' I ask, thinking of the small suitcase Harry abandoned in the middle of the hospital foyer as soon as she caught sight of her sister.

'Yes, case. The one we have to present to the magistrate's court to prove we should be allowed to start up again.'

'We'll talk about that tomorrow,' I say.

'There *is* a deadline—'

'We can discuss it first thing,' I say firmly.

'And what's happening with the ice-cream factory?' she asks. All I can think about is the scan and what it's for. Worry seeps up from my toes to my throat, making me swallow hard. I try not to be tetchy. 'Tomorrow,' I say again. 'Is that okay?'

Chapter 32

Billy

The nurse opens the pass door into Intensive Care apologising for the delay, explaining that they were dealing with a patient who'd just been admitted. Immediately I feel guilty that I was frustrated before, being kept apart from Richard for so long, and my perspective changes, thinking about another family, holding their breath over the fate of someone they love.

'Are you alright?' Mum asks me as I stand by the reception desk. She has her hand out, ready to press the door handle of the waiting room.

'Definitely,' I tell her. 'It's good to be here to have some respite from the reporters and those damn camera journalists.'

Mum nods. 'I didn't expect them to turn up so soon, it seemed like one second the police were ringing you to tell you they were interviewing Arthur, and the next, there was a pack of press people waiting outside the house. How did they know, and how did they get to Fox Halt so quickly?'

'Mum, I'll go and see Richard. Will you be okay in there?' I nod towards the waiting room.

My mother smiles, '*No comment,*' – and I laugh, thinking that's what we've all been telling the reporters. It's exhausting and intimidating the way they don't want to accept this answer. The only thing I did say was that they had to stay away from Hols and the cows, and I'll sue each and every one of them if any of our animals are upset.

I let them park in the yard because the lanes were blocked with their abandoned vehicles. No-one could get through. It's chaos. I hope they'll give up and leave us alone soon. I insisted Mum came to the hospital with me to get her away from them too. One of Mum's friends will take her home later. Jessie is besieged as well.

Jessie says she's managed to keep them behind the

massive wrought iron gates at the entrance to Culmfield. But it's bringing back bad memories for her of the days and weeks after Michael died when there was always someone desperate for an interview, a soundbite or a long-lensed photograph. Her youngest son, Max, was only eight then; he's sixteen now, and he is refusing to come out of his room, let alone go to school.

She promised to come in here this evening, the first time I've seen her since she told me I *had* to call the police. Jessie was vehement. 'Billy, if you don't, then I sure as hell will.' Her words keep ringing in my ears. She was fuming.

'Here,' Mum says, holding out a Tupperware container to the nurse who's about to escort me to see Richard. 'I made you all chocolate cookies with a few plain ones for Dr Marsh.' Mum rattles the box. 'And there is the recipe in there for Stacey; a special fruit cake I told her about.'

* * *

Each time I see Richard encircled by the seemingly interplanetary apparatus, I hope against hope that he'll be sitting in a chair rather than lying in bed. He's so much more like himself sitting up, more animated and alive. Today, I'm only half disappointed because although he's still in bed, he's propped up on three pillows. His face lights up as he sees me. 'I'm starving,' he says, and then he smiles at me. 'I couldn't have anything for the three hours before the scan, they said, food would make me feel sick – and the dye they used left a horrible metallic taste in my mouth.' He licks his lips and grimaces.

I'm so happy to hear him want to eat. This is also the most I've heard him say in days. My insides jump with optimism – he must be turning a corner. On the other hand, this is the second scan he's had in two days, and I'm worried about what the medical staff are looking for.

'I made you a sandwich, Richard.' His designated nurse steps quietly into the room holding out a plate; 'with extra cheese, hopefully it'll get rid of that nasty taste.' She leaves the food on his side table before slinking away again.

'Mum's in the waiting room with more cake for you,' I say, kissing him lightly on his lips. 'Do you want me to swap with her? Would you prefer a slice of cake to the sandwich?'

Richard holds out his hands to me, and I notice he keeps them raised above the bed covers. He must be stronger.

'It was so lovely to see Harry this morning—' He stops and frowns. 'It was this morning. She was here, wasn't it?'

'Yesterday afternoon,' I say, my elation waning because he seems confused again. 'Do you want me to get Mum so you can have cake instead?' I point at the sandwich. 'I'll have to sit in the waiting area while she sees you though, you can only have one visitor at a time. I'll be down the corridor, so I'll come straight back when she goes.' I can't gauge his lucidity, and I'm trying to avoid him being upset if I disappear.

'Darling, stay, please,' he says. 'Come here.'

I lean over to kiss him again, wrapping my hands around his neck, avoiding the pipe going into his nostrils - his full oxygen mask has been replaced since last night by the small tube feeding air into his nose. This has to be progress.

'Will Daniella come tomorrow?' he asks.

'She's here now, in the waiting area. I'll swap with her in a bit.' I collapse into the chair beside his bed, wishing this rollercoaster ride had an exit. I want to step off for a while - one minute noticing signs of improvement, thinking the drugs are beating the sepsis, the next deflated with the realisation he's still poorly and confused. Fear. Hope. Fear - *let me get off.*

Richard picks up the sandwich. 'Maybe only eat half of it,' I say gently. 'Mum will come and see you in a moment. She made a fresh Battenberg this—' *Beep Beep!* The alarm on the machine recording oxygen levels sounds loudly, and the sandwich falls from Richard's hand onto the blanket. His nurse is suddenly replacing the full oxygen mask. 'Please, go back to the waiting room,' she tells me. 'I'll come and fetch you when the stats have levelled off again.' She strokes Richard's hand in the way I want to.

'Is this bad?' I ask her.

'Maybe he forgot to breathe. Did he become excited? It's not what we were expecting. Richard's sepsis is getting better. We thought he was on his way out of here.' She waves her hand. 'Not out of here, *dead,* I didn't mean that!' She stumbles over her words. 'I meant back to the ward. Not now, though.'

'Another night in here, then?' I check, throwing my rucksack over my shoulder.

She nods, still holding Richard's hand. 'Seeing his daughter from New Zealand and the scans may have been too much. You and Daniella go. Get a coffee or maybe take a walk outside, it's a beautiful day; let him settle a bit.'

* * *

A little girl runs up to a beautiful Shetland sheepdog sitting by Mum's legs, and as I sit beside my mother, I watch the child pat the dog's silky head. 'Goggy,' she says and then she shuffles backwards, to stand stock still, gazing at the animal. The dog wags its tail hoping for another pat, but the girl doesn't move, her rosebud lips set in a thoughtful line as she continues to stare at the wagging dog.

The Sheltie's owner is on the other side of Mum, but it's Mum, not its owner, who reaches forward to stroke the dog. 'Nice doggy,' Mum says, her eyes on the enthralled child.

'Goggy.' The girl points.

'He's called Pippin.' The dog's owner speaks now, her voice gentle. 'He won't hurt you.'

Straight away, the child leaps towards the dog, embracing it in a tight hug. She rubs his head. 'Pippin, goggy, nice goggy,' she says into its neck as her parents suddenly appear, and I realise they are a couple whose daughter is in Intensive Care too. We spoke briefly in the waiting room yesterday. 'Is Jazmin improving?' I ask, hoping like mad they'll say yes.

'Another day, and she'll be back on Bramble Ward,' her dad says, kneeling next to the girl, and stroking the dog, too.

'Same with my husband,' I say quickly, in case they are too frightened to ask. 'Not the children's ward, back on a heart ward, the sepsis is seated on one of his heart valves.'

The little girl stares at Mum. 'We're getting goggy. I will call it Charlie, like Charlie in the Chocolate Factory.'

'We said we might get one, Bess,' her father corrects her, 'but because Jazzy's poorly at the moment, we have to be careful. A dog might make the house too dirty for her, and she could get ill again if everything isn't clean.'

'Wash hands,' Bess says, holding her hands up at her father. 'Wash hands before we see Jazz. We go see her now?'

* * *

Mum sighs. 'What a lovely family, such a shame,' she says.

I nod, watching Bess and her parents catch hold of each other's hands and walk towards the hospital entrance.

'Come on, Mum,' I say. 'I want to check Richard's okay.'

'One minute, Billy.'

'What?' I ask, noticing Pippin has his jaw pressed down on her lap. His eyes are on hers.

'The Jerseys.'

'I'm not discussing them—' I pull my feet in to get up. 'They're not my priority anymore. If you're set against them, I'll sell them, and we'll forget they were ever at Fox Halt.'

'But—'

'What?' I ask again, now feeling cross.

'Nothing,' she says. 'Come on, let's go.'

I feel sorry for being snappy. I'm tired and worried, and I'm taking it out on the nearest person. 'Mum, tell me,' I say, touching her hand.

'You can't kiss the hare's foot,' she says, and I stare back at her. I remember Grandad using this expression if I came in late for a meal, a saying like his dialect words that I grew up with, never asking what they meant, deciding on their meaning from the context of the sentences and the situations when he used them. I smile at Mum and nod. 'Grandad used to say that,' I say. It was something to do with being late or missing out on something because the moment was lost. Well, that's what I think he meant.'

Mum looks younger and, for a moment, the years fall away from her face. 'Yes, Dad did love that phrase. It's true, though.'

'A hare's footprint, that's all you'll kiss, if you try and kiss a hare's paw – the hare will have always raced away by the time you lean down. Darling, don't miss out, trying to grasp for something out of reach.'

I force another smile, unsure what's she's trying to tell me. Too tired to try to work it out.

Chapter 33

Billy

I study Jessie as she leaps out of the minibus, looking for any signs of weariness from the press intruding into her life. It's two weeks since I've seen her and she seems her usual lively self, bounding to the side door of the vehicle and opening it.

'Hello,' she says to me as I approach her, hanging on tightly to Betsy's and Bramble's collars. My wrists hurt. I've had the goats ready for Jessie to take with her for the last ten minutes, and they've been running circles around me, impatient to be doing something more interesting than standing waiting in the yard. Jessie walks up to Betsy first, bending down to look into her eyes before she speaks directly to the goat. Her voice is strict. 'I have to get the minibus clean again later. So, Betsy, keep the mess to a minimum, please.'

Betsy has a homemade nappy on, and as Jessie takes her lead, I offer up a prayer that the little goat will be good for the forty-minute drive to Culmfield. 'We'll put this monkey in first,' I say, lifting the much smaller Bramble into my arms and manoeuvring her so her front hooves are in the bus while her back ones rest on the footplate. One of Jessie's volunteers is already on the bus, and she grabs her lead.

In less than a second, Bramble is standing quietly at the back of the minibus, flanked by two helpers giving her lots of fuss as they stroke her sleek, smooth coat.

'Quick, we must get Betsy in before they get upset about being parted,' I say, but in that same moment Betsy kicks out her front legs and escapes, darting around to the driver's door.

'She wants to drive.' Jessie laughs.

'Probably, better than having you driving,' a volunteer calls out, making everyone laugh, including Jessie.

'Come on, Betsy.' I hold out a bucket of food. The goat snorts, dodges past me, and jumps straight into the bus, charging down the aisle to reach her friend.

As Jessie starts the engine, she winds down her window to speak to me. 'We're going to Bellever tomorrow,' she says, 'For a walk and afterwards, we're having lunch at Postbridge. Come to Bellever, Billy. Meet us at nine-thirty? There's something I need to discuss with you. Stay half an hour, that's all. It'll do you good to have a change of scene.'

I can't think about tomorrow, I'm living day to day, but I know it must be something important, so I quickly agree. 'Okay, I'll be there,' I say. 'And good luck with today.'

* * *

The courtyard gardens inside the curtilage of the hospital are maintained by a community group, and I'm so grateful to these volunteers because the open spaces they've created feel like the wards' lungs, like a place to breathe. We are in Richard's favourite garden and now that he is out of Intensive Care and staying on a ward, I wheel him here for an hour every day. 'They are like toy soldiers,' Richard says, pointing to two scarlet tulips standing tall next to his wheelchair. I smile even though he can't see my face whilst I push him.

We reach our special seat which has the kind of roof over it that you see on cutesy wishing wells – it might be over-quaint, but the roof means we can be out here even when it's raining, and in truth, I like it best when it's wet because it feels like a sanctuary, a tiny bit of private space. 'I have something to show you when we get back to the ward,' Richard says, lifting himself from the wheelchair onto the wooden seat. 'I think you'll be impressed.'

'What is it?' I ask, as I sit down next to him.

He hooks his little finger into mine. 'You'll see,' he says.

* * *

Derek and Garry, in the beds next to Richard, cheer as he completes his walk with a Zimmer-frame from his pillow around his bed and back to his pillow. I clap too, proud of the massive effort it took for Richard not to take a breather.

'See, Janette said you'd be able to do it again this afternoon,' Derek laughs. His words deflate me. I thought my encouragement the last few days when Richard felt he couldn't make it any further than the end of the bed had paid off. I was chuffed that we'd cracked this together.

I'm upset that Janette's been involved and what's more, that she witnessed Richard succeed before I did. This hang-up with Janette is silly and unfounded jealousy on my part, but I'm niggled because she's still at Fox Halt when Franklin has returned to Amersham, and the twins are staying in Sid's flat in Brighton. Richard is on the mend but Janette makes no indication she is thinking of leaving too. Mum keeps Franklin informed of his son's progress, while Janette talks to *'her'* girls each evening, filling them in too – and each evening I get home hoping Janette will have become fed up with our uneasy stand-off and have decided to leave as well.

I hope she'll take offence when I'm slightly too near the mark with a comment about her being a townie, unsuited for living on a farm, but each night when I get back from the hospital she'll be in the sitting room with Mum. They will be enjoying a television programme together, or Mum will be knitting something for the baby while Janette has her head in a novel. Crinkle is a traitor too – wherever Janette is, she is.

The doctors say the fluid is clearing from Richard's lungs, but they also tell us that once the sepsis is fully under control, he'll need a heart operation to replace the damaged valve, and this will probably be in a month's time.

As the weeks in hospital increases, Richard's belief that he will ever fully recover reduces. He's sleeping quite well, and as long as we supplement the hospital dishes with a few little extras, like Mum's pies, he's eating better. He is a couple of pounds under his normal weight now. He jokes with everyone, but underneath, I know he's desperate to be home. It feels like hurdle after hurdle, and when I think I see the finishing line, another obstacle is added – and the end line vanishes again. I don't know what I'd do without him, and the idea of a heart op terrifies me.

* * *

It's nine o'clock, and I'm about to leave. I kiss Richard good night. A kiss I never want to end. It's soft and lingering, not passionate. It's an *I will always love you* kiss.

'How's it all going?' he asks as I reach the end of Derek's bed, heading towards the exit.

'There's an inspection of the dairy tomorrow, and Environmental Health should approve everything,' I reply, wondering if I should go back and sit next to him to have a proper conversation. I don't think the nurses will mind if I'm here ten minutes after visiting time. I decide no, he's tired.

'How is Hols?' he asks, and now I'm curious why he didn't ask me all this earlier. I start to walk back, pulling my phone out of my pocket to show him a new app which Hols loaded onto it this morning. This new program should help us keep better track of the feed each cow requires.

Oddly, Richard doesn't seem interested, and I stare at him, wondering what this is all about. He normally insists I leave dead on nine. 'What's wrong?' I ask.

'I want to know about the ice-cream factory,' he says, sounding like he's genuinely keen to find out.

I shrug. 'Okay,' I say, putting my phone back into my pocket and looking at the clock, hoping he'll take the cue that it's getting late.

'Tell me,' he says as he sits up a little in the bed. I immediately make the pillows comfortable when he scrunches them up.

'I've done nothing since you came in he—' I stop because I am thinking how I fear he might die and therefore the factory means nothing to me anymore. Nothing matters except him getting well, but that would sound like I'm terrified of him dying - which I am - but I don't want him to know that.

'You have to get on with it, Billy,' he says. 'Don't let go of your dreams because I'm in here.'

'It's not my dream, not now,' I say. 'I want to get in that lovely motorhome parked up in the yard, reminding me that you're not there to drive it. I want us to get in it and just keep motoring.' My throat chokes up. 'Anywhere, Rich, as long as we're together.'

'That's not fair,' he says, throwing himself back on his pillows and looking up at the ceiling.

'What isn't?'

He continues to look up, trying to hide his eyes which I can see are welling up. 'You can't agree with what I want because I may die. We can't live like that.'

I lean over him. 'You're not going to die,' I say, my hand pressing lightly on his shoulder.

'No, I'm not.' He smiles, 'But you need a challenge, Billy, and the farm needs the ICF. You have to promise me that tomorrow you will get back in there - *and* tomorrow afternoon you will come in here with a new timeline, and you will talk me through all your plans for the grand opening.'

I want to tell him '*no,*' but I'm sure he won't listen, so I hatch a deal instead. 'Okay,' I say, 'And afterwards, we'll sit down with those.' I point to a stack of *Caravan Club* magazines Mum has brought in for him. 'And we'll plan a trip for the beginning of July.'

'July?' He frowns. 'We said October. You can't disappear straight after the ice-cream launch.'

'Freddy can take over. I'll only be in his way by then. He'll be fine. I can go in July. You're my priority, don't you see that? This moment now, this is what matters.'

Chapter 34

Billy

I'm twenty minutes early, but as I park amongst the tall evergreens at Bellever, I see the WhatIf minibus is here too, fifty metres away. Its passengers are crowded around it, kitting up for an adventure. I'm ready to go, so I stand next to my van and watch unnoticed.

Saffi is suddenly in my mind - often in a moments of peacefulness, he comes back, making me smile like he always did. In my imaginings, I leave the shelter of the trees, and I've travelled back to a day in November, twenty-four years ago in Paris. Saffi and I are outside the elegant perfumer Guerlain on the Avenue des Champs Élysées, its grand frontage reminding me of Harrods. Saffi grins at me – his black skin making his wide smile more dazzling. 'Let's go in,' he says, and I hesitate, overawed by how exclusive everything looks.

Inside, Saffi holds one of the expensive perfume bottles out to me. He laughs, throwing his head so far back that the ridiculous top hat he's worn all afternoon topples off his head onto the highly polished floor. His exposed hair is a nest of dreadlock and beads. 'This is so sexy and gorgeous, my darling, just like you - you must have it,' he says too loudly before spinning his wheelchair around and gliding towards the imposing marble counter to buy it for me. It's the minutes after this I remember most vividly when we were back outside, and Saffi gave me a fascinating lesson on perfume and the fragrance triangle - top, heart and base. 'There are so many things that alter our perception of a smell,' he said. 'The time of day, your mood, even the cup of coffee you drank an hour ago. It also depends where you are, the tranquillity or the distractions around you. And once you pick up the note of one smell, it's hard to discern another.'

My focus turns back to the smells around me this

morning and the strong scent from the pine trees, but there is a base note, a familiar and comforting smell. There are eight Dartmoor ponies, sheltering behind a high granite wall to the right of me, and the smell of the lanolin and sweat in their coats instantly reminds me of Banjo, my first pony, and riding him bareback around our fields.

There's a top note too, the smell of the water in the East Dart River, a stone's throw in front of me, the iron suspended in the water giving the faintest metallic taste of blood in my mouth. If I hadn't stood still and concentrated, I'd never have noticed this. *Thank you, Saffi.*

All of the ponies have one ear pointed forward and the other back. They are unbothered by the children who grow louder as their mothers try to dress them appropriately for hiking. Jessie hasn't seen me, too busy throwing provisions and safety gear into a large rucksack. I'm content here close to the ponies, so it's with reluctance that I move to meet her.

Jessie doesn't acknowledge me, still busy sorting her equipment, and I'm wary that I'm a stranger to the rest of the group - I could seem threatening to the children or their mums. I decide to introduce myself to the friendliest looking woman, her hair dyed a rainbow of colours. I notice how she keeps smiling at her two children, 'I'm Billy, Jessie's friend,' I say, holding out my hand. 'Jessie said, for me to come along for a little while, today.'

'Hello.' The *woman* greets me but then turns her attention back to her little boy.

* * *

'Right, I think we're ready; we'll head off.' Jessie throws the rucksack onto her back and starts to walk along a narrow path towards the river. Without a word, we follow her. Our leader soon stops again by a broken line of rocks in the river.

I've used these stepping stones many times - Mum often brought me to Bellever as a child, always picking up our neighbour Margaret, and Tom and his sister, Charlotte, on the way. On hot summer's days, the five of us would picnic on the expansive flood plain on the other side of the river - we'd play cricket or fish with homemade rods. Tom, Charlotte and I would build dams, paddling in the icy cold water for hours. There'd be other families here too, and it was common for someone to organise games of rounders or football with twenty or even thirty people involved – the improvised teams recruited from holidaymakers and locals who had never met before.

In a way, Margaret and Mum were like the ladies here today with no partners around to help them entertain their children, but my mother and her neighbour weren't here on their own due to violence or abandonment. It was simply that Pat, Margaret's husband, Dad, and Grandad, had no interest in leaving the farm, even for a halcyon day out.

'We won't use these now,' Jessie says, waving a hand towards the stepping stones. 'We'll cross here on the way back; no-one wants wet feet right from the start.' Two of the older boys frown at each other and start to whisper. Our leader turns towards the road which I drove down earlier and sets off again, marching along the grassy strip between the river and the forest. She storms past the ancient clapper bridge, which now only spans half the river. I expected her to stop and allow some photos to be taken. I always think this bridge is far better than the famous Postbridge, which is always swarming with tourists, but she strides on.

'Have I upset you?' I ask when I catch up with her.

'We can talk in a minute,' Jessie says, stopping and throwing her rucksack on the ground. 'I need everyone to regroup.' This takes a few minutes because the young whisperers have wet feet from trying to cross the stepping stones and are now sitting on the ground, refusing to budge unless their mum gives them the dry socks she has in her bag.

Jessie crouches down to the smallest child in the group, and pretends to whisper, speaking quite loudly, so everyone can hear. 'Shall I tell you a secret?' she says.

The child looks excited, and all the other children crowd around, wanting to know the secret too. 'It's about dragons and a wood cutter.' There is a buzz of excitement, as Jessie begins her tale, telling them the secret is about an endangered breed of dragons who hide out on Dartmoor during the day. There are very few of them left, but she still needs to warn us all that during daytime, when it's still light, *Tiff Dragons* disguise themselves as rocks or trees depending on how big they are – baby *Tiffs* may just look like a branch. She forbids us to sit on any rocks or branches because last night a wood cutter was going home late in the dark, and he shone his torch on a whole flight of dragons right here, exactly where we're standing. 'So, everyone, not just the children, *please* treat all rocks and any suspicious looking trees as sleeping dragons,' Jessie says, 'Be warned, if you do accidentally sit on one, they could suddenly wake up and breathe fire, toasting you to their preferred crispiness and then gobble you up in a single crackly and very crunchy mouthful!' I've never seen Jessie look so solemn.

Bellever's flood plain is sometimes used for overnight camping, and sadly a few irresponsible people leave behind the residue of their campfires, not lifting the turf first before they light their kindling. Jessie is next to a ring of stones encircling a tell-tale area of blackened ground. 'Please look at this.' She points to the burnt area. 'What do you think might have happened here?'

One of the whisperers shouts, 'Dragon!' his eyes wide open in delight.

'Exactly, so be careful,' Jessie says. 'No sitting on rocks or fallen tre—' Jessie stops and looks about two hundred metres ahead, to a giant oak tree that has fallen near the path. She looks back at the group, her serious face breaking into a big smile.

'Dragon!' Whispering Boy yells again, pointing at the tree before charging off towards it. All the children chase after him, desperate to climb on the tree, thrilled by the story.

'Jessie, I've been here well over half an hour. What do you want to talk about?' I ask as the rest of us start to follow.

'It's a three-mile walk, there is plenty of time,' she says.

'I've got to get back. We have an important inspection today, don't you remember?'

'Mary will deal with it, I told her last night, when she came home with Will, you wouldn't be back in time.'

'Will?'

'William. He told me to call him Will. Your neighbour, the young man who helps with your cows sometimes.'

'What do you want to talk about?' I ask again, trying to recall if I've ever heard William referred to as Will before.

Jessie turns her head to look me in the eye, not slowing her pace. 'Billy, please talk to everyone here today—' She pauses. 'No, don't talk, listen to them, ask about how they came to be with the WhatIf programme. Ask the children what they dream of and what their lives were like before. Do that for the next two miles, then I'll tell you what I want.'

'You said thirty minutes.'

'And you wouldn't have come if I'd said any longer.' Jessie replies and I nod because she's right.

* * *

'Was there really an earth tremor on Dartmoor in 1923 on Christmas Day?' I ask Jessie as we reach the two-mile marker and begin descending into the valley to head back to the car park.

She nods. 'There are accounts of pictures being rocked and Christmas decorations falling down. It was felt in south and central Dartmoor.'

'And the house where the two old ladies lived solely on a diet of slugs and snails, was the Snaily House true, too?'

'Yes, why are you questioning me?' Jessie frowns.

'We've had giants, and helpful little girl ghosts who always turn up with a lantern just in time to guide anyone home who is lost on the moor, two talking sheep and the story of the tin miner who accidentally dug a tunnel through to the basement of the Houses of Parliament, that's why.'

'And what about your crazy tale about the Magic Boo, Billy?' Jessie smiles. 'Are you glad you came out today?'

I smile back. 'I'd like to do it again, if you'll let me. I felt it helped the women talk more freely out here, where their words were whipped away by the wind, and their problems seemed smaller in the vastness of this landscape.'

'That's poetic.'

'It's how I felt.'

'Have you guessed what I want?' she asks.

I shake my head. 'Not a clue.'

She stands still for a moment. We are a little way in front of the others, so as we wait for them to catch up, she starts to explain. 'I love my son with all my heart, Billy. Arthur is clever, talented, funny, and so determined to succeed. I've seen him struggle, I've held his hand and encouraged him when he's been knocked down, and I've soaked up thrilling moments when he has won, but now, I'm scared.'

I frown, still not grasping what she's trying to tell me.

'I'm terrified of the person he might turn out to be.'

'You mean, like Michael or one of these women's former partners?' I check.

Jessie wrings her hands, something I often see Mary do

when she's worried about something. 'It's my fault,' she says. 'I know it is. I keep asking myself questions like did I spend enough time playing with him? Did he feel left out when he had three other siblings all vying for my attention? Could I have read more storybooks with him sitting on my knee? How much time did I waste writing, and hiding from Michael when I should have been holding my kids, teaching them lessons, cooking with them, helping with their school work-?'

'Don't torture yourself, Jessie. All your children know how much you love them. Look at Mary. What a beautiful woman she is. I mean beautiful inside; she's caring and compassionate.'

'My daughter's beautiful too.' Jessie laughs.

I nod. 'You cuddled Arthur as much as you cuddled Mary, probably more because he was younger than her, my little boy you used to call him—'

'But time rushes on, and the babies I held in my arms are making lives of their own. I've given in to Arthur's every whim. I let him take over the reins at O'Rowdes'. I even let him talk me into keeping the company.'

'You had to let him fly, Jessie. He's charismatic like Michael was, and he knows how to get what he wants. Nothing will stand in his way. Not you, me, Mary—'

'The shareholders can.'

I frown, 'What do you mean?' I ask as the stragglers catch up with us, and we let them pass - they can see the stepping stones and the minibus, so they know where to go.

'He's only got a twenty-five per cent share still. I hold twenty-six, I said I needed something to fund *WhatIf,* but in truth, I was wary of letting him take over completely. There's been an extraordinary meeting, asking Arthur to stand down because he's in breach of a conduct clause about bringing the company into disrepute. There's an explicit statement in the agreement that anyone with a twenty-five per cent stake or less can be voted out for unfit conduct. We asked him to withdraw.'

'You asked?'

'He refuses to step down, says he's not guilty, and we can't force him, but once he's convicted, he'll be out.'

We watch the Whispering Boys help the others across the stepping stones. They are doing a great job, delivering everyone across safely.

'By the way, Billy?'

I turn to her, surprised she's going to carry on talking about Arthur now we are in earshot of the others. 'Yes.'

'If you see Magic Boo again, tell her she can live with me. I have ten four-poster beds she can leap on to her heart's delight.

'Sorry, she wouldn't like Culmfield.' I make a sad face.

'Why not?' Jessie pushes out her lips.

'She's terrified of billiard tables. Something happened to her five thousand and seventeen years ago—'

'But they didn't have billiard tables five thousand and seventeen years ago.' Jessie laughs.

'In Chickenland, they did. In the Crimson Cockerel's Palace,' I say.

* * *

Jessie leans on my van, and as I unlock the door, I turn to her. 'So, you don't want me to hold back with my witness statement,' I say. 'You want your son to go to prison.'

'I want him to learn to be humble,' she says.

'But it could make him worse,' I warn her, 'He might come across comrades in arms.'

Jessie looks towards her group, who are filing onto the minibus. 'Billy, it can't be worse. I don't want my future daughter-in-law, whoever she might be, and Arthur's children stepping onto a *WhatIf* bus one day, hoping to rebuild their shattered lives, scarred or broken by my son. Love's hard sometimes.' I take a deep breath in, imagining how difficult this is for her, and then I put my arms out and hug her.

When Jessie releases me, I rustle in my pocket, pulling out a thin packet. I turn it over in my hand to show her the giant sunflowers pictured on the front. 'Would you do me a favour in the next couple of days?' I ask. I continue, knowing she'll agree whatever the favour might be. 'It's so frantic for me at the moment, I'm worried I won't get these in the ground in time. Will you sow them for me?'

Jessie smiles. 'I always wondered who it was. Do you place the gerbera on Saffi's headstone too?'

'Every year on his birthday,' I say, my eyes welling. 'I'll never forget him. Plant these an inch down, six inches apart, all around his grave.'

'I will.' Jessie takes the seeds. 'I'll give Saffi your love,' she says.

Chapter 35

Billy

Mary has slogged her heart out clearing the dairy - ensuring that everything that has to be disposed of is witnessed and recorded. Harry and Sid worked with her until they headed off to Brighton, and afterwards Grace, Mum, and the part-time ladies Gloria and June all helped cleaning all the equipment and every surface - scrubbing to the nth degree.

When I wasn't visiting Richard, I joined the cleaning crew. We have all been avoiding the press, who've gradually dwindled in numbers to leave a single journalist now - a freelancer called Phil. Mum keeps him supplied with biscuits and cake, and I don't think he really wants to leave.

I find it hard to sleep, my brain won't stop spinning, constantly worrying about Richard. I was up at four this morning, so I gave the dairy a final swab check before the inspector was due to arrive and before I set off to meet Jessie.

* * *

The inspector is climbing into his car when I arrive back at Fox Halt. I park next to him, jumping out and apologising for my absence. 'No worries, Mrs May,' he says, closing his door.

I tap on his window and feel relief as he winds it down.

'How was it?' I ask, my fingers crossed.

'I'm impressed,' he says.

My heart leaps. I barely get my words out. 'We passed?'

'All signed off.'

I stare at him while his words sink in. 'So, we just have to wait for your report to be rubber-stamped by the magistrates court tomorrow - and then we can start up again?' I lean against my van, my legs feeling like they could give way.

'That's the gist of it.' He moves to press the button to wind his window up. 'Sorry, Mrs May, I do have another appointment to get to.'

* * *

In the dairy, Mary throws her arms around me. 'We did it,' she says, pulling my neck forward as she jumps her feet off the floor. 'Where do you think we should start tomorrow?'

'You're in charge,' I say, relieved she's no longer yanking my neck.

'Yoghurt.' Mary smiles – it's fabulous to see her re-energised. 'We'll start once the bulk milk tank is filled tomorrow morning.'

I nod, but before I can say anything else, Mary holds out a scrunched-up piece of paper. 'Read this,' she says.

I take the note and stare at it blankly. 'Just tell me what it says, please, I haven't got my glasses.'

'It's a recipe for a goats' milk yoghurt.' Mary smirks.

I lift an eyebrow. 'Goats' milk?'

'I think we should cash in on Fox Halt being in all the papers. There's no such thing as bad publicity, and I have a little plan to make Betsy and Bramble Yoghurts, just two flavours, vanilla and strawberry. They're our two most popular cows' yoghurts.'

I shake my head. She reminds me of her former self, the thirteen-year-old who kept designing new labels and logos for me when she first got involved with the dairy, excited and earnest both at once. Mary grins. 'I've sourced some goats' milk and I confirmed the order as soon as we got the all-clear.' She glances at the clock. 'It'll be here in about ten minutes. I plan on us making it for a few days.'

'Okay,' I say, not really caring what she does. After the heartbreak of the dairy closing and the struggle to get it pristine again, it's just great to see her happy.

'Read the back,' she says.

I shake my head, turning over the crumpled sheet as instructed. I frown at her. 'I've still got no glasses.'

'It's a list of customers who've ordered a batch for next Wednesday. She stresses *Wednesday* – as if it's significant.

'And –' I shrug.

'Arthur has his first court hearing next Wednesday.'

I'm trying to keep up, but I'm lost. 'Okay,' I say again.

'And this –' Mary plucks her note from my hand, waving it in front of my face, 'will *accidentally* fall out of my pocket in a minute, while I take delivery of the goats' milk. Perhaps someone who's hanging around the yard – called Phil – will find it and he's bound to see it as a new angle on the story.'

I smile. *Let her have some fun. She deserves it.*

'Mmm, I can't decide how much to make,' she says.

I press my fingers into my neck, thinking how she's not upset at all that Arthur is probably going to prison. I touch her shoulder. 'I don't know what I'd do without you,' I say.

She smiles back at me as she makes the scrappy bit of paper hang precariously out of her trouser pocket. 'Don't worry,' she says. 'The dairy; it'll be better than ever, soon.'

'Then I ought to get the ice-cream factory sorted too.' I make my hands into fists and shake them at Mary, trying to appear as motivated as her. My heart isn't in it though, I'm only heading in there because I said I'd report back to Richard later. 'I'm going over there now,' I tell her. 'I need to list everything outstanding and make a revised project plan.'

As I'm about to walk out, I turn around and see Mary is working on a line drawing of a goat, designing her new yoghurt pots. 'You really do love this place, don't you?' I say, but she doesn't hear me, too engrossed in her new venture.

* * *

I've written, *1) Test line from cow to ice-* when I hear the latch on the outer door being pulled back. Half a second later, Crinkle is with me. 'You can't be in here,' I say, lifting her up.

'She darted past me.' Janette walks towards me, her hands outstretched, 'I'll take her back to the house.'

As I lean forward, Janette slides her hands under Crinkle and over mine, and suddenly I'm remembering how I passed my goddaughter Anouk to Richard at her christening, that was the day when we first kissed, I can see the fountain and feel his lips on mine…

'Let her go,' Janette says, crashing into my memory.

I release Crinkle into her arms. 'I was daydreaming,' I say. 'I'm sorry.' Janette nods, turns away and leaves, cooing all the time to the dog cradled in her arms – it's no wonder Crinkle has taken to her.

* * *

2) Fit inner door, 3) Order health and safety notices. Janette is back, standing in front of me, and I guess she's waiting for me to look up but I don't. Surely, she can see I am busy, and I want to carry on with what I'm doing. 'I wanted to talk,' she says.

I raise my eyes now. 'To me?' I check.

Janette stares back. 'We are like ships that pass in the night, you and me - Mornings, I'm at the hospital, and you are here, at the farm - afternoons and evenings, you're with Richard, and I'm here.'

'Not today, though,' I say, lifting my eyebrows, hoping she'll decide that she doesn't want to talk after all because I'm too bristly. Janette wipes her hand over the edge of a stack of pallets and perches on them, not giving the impression she's about to leave me alone. Another thought strikes me. *Has she come to say goodbye?* Richard is getting better, so it's possible.

I make my voice friendly. 'What would you like to talk about?' I ask.

Chapter 36

Billy

Janette's lips are slightly apart as though she wants to say something, but her words won't come. Her eyes well up and I dismiss the idea she's here to say cheerio. 'Do you fancy a walk?' I say without thinking – it's just a reflex reaction. I watch a single tear run down her cheek. She nods. 'Please,' she says.

* * *

'T M,' Janette reads aloud as she runs her fingers over the letters crudely cut into one of the ancient wooden pews. 'T. May perhaps? An ancestor of yours?' she suggests.

I tap the seat next to me, beckoning her to sit down. 'What did you want to talk to me about?' I try not to sound impatient. We've walked from the farm to the church; just under half a mile, and she hasn't said anything that ties in with how she looked earlier. She's mentioned the weather, the prettiness of the village, the wheatsheaf weather vane on top of the church tower – nothing that would make her cry.

Janette sits and bows her head for a moment, and I wonder if like I did just now, she's asking God to help Richard. I'm not religious, not in a formal way – not like Mum, who comes here every Sunday. I do believe in some greater force that we can't see or fully understand, but I shrink away from the pomp and ceremony which goes with coming here for services. I find closeness to my God simply sitting atop Primrose Mound or seeing a newborn lamb being nuzzled by its mother, but still, it felt good to say a prayer for Richard.

'The baby.' Janette stops and gazes at up at the wooden vaulted the ceiling, and my heart crashes into my mouth, terrified she wants to discuss *the baby*, Richard's child – the baby I lost when they were still married. I breathe in deeply, start to count, *one and... two and...* No-one ever talks to me about Ross – I won't let them. My pulse throbs into my fingertips. Twice

I've spoken to Mary about the child I lost and both times, I cried more than talked but I've never explained how much it still hurts to anyone else, not Richard, Jessie or Mum. I definitely won't discuss him with Janette.

She is staring at me now. 'Are you alright?' she asks and I nod a quick response so she carries on. 'Freddy and Grace say I can have the third bedroom in the holiday cottage. I want to be here when the baby is born.'

Relief gushes in my veins that this is about Tom. 'You're telling me that you are going to leave Mum and me to move across the yard?' I ask.

'Yes.'

I frown. 'You can hardly squeeze a single bed in that room, and if you do manage it, that's all you'll get in - it's tiny.'

'Don't you mind?' She stands up and frowns at me.

'Mind what?' I ask. My brain on a go-slow, still suffering from the trepidation of Janette wanting to talk about Ross.

'Me staying on?' She sits back down, but now her eyes are on the floor. 'I offered to buy them a place in Amersham. I told Freddy he'd have better prospects nearer London.'

'You did what?' I'm on my feet, and I've just shouted in church.

Despite my reaction, she doesn't look up. 'They refused straight up. I'm sorry, Billy, I wanted them closer to me. But I get it now—'

I feel awkward standing next to her - and she did say they refused her offer, so I sit down next to her, cross my arms and legs and lean back in the seat, my fury ebbing.

'They won't leave.' Janette's eyes are full of tears again as she looks at me.

'You aren't expecting me to change their minds, are you?' My anger fires up again. 'Never.'

She shakes her head. 'Grace won't leave Hamsgate, her family's here, and she's so close to her mum, I see that now.'

I push back farther until the hard upright seat becomes uncomfortable against my spine. My mind spins. 'What about Martin? His tour finishes next Tuesday - that's what Mum said - is he coming down? You won't both fit in that box room.'

'Martin and I are finished.' In one graceful movement, Janette slides along the bench, stands up and then steps behind the mahogany lectern. She can just see over the top, dwarfed by the magnificent fan arched rood screen which frames her.

'Finished?' I blink.

She clears her throat. 'I should've ended it ages ago. When I first discovered—'

I get up too and stride towards her. 'Martin's been unfaithful?' I ask, immediately feeling like a double-dealer, remembering about Richard and me.

She nods. 'Who do you think he's been swanning around the States with?'

'I don't know.' I take a step back.

'She was his student.'

I stare at her, unsure what to say.

'It's not the first time.' Janette straightens her back and sniffs. 'Usually, he ends it straight away, promising it won't happen again, saying how much he loves me and how stupid he's been, but this time he believes there's a future with her - blinded by an intelligent young woman finding him attractive. She's a year younger than Harry and Sid.'

I press my hand to my mouth, still struggling for the right words.

'Once the divorce goes through,' she says. 'I'll buy something - maybe not in Hamsgate, but close by. I don't think it'll take long to sort out, I've paid for everything since Martin and I got together.' She pauses. 'I've been a fool.'

'Don't be hard on yourself,' I say at last.

She shrugs.

'It's easy to be taken advantage of when you love someone. You are no fool, Janette.' I look at my watch, hoping she'll take the hint that I need to get back to Fox Halt and then to the hospital. 'Thanks for letting me know your plans,' I say. 'It couldn't have been easy, telling me about Martin.'

'You need to go?'

I nod. 'I do.'

'One more thing—' She examines her perfect nails. 'Can I cover Grace's maternity leave?'

I frown. 'To be honest,' I say, 'With everything that's been going on, I hadn't thought about what we'd do without her—'

Janette cuts in. 'You need someone, though, don't you?' Her focus moves to the end of the bench in front of her and the carved initials. 'The baby,' she says. 'Tom MarcFenn, T M, it was obviously meant to be, wasn't it?

Tom Ross *MarcFenn,* I think, but I don't correct her.

* * *

'Do you mind?' I ask Richard when I've told him about Janette.

He smiles. 'She has already spoken to me about staying on. I told her to ask you to make sure you are happy about it.'

My heart jumps, angry that Janette has already confided in him. 'Why don't I do that?' I ask, my voice croaking a little.

'What?'

'Think to ask you before I delve into things head first.'

'You can't help it, Billy. You're selfish and thoughtless. It's okay, though, I wouldn't love you any other way—' He pauses and looks at my concerned face. 'I'm joking,' he says.

'Are you?'

'I can't imagine anyone caring for me like you have the last few weeks. You've got me through this.'

'Everyone - Janette, Jessie, my mother, Freddy… It wasn't just me,' I say, refilling his plastic glass with the Westcott's apple juice that I've brought in for him. William presses the juice alongside making his cider, and I know Richard likes it. His doctor says he needs to drink more.

'You're the one I look forward to seeing every day.' He stands up and puts his arms out for a hug. As I step into his arms, I think how amazing it is that he can get up so easily now.

I glance at Garry and then at Derek - and then around the ward. 'Can you walk all the way to the garden?' I ask.

He nods and points to my bag. 'Bring your task list.'

'I haven't done it.'

Richard huffs and seems to deflate as he sits back down in his chair again. 'Why?' His brightness has gone.

'Jessie, Bellever, then the inspection and then Janette—'

'If you wanted to do it, you'd have found time, Billy.'

I gather up a handful of caravanning magazines, 'I'll explain in a moment, in the garden,' I say, 'And we can look at these too.' I wave one of the books at him.

'Leave those here, please.' Richard frowns, and then nods towards one of the nurses who looks as if she's filling in a report as she stands behind the ward's reception desk. 'See if you can borrow a pen and paper from Rowena,' he says. 'Then while we're in the garden, we can brainstorm the outstanding works together.'

As I let the magazines drop back down onto Richard's

bedside cabinet, I notice a pull-out supplement from the Daily Mail newspaper lying on the floor by the foot of Derek's bed. There's a photo of two familiar animals on the front cover, with the headline, *'Will Goats Topple Top Supermarket Boss?'*

I look at Derek. 'Do you mind if I have those pages when you finish with them?' I ask him, pointing at the goats.

Derek fumbles with a button on his pyjama top but doesn't reply.

'It's for Mum,' I add quickly. 'She'll probably put it in a silver frame and give it pride of place on our sideboard.'

'For Daniella? Take it now. Hope it makes her smile,' he says. 'That's the famous duo, is it, Betsy and Bramble? Your mum's told me all about them.' Derek nods his head towards Richard. 'He's got a date, did he say?' A grin creeps over Derek's face, made funnier by the front tooth he's missing. 'A date for the heart op, I mean, not with one of the nurses.' He glances at Rowena. 'Looks to me like Richard's got enough women chasing after him already, you, Janette, Daniella…'

I laugh – it's embarrassing how Richard's visitors have multiplied whilst Derek only has his son visiting him, who comes in for exactly fifty minutes every other day, and most of that time, it feels like the two men struggle to find anything to say. Sometimes Mum chats more with Richard's lonely neighbour than she does with her son-in-law. She brings in photos of the plants in her garden to show Derek, so he can advise her how to look after them. He's missing his own garden terribly, worried how it will look when he gets home. His son assures him that he's keeping an eye on everything, but he longs to be tending it himself. *'I've a lovely garden, my wife Eileen and I started it from scratch. It was such a mess when we first cleared the site, smothered in brambles – that was forty-two years ago come July,'* Derek tells anyone he manages to have a fleeting conversation with.

* * *

The first bud has opened on the yellow climbing rose that scrambles over the roof of our garden seat. 'Does it smell?' Richard asks.

I sniff the delicate flower. 'A little, it's a bit like almonds,' I say, watching Richard almost collapse onto the seat. He walked too quickly even though I kept saying to slow down. 'When is your op?' I ask when he's caught his breath.

'Fifteenth of May.' He places his hand on my knee and I savour his touch – the weight and the feel of it.

'That's the day before Tom is due,' I say immediately, hoping Richard will be well enough to see the newborn as soon as he arrives. Hoping too that the sight of his grandson will instantly melt his heart.

'A bit less than three weeks away,' he says – as if he needs to tell me how far off it is when it's such an important date. I count down the days, desperate for Tom to be born safely and for Grace to be okay.

'…like it.' Richard's voice trails off.

'What's wrong?' I ask.

He glares at me. 'Are you listening?

* * *

Richard

I adjust the cannula, trying to ease the stabbing sensation. My arm is so bruised that the smallest non-alignment is painful. Billy is frowning at me. 'You won't like it,' I say again now that I have her attention.

Her frown deepens. 'What won't I like?'

'The heart operation will be in Plymouth,' I say, waiting for her to be upset about having to travel even further each day to see me. Instead, Billy exhales hard and drops her shoulders. 'I knew it'd be there. That's not a problem,' she says.

I squeeze her knee gently. 'It's after the operat—'

'You'll be home,' she cuts in, 'and I'll take care of you. I know you'll be weak, but I'll be there. It'll be fine.'

I shake my head, 'I have to come back here afterwards. I have to be completely free of the infection before I can come home – that is likely to be at least three weeks after the op.'

Billy's hips were pressed against mine, but now she turns to stare into my eyes. 'I'm worried about you, Rich – it's so depressing in here.'

'But I have an end date to focus on and there is something else—'

'The baby?' she interrupts, smiling, her voice hopeful that I'm suddenly looking forward to the child's arrival.

'Not the baby, the ice-cream factory, I want to know every last detail. It'll be something for me to think about.'

'Really? You want me to go ahead with it?'

I nod. 'I've been out of order, Billy. I want to be involved with everything you do.'

She smiles at me, but it's a fake smile, where she pulls her cheeks up, trying to make it look like she is happy.

'What's wrong?'

'I'm fine – I'm glad you want to help me.' Not even a smile now. Nothing about her body language says she's fine. I try another tack. 'So, Grand Launch Day, are you planning on the Queen opening it this time? After all, you are famous now.'

Billy answers quickly, and now her voice is animated. 'Far more spectacular than that,' she says, 'I've got in mind a double act, a famous pair of rascals who now have their own blog, want to see?' She holds up her phone. 'Here.' She presses the play arrow on the screen.

My mouth opens wide as I watch a video. 'That is the Great Hall at Culmfield?' I am transfixed by what I'm watching…'Oh no, they *can't* do that!' I see Betsy leap from the piano stall onto the keys of the Steinway and then she and Bramble bleat excitedly, sliding on the piano's polished cover. In the background, I hear children giggling and clapping at their terrible behaviour. Billy looks over my shoulder at the screen, '1,719 hits so far,' she says. 'Comments too – look, they are asking if they are available for more bookings —those two rascals have quite a future as therapy goats.'

'You haven't got time, Billy.'

'I'm joking. Jessie picked them up from the farm. I didn't do anything other than help her load them on the minibus. She said other than the piano incident, they were as good as gold. The children adored them.'

'What about making goats' milk ice-cream too?' I ask and she laughs. 'Maybe?'

Chapter 37

Billy

I shield my eyes from the camera flashes which make it hard to follow Arthur and his barrister down the outside steps of the Court. Arthur has his head high, in the same defiant stance he maintained throughout the hearing. His arrogant swagger in front of the journalists would never give away that just a few minutes ago, it was decided there's enough evidence to try him, and a date's been set for his trial in six months.

There is the only one question I answer as microphones and cameras open fire on me, 'Yes, I've tried them, Betsy Yoghurt and Bramble Yoghurt. They are both delicious,' I say.

* * *

It feels like hours and hours since Richard went into surgery, but the clock on the welcome desk in the Plymouth hospital says it's only six o'clock. As I walk into the Intensive Care ward, the number of hi-tech machines and computers around each patient makes me shudder. I thought the equipment when Richard was in Intensive Care in Exeter was impressive but this is on a whole new level. Franklin is with me, and I grab his arm when I realise that the first patient inside the door is Richard. His dedicated nurse speaks to me, but all I can focus on is my unconscious husband.

'…fine and stable. We'll be able to take him off the ventilator in a couple of hours.' The nurse tells Franklin. I suppose she realised I wasn't listening, my eyes fixed on Richard and the ventilator filling his lungs. I stroke the back of Richard's hand and say his name, watching all the lit-up machines he's connected up to and expecting the display screens to register a change – but the lines and charts remain static, and the numbers on the dials don't move. He doesn't know I'm here. He can't feel my touch. Can't hear his name. I swallow hard as a single tear starts to run down my face.

'Son, I admire the fighting spirit. Keep it up.' Franklin kisses Richard on the cheek and still nothing. I've never seen Franklin embrace his son before, let alone kiss him. They love each other, but they don't touch.

'I thought he'd hear us.' I run the tip of my tongue along the inside of my lower lip, trying to stop more tears.

'The nurse explained this is what we should expect.' Franklin nods slowly.

'But I'm glad I'm here,' I say, realising I'm still clutching my father-in-law's arm. 'It's good to physically see that Richard has come through safely, to see and touch him, not be told on the phone that he's doing alright.' I swallow hard again and wipe my hand across my cheek to wipe away another tear. 'I never imagined anything like this, though, did you?' I look at Franklin then nod at the decks of machines. 'It's like every organ in his body, and all his vital signs are being monitored and regulated.'

Franklin rustles in a pocket of his tweed jacket and pulls out a bag of barley sugars. He offers one to me. 'Come on, girl, nothing more we can do here. Let's get back to Fox Halt Farm.' He shakes the bag, making the sweets rattle together. 'Sugar always makes one feel better.'

'Thank you,' I say, fishing a sweet out, fairly certain we shouldn't be eating anything in this sterile environment. I kiss Richard's forehead. 'Love you,' I whisper.

* * *

Richard

Bright light… The hands of the clock are wavy. They move backwards.

A man speaks. 'Ventilator –'

Long thin fingers, like a pianist's hands.

Words drift over me. I focus on his black eyes trying to keep mine open. Mo Farah but he has a younger face, filled out, smooth skin.

Focus on his eyes. Large. Caring. He smiles. Arching eyebrows. Black eyes smiling – No, not Mo. I know these eyes, this face. *Who is he?*

Sharmarke?

No.

Chapter 38

Billy

While Janette and Franklin are with Richard in the High Dependency Unit, I'm with Grace in the waiting area. For a moment, Grace stops pacing to reach for a holdall by my feet. 'Do you need a hand?' I ask her as she searches for something inside the bag, her massive bump making it awkward. She dumps the bag on my lap. 'Dig out the plastic tub in there, will you?' she says. 'Oh, and there's a fork too.'

I hold the requested items up to her, then change my mind, deciding to remove the lid of the container too. My nostrils tingle with the sweet smell. 'Pineapple?' I ask Grace.

'Yeah,' she says, taking the fork. 'It's something Freddy read about last night. It's got an enzyme in it which supposedly softens the cervix and should make it easier for little Tom to get out. I can't wait for him to be here, and Freddy's just the same.' Grace arches her back, pressing a flattened hand on her spine. 'Cor, I hope he comes soon. This is bloody ridiculous.'

'Can I rub your back?' I say, desperate to help.

'Gracie needs to keep walking around and stuffing her face with the pineapple, and he'll be with us by the stroke of midnight, right on time,' Freddy says, striding into the room. 'Here, Billy.' He hands me my coffee as he sits next to me. He mirrors my crossed legs, his back upright against the chair. Freddy never sits like this. He slouches. He makes me think of Franklin, who I'm sure has never slouched in his life.

I sip my coffee, noticing how it tastes of tea *and* coffee with a subtle hint of tar. It's hot, though, so that's a bonus.

'The point of sale stuff you emailed me on Monday,' Freddy says, turning his head stiffly towards me. 'You wanted my comments by tomorrow?' He glances at Grace and then his eyes dart back to mine.

'Did you like it all?' I ask – I'm feeling quite proud of the designs I roughed out for him, everything's been so hectic, but I managed to concentrate on them for two uninterrupted hours, and I was pleased with what I'd created.

'Yes.' His voice lacks the enthusiasm I'd anticipated.

'Good,' I say, still hoping for a comment about how imaginative I'd been.

Grace sits down on the other side of me, dropping the tub back into the bag. 'He doesn't like the name,' she says, gazing across at Freddy.

My heart jumps to my mouth. 'You've changed your mind. You don't want to call the baby Tom Ross?' I lean down to pick up the tub, pretending to see if Grace has put the lid back on correctly, not wanting them to see my disappointment. Grace touches my hand. 'No, we both adore Ross. It's the name for the ice-cream. Fox Halt Farm Ice-Cream. Freddy hates it.'

'That's a bit strong, Gracie.' Freddy uncrosses his legs and gets up, walking across the room to stare at a model of a heart which is standing on a small table pushed up against the wall. It's a life-size heart, an anatomy model showing the heart chambers, valves and vessels. Its vibrant blue and bright red colours make me look away; I know it's just what's inside us all and a totally vital organ, but it looks grotesque to me.

I'm sure Freddy's only examining it to avoid my gaze.

'You said, 'Hate, you do hate it.' I'm glad we are the only people here because Grace is almost shouting at him.

I watch Freddy's back as he takes in a deep breath. He turns around and looks at me, and I see he's lifted the heart off its stand and pulled it apart. His index finger smooths the valve that Richard has had replaced with a mechanical one. He keeps stroking it as he talks. 'Foxes and ice-cream feels wrong to me. People perceive foxes as sly and cunning. Ice-cream is honest and generous. I don't like *Foxy Lady* either. I think we should get away from foxes all together and think of a name that conjures up authenticity, is traditional and Devonian—'

'Daniella May's Ice-Cream, no, Great-Granny May's Ice-cream,' Grace says, standing up slowly and straight away placing her hand on her bump.

'We already have a presence in the market with Fox Halt,' I tell Freddy, trying to keep my eyes on his face when something macabre inside my brain keeps drawing them towards his hands and the heart. 'The farm shop, our milk, the cheeses and the yoghurt, they're all branded Fox Halt. We should capitalise on that and hit the ground running as it were, not start up a new brand.' I uncross my legs, trying not to look negative as though I'm putting up a barrier to the first idea he's come up with.

'I don't agree,' he says, 'Nor with you, Gracie.' He waves half the model at me and the other half at Grace, and for a split second I think he's going to throw one part to each of us. I feel relief as he puts them down gently on the table instead. I didn't want to touch it.

Freddy brings his hands together as if he's praying. 'I think we need a local surname, yes, but May is too generic. We want people to know they're buying a local product.'

'Westcott,' Grace chips in. 'My surname, you don't get more Devon than that, and it's not too long either.' She moves towards Freddy, more marching than waddling, and I smile. I love this girl, she always has so much energy, and I suspect she's trying to make me laugh.

'But William's cider and apple juice is Westcott's,' I say, beginning to suspect the pair have rehearsed this argument; it all feels too smooth. Grace is always quick with quips and comebacks, but her responses are lightning fast.

'Granny Westcott, *I like it*,' Freddy says, 'But maybe, it's a little too quaint, Gran Westcott's would be better.' He looks at Grace, who stands still and throws her arms down to her sides. 'Gosh, that's lucky,' she says, holding her hands out and starting to count on her fingers.

'What is?' Freddy asks.

'Gran Westcott's got exactly the same number of characters in the name as Fox Halt Farm. It'll be so easy to change on all Billy's designs.'

I clap my hands, now convinced I've been an unwitting extra in this carefully choreographed scene. I don't want to argue with them, Freddy will have to sell the ice-cream, and I'm thrilled they've put so much thought into its name, especially with everything they've been dealing with lately – Richard's illness, Freddy's exams, moving in together, Janette living with them and all the things that they've had to sort out ready for Tom's arrival.

'Does William mind you using Westcott's?' I ask Grace.

'He's fine about it.' She laughs, recognising that the game is up, and I know this rehearsed conversation was all a ruse. 'We can piggyback off each other's reputations, 'Should give more exposure to both brands.' That's what he said.'

Freddy smiles at the young woman who's about to have his child, like he's just met her and has instantly fallen in love, 'William's exact words,' he says, staring into Grace's eyes.

'And Mum loves it too,' Grace says. 'She's offered to be the original Gran Westcott - of course she's Mrs O'Sullivan now, but she was Mrs Westcott, and she is going to be a granny very soon. Mum said she'd come to the launch wearing her hair up in a bun, using a walking stick and wearing a pair of those black wrinkly tights that sweet grandmothers have in all the fairy tales - and the little round wired spectacles too. She had Sean in creases as we watched her bent over, shuffling around the feed silo, asking us in a withered old lady voice if we'd tried her delicious ice-cream.'

'I think it's a great name,' I say. 'But before we go and see Richard, would you mind putting that back together?' I ask Freddy, pointing at the pieces of heart.

* * *

Richard grasps my arm. 'Can you take a video—' He pauses to breathe in slowly, 'On your phone before you go?' His eyes are fixed on mine, making me feel like I never want to leave.

'A video?' I frown at him.

'Of me, it's for Daniella—' Another pause, and he smiles, 'I want to send her a message.' Poor Mum thought she was starting a cold this morning, so she stayed home. Franklin, Janette, Freddy, Grace and I all came together, crammed in Franklin's Wolseley - which is lovely looking on the outside and luxurious inside. But its engine hisses like there are a hundred snakes under the bonnet, and I wasn't convinced we would make it. My only reassurance was that Grace would be out of the passenger seat and checking out the snakes in a flash if we did break down. Franklin, however, was blasé telling us all, 'This old lady has always sounded the same way,' saying she had never let him down. Not once in forty-seven years. *The car is the same age as me!*

'All set,' I say, holding up my phone, ready to record.

'Get well soon, Daniella,' Richard smiles and waves.

* * *

It's eight o'clock now, and the hospital feels very different from this morning. The small charity shop in the foyer which is run by the Friends of Derriford is shut up for the night, and the buzz of earlier has faded away. I walk slowly, in a fog. The worry of Richard being cut open yesterday and lack of sleep clouds my mind. I won't use the stairs. I'll save my energy and take the lift instead.

As the lift doors close, two men dart in next to me. The man facing me passes his headphones to the other. 'You won't get this one,' he says, tapping his mobile phone, I guess to play the intro to a song. His friend has his back to me. ''Girl with Fire in her Stomach', by *Pokémon* something,' his friend says.

The quiz master snatches the earphones back, almost tearing them out of the other man's ears. 'How did you know that? Yana only sent me the link seconds ago. It's a band her friend is in.'

'She sent it to me on Monday. I thought they were good.' His friend laughs. As the lift jolts to a halt, I think how Mary would love this game, she's our music queen in the monthly charity quiz at The Hamsgate, astounding me every time with her knowledge, not only of songs but also her encyclopaedic knowledge about when it was a hit and the artist. She can even identify if it's a cover or the original band.

Leaving the lift together, I see the music guru's face. He stares at me then turns away. I have a sense I know him, but I can't place him. I glance at the identity card hung on a rainbow-striped ribbon around his neck —his name is *'Asad Umar.'*

I follow the pair down the corridor until I see Asad's companion use his pass to enter the Intensive Care Unit.

'Pokémon Stint,' Asad says, remembering the band's name as he pushes the door open so his friend can enter first.

'Pokémon Stitch, close though,' his friend says, and I hear them laugh. I continue along the corridor to the next door that will take me into Richard's ward and then, while I wait to be let in, I think about Asad Umar, racking my brains where I might have seen him before. He was wearing a pink checked shirt and chinos, so I presume he was a doctor. Sharmarke flashes into mind - I haven't seen him since he was fifteen, but Asad did look like a grown-up version of the boy. He'd be a year older than Mary. Deciding quickly, he might have changed his name, I tap into my phone's search engine, *'How long does it take to become a doctor in a hospital?'*

The search result appears straight away, and as I scan the

page, I see it's ten years, so it couldn't have been him.

'Which patient are you visiting, please?' a female voice asks through the telecom.

'Richard May,' I say, holding my hand under the bottle of antiseptic cleanser hung up in front of me and squeezing the lever, dispensing a pine-scented gel onto my palms.

The door clicks open, and I think later, I will look up 'Girl with Fire in her Stomach' on my phone. I'll listen to it on the way home.

* * *

RICHARD

'Eight pounds something,' I tell my ward neighbour Kamil, as he shuffles towards my chair in his brand new slippers— a present from his sister yesterday, beautifully wrapped with a red bow, he did not have the heart to say they were too small. He is walking with his toes curled up inside them, determined to get to me and my chubby black-haired grandson.

When Freddy and Grace walked into the ward with baby Tom, I could see their joy and the bond already between them - I saw too, how wrong I've been. Everything will work out for them. I'm sure it will. My newly repaired heart beats hard, as I look down at the baby lying in my lap. 'You are just perfect,' I say, staring into his eyes. I know he probably isn't focusing on me, but it feels like he is.

'Even smells quite good.' Freddy smiles from ear to ear and leans over me, taking his son away before Grace has a chance to. 'Nothing heavier than a half-filled kettle, that's what the doctors said, Dad.' He lifts Tom up and holds him against his chest, his hand supporting the baby's head.

Billy has gone to find out why I'm on this ward. It's horrible. It feels like I have been dumped here because there was nowhere else to put me. This might be the truth, the Plymouth hospital wanted to send me back here, to Exeter, three days ago, but there were no spare beds.

I have a pervasive fear that other than Kamil, my companions are terribly ill and close to death. To make it worse they are all suffering with dementia, Alzheimer's or severe learning difficulties which means that there are two hospital staff stationed on chairs by the entrance to the ward. The nurses are permanently here just in case someone gets out of bed, accidently pulling out their cannulas, urinary catheters or oxygen tubes.

Kamil's predecessor passed away in the early hours of yesterday morning. I feel trapped in a living nightmare. To add to this, the lighting is dimmer in this ward than on any of the rooms that I've stayed in, and the two tiny windows are so high up, we can't see outside. I even have to enter a door key code to get in and out of my dreadful prison.

I'm nowhere near death, I can climb two flights of stairs without getting out of breath - and yesterday, I walked a circuit of the outside of the hospital, but this place is bringing my spirits down, and I have to keep on reminding myself, *five more days, that's all.*

Billy has a massive smile on her face as she rushes past the nurses at the door. Her smile takes me back to the day when I saw her walking up the aisle of the Culmfield Chapel on the day we were married. 'I can take you home,' she says, nearly diving onto me, 'Tomorrow, they've agreed to let you out. Can you believe it, Rich?'

I stare at her open-mouthed that tomorrow, I'll be standing in the farm kitchen, and I can sleep in my own bed lying next to her.

Billy is still smiling, 'I have to bring you in every day for the next two weeks so they can administer your antibiotics, but that will be just an hour's appointment,' she says.

I grin back, a hundred thoughts of Fox Halt Farm flashing in my mind. Billy sighs. 'There is a bit of bad news.'

My new heart valve misses a beat as I imagine some unattainable condition for my freedom, like leaving my right arm behind for a medical survey into sepsis, or the only doctor who can sign my release papers has just left for a three-month trek in Tibet. I'm sweating, suddenly feeling faint. Billy holds out her hands. 'Are you okay?' She frowns.

'What is it?' I ask, my mind spinning cartwheels.

'I have to stab you morning and evening.' She touches my hand. 'Like the nurses are doing, inject you in the stomach. I'll be a bit of an amateur at it, I'm afraid. Do you mind?'

Chapter 39

BILLY

I reckon Richard has been through every type of scanner they have in Exeter hospital at least once, some twice or three times. He's had two stays in Intensive Care and experienced a level of attention from the nurses, doctors and auxiliaries that's been second to none, but it's clear that the high standards were often down to the staff working harder than they are paid to be.

Many times staff shortages have been evident, like the nursing sister crying at the front desk because she can't get anyone to cover the two nurses who've called in sick, and the countless times when Richard waited to get simple problems dealt with – a bag emptied or an infusion alarm reset. Now we are waiting for Richard's discharge drugs to be signed off by a doctor, so I can fetch them from the pharmacy – three hours, we've sat in this dingy ward thinking, any moment we can leave. We are stuck in the arms of the system that has kept Richard alive all these months, yet we just want to be free.

A doctor finally walks into the ward, and I assume he's the elusive person we've waited for, but as he approaches us, Richard and I say his name at the same time. 'Sharmarke.'

'I'm Dr Umar,' he says, holding out his identity card, his eyes begging us not to challenge him. 'I have this for you, Mr May.' He hands Richard the long awaited prescription. 'I thought I could walk with your wife to the dispensary to collect them for you,' he says and I notice how he swallows hard before he continues. 'In case there are any queries – you'll be on your way soon, I promise.'

'Right,' Richard says in a tone much more composed than I could muster, still convinced he's an imposter.

The doctor who I think might be Sharmarke lets the security door to the ward slam behind us, and then he opens his shoulder bag. 'Here,' he says, holding out two stuffed full paper bags with a pharmacy logo on them. Automatically, I take the bags from him with my hands shaking.

'That's everything,' he says. 'That's the whole of Richard's prescription.'

'You fetched it from the pharmacy?' I ask, totally convinced now he *is* Sharmarke not just by the way he looks, it's the way he walks too, and because he lied about us collecting the prescription together.

He nods. 'Can we go outside?' Sharmarke points through the window to a metal bench. 'I need to talk to you.'

* * *

He keeps his hands pressed together as we sit down 'Sharmarke, are you a real doctor?' I ask, so many questions rushing through my brain. It's so strange to say his name again.

He doesn't ask me to call him Asad or Dr Umar. 'Still in training,' he says. 'I've completed my medical degree, and I'm in the second year of my foundation training. I've just started acute medicine in Plymouth.'

'So, why are you here?' A shiver runs through my body, remembering the last time I saw him, the night his father threw me in the boot of a Rolls Royce, later abandoning me terrified in a forest in Cumbria. It feels like a lifetime ago, but I look at my wrists, remembering how they were tied, and I run my tongue over my lips, recalling the fear, the tape over my mouth and the thirst. I believed I was going to die that night.

'To speak to you, I wasn't sure if I should, I have a new life now...' I struggle to concentrate on what Sharmarke is telling me. I remember the knife pressed to my throat and my panic that his father, Amir, would kill me and then afterwards kill Mary too. As if he's read my mind, he refers to his father. 'Dad did this,' he says, turning his identity card so I can read it, but all I can think of is *his dad* murdering Michael O'Rowde, *his dad* did that. *His dad* did his best to frame me for the murder as well. *His dad...* but he *didn't* kill me though, did he? He spared me, left me food and water and gave me a chance to live - making it crystal clear I must never reveal the truth. *His dad* let me live.

Sharmarke is talking again. 'I've no idea what happened to the real Asad or his parents,' he says. 'They were Somali; that's all I know.' He mutters something under his breath, staring straight ahead.

'What happened after you left Culmfield?' I touch his

arm to bring his attention back to me. Sharmarke looks up at the cloudless sky, and I guess he is remembering that night too. 'We ended up in a massive scrapyard on the outskirts of Birmingham,' he says. 'The man Dad got our new passports from owned it. He had Somali, Ethiopian and Syrian workers there. It was a horrific place where no-one dared to ask questions. We stayed two days there, and they were the most terrifying days of my life. Mum and I locked in a shipping container. I still have nightmares recalling the smell of it. I'm sure there were dead bodies hidden under the sacks in there. The smell of a corpse—'

'Why did you want to see me?' I cut in, not wanting to hear any more. I answer my own question. 'To check if your secret's safe, that no-one else knows what your father did?'

'*She's* why I'm here,' Sharmarke says.

I close my eyes and suck in a breath, my heart thumping.

'Mary is fine, she's happy,' I tell him. 'She works for me now, virtually full time.'

'Is she seeing someone?'

'Yes.' The hairs on the back of my neck stand on end and I notice how he has tears in his eyes.

'I can't forget her. Mary's in here.' Sharmarke places his hand on his chest. 'I still love her.'

'You have to leave her alone.' I stand up, letting all the contents of one of the paper bags spill onto the ground. I ignore them at my feet, staring at Sharmarke instead, desperate for him to listen to me. 'She's happy. It's taken a long time for her to come to terms with what happened and if you really love her, you have to let Mary have some normality in her life. She may be your stepsister, but you can't see her. It'll upset her too much.' Sharmarke moves to clear up the boxes of drugs.

'Leave them!' I shout, kicking everything out of his reach. 'Did you hear me, Sharmarke?'

Two nurses walk past, and I'm yelling at a doctor, and there are packets and boxes of drugs scattered around us. *What must they think?* Sharmarke raises a hand to them and smiles as if to say, *'I'm dealing with this.'* They smile back at the attractive young man and then walk on continuing their conversation.

'I'm not her brother. I had a DNA test - I'm sure Michael O'Rowde raped Mum, but I'm not his son.'

I nod, trying to grasp what he's just said.

'I'm not Mary's brother,' Sharmarke speaks softly as he gathers up all the boxes and packets. He hands them back to me, but the bag is torn, so I clutch it all to my chest.

'No,' I say, and I start to walk away. Now running, heading back to Richard. I have to get away from him.

Sharmarke catches up easily. 'Will you give her something, please?' His eyes are pleading.

I stop and stare at the strip of paper he has in an outstretched hand, and I can see there is a phone number written on it. I shake my head. 'No.'

* * *

RICHARD

Billy places a pillow diagonally across my chest before pulling the seatbelt over me and the padding. 'It's like I'm stealing you,' she says.

I laugh. 'This is your getaway van, then?'

She turns away to stare out the windscreen, not putting her seat belt on or slipping the key in the ignition, and it's a moment or two before she speaks again. 'If this is a getaway vehicle, then Jessie should be sat here. She'd make a much faster exit than me.'

'My heart's not yet up to Jessie's driving. ' I laugh again, aware of the pressure on my wound.

'No.' Billy turns back to me, leaning forward and kissing me on the mouth. As I push my lips against her, I see her eyes are staring past me.

'What are you thinking about?' I ask.

She looks at me and smiles. 'How wonderful it is to be taking you home.'

'Hope you're hungry,' I say.

Billy starts the engine and frowns at me. 'Why?'

'While you fetched my meds, I texted Daniella, and she messaged back all the things she has made for tea. I told her I couldn't wait. But all I really fancy is a piece of to— Stop!' I shout. A man nearly stepped out in front of us - someone probably rushing to a loved one's bedside and not concentrating, but Billy wasn't paying attention either. She should have seen him and braked before I shouted.

'What's wrong?' I ask her, certain something is distracting her.

'Can I get you home first? I think I've just proved I can't think about two things at once at the moment!'

'It was Sharmarke, wasn't it?'

She nods, focusing ahead of her, driving at twenty miles an hour in the thirty limit.

'I thought I was hallucinating when I saw him before – I reckoned the anaesthetic was making me woozy and I was seeing things.'

Billy glances at me. 'You saw him before today?'

'He took my ventilator off after I had the heart op. I was so groggy, I thought I dreamt it.'

'He was in the lift the day after your op too,' she says. 'When you were in the High Dependency Ward. I dismissed it as well – I thought he was too young to be a doctor.'

I lean forward to pick up the parking ticket on the dashboard, and I start to fold it into tinier and tinier pieces. Billy keeps driving slowly like I'm some iced celebration cake, she doesn't want to slide off the passenger seat. 'I decided he just reminded me of Sharmarke,' she says, 'but I should've realised; that graceful walk of his, it's unmistakeable really. Richard, can we talk about something else for now? What are you most looking forward to when we get back?' she asks.

'I'd like to stop at the top of the lane. I love that view of the farm and the anticipation of arriving home.'

'I thought you'd say little Tom. You've fallen in love with him, haven't you?'

'I can't wait to see him,' I confess, and I smile at her. 'I'm looking forward to seeing Piggy too. Sounds like I have to win her affections back from Janette, though.'

'She's missed you, don't worry,' Billy says.

'I've missed *you*,' I tell her, watching as she drives, not taking her eyes off the road in front.

'You've seen me every day.' She laughs.

'Not lying next to you. That's what I've missed.' I touch her thigh, and suddenly nothing matters in the world but us. 'I've really missed you, darling,' I tell her again.

She takes a hand off the steering wheel and places it on mine. 'You still have to lie on your back, don't forget.'

I nod, and neither of us speaks for several minutes, her hand rested on mine.

I break the silence. 'Do you think, if we took it slow, I'd get as far as Primrose Mound tomorrow?' I ask her. 'They say I must walk each day.' I can't fold the ticket anymore, and instead, I start to roll it between my thumb and index finger.

Billy still doesn't look at me. 'But not back again,' she says. 'That's too far. I'll drive the quad bike up there first thing tomorrow morning and leave it there, so I can bring you home on that. Is that okay?'

I grin back. 'It is so nice to be asked what I want, rather than be told, for example, I have to take this tablet, I have to eat my lunch at twelve o'clock.' I groan.

Billy frowns. 'Sorry, it was so awful.'

'I've almost forgotten to think for myself. We won't have to ask if we can go to the garden. We don't have to be back to the ward in time for the doctors' rounds or dinner. Do you know, maybe when we head to Primrose Mound, we won't tell anyone we are going or what time we'll be back.' I squeeze her thigh, remembering times when we've sneaked up there, squashing the primroses flat, my body on Billy's giggling and whispering - unlikely we'd be discovered, but still the risk of it firing up our senses.

Chapter 40

Billy

Mum knocks on our bedroom door, her words crystal clear. 'If any of us are going to get some sleep tonight, you'll have to bring Crinkle up. Just this once won't hurt.'

I scramble out from under the duvet to find Mum has a clean dog bed in her hand. 'I'm not getting her,' I say. 'She'll expect to be up here every night with us, otherwise. She'll give up making that racket in a moment.'

Twenty minutes later, I'm nuzzled into Richard's side as he lies on his back - as he's been instructed to lie for the next week. I revel in the smell of him and the touch of my skin against his, but the howling is growing louder, and I can't bear it any longer. 'I have to get her,' I say.

I get up again and fetch the dog bed, putting it next to Richard's side of the bed. Crinkle is lying next to Richard with her head on my pillow before I get back upstairs. I shake my head. 'No, Crinkle,' I say, bundling her up and lowering her gently into her own bed. 'Stay,' I tell her as she rolls onto her back with her legs in the air.

'Are you okay, Richard?' I ask, kneeling beside him next to Crinkle. He's been staring at the ceiling for a little while now.

'My sleep pattern is shot. I am not sleepy at all.'

I kiss his cheek. 'I've not told you about Sharmarke.'

He turns his head towards me. 'I was wondering about him, and where Amir and Nala are, did he tell you?'

'I didn't speak to him for very long.'

'You weren't curious?' He frowns at me.

'He told me he wanted to get in touch with Mary, and after that, I just wanted to get away. It upset me, and you were waiting to go. He said he's not her brother.'

'Not her half-brother?' Richard reaches his hand out to me and I see that he wants to sit up. I help, pulling at his pillows when he's more upright.

'He's done a DNA test,' I say. 'He was sure Michael raped his mother, though, and I think it's true too – his parents wouldn't have had the leverage they had over Michael, otherwise.'

Richard slumps down a little. 'There's nothing to stop Sharmarke contacting Mary, you know? He didn't need to ask you to arrange it for him. He could go to Culmfield—' He pauses as I climb back into bed beside him. 'Actually, I suppose he wouldn't go there,' he says.

I shrug. 'He wanted me to give her his mobile number.'

'You didn't agree, did you?'

I get up again and pick my jeans up from the floor, rummaging in the pockets. 'I have this – Sharmarke looked so miserable, I took it from him.' I hold up a slip of paper.

'That's his number?' Richard asks, suddenly throwing his legs over the side of the bed. He snatches the piece of paper from me. I watch in disbelief as he heads for the door, carefully pulling on his dressing gown.

'Where are you going?'

'To the kitchen.'

'Why?' I whisper so Mum doesn't overhear.

He doesn't reply as he toddles down the stairs, Crinkle and me following on his heels.

In the kitchen, he opens the Rayburn door and tosses the paper onto the fire inside. 'Promise me, Billy, you won't contact him again, and also promise me you won't tell Mary you've seen him. She is happy with William, and it is obvious how deep William's feeling are for her. Leave this alone.'

I cross my fingers behind my back, ready to pledge, but I can't say the words. I pick up the kettle instead, placing it onto the hot plate to boil. 'Do you want a cuppa while we're down here?' I ask. 'There's decaf coffee. Mum got it for Jakub.'

'Billy,' he says, fixing his eyes on me.

'How can you ask me not to tell her? Mary is like my daughter, and she'll hate me if she discovered I hid this from her. Our history of keeping secrets is not the best, is it?'

'Billy, no.' He says *no* so sharply that Crinkle barks and sits between us. 'Sshsh,' we both tell her at the same time. She thumps her chin on the floor and lets out a long whine.

'I understand what you are saying, Richard,' I tell him as I make two cups of tea, trying to avoid looking at him, 'but it's up to Mary to make her own decision; we can't decide for her.'

He walks towards me and then leans past my shoulder to reach for the tin Mum keeps her homemade cookies in. 'Maybe,' he says, as he lifts the lid, making a show of breathing in the familiar smell of chocolate this special tin always releases. Crinkle looks up and wags her tail in anticipation of a biscuit. 'No chocolate for you, Piggy,' he says, biting into a cookie himself. I watch him savour it as he heads for the larder to find Crinkle one of the Rich Tea biscuits I keep for the sheep.

'Think about what we did to William,' I say. 'Keeping him in the dark all those years about his father's death, and who knows how it will affect Grace when she finds out too?'

'So, you've told Martha, have you?'

'Yes.'

'You went against my wishes, even when I expressly said not to. Did you forget?' He holds a hand over his scar.

'I didn't forget. It just wasn't worth arguing with you. Damn it,' I say, tipping my mug of tea down the sink. I'm so upset now, I won't be able to swallow it. I hate arguing with him. 'Mum's right. Secrets only cause more trouble in the end,' I say. 'I'm going back to bed, and I'm telling Mary tomorrow morning - when you and I get back from Outpatients. She has to work out for herself what she wants to do. I'll tell her we are here for her, whatever choice she makes.'

'It's Saturday tomorrow.' Richard looks triumphant.

'Yes.'

'Outpatients is closed on Saturdays. We only have to go in from Monday to Friday each week.'

'I thought it was every day?' I frown.

'Nope.'

We stare at each other. Crinkle eyes me then Richard.

'Have you forgotten that I just burnt the number?' Richard moves towards the stairs, his hand on the light switch.

'I put his number in my phone,' I say. 'She'll want to meet up with him, I'm sure.'

Richard leans down to rub Crinkle's ear. 'I wouldn't like to put money on it, would you, Piggy?' he says and I'm sure she nods her head at him.

Chapter 41

Billy

'Twenty-one days to lift off,' is scrawled in Richard's handwriting on a luminous note stuck to our action plan for today. Three weeks until our launch, and there isn't a mouthful of Gran Westcott's ice-cream in stock!

Richard and I keep revising the project plan because other things crop up which are more important than making ice-cream. Today was earmarked for me to start filling the smallest tubs we will sell with our most basic flavour, vanilla. Seemingly a simple task. The Jersey milk was delivered yesterday, and our own milk is waiting in the new refrigerated bulk tank, both ready to be pasteurised - the first part of the process, but I'm not in the factory. Instead, I'm in the dairy putting lids on yoghurt pots before they're sealed and packed. Although we never used to work weekends in the dairy, since we got the all-clear from the health inspector Mary has added Saturday mornings to the schedule for the next month, to help catch up with all the stock we've lost.

Mary is walking towards me. 'Where's Nan-Dan?' she asks. 'I thought she'd be doing this.'

'She's exhausted. You should have seen the spread she laid out last night. I made her have another hour in bed,' I say.

'Gloria and June seem to be having a lie in too. Neither one is answering their phone. It's certainly unlike them to be late or to ignore my calls for that matter.' Mary is sarcastic. 'I take it you're behind their absence? What's going on, Auntie?' she asks.

I kick a stool towards her. 'Sit down, please.'

'Are you going to interrogate me? Has something happened?' She flounces onto the stool.

'It's Sharmarke,' I say, desperate to get this over with.

She's back on her feet. 'What about him?'

* * *

'I'm glad you stayed in bed, Rich,' I say. 'I don't think you slept more than an hour last night.' I throw my shoes and socks off and unzip my jeans before diving in next to him.

My cold toes find his boiling hot legs. 'Yours and Crinkle's money is safe, by the way,' I tell him, my head crashing onto the pillow.

He smiles as he puts out his arm for me to lie on. 'So, Mary doesn't want to contact him?'

I burrow into his neck, not willing to say he was right, 'It feels like it's just us against the whole world,' I say. 'Like we are supposed to be here together in this moment.'

Richard makes a contented grunt.

Pushing myself up onto my arms, I stare into his eyes. 'She might change her mind,' I say.

'I don't think so.' Richard pushes my hair off my face. 'William and Mary came in to see me, ten, maybe a dozen, times while I was in hospital. They thought I wasn't watching them, but I was. Those two are right for each other. They complement one another and spark off each other too. Laughing together. It's something pretty special they have.'

'Like us,' I say, kissing him on the lips to make sure he can't say *no*. I run my finger lightly down one side of his long scar. '*My zip,*' he's nicknamed it, after one of the nurses told him he was a member of the Zipper Club – his open-heart surgery leaving him with a tell-tale calling card, a *zip* from below his chin down to his belly button. 'How about breakfast and then a walk?' I ask him.

'Billy, you should be making ice-cream right now, not here with me. We'll go for a walk around four, after you've got the first one hundred tubs done. You can bring a couple with you, and we can demolish them up on Primrose Mound.'

'I'll make your breakfast first,' I say, and I kiss him again, relishing that he is home.

Richard moves to get up, rolling onto his side, not using his arms in the way the hospital staff showed him. 'I can put cereal in a bowl,' he says as he gets to his feet. 'And I can make toast and brew coffee. You go, Billy, you're far enough behind already. I'm not an invalid. I'm allowed to lift light stuff; Cheerios aren't heavy.'

'But this is our second chance. Ice-cream seems so insignificant. I want to be with you.' I reach out to him, but he steps away.

'We have time. Go, please.'

As I'm about to head out the bedroom door, I notice a lump in the bed. At first, I think Richard placed a pillow next to him to stop him turning over during the night, but then I spy Crinkle's empty bed. I shake my head. *You rascal dog*, I say under my breath.

* * *

As I fill the hundredth carton of ice-cream from Brenda the blender, a shiver of sheer delight runs through me. I'm proud of the job I've done putting everything together. The equipment is noisy, but it works perfectly. With all the machines running, earplugs are a must, it's going to be different working in here than in the dairy, which isn't really mechanised at all - but still, the decibels are bearable. Especially bearing in mind the youngest device in my factory is at least fifteen years old - Gino said Andrew bought some of it second hand himself - and I never could have justified the hundred thousand pound set-up cost if I'd bought it all new. Brand new machines would be quieter, but nonetheless, it's all been well maintained, and it works like a dream.

Gino helped me get the actual mix of ingredients just right - the exact proportions of milk, dried skimmed milk powder, sugar and cream, and before the tasting party with his family, I spent a week making up batches of two litres of each flavour at a time - each day Gino popped in to give me feedback and tips to get the taste and creaminess just so. My final vanilla recipe melts in my mouth, the same way my dessert did in Polpeor Café on Valentine's Day. I could say it tasted better than the Cornish ice-cream, but like perfume, the enjoyment and perception will always be tempered by the particular circumstances of the moment it's experienced in - and Cornwall with Richard will always give that particular mouthful the edge.

* * *

Normally, when Buttercup spies me, she dips her head and stretches out her front legs like a puppy who wants to play. After her playful bow, she will rush up to me, nosing my pockets for a treat. I'll rub her forehead and feed her a piece of biscuit but now, as I watch her, she remains lying down, not moving to get up, and I'm sure she sees me.

Richard looks from Buttercup to me. 'Oh dear, you've spent so long in hospital it seems your favourite cow has forgotten you.'

For a split second, I think he's right – Daisy Mae usually follows her friend. She is more timid than Buttercup and normally hangs back a little bit but she's not approaching us either. As I open the gate, Buttercup still doesn't move and Daisy Mae stands next to her, their noses close together reminding me of the day when Jessie and I fetched them from Wales when Jessie said they were like two teenagers conspiring.

'Something's wrong with Buttercup!' I shout as I run towards them, my heart pumping. I call back to Richard. 'Look how she keeps swinging her head towards her belly. Her stomach's bloated.'

The other Jerseys have made an outer circle around Buttercup and Daisy Mae, all watching the pair closely. One makes a low moo at Buttercup, but she doesn't seem to notice. Daisy Mae kicks her hind leg up at her belly; she looks uncomfortable too. I kneel next to Buttercup, rubbing her between her ears but she pulls her head away from me. I look up at Richard, who's now just a few steps away from me. 'Call the vet, beg them to send someone fast, please,' I say. 'This is really serious.'

For twenty or thirty seconds Buttercup thrashes, trying to get up and then, exhausted, she lies flat on the ground. Her heart is trembling under her skin, and when her beautiful black eyes start to flicker, I feel sure she's giving up.

Richard is on the phone to the vet again, describing what is happening, mucus bubbles around Buttercup's mouth and nostrils. I shout at him, 'Say to hurry!' I throw my arms around my beautiful cow's neck, pushing my fingers into her skin. 'I love you. Please don't die,' I sob into her fur. 'No!'

Chapter 42

Billy

I've not met Eva Smith, the new vet, before - she's only been working for our local practice for three days, but I'm already impressed. Eva arrived in minutes, driving her 4x4 across the field to reach us. The first thing she did, though, was make Richard sit in her vehicle. She told him she wasn't looking at the cow until he did. With the shock of Buttercup in distress and being standing up for so long, Richard was grey and shivering. I was so caught up with my sick cow, I hadn't noticed, but Eva saw before she was even out of her car.

'Something's poisoned her, that's my first guess, is that what you think, Mrs May?' Eva asks.

I try to speak, but I can't. I nod at her. All I want to do is stroke Buttercup's sweaty neck. I want to massage her until she wakes up. I can't believe my gorgeous, clever cow is dead.

'From all you told me, I'm sure it is poisoning and the PM will just confirm it.' Eva scans the field. 'What could she have eaten?'

There is a voice behind us. 'These,' Mum says, holding up two tall stems of her pink and yellow lupins. *'Manhattan Lights, they give a real show and such a sweet scent.'* I recall Derek telling Mum, saying he grew exactly the same variety and what a picture they'd be in his garden if he was able to see them.

I frown at Mum. 'But she hasn't been in your garden.'

'No, but someone has. These are all I have left. My whole show has been hacked to the ground and cleared away. I noticed the destruction when I went out in the garden just now, looking for you two, and then I saw this young lady in the yard.' Mum waves a hand towards Eva now crouched next to Buttercup, examining inside her mouth - the vet's long dark blond hair is smeared in saliva and phlegm. 'She explained about Buttercup, so I opened the gate for her, telling her where you'd be.'

'Lupins are poisonous, aren't they?' I look at Eva.

'Very,' she agrees. 'Especially the seeds.' She turns to Mum. 'Had some of yours gone to seed?'

'Most of them,' Mum says as she kneels down next to me. She places a hand gently on my shoulder before she starts to stroke Buttercup's neck too.

The vet shakes her head. 'I'm sorry I was too late, Mrs May, actually by the time you discovered her, that would have been too late as well.' She gets up and walks towards Daisy Mae. 'I'm sure I can help this one though, maybe she didn't ingest as much.'

My insides feel wrung out. I shouldn't have allowed this to happen. I failed my darling cow. She was so important to me, like all my animals are. They are my friends, my children and my family.

'Arthur,' I say under my breath. 'You must have broken your parole – you should be nowhere near Fox Halt. *How could you kill her? They could all be dead!'*

A terrible crime has happened here – a crime I should have anticipated and prevented somehow. The stench of death and guilt overrides my senses. I feel helpless, unable to leave Buttercup's side, paralysed with grief and shock, and I watch in a haze as Mum slips a halter onto Daisy Mae.

My mum listens intently to Eva, who's giving her careful instructions about what we need to do to prevent Daisy Mae from suffering the same fate as her friend.

* * *

Twenty minutes later Eva has left, and Mum walks Daisy Mae back with Richard and me. I don't think the cow has ever been halter trained, but Mum is a bit of a Doctor Doolittle, and the poorly animal walks steadily by her side. Maybe the Jersey knows she needs to get to the stable so we can help her.

Her head is low, and I'm sure she, like all of us, is heartbroken about her pal. Buttercup was always the greedy one of the pair, Daisy Mae probably nibbled at the plants while her friend scoffed away, and that saved her life.

Chapter 43

Billy

It was easier in Outpatients this morning with no forms to sign or procedures to be briefed on, no wait for the doctor to check how Richard's bloods have been affected by the intravenous antibiotics. No rigorous monitoring; everything felt more relaxed. After yesterday's visit, we knew where we were going, the best place to park and how long we'd be expected to stay.

We spent only two and a half hours away from the farm. All the hospital staff were lovely, but it was another lesson in how lucky we are - each of the six chairs in the Outpatients room was booked for individual patients for an allotted time. The time it takes for their particular intravenous drip to run into their bodies. Over the last two mornings, we have spoken to many different people with many ongoing and long-term illnesses.

Richard will be attending the Medical Outpatients for the next few days, and then he's assured that the sepsis will be obliterated for good, but some patients we met, like those on kidney dialysis, have been visiting the unit at regular intervals for months, even years, requiring continuous treatment to help their bodies function. It is humbling, realising how they get on with living, despite being very ill. I take too much for granted.

Crinkle is still being a pain. Yesterday, she dived into the van before Richard had a chance to get in, and when I took her back to the house, she barked and whined until I said she could come with us. She won't leave Richard's side.

The solution I worked out so Crinkle could come to the hospital too, involved both Janette and Grace. Janette came with us to Exeter, holding Crinkle on her lap, while Grace with baby Tom manned the office. When we arrived at Outpatients, Janette stayed in the van with the little dog, reading Crinkle her latest novel to distract her. This morning, we've made the exact same arrangements.

I've called in the troops today, including Gino, who didn't need me to fetch him because his sister-in-law, Stella, offered to drive him over to Fox Halt, even offering to help me too. In addition to these two, I've recruited my cousin Tanya, Mum, Gloria and June, and the whole crew were chomping at the bit, ready to start at eight this morning, before I drove Richard to the hospital. I explained what I hoped they'd do. Gino knows the whole process inside out anyway, so I feel like I left everything in very safe hands.

Mum grabbed my arm just before I abandoned them, telling me in no uncertain terms that Daisy Mae was her priority, so if she needed to, she might be with her for the rest of the morning and not helping in the factory. The police are due to visit, and she is also going to show them the part of the garden where the lupins were. My mum's determined that Arthur should pay for his crimes. He hurt her beloved goats, wrecked her garden and I think she secretly loved Buttercup too – from all the attention she's lavishing on Daisy Mae, I can see she definitely adores her.

Richard isn't allowed to drive for another three weeks, not until he's been signed off by our GP, so he's been offering to get a taxi instead of me driving him, but I can't let him do that. I want to be there to keep him company while they administer his drugs. It's a long time for him to be sitting in the chair alone.

* * *

I walk into the factory, and I see all my apprentices working on different processes to the ones I expected. I imagined that the smallest tubs of rum and raisin would be finished by now, and they'd be filling more of the small tubs with honeycomb, but there is no sign of either flavour. Double chocolate chip is sliding out of Brenda into five-litre containers. I tap Gino on the shoulder. 'Where are the rum and raisin tubs?' I ask.

Gino shrugs. He has earplugs in, but I'm sure he's pretending not to hear. I signal for him to come closer. 'Could we pop outside?' I shout, mouthing my words carefully, so he has to understand.

He nods.

* * *

'Blimey, scorchio out here!' Gino says as the heat from the hottest day of the year so far hits our faces. The processing area in the factory is kept at nineteen degrees, but they said on the radio, it could reach thirty today.

'Where's the rum and raisin?' I ask again.

'I thought it was the wrong thing to concentrate on.' He casts his eyes to the floor, reminding me of Crinkle when she's done something she knows she shouldn't have done.

'I see,' I say, breathing in deeply, knowing I should be grateful he's helping me. 'But you did realise that I wanted the rum and raisin done first.' My attention turns to Mary as she opens the door of the dairy, stepping outside. She looks at me, waves and starts to walk towards us.

'But it's not one of the first ten flavours you've decided to stock.' Gino shrugs.

'It was what I wanted, and I'd specifically left those instructions—' I pause to look briefly again at Mary, and Gino turns away from me. 'Where are you going?' I frown at him.

'To get Stella, we'll go home now.'

'No, don't, please.' I grab his arm. 'I'm so grateful to you for coming today.'

'But I can't do as I'm told,' he replies, staring at Mary, who's standing beside us now. I watch as Mary presses her hand along her eyebrow as if to signal she doesn't want to get involved in an argument, and I assume too that she's waiting to speak to me.

'It's my fault,' I say to Gino, 'I didn't tell you why I needed the rum and raisin. It's a present.'

'A hundred tubs?' His eyebrows meet, forming a black line across his forehead.

'I don't need it all, but that's the smallest amount we can produce in one go. It's promised to the lady who sorted out the planning for me. I owe her a thank you, and it's her birthday today. I wanted to surprise her and deliver it this evening.'

'We better get back in there, then - pull the chocolate—' Gino starts to head back inside.

'But I need to explain why I only want the small tubs rather than the larger quantities,' I call after him.

He holds his hand up. 'Don't waste time on that now. Let me get this sorted first.'

'Are you sure?'

Gino smiles. 'We can empty the large containers back into Brenda and fill up small tubs instead. Then, we'll do rum and raisin. We'll have it ready by four, if I can persuade Gloria and June to let the machine keep streaming out the ice-cream without stopping between fills. They've had a bit of practice now, so it's a matter of concentrating and they must—'

'Stop chatting,' I cut in and laugh. 'Good luck with that. Two minutes, I'll help too. I just need to talk to Mary.'

Chapter 44

Billy

'I would like that number, please,' Mary says, nodding towards the pocket where I keep my phone.

I shake my head. 'No.'

'You said it was up to me to decide, and I've chosen to contact him.'

'I deleted it,' I say.

'You didn't.' She lifts my phone out of my pocket, enters my code before scanning my contacts list, and then she looks up and frowns at me.

'I changed my mind. You shouldn't contact him,' I say.

'I'm twenty-two, Auntie.' She stamps her foot. 'I know what I'm doing, and I want to speak to Sharmarke.'

'And what about William?'

'I told him last night.'

'I'm sure he wasn't happy about it, was he? How would you feel if he went off for the evening with Cara or Lorna?'

'He can go off with whoever he likes whenever he wants because I trust him – like he trusts me. I need to speak to Sharmarke just once. I want to know that he's okay.'

'Sweetheart, you've only just let yourself love again. Are you honestly strong enough to go through all the heartbreak of contacting Sharmarke, dredging up all that hurt?' A police car pulls up right next to us, and a policeman and a female PSO get out. 'Mrs May?' the support officer says, looking at me.

'You need to speak to my mother,' I say, pointing towards the ICF. 'She is working in there this morning.' I want to continue my conversation with Mary, and Mum can show them the garden.

Actually, I don't want to talk about Buttercup, I can't stop crying every time I think about her. I keep picturing her dying – and the anger inside me keeps bubbling up each time I think of Arthur killing such a trusting and gentle creature. My chest knots into a tight ball as I imagine him watching her eat the lupins. Her happily munching and him so evil, knowing the plants he'd fed her were toxic.

The PSO has not gone into the ICF but is now talking to her colleague, and the amount of head shaking makes me think they are disagreeing with one another.

Mary looks at me. 'I want to know what Sharmarke's been doing all these years, surely you understand that? I've question after question. My brain won't stop thinking about him. I loved him so much—'

'But you're with William. You need to appreciate what you have. You and Sharmarke are different people now—' The PSO interrupts me.

'Mrs May, we need to talk to you, not your mother,' she says.

'But Mum'll show you the garden. She'll show you where the lupins were cut from.' Once more, I point to the door of the factory, and this time she walks a few steps towards it before her companion catches up with her, making her stop.

I turn back to Mary. 'You're not children anymore. So much has happened. So much heartache since you were together. Do you think it can ever be the same?'

'It's my decision, Auntie. I have to know for sure.'

'Forget it, please, darling,' I say. 'Tell me you will—' The PSO and the policeman are standing next to me now. I turn to them and sigh, 'Okay, I'll show you the garden,' I say, and Mary walks away.

* * *

The doctor holds up the result sheet. 'That's it, Richard, we are happy with your blood result. No more sepsis, no more visits and no infusion today. You can turn around and go home, we don't need to see you again.'

'I had a feeling you would say that.' Richard smiles, and the doctor frowns. 'My dog hasn't left my side since I went home - but since yesterday morning, she hasn't bothered with me at all. She didn't sleep next to me last night, nor has she started howling as soon as we are separated. I feel sure she sensed I was healthy again.'

* * *

Mum insisted on a celebratory meal tonight to mark Richard being well again, and the old Friday night crew are in the farmhouse kitchen. Tom is asleep in a car seat by Crinkle's chair.

Janette was invited too, but it's her Pilates class tonight, and she didn't want to miss it. All afternoon Mum has been in her element, delighted to have so many mouths to feed and looking forward to all the chatter and laughter - and now, at last, our plates are loaded up with roast chicken dinner. Mum can't stop smiling at each of us in turn around the table.

I look across at William, noticing he hasn't lifted his knife and fork. Mary picks up on it too, and she nudges him and smiles. Suddenly, he is on his feet, his plate in his hand, 'Sorry, Daniella, I'm not feeling very sociable tonight, I'm going to head home.' He places his untouched meal next to the sink, and Mum is already standing next to him. 'Don't worry, William, you can take it with you,' she says. The rest of us watch as Mum finds an empty plate from nowhere and plonks it over William's meal, covering it up in Clingfilm in seconds. 'Here,' she says to him, wrapping two tea towels around it to keep it warm and holding it out to him.

'Thanks.' William takes the parcel, his eyes fixed on Mum but as he reaches the door, he turns to Mary, 'If I asked you to marry me, then would you not see *him* tomorrow?'

Mary doesn't look at him and says nothing.

'I can build us a house at Foxlands, or we can go to Culmfield, I don't mind.' He glances at the sleeping baby, 'We'll have kids, a bab—'

Mary beams at him, her whole face lights up, and I see William's eyes welling.

'You won't go?' he says.

'I'll marry you, William, but I'm seeing Sharmarke tomorrow; that's final. Not seeing him can't be a condition. It's not fair!' Mary's knife and fork are still in her hands, and I don't think she believes he's going to leave. However, William opens the door, turning back to Mary one last time. 'Please don't see him, I beg you.' His voice is crackly, sounding like he is about to cry.

Mary gets up. 'Auntie is coming with me,' she tells him, and suddenly her eyes are full of tears too but then she sits down again. 'No,' she cries out. 'How can I ever be with someone who doesn't trust me?' This is the first I've heard about Mary arranging to meet Sharmarke, or that she wants me to go with her. My eyes dart between her and William. It's as though a storm has risen out of a flat calm sea.

'Last chance, Mary?' he says, but she doesn't reply.

She doesn't even lift her head to look at him. The kitchen door shuts quietly, and our meal is eaten in silence, any thoughts of celebration disappearing with William.

* * *

'Come in.' Sharmarke's voice is light-hearted as if he'd just opened his front door to friends from the hospital. Mary doesn't move, mute and rooted to the spot.

'Nice house,' I tell him, giving Mary time to compose herself. 'There's a *Grand Design* look about it,' I stall. The house is impressive – its three-storey facade is snow-white as if it's just been painted. It's much bigger than any of its neighbours, detached with sweeping, manicured lawns running the five hundred metres down to the River Dart.

'It's not mine; we are renting it. I share it with a colleague,' he says.

'Oh,' I say, still wondering about the fortune it must cost to rent, right on the edge of Dartmouth.

'Would you like drinks?' he asks.

I wait for Mary to answer, but now she is staring at Sharmarke, and still no reply is forthcoming, she seems transfixed by his face.

'Tea would be nice,' I say. 'No sugar, please.'

He looks at Mary but I can see she isn't going to answer. 'For *both* of us, thanks,' I tell him.

Sharmarke pulls his eyes away from Mary. 'Do you want to wait in there?' He waves towards the entrance of a green oak conservatory which spans the width of the house.

'Can you hear it, Auntie?' Mary says as Sharmarke disappears into the kitchen.

'Hear what?'

'My heart, it is beating so loudly.' Mary throws herself into a comfortable looking armchair. 'I keep picturing us as kids,' she says, picking up a toy police car from the table next to her. It has a pair of happy eyes on the windscreen and a grinning mouth on the front bumper. She presses its wheel backwards on the table, and the car shoots forward, crashing onto the slated floor. She gets up to rescue it, then dives back into her chair.

'Me too,' I say, my mind now full of pictures of my days at Culmfield. 'On your horses, in grubby jodhpurs.'

'And later when we were teenagers—' Mary whispers, 'a hug, a nervous kiss, and the easy way we were together.'

'But you aren't children anymore,' I say, putting a toy lorry I've just stepped on next to the little police car.

Mary's on her feet again, walking towards the gap in the open bi-fold doors. She stands still watching the scene outside, and I move next to her. I stare across the river at the busy marina, full of yachts, and watch the ferry disgorging cars and foot passengers onto the Kingsweare bank of the estuary.

Sunlight sparkles off the various craft travelling up and down the wide watercourse. It looks idyllic, but it's far from peaceful - the rigging of the yachts corralled in the marina rattle in the breeze, like they are all quivering, desperate to escape their moorings. Voices of excited children carry across the water as the departing cars on the ferry turn off their engines. There are three mallard drakes quarrelling over a single female, and a moorhen whistles continually at her adventurous chicks, warning them to stay close to her.

'Here you are.' Sharmarke puts a tray onto a white, angular table that matches all the other chairs in the room except for the pretty ancient looking armchair Mary sat in. She walks towards Sharmarke. *A moth to a flame?* I hope not. I want to run away. *I must have been insane to have agreed to come.*

'I like your shoes,' Mary says to him, immediately blushing and looking back out through the doors to the river.

'Where is your house-mate, Sharmarke?' I ask, trying to distract him from Mary who's looking terrified again, hoping too that his friend might join us and make me feel less uncomfortable being here with them both.

'Marcus is with his boys, down there.' He waves towards the town centre, 'He only sees them once a fortnight, so he'll be buying them burgers and generally spoiling them rotten. Please call me Asad - I'm used to it now. Sharmarke was a lifetime ago.' His voice isn't as bright as it was, as though his confidence has gone. He's probably as nervous as Mary, just hiding it better.

'I was a lifetime ago,' Mary tells him.

'I've never forgotten you, Mary,' Sharmarke says, placing his hands on the table.

'You still ride?' Mary asks, sitting down opposite him, her hands on the table too, mirroring his action.

'No, I couldn't – are Braveheart and Steel still at Culmfield, are they pensioned out in one of the fields?'

Mary shakes her head, her eyes set on his. 'There are no horses or ponies there now. Both your horses were sold a month after you left. I wasn't interested in riding without you, and Charlotte wasn't there to look after the other animals – she and Grégoire moved to Paris.' She picks up her mug. 'Where are your parents, now?' she asks, putting the drink down, not even sipping it, her hands firmly pressed on the table again.

'Scotland, Dumfries,' he tells her. 'They work for this quirky museum – Dad does all the maintenance work there, and Mum's in the café – they've lived in the same house ever since we left.'

'Scotland?' Mary frowns, 'I imagined you'd be living in Birmingham. Your mum had a friend there, didn't she?'

'She did, but no. We lived in a village just over the border. I was at Cambridge.'

Mary frowns again, 'University?' She pauses. 'Really?'

Sharmarke nods.

'You were always clever, but wowee, that's impressive.'

'I was lucky, that's all, Mary. When we arrived in Dumfries, Mum and Dad put me in a secondary comprehensive school which, to be fair to them, looked pretty impressive with its quadrangle and bell tower, reminding us a bit of Exeter School, but it turned out that was where the similarity ended. It was shit, the lowest-rated school in the county – the teachers expected nothing. If the pupils didn't want to work, that was fine, and what they gave me to do, I'd covered the year before at Exeter. I was bullied from day one, called teacher's pet and a geek because I wanted to learn.'

'But you did okay.' Mary leans forward to touch his hands, and then recoils.

'I scrapped with the bullies, kept on landing myself in detention. I was in detention all the time. But it suited me because I could work there without being hassled.' Sharmarke smiles at Mary, a massive smile that would melt anyone's heart. He continues, 'That's how the deputy headmistress got to know me. I kept landing up in her office, explaining why I was in trouble again.'

'And that was a good thing?' Mary frowns.

'She felt sorry for me and she started to help me through my Nationals. Later on, she insisted on paying the majority of the fees for me to go to her son's private school to complete my Advanced levels. I got to Cambridge on a scholarship. Her son Marcus, got into Cambridge too, and I just followed him into becoming a doctor, without thinking about it really.'

'Marcus is only twenty-three,' I say, my interest suddenly piqued, 'and he has two children?'

'He's a rebel, I think that's why his mum took to me. He got his girlfriend pregnant when she was sixteen and again when she was eighteen. His poor mother tears her hair out, but Marcus and I got on as soon as we met, and we've ended up here. No grand plan or anything like that.'

I have so many questions, and while I'm here, seeing Mary and him falter over their words, I become impatient to know more. 'The four million pounds Jessie gave your dad, that would have paid for a good school?' I say, getting up from the table and taking my drink back to the bi-fold doors.

'It's still in the offshore account. Dad won't touch it. He's terrified the police would track him down if he tried to use it.'

Mary jumps up. 'It's *your* money – my father wanted *you* to have it.' She strides across the room to stand beside me.

Sharmarke stays put, making his hands into fists as Mary walks away from him. 'My parents rented a tiny two-bed terrace, the kind of place you might expect an immigrant family to live in, like everything my parents do – they stay under the radar, nothing is remarkable about them. New names and a new life,' he says. He looks at Mary. 'Are you still friends with Mollie?'

Mary nods her answer. 'I imagined you qualifying for the Olympic show jumping team,' she says.

Sharmarke laughs. 'Dad wasn't sure our passports were kosher. He didn't want scrutiny. Anyway, we'd have to be rich to have horses, especially top class showjumpers and Dad never wanted to give that impression to anyone.'

'Oh.' Mary looks sad. She knows what an amazing horseman he was. She must think of the wasted opportunity.

Sharmarke shakes his head. 'That was also the reason why Dad was set against me attending the private school. When I did go, Mum and he paid as much as they could from their wages, but Dad made sure everyone knew Mrs Adair was funding the rest of my fees.'

'Do you miss it?'

'School?' He frowns.

'No, riding.' Mary takes a step closer to me. 'Ouch!' She's standing on another toy, and straight away, she bends down to retrieve it. I watch as she takes a cute Lego hedgehog to the table, placing it between the lorry and the police car, putting it down carefully like it's made of glass. She sits down in the armchair again.

'For the first year, I missed the horses terribly,' he says. Sharmarke can't see Mary from where he's sitting, so he moves to stand next to the armchair, his back pressed against the wall and his hands tucked in behind him. 'Did you stay on at school?' he asks, now leaning down to pick up the police car.

'No.' Mary stares at the toy in his hand. 'I was lost. It took me a long time to get over you.' She glances up at him before her eyes dart to the car in his hands. 'And everything else that happened,' she says. 'I started working at Fox Halt Farm as soon as I left school. I needed to get away – there were just too many hurtful memories at Culmfield for me to stay. I live there still, but it's just a place to sleep, that's all.'

'We were deeply in love, weren't we?' Sharmarke twists the car over and over in his hand.

'Young love, an extraordinary love,' she says, looking up at him again, this time leaving her eyes on his. 'I was devastated when your mother told me you were my half-brother. It was physical pain I felt. Like a real broken heart.'

'I'm not your brother.' His voice is soft.

'Auntie told me.'

'So that changes everything,' he says, moving to sit on the arm of her chair.

'It changes nothing. You're Asad now.' Mary touches his hand, the one holding the car, and her words start to tumble out. 'I was in love with *Sharmarke*. I'm not in love with Asad. You've done a hundred new things since we were together, experienced new places, had new girlfriends. You and I are different people now. I was curious to know you were okay. That's why I'm here. We can't go back to the way we were.'

'No girlfriends. No-one ever measured up to you.' He releases the toy car into Mary's hand.

'But I'm not the person you remember. Your memories

are made up of all the good bits. You've forgotten all my wicked habits, how I used to put you down, all our fights, how I teased you and exploited your feelings for me. You never said no to me. What sort of relationship was that really?'

'It was special, Mary. It could be good again. I'm *not* your brother. We love each other.'

She lifts her hand away. 'I'm glad I'm here today, Asad, but this is it.' Mary stands up. 'When I leave in a minute, we return to our new worlds.'

He gets up too, which I take as my cue to leave, but then he moves towards her and tries to kiss her. Mary turns her head away. Her hands are shaking as they stand apart, staring at one another. 'Does William know you're here?' he asks, stepping back a little.

'Yes.' Mary looks at me again, 'but even with Auntie here, this still feels illicit - it shouldn't do, but it does.' Mary's hands tremble even more. 'Sharmarke, I have to go,' she says.

'No.' He grabs her hand, enfolding it in his. 'We'll rekindle what we had?' he says. 'Reignite the sparks.' Sharmarke smiles. 'Listen, I'm on holiday from Friday and heading back to Annan to see Mum and Dad. Come with me, spend a week with me. See if you truly have no feelings for me anymore. It was so fierce for us, Mary. No way can that have just evaporated away.'

'No—' she says, her voice firm.

'We can see my parents and then I'll take you to Cambridge to show you all my favourite places. We can fill in all the missing gaps in our lives.'

'Sorry, Sharmarke, I won't open old wounds. I'm with William now. Ours was young love, that's all.' She pauses, 'Yes, you *were* the world to me, but that's no longer true. On the outside, I see Sharmarke but inside you and I've changed too much.' Mary looks at me. 'Auntie, we'll go?' she says.

Chapter 45

Billy

Mary stops rinsing the muslins as soon as she realises I'm behind her. 'I've blocked his number. He kept texting me, begging to see me again. Each time his name flashed up, it made my heart beat so fast, but I didn't answer – not once.'

'Poor you.' I touch her arm.

'It's like I'm drugged. I can't get him out of my mind. My head's throbbing, and I keep feeling sick or bursting into tears,' she says, drying her hands on a paper towel, wiping each finger and her thumb meticulously as she looks at me.

I pick up the muslins to take them to the drying area. 'It's brought back a lot of emotions. It will get easier.'

'Auntie, I know his face by heart,' she says, pulling out another paper towel as though she's forgotten her hands are already dry. 'I know the lines on his fingers. I can see every eyelash. I keep thinking about how he blinks when he's listening to me.' She throws her arms down by her sides. 'I keep wondering if I've got it wrong.' She points at the windowsill. 'Look!'

I shake my head, and then I reach for the little police car on the window ledge. I drop it in my pocket. Mary looks at me. 'Thank you,' she says, her face earnest. 'That darn thing has followed me around for days. It was by my mug at breakfast. It's been on the edge of my bath. It was even on my pillow all last night!'

I tap my pocket. 'I'll put it in an envelope and post it back.' I smile, wishing I could take her pain away too and mail it somewhere far away. 'I know Sharmarke's happiness is important to you,' I say, 'but you have to look after yourself. You weren't expecting this, were you? The hurt all over again or the quandary about what it would be like to be with him?'

She shakes her head. 'I don't even know if he's being honest with me. Every nurse must swoon over him. He can't be single, can he?' Mary stares at my pocket. 'I feel thirteen again. It's like when Nala told me I had to break up with him.'

* * *

The following morning, I open my eyes to see Richard standing beside the bed. 'Happy birthday,' he says, holding out a china pineapple to me - the single item Saffi left Richard in his will. The ugly thing sits on our sideboard in the sitting room, and whenever I look at it I smile, remembering Saffi and the wonderful surprise he concealed inside it, tickets for the Paris opera - to go with him and Richard. I swallow hard as a tear starts to run down my face.

Richard has leaned down to kiss me, but I dive away, 'Are you kidding me?' My voice is low.

'Billy, What—'

I hold up my hands, breathing in slowly, staring back at him. 'It's not my birthd—' I gulp for air, trying to keep a sob from coming. I'm upset that Saffi is no longer here, upset too that Richard doesn't know when my birthday is after all these years together. *We are leaving on my birthday for our trip around Europe, that's ten days away.*

He's frowning, open-mouthed.

Pictures rush into my mind, Saffi in the bath, the bloody water soaking into my clothes, more blood. My miscarriage, the pain and the loss, and now on top of all this horror. Disgust that my husband hasn't even bothered to think of a novel way to wrap my present and that he is giving me on the *wrong* day. That was Saffi's idea, not his! *I hate surprises... He should know that.* Tears are coming now from my feet and emptying up from my stomach. I'm hyperventilating. All I can do is sob and gasp, sob and gasp...

Richard puts the pineapple down on the bedside cabinet and grabs my arm. 'Billy, stop this.' He yanks my wrist, but I don't stop, my anger firing out between gasping for air and sobbing my heart out. 'Do you know anything about me? Do you know how much you hurt me wanting Grace to get rid of Tom? Did you once think of that?'

It's like my chest is collapsing in on itself. I can't get enough air into my lungs. I keep on though, shooting hurt after hurt at him, 'Saffi... Tom... Dad, all of them dead. Why do you think I want to work all the time? I need to blank it out. Sitting still is hell for me… You can't even get my birthday right!' I slide out of bed and onto the carpet, pushing my back up against the side of the bed. I sit on the floor, hugging my knees and rocking.

'I know it's not your birthday.' Richard jumps back like I've just hit him. 'How senseless do you think I am?'

But I'm not taking in what he's saying. I'm sitting with my back to the bath. I'm with Saffi, crying my heart out over him killing himself and crying about Ross too. 'Saffi, Ross—' I sob and Richard cuts in kneeling down beside me. 'I loved Saffi too. I wish Ross was here too,' he says.

Something about him saying our baby's name makes me laugh. I'm up on my feet in a flash, staring down at him. 'You have no idea,' I say through gritted teeth, throwing my arms back. My hands catch the pineapple, cracking it against the wall. 'You have no idea—' The shock of seeing that I've broken the treasured pineapple makes me stand there gazing at it, my face hot, snot running under my nose, my eyes full of tears.

'That's *not* how it is…' Richard is up and he is trying to catch hold of my hands, but I keep pulling away.

'It hurts all the time,' I yell at his face, and then I wipe my nose on the cap sleeve of my nightshirt.

He looks away. 'I've lost them too.' I hear him sob. He is looking around the room, everywhere but me and now, he leans down and picks up a small gold envelope from the floor - it must have been hidden inside the pineapple just like Saffi's gold envelopes were. 'Here,' he says, opening the envelope and sliding a card out from inside.

When I don't take it, he places the card where the pineapple was before I knocked it. 'I thought it would be best to give you your present early, so you could enjoy it before we go.' He is crying, and he wipes his face with his fingers.

His tears make me feel like I've punched him in the gut. I am suddenly so sorry for my outburst and so full of love for him. Wishing I could take all my evil words back. The card has a buttercup on the front. I sigh as I stare at it. 'Buttercup!' I say, my throat sore and my words hoarse.

'We need to talk about Ross.' He wipes his eyes again.

'Our baby,' I say, reaching out for Richard to hold me.

'Yes, our Ross.' I look into Richard's eyes. 'Please. I want to talk about him…' My husband wraps his arms around me, and holds me so tight. 'Ross,' I say again. 'Ross…

* * *

The Jersey cow blinks her long lashes as she pushes her head over the stable door. 'Say hello to Lowencombe's Circus Lady,' Richard says, kissing me on the cheek. 'Happy birthday, darling.' I recognise her first name immediately because I didn't choose my small Jersey herd at random. They were all sired by a particular Lowencombe bull, who'd won best in breed at four major agricultural shows three years ago.

'She's beautiful,' I say, rubbing her forehead like I used to with Buttercup. 'So tame too, she's even looking for a biscuit just like Buttercup did.'

'That's all the showing she's done. She won Devon County, last month.' Richard smiles.

'She's from me too.' Mum walks up to us.

I frown at her. 'But you don't want the Jerseys here.'

'I've had a lot of time to think, Billy, if you introduce them gradually, ease them into the herd over the next few years until they make up half, then that'll be okay with me. I've been keeping a beady eye on them whilst you were with Richard in hospital, and when Buttercup died, I realised how fond I had grown of them all. Daisy Mae has been my reason to get out of bed this last week.' She smiles, a really big smile, and her eyes glitter. 'We should try something new, keep on taking the farm forward, we can't live in the past,' she says.

Richard slides a hand around my waist, patting Circus Lady's neck with the other. 'Daniella knows the farmers at Lowencombe, so she bought her. She wasn't even for sale, but when I said to your mum about buying her for your birthday, she was determined to get her for you. All I did was provide the money for her to complete the deal last week.'

'You're joking?' I laugh. 'My mother could never have kept that secret, not for a whole week.'

Richard smiles. 'She did.'

'That is a bigger surprise than Circus Lady here,' I say, shaking my head.

Mum laughs. 'Love you so much, Billy,' she says, touching my cheek.

'Love you too,' I say and I look from Mum to Richard, and then to my birthday present.

* * *

While I'm bolting the stable door, having just fed Circus Lady and given her a cuddle, I notice Mary climb into her car. She doesn't look up at me, and in a few seconds, she speeds out of the yard without a backward glance.

* * *

In the office, sitting in Grace's chair, Janette looks up from her mobile and smiles at me.

'Is something wrong at Culmfield? Is that why Mary left in such a rush? Do you know where she was going?' I fire my questions at Janette before I'm even halfway through the door.

Janette shrugs. 'She said she'd done everything for the day and that she was off. She wished me a good time with Paulo tonight.' Janette lifts her mobile off the desk and waves it at me as if to indicate it was Paulo she was messaging when I walked in – Mary has kept me posted about Janette's burgeoning romance with her Pilates instructor, but I feel uncomfortable talking to my husband's ex-wife about her love life. 'Okay,' I say, 'If you have any questions during the rest of the day, just text me.'

She nods, her eyes scanning a new message that's just pinged in.

Suddenly dread creeps over me; it's Friday, and *he* invited her to Scotland today. *Is Mary heading to see Sharmarke? Did she not want me to have the opportunity to change her mind?*

* * *

Monday, and I feel I haven't slept all weekend, anxious about Mary, but my brain is now switching between concern for Mary and worrying about a couple of health and safety folders I need to make up for the ICF before the launch. It will be another *little job* I can cross off the thirty or so items on my *'little jobs list'* which I need to sort out before Saturday.

As I creep across the yard to the ice-cream factory, trying not to disturb the visitors in the holiday cottages, I feel a vibration against my thigh. My phone is always on silent, and often I imagine the pulse of a text, so when I lift my mobile out of my pocket to check, I'm not expecting anything. No-one will be contacting me this early in the morning.

'Sorry, I can't make it back today xxx' This is all Mary's message says.

I hesitate before replying, *'Okay, I am always here for you.'*

There's nothing to be gained from questions or expressing my disappointment about the path she's chosen. I take in a deep breath, thinking how I'll have to step into her shoes today.

As I start working out the logistics of running the dairy and making deliveries on top of everything else on my list, a tightness builds in my chest. I think how William told me he didn't know where she was, and how Jessie said the same thing. I'm sure though, in truth, all of us know where she is, and who she is with. I fear the repercussions. Have I lost my *darling girl* for good? *Will she be happy?*

Chapter 46

RICHARD

Each day, we add two minutes to the length of our late afternoon walk - it's a special time to catch up on what Billy is organising for the ice-cream launch and a precious time to chat about all the things I'm doing to prepare for our motorhome trip. We have agreed that we will leave early on the twenty-seventh just two days after the launch. Billy has enough on her plate with the ice-cream and everything else, and I'm pleased to have a project of my own. All sorts of items keep being delivered to the farm, which I have seen recommended on caravanning forums or in magazines, declaring it's *the best*, or we *shouldn't be without*.

I have booked our ferry tickets and the first three camp sites, but although our trip is all planned out, I'm not booking any more places to stay. We want it to feel like a holiday - untied to a fixed itinerary.

I haven't told Billy, but as soon as I hear her footsteps in the yard in the mornings, I jump out of bed to go to see the sheep - it's an additional bit of exercise on top of the amount the hospital has recommended for me to do each day. I don't want Billy worrying I am doing too much, but I'm determined to be fit by the time we leave. On the walk, I spend ten minutes, just with my back to the field gate, gazing at the Jerseys. It's life-affirming, making me grateful for being well again and for living in this incredible place.

The early morning sun reflects off Daisy Mae's coat, and as her warm breath condenses in the cool air, it's like she's having a crafty cigarette - the 'smoke' from her mouth giving away her guilty crime. I look from her to the rest of the heard and realise she's on her own. Even Nutmeg isn't with her. Since Buttercup died, Daisy Mae and Nutmeg are new best friends. All the other heifers, except Daisy Mae, are lying down in a group under a horse chestnut tree. I stride towards Daisy Mae, wondering what's wrong, the nightmare of Buttercup being poisoned at the forefront of my mind, but with two more steps, I relax a little. I can see a calf's two white-tipped hooves inside Daisy Mae's ballooning birthing sack. This is all I can see. There is no nose yet, so I don't know if the calf is the right way around, it could be a breech birth where the calf is backwards, and if this is the case, it will probably need help to be born.

I panic again. Billy always gets the Friesians in the shed a day or two before they are due to calf so she can monitor them, making sure the cow is alright, and someone is on hand in case there are any problems. I text Billy, *Daisy Mae is calving – what shall I do?*

* * *

BILLY

The calf instinctively struggles to get up. She can't, and Daisy Mae starts to nuzzle her, licking her soaking wet fur as she lies on the ground. The other cows have come to investigate, standing a few feet away now, pushing their noses out toward the calf and sniffing the air. Their ears forward, their eyes wide, curious about what Daisy Mae has found, keeping their distance in case it's dangerous. Even Nutmeg hangs back.

Five minutes later, and the new baby is kneeling on her front legs, her back legs straight, her mother still frantically licking her like she tastes better than anything Daisy Mae has ever licked in her life. She's up. She's down again, and still Daisy Mae licks. Up again, seeming to know right away where her breakfast can be found. Stepping towards her mother's tail before crashing back onto the floor.

Eight minutes and the calf finds a teat. Daisy Mae nudges her into a better position to drink before starting to graze contentedly as though this happens every day. While she sucks, the calf keeps a wary eye on Richard and me, her lower jaw rhythmically squeezing milk from her mum's udder, her mouth frothing with the creamy liquid.

The baby stops guzzling and starts to walk towards the other cows, but Daisy Mae heads her off, making her stay close to her. Richard reaches for my hand as we watch, spellbound by the new arrival. The first Jersey to be born on the farm. 'I'm so glad we witnessed this,' I say.

'And all on video,' Mum is standing behind us, waving her phone. We had no idea she was there, and she's filmed the whole birth. She has the biggest grin on her face. 'If we take the pair of them down to the shed, I could get a shot of the farm's newest baby with Betsy and Bramble. It will be a great post for the blog.' – Mum hasn't sewn or knitted a thing since I created the blog page on the Fox Halt Farm website. Every night she writes a four-hundred-word update, as though the clever goats tell the world about their day on the farm. She's always taking photos or videos – and now Mum spends each evening answering comments too. Betsy and Bramble have their own Facebook page, and a Twitter account and Mum manages it all.

Mum loves it, communicating with the world, and her audience grows every day. There are trolls and negative comments, but Mum seems to delight in blocking them, concentrating on the goats' hundreds of fans instead.

'I'm not sure about taking them to the shed,' I tell Mum.

'Why not?' Richard asks, looking up from the video Mum is showing him.

'Because I'm wondering if they'll be better off here. They have the mobile milker, so Daisy Mae can choose to get rid of her excess milk whenever she wants to.'

'But you need to wean the calf off Daisy Mae in a couple of days,' Mum says, taking some photos of the calf. 'How will you know this little mite is getting enough milk otherwise? It's so easy to keep a careful eye on the young ones in their pens.'

'Mum, I want to try leaving them with their mothers. It'll cut down on the labour needed to look after them, and I want to see how the calves fare being with their mum's for longer.

'But—' Richard looks at me and frowns.

'What?' I say, cutting him off, feeling defensive and outnumbered. This is something I've been considering ever since the Jerseys arrived, something else new I'd like to try.

'But look at Daisy Mae,' Richard says, 'She won't let anyone near her calf. If you do this, the young stock will miss out on the human contact that the Friesian calves have. How tricky will it be to handle the Jerseys in the future?'

'I honestly don't know, Rich, but other farmers are doing it. I think if we are around them enough, they'll get to know us. I plan to give them two months with their mothers before we wean them. The mums will be pretty fed up with them by then.

We'll keep all the youngsters together for a while after that, and the cows can be back in their little herd too. I think it'll work. I want to try it.'

'You'll lose two months' milk,' Mum says.

'Not completely,' I snap back. 'The cows will produce more than the calves drink every day, and we'll have that.'

Richard opens his mouth, closes it again, then he looks at Daisy Mae and her calf before looking back at me. At last, he says, 'You won't be here, Billy. You could be leaving Hols with a right mess to sort out in a week or two, once all of the Jerseys have calved. Is that fair on her?'

'If it works, she'll have less to manage,' I say quickly.

'*If* it works.' Mum is staring at me too. 'And Hols has Circus Lady to integrate in with this lot once she's finished her quarantine. She is only nineteen, remember, that's a lot to deal with if this new system starts to fall apart, especially on top of what she's already doing.'

'I don't think it will fall apart,' I say, 'Let's see what happens in the next day or two, I'll keep a close watch on them, if problems start, I'll wean Magic Boo, and that'll be it, we'll go back to the way we've always done it.'

'Magic Boo?' Richard frowns at me.

'Do you like it? It's what I wanted to name our first calf.'

'What's a *boo*?' Mum takes another photograph.

I point at the calf, now nose to nose with Crinkle - who, like Mum, has appeared from nowhere. 'That's a boo,' I say. A magic one.' In this moment, my phone vibrates. It's a new text from Mary, saying she won't be here today, either. I don't reply. I just send '*xxx*'.

Another text and I guess it's Mary again, but it's not, it's from Jessie - '*Mary is here, can you come over?*'

I scratch my head, running through possible new arrangements for the day. Gloria and June helped last week in the factory, but this week they are scheduled to be back in the dairy. I feel as if I am being pulled every which way. I'd like to stay here with Daisy Mae and Boo, stay here next to Richard and Mum and just stand and stare - drink it all in, forget the rest of the places I need to be, and all the things I still have left to organise for the launch, but instead, I send a reply text to Jessie. '*I'll be with you in an hour x,*'

* * *

'So, essentially, you can't come back to Fox Halt because of William?' I ask, trying to summarise the words between Mary's sobs.

She nods, keeping her eyes on the floor.

'I have to go,' Jessie says. 'I'm sorry, but I've got a new case – I need to be at Killerton House in ten minutes to meet a mum and her son. She told her husband she'd been given a free family ticket in the supermarket.' Jessie pulls on a Doc Marten boot over a sock with a hole in the toe. I guess the rambling detail is because she feels guilty about leaving her daughter in such a state. 'I'll be back by one. Text me if you need anything,' she tells us, but it's only me who acknowledges her. Mary is still crying into my neck.

Jessie gives me a thumbs up.

I shrug at her, wondering what to do next.

'…and Grace.' Mary's voice is so quiet I can hardly hear. We are sitting at the kitchen table – the same table I've sat at a hundred times before, drinking tea with Jessie debating plans for Culmfield, even before Mary was born.

'Are you glad you saw Nala and Amir?' I ask. I have no idea where to start, I know she needs to talk, but I don't want to give her answers. She must work this out herself. She doesn't reply. I try again. 'Were they surprised to see you?'

'He'll never forgive me, will he, Auntie?' Mary says, looking at me through her mess of red hair. Her curls have sagged and knotted together, and I imagine her rubbing her head into her pillow for hours last night. I'm not going to say that William will forgive her. He'll be hurting, knowing she has been with Sharmarke for the last four days. I stare back, not saying anything.

'What a mess,' she says. 'What would you do?'

I've run headlong into one disaster after another. No, not run, I fell into most of the things that have happened to me, allowing myself to be dragged along, letting things happen that I should have faced up to and dealt with. 'I'd probably still be in Cambridge,' I say.

Her eyes are wide. 'You think I should be with Shar—'

'No—' I cut in. 'You asked me what I'd do, and I'm saying what I would've done, I'd never have had the guts or the sense to seek my own goals or realise what was wrong. I wouldn't be here, admitting I'd made a mistake.'

She sighs, putting her head in her hands.

'But you wouldn't have known it was a mistake if you hadn't had the guts to try,' I say. 'Whatever happens, you know now.'

'I suppose.'

'And you walked away, that's good too.'

She sips her tea. 'Are there any biscuits?' she asks.

I get up, instinctively opening the cupboard above the sink to find them.

'This is where you are hiding.' Max, Mary's youngest brother, walks in and sits at the table next to his sister. 'I'll have a couple of those, please,' he says when he spies me opening a new packet of chocolate digestives.

'Have you just got up?' Mary asks Max.

'Yes.' Max lays his head on the table, looking as though he'd like to go back to sleep right away.

Mary pushes his shoulder. 'I thought you were supposed to be revising.'

'One's got to eat,' he says, picking up the two biscuits I've laid in front of him. He bites into both at once like a sandwich. 'Wish Mum would only buy milk chocolate ones. She knows I prefer milk chocolate.' He sits up and pretends to punch his sister in her chest. 'And you ate all the *milk* chocolate ones last night.'

'You were here yesterday?' I ask Mary, who's scowling at Max.

'Came back at lunchtime,' Max tells me, 'Ate most of *my* biscuits then. She said she didn't want lunch, but then she kept on stuffing her face with *my* biscuits while she moaned on and on about how stupid she was. She could have had the dark chocolate ones instead. I told her they were better for stress, more cocoa.'

Mary stands up. 'Shall we go in the drawing-room, Auntie? It's much quieter in there.' She looks at her brother and seizes the packet of biscuits. 'Max, you don't like these, remember.'

The drawing-room has always been my favourite room at Culmfield. The light oak panelling runs floor to ceiling, but it's the plasterwork around the cornices and the fireplace that makes it breath-taking. The ornate decoration is a copy of the master sculptor and woodcarver Grinling Gibbon's work in

Hampton Court Palace, moulded with such natural-looking acorns, flowers, and fir cones, you feel you could pick them.

In stark contrast to the elegant walls and ceilings, Jessie's tatty furniture and curtains look like they came from a clearance sale. I pause to gaze at the carving. I know Jessie hates spending money on herself, thinking it would be better saved for *WhatIf,* but it would be nice if just this special room could be furnished properly.

Mary sits down heavily on the threadbare sofa, picking up a leopard print cushion which she holds against her skinny body like a shield. I sit on the same sofa but as far away as I can from her so I can twist my body to talk face to face.

'You'll have to manage without me, Auntie,' she says. 'I'll never be able to come back to Fox Halt. It's not fair on William – I don't want to bump into him. I don't want it to be awkward for him.'

'But he won't be at Fox Halt if you aren't there. I haven't seen him since Friday. He has no reason to come over.'

'He'll be doing the milking at weekends while you and Richard are away in the motorhome, won't he?'

'At weekends, yes, but you won't be working in the dairy then.'

'Grace will kill me. She warned me never to hurt her brother, and that's what I've done, haven't I?'

'Grace will probably stop talking to you for a week, but that's all,' I say, sliding towards her a little. 'She won't be able to help herself, you know she can never stop talking, and she cares about you, Mary.'

'I can't,' she says, throwing the cushion at me.

I let the missile roll onto the floor. 'But you have to come back, Mary. Even if you've lost William, you can't give up on Fox Halt. The farm needs you. I need you.' I slide off the raggedy sofa to kneel on the floor in front of her. 'I need you.' I stare up into her eyes. 'And Richard, and Nan-Dan, they need you too. Fox Halt Farm is empty without you. Please come back.'

Chapter 47

Billy

The boy scrambles up into the *WhatIf* bus, and I watch his mother climb in next to him, pulling out a furry penguin from her handbag and passing it to him. 'Peter,' he says and smiles.

'Are they allowed in the front seats?' I whisper to Jessie.

'No, but I can't put them in the back on their own, the poor woman's terrified. I need to keep reassuring her.'

'Do you have time to talk to me?' I ask.

Jessie nods. 'For a minute. How's Mary?'

'I didn't push her,' I say. 'She has to work this out for herself.' My eyes move back to the woman and child. 'Look, I think you need to go, Jessie,' I say, nodding towards the bus. 'I told her that I hoped she'll talk to William.'

I'm not sure Jessie is listening. Her eyes are on her passengers, waiting for her to drive the bus away, but another question bubbles into my mind. 'How's Arthur?' I ask,

'He's telling everyone life's not fair. Says he should have been fined and his case shouldn't be going to court. I'm not giving him any sympathy, though. His barrister has warned him it could be treated as a bit of a show case. His entitled attitude and his privileged background, taking over *his daddy's* company could be used by the judge as a stark lesson to others thinking of hurting others. He's likely to get a long sentence.'

'Is he in Richmond?' I ask.

'Yes. He's not welcome at Culmfield.'

* * *

Launch day dawns with William milking the Friesians for me while I check the Jerseys.

There are four calves now, one bull calf and three heifers. All four, healthy, strong and beautiful - a few days after the Jerseys arrived, Grace and I set up the robotic milker so that when the cows entered it, they'd receive some food as a reward, the cows' individual ear tags signalling to the machine which animal has entered, and then it provides each cow with its correct ration of food. Two weeks later, Grace reprogrammed the robot to still feed the cows but also for the robot to wash their udders while they ate - and a month after that, she made it clamp on the milking cups for ten seconds to get them used to that too - it couldn't milk them because they didn't have any milk.

Now that some of the cows have calved, the robot is reprogrammed to milk three of the Jerseys' four teats, and in addition to this, I adapted the physical shape of the machine so that their calves can enter too, waiting beside their mother without interfering with the milking machine.

I've been checking on the Jerseys for half an hour each morning and evening, looking to see if the robotic machine is working properly. I have a wildlife camera that takes photos when it senses movement, and this allows me to see what's happening when I'm not around. The times each cow enters the machine is recorded, but I want to be sure the calves are happy when their mums are being milked. So far, so good, but I'm keeping my fingers and toes crossed it will stay that way. If it continues to work, I can leave the calves with their mothers for a longer period of time.

For the first two weeks after the calves are born, the mother's milk has a high level of bacteria in it so it won't be used for human consumption, but after that, all the milk can be used for Gran Westcott's ice-cream, but sadly I'll be away with Richard when we reach this exciting milestone.

I've used every avenue I can think of to promote the Fox Halt Farm Open Day with the Special Launch of the ice-cream set for twelve o'clock mid-day. Everyone's invited to see the animals, dairy, and the factory and to try our new ice-cream.

So many people are helping today. William's giving trailer rides mainly because it gave him an excuse to drive Grandad's old tractor - which his father helped my dad restore. Janette's set up a scavenger hunt, and Mum has organised a chicken egg hunt, where families seek out hard-boiled eggs she's hidden in Home Field - there's a free ice-cream for every twelve eggs they discover.

Freddy put together a game he's named Poo Snap where the children have to match poo in plastic bags with cut-out shapes of the animals who made the poo, but I have a sneaky suspicion that Jessie and Herbie will be the busiest of all my helpers today because they're introducing Betsy and Bramble to everyone. I'm sure the goats will be the main attraction, maybe more so than the ice-cream!

There's a hog roast and hot dogs which another local farm has organised, and the local producers of the goods we sell in the farm shop - like honey, wine, and chutneys have all set up stands too. The makers will be able to talk about their artisan goodies and explain all about how and where it's made, and they're handing out lots of freebies too.

Gino and his extended family are the first to arrive, and as the day speeds along, there is lots of laughter and chatter' it is fabulous to share Fox Halt Farm with so many others.

When Jazmin, the young girl who was in Intensive Care with Richard, and her sister Bess turn up with their parents, Richard takes them for a private trip around the farm in William's Land Rover.

Afterwards, he gives the sisters their own individual tour around the ice-cream factory, letting them use Bertie to fill their own tubs of ice-cream. 'It wasn't like Willy Wonka's chocolate factory,' Bess is telling me, but Crinkle wearing a goat-patterned onesie soon cheers her up with a big lick across her face - I gave Crinkle a bath this morning and as soon as Jazmin arrived, Richard slipped the dog into the onesie (Mum made the outfit). The girls take it in turns to cuddle the dog in pyjamas, and Jazmin's not worrying about all the dirt and dust Crinkle usually carries around in her coat.

I have set up a piece for Spotlight, our Devon BBC News television channel with Jazmin, Bess and all Gino's nephews and nieces holding an ice-cream cone, each filled with different flavours of Gran Westcott's Ice-Cream. Of course, Betsy and Bramble are in the picture too. A far cry from our newspaper disgrace and the humiliation of the closure notice.

They say never work with children and animals, but I have an extension to this piece of advice, never work with children, animals *and ice-cream*. It is near impossible making two minutes' worth of video with all the children wanting their favourite flavours of ice-cream, getting them in the places we need them to stand - and all the time, while the ice-cream melts in the hot sunshine, the two rascal goats try helping themselves to the children's cornets. We end up with a lot of giggling and bleating, an exasperated cameraman and a creased-up reporter.

Mum videos the chaos. 'That'll be perfect for the blog,' she says, pocketing her phone with a smile.

I listen as Freddy asks Gino if he will help him occasionally, and I continue to eavesdrop as Gino provides him with a complete list of Andrew Arscott's former customers and what he remembers they used to order. It's a poignant moment, witnessing Gino's enthusiasm and seeing young Freddy hang on his every word.

'That's the last tour,' William tells me, 'I'll put the tractor away and head home.'

'Thanks for everything you've done today,' I say when I follow him into the tractor shed.

'I'll disconnect the battery. It might be a while before she's used again.' William doesn't look at me as he lifts the bonnet of the Fordson Major.

'Have you heard from Mary?' I ask.

His attention remains on the tractor. 'It's too hot. I can't put the dust cover over her yet,' he says.

'She's at Culmfield. She came back on Monday. She knows she has hurt you terribly. The girl was in bits when I saw her. Jessie says she can't stop crying.'

'You might want to put her up on blocks, take the pressure off the tyres if you are not planning on using her for a while.' William holds out the tractor's ignition key to me.

'Mary knows how much she has hurt you, William. She had to work things out in her own mind, but she realises how much she loves you, that's why she didn't stay in Cambridge, but she's too scared of rejection to face you. Too frightened, you'll not forgive her.' I touch his sleeve.

'She is such a great tractor, Billy. Some of the old boys say to wipe them down with a rag soaked in diesel. They swear it helps to stop rus—' There's a crashing noise outside the shed and then a yelp. William and I rush to investigate and see Mum standing next to an old trestle table that she must have been trying to fold up. The table lies on the ground beside her. William rushes to Mum, who's shaking a hand out.

'Are you okay?' he asks her, picking up the heavy table with one hand, the other lightly rubbing Mum's shoulder.

'Yes, dear boy.' My mother holds two of her fingers, squeezing them together.

'Have you hurt yourself, Mum?' I ask.

'I'm fine,' she says. 'Should have left the clear up to the youngsters.'

Mum smiles at William then at me. 'Can you two take this table up to my bedroom, please?'

'I'll do it.' William is about to pick it up, but Mum swipes his hand away.

'Both of you carry it, it's heavy, and I'd rather not have the wallpaper scratched off the walls with those sharp corners. I know you'd be careful, William, but with two of you, it will be easier.'

'Why do you want this old thing in your room?' I ask.

'I just do,' she says, giving me the Mum stare that says *do it and don't argue.*

* * *

As I push open Mum's bedroom door, I'm relieved we had the two of us to carry it. The old table's iron legs grew heavier as we lifted it up the steep stairs.

'Can you set it up under the window, please,' Mum calls up to us from the kitchen.

As we carry it to the window, I realise at last what she is up to. 'Look at that,' I say, pointing out the window to a tractor working in Gully Field. We can clearly see the ploughed-up mud, creating dark brown letters in the grass. The letters spell out, WILL U MARRY ME?

'That's Mary!' William shouts. 'She shouldn't be on that ground. It's too steep. The tractor could turn over.' He rushes to the door.

'Where are you going?' I hear Mum ask him.

'To stop that crazy girl from killing herself.'

'And tell her, yes?' Mum checks.

I hold my breath and a whole minute seems to go by, but then I hear, 'Yes.'

Chapter 48

Billy

It's my birthday, and Jersey calf number five has just been born. Hols discovered him ten minutes ago and she's just called me to come and look.

When I get to her, Hols scratches her head as she explains why she phoned me. 'His front legs are bent over at the ankles. He can't stand up properly, and he can't reach his mum's teats, I'm worried about the colostrum,' she says, 'Shall I contact Eva, and ask her to have a look at him?'

Newborn calves have little to no immunity, and the colostrum in their mum's first milk is full of antibodies, white blood cells, growth hormones and nutrients, so it's vital we get this little one to drink soon, not just because of how good the milk will be for his health but also because the calf's intestines' ability to absorb the antibodies is best after birth and decreases drastically within six hours. 'You start milking the Friesians,' I say, 'I'll sort this little fellow out.'

I find Richard sitting at the table in the motorhome checking his list of last-minute things to do before we set off in just two hours' time. He looks up. 'What's wrong?' he asks as soon as he sees me.

'Can you help, please? I need to get one of the Jerseys into the stable.'

'What's wrong?' he repeats, sitting down on the caravan step to pull on his wellington boots.

'We have a new baby Jersey and he has a problem with his front legs. I can't do anything about it while they're in the field. We need to get them in. If we put him in the trailer behind the quad bike, his Mum will follow.'

In the stable, I use a couple of hurdles to keep the cow in one corner while I create a makeshift sling to hold up the calf while he drinks. We can almost see him grow stronger as he takes his first guzzle of his mother's warm milk. 'I'll show Hols how to do this later,' I say.

'What about his legs?' Richard asks. 'Will—'

I cut in. 'I've seen this before,' I say. 'He was cramped up inside his mum. They'll straighten out on their own in four or five days.' I hold up the calf's bent ankle and massage it while still holding it into the correct position. 'I'll get Hols to do this too, for a few minutes morning and evening. Could you do something else for me?' I ask, still rubbing the ankle.

He nods as he watches me knead the joint.

'Can you get some sawdust over here? It will be easier on his knees than straw, just until he's better.'

* * *

It feels as if we are lord and lady of the manor as I drive the motorhome out of the yard. Checking the wing mirror, I see everyone lined up behind us, like servants in period dramas. William, Mary, Grace and Freddy, Janette and Mum stand shoulder to shoulder all waving us off.

'Turn into the farm shop, Billy,' Richard says when we reach the main road. I'm not surprised, I expect he's planning for us to say goodbye to Herbie and the staff. He probably wants to drive from here, too.

I switch off the engine and am about to hop out, but he presses my arm. 'Wait.' I look at him and frown, wondering what's wrong. He's done everything to set up today. Organised our whole trip and got everything we need. 'We can't go,' he says, now leaning forward to touch my cheek.

I move my eyes from side to side, enjoying the feel of his fingertips on my skin. I'm racking my brains trying to think why he is telling me we can't go.

'You are only doing this for me.' Richard rubs his chin.

Our phones both ping at the same time and I can't help glancing at Richard's phone in its cradle on the dashboard. 'Jessie,' I say seeing her name on the screen.

Richard turns to lift the phone and reads the message. He finishes reading, looks at me and smiles. 'She says she's just received a large anonymous donation to *WhatIf*.'

'That's great,' I say, taking the phone which he is now offering to me, so I can read her message too. '*Over four million pounds!*' I suck in a deep breath, realising immediately who it must be from. 'I hope Sharmarke is alright,' I say.

'Asad will be fine.' Richard straightens his back.

'You think so?'

Richard nods. 'That young man has the world at his feet.'

The hair on the back of my neck stands on end, remembering another young man who had the world at his feet, another life destroyed by Michael. I swallow hard but then smile, recalling the fateful night Ed and I played draughts together.

'I hope he gets over Mary,' I say, putting my hand on Richard's knee. 'I want to go,' I tell him. 'We've got the world waiting for us too, we've got two months, all to ourselves.' I look down at Crinkle sitting on the floor at Richard's feet. Her ears are up, making her look like she's all set for an adventure. 'All that time in hospital, we dreamt of today.'

'All that time, I wanted to get back to Fox Halt,' Richard corrects me. 'Look, Billy, I watched you with that calf this morning.' He looks serious now, not even the ghost of a smile.

I sniff, still a bit upset inside, remembering Ed. I look into Richard's eyes, trying to think what is stopping us from going away.

'You need to be at the farm, darling,' he says. 'All that knowledge, all that love you have for your animals. The way you care for them, you need to be at Fox Halt, and the farm needs you back there. We can't go.'

Tears are in my eyes now, but this is emotion that Richard is bringing to the surface, his sympathy giving me permission to cry. 'I would love to see the rest of the calves born,' I say. 'I'd love to see Circus Lady join the herd, and I would love to be managing the cows again, with Hols helping out as much as she can, but I love you more, Rich, and we need this holiday. We can have day after day being close to one another, laughing together. No problems to deal with every five minutes—'

'But I can't let you. I will ask the caravan company to buy this vehicle back. Our place is at the farm with our little grandson. I can help you like I did this morning. We can be with your mum too. She will miss you like mad,' he says.

'She'll miss *you* like mad, that's true,' I say, 'But you can't sell our motorhome.'

'I have been thinking, Billy - we would be better off hiring vehicles when we arrive in these far-flung destinations.

We can still travel around Canada, explore the east coast of Australia, see the Northern lights or travel round South Africa in motorhomes that are already there, not waste precious time driving to these places. We'll go for two weeks either side of Valentine's each year when it's quiet on the farm, and we'll be glad of some warmth.'

'You've thought this through, haven't you?' I say, holding on tightly to the armrests of my plush leather seat.

He nods, and at last he smiles. 'Watching you this morning made me finally decide. We need to turn around, and you can give that little calf another leg massage and another drink.'

'Can we take Mum with us next time?' I ask.

'My dad too if you like.' He laughs.

I grin back at him. 'That'll never happen, you know that, your dad's far too content in Amersham having all the local ladies chasing around after him.'

Richard leans forward and kisses me, pressing his lips onto mine. 'Turn this thing around, Billy,' he says, and for once, I do exactly what he asks me to do.

Epilogue

3 February 2021 – Billy

Captain Sir Tom Moore died yesterday. I was driving my van, having finished the last delivery of the day, when they announced his passing on Radio Devon. As ever, his family, just like Sir Tom would have done himself, made a humble and life-affirming statement. I was in pieces when I got back to Fox Halt, as like so many I'd taken the amazing one-hundred-year-old into my heart and felt bereft at his death.

I cried my way through the milking – throwing my arms around Petunia 717, sobbing into her neck like I used to with my ponies when I was a child, my tears soaking her thin fur, her warmth and solidity reassuring.

Mum was inspired so much by Captain Tom that she did her own walk, walking from the house to Primrose Mound every day until his 100th birthday. She is ninety-one, and with all her social media following, she raised just over thirty thousand pounds for Devon, Cornwall and Somerset food banks. Everyone on the farm felt it yesterday, but Mum didn't even manage to post more than a single photo of Sir Tom receiving his knighthood from the Queen. This morning though, she was busy writing again, catching up on all the words she didn't use yesterday – all the messages she had were so heartening, it's obvious the whole country feels the same.

It's our third lockdown. Everyone advised to social distance, wash hands and stay home if they can. The first time the Coronavirus and Covid 19 restrictions hit us in March last year, we created a drive-through at the farm shop, which was amazingly successful and still is; our customers phone or email us, and when they drive to the shop, Herbie happily loads their car boots for them without them needing to get out of their cars. Richard and I devised a regular delivery service too for people isolating at home.

Our milk vending machine is doing a roaring trade, and we struggle at times to keep up with demand. But it's not just about us keeping the businesses going – it's much more than that…

Our ice-cream production has ceased for now, so Freddy and Grace and their little ones – Tom and Emily, who is nearly two – are making up top-up packs for local school lunches and hampers are available for anyone in the EX20 postcode who needs them. No question asked; if families say they're struggling, we believe them.

Grace, Freddy, Tom and Emily keep themselves to themselves, isolating as much as possible, but Mary and Will's little Billie is with Richard and me most days; the three-year-old calls me Big Billy, but she's adopted Richard as her stand-in grandad and the pair adore each other. Normally, if you find one, the other isn't far away.

The cows keep us as busy as ever, and I think Mum is as proud of our Jersey's lineage now as she is of the Friesians. Her social media pages are certainly full of stories about them.

The motorhome is gone, and we have not managed to find time to go travelling yet. Every day is so full of work, and Richard and I work on everything together. We are always talking about the past and the future.

Arthur was given ten years, so he has at least a year to serve. Every day his freedom draws nearer; I wonder how we will tell him the truth about what really happened to his dad. I can't bear him hating me, and I don't want this to come between Jessie and me either. No more secrets anymore – well, just one, we can't tell Arthur where Sharmarke, Nala and Amir are now.

There are early primroses dotted around us as Richard carries Billie to the top of Primrose Mound on his shoulders. The brave flowers are especially welcome today because the early morning mist is lingering in the valleys, and the yellow dots feel like little beacons of hope.

I spread two thick blankets on the ground under the gnarled tree at the top, pulling my small rucksack off my back to pour Richard and me a cup of tea. This is our morning ritual now. Billie presses her red-cheeked face into Richard's coat and pats his shoulders with mittened hands. 'Tell me one of your stories, Grumps,' she says, 'the one about the horrible hobgoblin who used to live on Fox Halt Farm.'

Richard frowns at her. 'No, I've never heard of any hobgoblins around here.' He sips at his steaming drink.

I scratch Crinkle's ever more greying ears. 'The Butterfly Catcher,' I say.

'Yes, Grumps, Butterfy Catch-er. Tell me the story about him.' She cuddles into Richard's chest and sighs, and the story begins.

Can I Ask for Your Help, Please?

I hope you enjoyed this book. If you did, please post a short review on Amazon and/or on Goodreads. Reviews make a huge difference in helping others discover my books. They help a good deal with the success of my novels too.

Your review doesn't need to be long, just a couple of lines would be great. I assure you each and every one will be read and is greatly appreciated!

Please recommend my books to your friends.

Inspiration for this Trilogy

My debut novel *Fox Halt Farm* includes many things that happened to me, but the events are all muddled up. The characters are composites of many people - and outcomes are different - what I tried to capture is feelings and an understanding of the search for the elusive happiness we all seek. I can't say I wrote *Fox Halt Farm* because it's more I dreamt it. The outline of the story came to me one night, and it wouldn't go away.

I cried my heart out at times while I typed, believing before I started writing, I had my fabulous father's sudden death sussed, happy in the knowledge he was always looking over my shoulder, checking on me. I know now I had more grieving to do, and I needed to remember the incredible man he was and the things he did. I needed to cry over other losses too, and properly recognise the precious people and the extraordinary moments which have moulded my life so far.

Before *Fox Halt*, I thought you get on with life and live for the day, but I see now we all have to take time to reflect and wonder at the past times too. Writing has opened up a whole new world to me, learning how to create stories people can relate to and enjoy and meeting so many new friends. Thank you again for reading my books, and I hope you enjoyed them.

Other Books by Celia Moore

Fox Halt Farm & Culmfield Cuckoo - Part 1 and 2 of this Fox Halt Trilogy

Acknowledgements

I have to thank my husband, my daughter, my mother, Peter, Tracey Lee and Jenny Ford for their endless support and encouragement.

Thank you too to Julie and Mark Heslington, Beth Webb, Melissa Eveleigh, Carol Noble-Smith, Jomie Gee, Celia and Marj Rundle, Graham Sercombe, Anne Williams, Debbie Johnson and Rachel Gilbey.

I painted the picture on the front cover but the amazing Harrison Pidgeon put the design together.

Thank you to my editor, Amanda Horan at Let's Get Booked, who is totally brilliant. Without her extraordinary help and knowledge, I could never have felt the delight I have for my writing.

Thank you, Julia Gibbs, for proofreading – finding all the mistakes I would never have seen.

Thank you, Woodleigh Café, for all your support, and Geoff Brooks, Carilyn and Ross Govier and Farmer Tom's Ice-cream for allowing me time with you behind the scenes to research this book.

A special thank you to the Artful Farmer's Wife Facebook group, whose support for my books is beyond incredible.

And finally, thank *you* for reading my books. Without you, I couldn't share my love of writing.

If you would like to know when more books will be available, or have questions about the author's writing, or her talks about writing her novels, please contact Celia: she would love to hear from you.

Website www.celiascosmos.com **Facebook Celia Moore Books**

Printed in Great Britain
by Amazon

18557101R00159